.... And it is time to go, to bid farewell
to one's own self, and find an exit
from the fallen self ....

D. H. Lawrence, *The Ship of Death*

Let's spin the bottle
No I don't want to be kissed

Sometimes I feel my arm
Is turning into a tree

Or hardening to stone
Past memory of green

I've a long way to go
Who never learned to pray

O the night is coming on
And I'm nobody's son

Father it's true
But only for a day

Stanley Kunitz, *The Game*

Gemini

Michael Burns

Poncha Press
Morrison, CO
www.ponchapress.com

First printing 2001
Printed in the United States of America

Published in the United States by:
Poncha Press
P.O. Box 280
Morrison, CO 80465
SAN: 253-3588
www.ponchapress.com

ISBN: 0-9701862-4-X (hardbound)
Library Of Congress control number: 2001 131102

Cover illustration by Geoffrey Zipoli
Jacket design by Dave Hoffman
Author portrait by Wendy Cahill

To my wife Nancy

ACKNOWLEDGMENTS

I would like to thank Kathryn Davis, Rosemary Mahoney, Jamie Neilson, and a very special thanks to Sandy Smoller, Gemini's "Godfather."

Prologue

New Year's Eve, 1967

What would forever stick in Scanlon's mind was the sight of Katie, little Katie, his child bride sitting in the middle of the overstuffed sofa balancing a wine glass on her bare knee. She had on the black shift Scanlon had bought her for her nineteenth birthday. He didn't think anything of it because it was New Year's Eve, and they had guests coming. But Katie was no drinker and here it was the middle of the afternoon and she was drinking wine. She was so tiny, so insignificant, swallowed up in the nubby fabric of that enormous sofa.

Katie was a pretty girl and the fact that she had recently begun to take pains with her appearance probably should have tipped him off, but it hadn't. Or maybe it had, somewhere in the corners of his subconscious. The truth was he didn't care. So, she was getting better with makeup. When they first met she used too much of everything: too much eye shadow, too much mascara, too much lipstick. It made her look like a slut, a street-walker. Then she was seventeen. She was now twenty-two and had learned to tone down the makeup.

She was so petite. So petite that all the furniture in their furnished apartment had the effect of making her look tinier. She was like a child in the big drafty apartment with its high, molded tin ceilings, its dark woodwork, its faded wallpaper with vases of faded flowers.

She was looking at him, her head cocked, a smile on her face that conveyed no mirth, no joy, no playfulness. What would they have said to each other? The way they were with each other at the time it could have gone like this ...

Scanlon: What the fuck is it with you? Aren't the Stacys supposed to be here? You're on your way to being shitfaced and the place is a pit. What is it with you?

Katie: I'm leaving you, Jack. That's what it is with me. I mean it this time.

Scanlon: Don't do me any favors. How come you're drinking? You never drink by yourself.

Katie: I plan on doing a lot of things by myself from now on.

Scanlon: Where's Lucy?

Katie: Having her nap.

And Scanlon would have flung his coat onto the armchair across the room because by now he would have begun to get angry, and yes, a little scared. It was not that Katie hadn't announced a hundred times her intention of leaving him, and he supposed it was clear to both of them that it was only a matter of time before they actually broke up, but Scanlon always imagined that he would be the one to walk.

There was something different about her today, something calm and self-possessed. She was in control the way she had never been in control before. Scanlon understood that this time she meant business, and he was unprepared. In anger he flung his coat because that was the way he was in those days whenever he felt cornered, confused, outwitted, threatened and out of control. Then he would have stalked into the kitchen to make himself a drink. He'd already had plenty to drink at the office party, but Jack Scanlon could always find room for another drink.

The kitchen was a mess: last night's dishes strewn all over the countertop and kitchen table; ashtrays overflowing with butts (they both smoked like fiends); the garbage can spilling over onto the linoleum. It was his job to take out the garbage, a job he could not be depended on to do. But Katie? Katie was a fanatic where housekeeping was concerned. It was simply not in her nature to let a kitchen get like this. Scanlon pried a tray of ice cubes out of the glacier they called a freezer and got the whiskey down from the cupboard. He knocked down a sturdy hooker, then poured himself another generous portion over ice.

Scanlon returned to the living room stirring his drink with his finger. Katie was in the same exact position he had left her. She had a finger pressed into her chin, the same hateful smile on her pretty face. Except, to Scanlon, she was no longer pretty and had not been for a long time. In fact, he found her grotesque with her turned-up nose and small mouth. Did she imagine she taunted him with the bare thigh? They no longer slept together. She couldn't bear to have him touch her, and he no longer had the wish to. Their marriage had been bad from the start. How could it have been otherwise? Lucy was all that had kept them together for the past five years. As he thought about Lucy, Scanlon felt a chill as if the ice in his whiskey had drained off his body heat. Then he thought about the Stacys and things began to fall into place. It had been Katie's idea to invite them down from New Hampshire for New Year's Eve and Scanlon had been too obtuse to see that it was a setup. Katie despised the Stacys. She despised all of Scanlon's friends but especially she despised the Stacys. It had to do with the fact that George Stacy's sister used to be her best friend and that George and Elaine and Scanlon were older than she was and college educated, and she thought they condescended to her when they were all together which Scanlon supposed was true. But he didn't care anymore and probably never did.

There was a knock on the door. When Scanlon didn't move to answer the door, Katie asked him in her superciliously sweet voice if he intended to let his friends in.

The Stacys were framed in the doorway, the low-watt bulb on the landing casting them in an oily light. Elaine was a dresser and for this occasion she had on a gray, suede coat with a fur collar, calf-length suede boots to match her coat, even matching suede gloves. George Stacy, in shabby contrast, wore his old, too large car coat with the wooden buttons. He needed a shave. George always needed a shave, even after he had just shaved. His hairline had receded drastically since Scanlon had seen him last. He cradled a beribboned bottle of champagne and Scanlon could tell from his wide-open eyes that George sensed danger.

Elaine pushed past Scanlon into the living room; George hung back. Elaine wanted to know where her little girl was. She meant Scanlon's little girl Lucy, not Katie.

"I'm leaving your friend," Katie said to Elaine. "Happy New Year."

George Stacy's eyes rolled. He muttered something under his breath. Scanlon invited him inside. George stood his ground on the landing, a blank look on his unshaved face, just stood there in his ridiculous car coat with its silly wooden buttons, holding the absurd bottle of champagne with its gay red ribbon. Scanlon invited him in again. He continued to look stricken and it was Elaine, finally, who ordered him into the room.

George said, "Jesus Christ, Jack," and Scanlon invited him to take off his coat. Scanlon, profoundly embarrassed and humiliated, tried to apologize to his friend. George Stacy looked at him, unblinking.

Elaine took off her coat and told George to take his off. She removed her stylish gloves in dramatic fashion, pulling each finger out separately, all the time looking directly at Katie who held her gaze without a flinch. George put the champagne bottle on the coffee table next to the tabloids Katie always put out whenever Scanlon had over friends who were educated beyond tenth grade. She did it only to annoy him.

Katie stared down Elaine, her thin lips pressed defiantly together, her head thrown back like a fighting cock. Elaine reached out and put a hand on Katie's arm. Scanlon expected Katie to pull away but she did not. The next thing they were up and moving toward the kitchen.

Scanlon pleaded with George Stacy to please take off his goddamned coat. He unfastened the buttons, then started to mutter and pace. Did Scanlon think that they would be amused by this scene? Were they invited all the way down here on purpose to be witness to the event? He paced back and forth in front of the window, the one window they had in the living room, a window that looked out on an alley between the triple-decker apartment buildings where tenants who had them were allowed to park their cars. Maybe if Scanlon had owned a car things would have been different. He was a drunk and he knew it. Even if he was a drunk he was a responsible one, one who knew better than to put himself in charge of a lethal weapon. The truth was that he had been taking driving lessons.

Now that he was finally starting to get somewhere in the company, he'd planned to take his driver's test, buy a used car. By June he would be making nine bills; he was going to get a car like normal people.

Scanlon repeated his apologies to George and informed him that it had been Katie who invited them down, not him. This news had the effect of getting George to take off his coat. He dropped it absently on top of Scanlon's. Elaine apparently had not told him that Katie had been the one with the invitation. He told Scanlon that if he had known he would have smelled the rat at once.

Scanlon went to the kitchen to fetch the bottle, some ice and glasses. He didn't have to ask George Stacy if he needed a drink. Katie and Elaine were at the kitchen table, which had been cleared of dishes and crumbs. On the stove a kettle of water was heating.

Elaine greeted Scanlon again as if she were seeing him for the first time today. He had to go after the freezer with a screwdriver to get to a tray of ice cubes. He was so upset with anger he made a mess of it.

He was sarcastic with Elaine and before she could come back at Scanlon Katie was all over him, telling him how she was taking Lucy and that there was not one single thing on earth that he could do about it. She sounded very sure of herself, so sure that Scanlon felt something happen to his stomach. He felt a powerful urge to throw up.

He retreated with glasses, ice and bottle with Katie yelling after him, reminding him that she was free of him, free of his put-downs, free of his filthy habits, free of his sarcasm, and free of his body. She put special emphasis on the word body. This was for the Stacys' benefit because she had been free of his body for a long time.

Scanlon poured his pal George Stacy half a glass of whiskey. George was perched on the edge of the sofa pulling at what remained of his wiry hair, a study in misery. Scanlon reminded him that it could be a long night. He had better get busy with his drink.

George did as he was told and drank up. What they did best together was drink. They had always drunk well together, ever since they met back in high school. They drank their way through high school and freshman year in college; they parted company for four years while Scanlon represented the U.S. Navy in the Far East, then they were back at it, drinking their way through Scanlon's bad marriage.

Scanlon told George that he must feel like a prophet, remembering how back in L.A. when he told his friend about Katie and himself George had predicted that nothing good would come of his marriage. George had been incredulous. What could he have done? Scanlon wanted to know. She was pregnant and he was the product of New England ethical training. Scanlon felt that he had no choice but to marry her. George disagreed. He claimed he could have gotten a dozen affidavits signed by guys who had banged her. She's my sister's age, for the love of Christ, he had wailed. She's jailbait! Indeed. Another cogent reason for Scanlon to agree to marry her. George told him he would live to regret it. Nothing good could come of it.

Don't make me say I told you so, George told him. He added that it was probably for the best, that he and Elaine were frankly surprised that they had lasted this long.

Scanlon went to the window. It was only five o'clock in the afternoon but already very dark outside. The wind howled through the alley rattling the window in its frame. Paper trash flew like demons, parked cars were pelted with street grit. Katie had put up plastic on the inside of the window to keep out the draft. It billowed into the room like a sail. The heat came with the rent and they had their own thermostat. Katie kept the temperature in the eighties because she worried Lucy would catch cold from the drafts.

Scanlon invited George Stacy to put on some music if he felt like it, remembering that the last time he had fought with Katie she had scaled a stack of his favorite records off the back porch. Since George and Scanlon shared the same taste in music, many of his favorites were gone, too. It didn't matter because George was not in the mood for music under the circumstances. And he didn't feel like watching TV. There was nothing on at that time of day anyway unless he wanted to watch the stuff Katie liked to watch in the afternoon.

Scanlon poured more whiskey for George and himself. The bottle was almost finished. Scanlon realized that he must be drunk. He didn't feel drunk. George took his drink down fast; they killed the bottle and went in George's car to the package store for a new fifth and a case of beer.

The women were still in the kitchen when they returned. Scanlon could hear their muffled voices through the door. What could they possibly have to discuss, these women who had never had more than words of greeting and good-bye before? Whenever the Stacys were down, it would be just the three of them, George, Elaine, and Scanlon. Katie was on the outside looking in, and don't think she didn't resent it. It would be fair to say that Elaine had tried often enough to include her. Katie had always resisted. Scanlon supposed the fault was his; he went out of his way to see to it that Katie was excluded, to treat the Stacys as if they were his allies against this small woman who had trapped him with her sexual guile. Now, she threatened to take away the only thing he cared about, and as she so eloquently put it in the kitchen, there was not one thing he could do about it. This was Massachusetts where the husband had virtually no rights in a divorce or custody case.

In this mood of desolation, Scanlon went into Lucy's bedroom to get his daughter up from her nap. She was already awake, sitting up in bed with two pillows behind her back. She had her little thumb in her mouth, pumping at it for all she was worth. She held onto the filthy knot of her security cloth with a death grip in her thumb-sucking hand and tugged at her ear with the other.

Whatcha doing, sweetpea? Scanlon would say whenever he got her up from her naps, and take her in his arms and ask her to tell him that she loved him. She was all damp and sleep-rumpled, smelling of stale pee. She was a bed-wetter, a thumb-sucker, and Scanlon supposed this was because she was insecure on account of her parents' crummy marriage. The thought of this and the feel of his little girl broke his heart. His throat constricted. Scanlon wondered if the alcohol on his breath offended her. Would her most vivid memories of childhood be the smell of her old man's alcoholic breath as he whispered endearments in her bedroom?

Lucy sucked fiercely at her thumb and pulled at her ear. She knew something was up. Scanlon told her there was a surprise for her in the other room. Like any kid, she loved surprises. She gave Scanlon those big brown eyes and he almost lost it. He held out his arms and Lucy allowed him to pick her up. She hung onto the dirty cloth for dear life, her thumb still buried in her small mouth.

He took her to the living room first to show her to George. George was not fond of kids and Lucy sensed this. She stared past his shoulder as he tickled her under the chin, asked her if she would like to suck on his thumb for awhile for variety. Now that he had some whiskey in his belly, George was more relaxed. He sat down on the wing chair, on top of their coats, and Scanlon took Lucy into the kitchen where he had been dying to go. Lucy made for a good excuse to butt in on the women, to see what they were up to.

Lucy had always taken a fancy to Elaine; for her part Elaine adored the child. She scooped her from Scanlon's arms and smothered her with hugs and kisses. Scanlon could see peripherally that Katie had her eye on him, measuring him. Scanlon thought of things like alimony, child support, and he felt again like throwing up.

Back in the living room, Scanlon found a thoroughly relaxed George Stacy conducting Mahler's Fifth Symphony with a beer bottle. With his unruly hair and rumpled clothes, he looked the part of conductor. Scanlon asked George to help him with his options. George reminded him that he lived in the Commonwealth of Massachusetts and that he could expect to take it up the ass if Katie followed through and filed for divorce. Then Scanlon started raving about absconding with Lucy because George got on his serious face and told him to calm down, not do anything rash, not compound his troubles. Then he waxed philosophical about marriage and family. In George's opinion Scanlon was no family man, and neither was he for that matter. Neither of them was cut out to bear the burden of family responsibility. They were isolates, better off on their own. If Elaine could have heard him carrying on in that fashion, she would have made him pay. George sat down beside his friend on the sofa. His lips were wet and his eyes moist from all he had had to drink. He made Scanlon promise not to do anything weird. Scanlon told him he was an unfeeling prick.

George leaned back, looking smug, and peeled a swath of beer bottle label down the middle, then worked inward from the edges. Little piles of labels were accumulating on the coffee table. Scanlon idly considered putting the champagne in the refrigerator though the prospects of a New Year's champagne toast looked remote. What would 1968 have in store for him? Scanlon wondered, his heart leaden in his chest. He got up and paced the floor. George closed his eyes, moved his head to Mahler. Scanlon knew that he should kick him out of his house, him and his well-dressed, meddling wife. He would do nothing of the sort, of course. If he was not one to speak his mind in those days, he was also averse to confrontation.

George asked him if he had a lawyer. Of course he didn't have a lawyer. Scanlon told him that he was pretty sure Katie had one though. George, of course, could not believe that Scanlon would have been so taken by surprise by little Katie. He laughed with the same incredulity he had in L.A. when Scanlon told him about Katie and his plan to marry her. Scanlon reminded him that they had been at each other's throats every day for the five years they had been together. Why should it be any different now? So how did Scanlon know it was different now? George asked. For all Scanlon knew she could have been bluffing, George reasoned, just busting his balls. Scanlon told him this time it was no drill. This he knew in his gut. He should have seen it coming a long time ago, George said. He got up off the sofa and paced the floor with Scanlon. As for lawyers, Scanlon said that George should know him better than to think he'd hire a lawyer any more than he would consult a shrink. George told him not to come crying to him when he got hosed. If Scanlon had taken care of business he might have stood a better chance, not a good chance, but a better one than he had now.

George spoke the truth. Scanlon knew this in his heart. It was because he had become so inured to a life filled with bad words, bad intentions—bad karma as the hippies would call it—that it had taken on the deadness of routine, a routine he had not been able to see or imagine beyond. He was a victim of inertia. Now it was out of his hands, out of his control. What if Katie really was only bluffing? Or what if Elaine were to talk her out of it, if that was what she was trying to do in there? He had no assurance that Elaine would want to talk Katie out of leaving him. She was of the same mind as George where it concerned Scanlon's married life; he would be better off on his own. Elaine seemed not to appreciate what it would mean to him to lose his daughter.

Elaine appeared, carrying Lucy. She said she was going to put Lucy down for the night. What had they been saying in there all this time for Lucy to hear? Scanlon told Elaine that he would put Lucy down himself, and took her in his arms. She resisted and he had to exert some force. Lucy began to whimper. Come on, darling, he remembered saying, let daddy put you to bed. On the way to Lucy's bedroom, Scanlon thought idly of sleeping arrangements. The Stacys would have to spend the night. George and Elaine would sleep in Scanlon's bedroom; Katie would crawl in with Lucy. That would leave the sofa for him. He didn't mind the sofa because he would not be able to sleep in any case.

Scanlon laid his daughter down on the bed, tucked in the bedclothes around her. She asked him if he was drunk, and Scanlon asked his daughter if mommy had told her to say that. She stabbed her thumb in her mouth and stared at him as if he were someone she didn't know or care about. Scanlon put his face down in the blanket and wept. Lucy must have thought he was playing their crybaby game. But after awhile, with him slobbering out of control, she got afraid and started to hit the top of his head with the heel of her little hand. Stop it, daddy, she said, stop your crying. Scanlon took her in his arms, hugged her so hard she complained he was hurting her.

After putting Lucy down Scanlon stopped in the bathroom for a look at himself in the mirror. He was puffy around the eyes from booze and crying. His eyes reminded this chick, Donna, over at the plant, of Tommy Smothers. She should get a look at Tommy Smothers' bloodshot eyes now. Scanlon hated his eyes. As a kid, he should have had an operation. If he'd had any kind of parents, he wouldn't have to spend every morning of his life in front of a bathroom mirror hating his own looks because of one wandering eye. And when he was torched, it really moved off course. He wished the Stacys would leave, get out of his private life. It wouldn't have been so bad if it were only George. Elaine would probe and cross-examine and not be satisfied until she knew everything. She was the type who had to share everything with her husband, and then they would both know everything about his private life, things nobody had a right to know. What else could she be doing in the kitchen with his wife all this time except gathering facts about his wretched marriage?

In the living room George was hunched over his beer. He looked morose the way only George Stacy could. What did he have to be morose about? Scanlon was the one being abandoned, his child taken away from him. Scanlon told him to put on some more music, something more life-affirming than Mahler. George told Scanlon that he didn't look very pretty. Well, Scanlon replied, I don't feel that pretty. It had to be close to midnight. What were the women doing in there?

The champagne with the gay ribbon was still on the coffee table. Beer bottles had accumulated on the floor, on the arms of the sofa, on the mantle of the boarded up fireplace, on the window sill. The whiskey was gone. As drunk as he looked in the mirror, as legitimately drunk as he had a right to be, Scanlon felt oddly sober and clearheaded.

He said to George that he thought Elaine was his friend, implying that he now thought otherwise. George didn't seem to understand. Of course she was his friend, George said. If she was such a friend then how come she was in his kitchen collaborating with the enemy? George told him he was acting like an asshole. But Scanlon couldn't take anymore waiting and wondering what was going on behind that kitchen door. He announced that he was going in there to have it out. As if on cue, Katie pushed through the door and marched past him to Lucy's bedroom, her turned-up nose in the air. Scanlon started to follow her. Elaine was there with a grip on his arm telling him to let her go, he was in no condition to be dealing with her now. Wait until morning. He'd be better off, Elaine told him. Scanlon asked her what Katie had said about him. Elaine looked at him as if he were demented. He was confused; he didn't know what to do. His nose and extremities were cold. He felt numb.

Elaine appraised the room like an interior decorator. She shook her head, claimed she hadn't seen a room like this since her last fraternity party. George and Scanlon sat on the sofa like naughty boys. They both knew how Elaine disapproved of the way they were when they got together. This was why they had not got together much lately. Scanlon had begun to think that they were both put off with the way he and Katie were with each other.

Scanlon asked Elaine if she wanted a drink. They were out of whiskey and what was left of the beer had gone warm. Did she want warm beer or did she prefer warm champagne? She wanted neither. She blew smoke at the ceiling, inspected her nails, her forehead creased in a frown. When she finally looked at Scanlon, it was with a coldness that he wasn't used to seeing from her. What stories had Katie told about him? They would be true stories because whatever else Katie was she was not a liar. Scanlon was the liar in the family. Besides, to make him look bad she wouldn't have to stretch the truth. And if there was one person she would delight in painting him black to, it would be Elaine Stacy. To Katie it would have been like killing two birds with one stone because of her intense dislike of Elaine. Scanlon was frankly surprised they had lasted so long together in that kitchen tonight. Surprised and worried.

He wanted to know from Elaine what they had talked about all night in there. Had Katie been boring her with stories about what a swell husband he'd been, or what? He heard his voice come out phlegmy and squeaky. Elaine said nothing for a long time. She just stared at him in a way he couldn't remember ever being stared at by her, when he'd given her plenty of reasons in the past to look hard at him. Then, with a sigh, she told him she loved him dearly but had never been blind to his faults.

What Scanlon wanted very much to tell her was that his faults were none of her business, and that she had no right forcing her way into his life, judging him for the way he lived, no right at all. But in those days he could not say things like that. If he had been the type to make New Year's resolutions he would resolve to start telling people exactly what he felt and thought. No more mister nice guy, no more oblique. He kept his mouth shut.

George piped in to remind his friend to face facts, that Jack Scanlon was no family man. Scanlon reminded him that he had already pointed that out. George suddenly looked very drunk. Then Elaine had to tell him that as cruel as it may sound he would eventually get over Lucy. So there it was. Scanlon's heart lurched in his chest. George and Elaine looked at each other, passed little head and eye signals. Scanlon let this go without comment.

Elaine sat down next to Scanlon and put her hand on his sleeve, her other arm around his shoulders. She invited him to come up to Garrison for a few days to just do nothing. Scanlon noticed how she emphasized "few days," no doubt remembering the last time he had spent time with them four years ago when he came back from California. They were newly married and George told Scanlon a couple of years later that his little visit had nearly cost him his marriage. Scanlon had not told him then that he would probably be better off if it had.

Scanlon said to Elaine that he didn't know how that would be possible, his coming to Garrison. He thought he saw a flicker of relief in her eyes. Besides, what made her think he would want to subject himself to their domestic strife? Still, she told him to give the invitation some thought.

Happy New Year, Scanlon said with mock joviality, and swallowed the dregs of some warm beer. Elaine wouldn't look at him now. Neither would George. Suddenly he was an embarrassment to his best friends. He couldn't bear to look at them anymore either. He announced that he was tired and wanted to go to sleep. Elaine got up quickly and went to the closet where Katie kept sheets and extra blankets, then headed straight for the master bedroom as if it were understood that was where they would sleep. It was all right with Scanlon except it irked him sometimes how people took certain things for granted. Elaine called from the bedroom for George to come in and help make up the bed. George rolled his eyes and with a supreme effort, as if he were pulling himself out of quicksand, got up from the sofa to help his wife make up Scanlon's bed. Elaine came back with some sheets, a blanket, and a pillow for Scanlon. She told him to get some sleep, told him he would feel better in the morning. Sure, he'd feel better in the morning. She dropped the bedclothes in his lap, gave him a sisterly kiss on the top of the head. I mean it, Jack, she said, come spend some time with us. Give yourself a chance to deal with this. Then, as an afterthought, she told him in this soft voice that maybe he should give some thought to seeing someone.

Scanlon thanked her, not sure what she meant by seeing someone, though knowing her she probably referred to a shrink. He told her he'd think about it. Then, she actually told him to go to sleep, told him again that things would look brighter in the morning. Go to bed yourself, Elaine, he thought, before you make me puke.

He threw the bedclothes on the floor and lay down on the sofa. He was wide-awake with a buzzing in the back of his head. If he had had any gumption, he would have gotten Lucy and taken off with her to where nobody would ever think to look for them. Where on earth that would be he had no idea. Elaine knew everything about him, things she should not know. And now George would know, too. It would be impossible for them ever to be friends again.

New Year's Day, 1968. The sun was bright in Scanlon's eyes. He could hear George snoring in his bedroom. Lucy's door was open. Scanlon went in to find the neatly made bed, the bureau drawers open and empty, empty coathangers in the closet. She had been quiet, so quiet that not even Elaine Stacy, a notorious light sleeper, had heard them go.

Chapter One

In the bathroom mirror Jack Scanlon studied the progress of his new mustache, the mustache that Winship had stared at this morning as if it were a third eye. His look had said to Scanlon, I ordered clean-shaved goods in April, how come in September I get a mustache? His unspoken message had been, get rid of the mustache, and while you're at it you can get rid of the sideburns, too. There was an obstinate part of Scanlon that would have refused had it come to that. When he was hired in April by Sumner Purnell, the district superintendent, Scanlon was under the impression that Fairfield was desperate for a science teacher. In Scanlon's opinion, desperate people shouldn't sweat small things like mustaches and sideburns.

He'd interviewed with Winship right after he finished with the superintendent and had taken an instant dislike to the principal. That dislike was still intact after this morning's meeting. Winship had asked him to come over to school to discuss the textbooks he would be using in his courses. Scanlon arrived on time, powerfully hungover, only to discover that the textbooks had not arrived because of a screw-up on the part of Winship's new secretary. The principal offered no apologies for dragging his new teacher to the school for nothing, seeming capable only of staring at Scanlon's facial hair. In an hour he was due at Winship's house for the welcoming party for the faculty, none of whom Scanlon had met.

Aunt Alice had left a stack of clean underwear neatly folded on his lumpy bed, and three freshly pressed shirts hanging in the closet. His aunt and uncle had opened two of the three upstairs rooms for his use. He also had the use of the upstairs bathroom, poorly lighted as it was, and with a hot-pink paint job—it was at least private. There was a claw-footed bathtub but no shower. He missed his shower, but he was in no position to be fussy. Ira and Alice had refused his feeble offer of room and board, and in the nearly three weeks that he had been here hadn't pressured him to find another place. On his income as a schoolteacher, decent places to live weren't easy to find. He must start looking in earnest soon, before he began to wear out his welcome if he hadn't already.

Scanlon sighed, stowed his underwear in the spicy-smelling top drawer of the oak bureau, checked the knot of his tie in the mirror, and went downstairs. He brought along a jacket to wear, despite the unseasonably humid weather, in case the Fairfield High teachers had pretenses to formality.

Alice was ensconced on the sofa, flanked by two of her five cats whose names Scanlon could not keep straight. She was talking on the telephone. Alice spent a good part of every afternoon talking on the phone to her mother or to one or the other of the two sisters still living in Groveton. The afternoon routine also included her soaps and of course the Merv Griffin Show.

Lucky, a spaniel-beagle mongrel, lay on the braided rug at Alice's feet and in her lap was Nanette, a white toy poodle. It was three o'clock in the afternoon, but Alice still had on her pink housecoat, and her hair was done up in huge, pink, plastic curlers. Alice winked at Scanlon over the beer bottle she had to her lips. Alice sipped her way through a couple of six-packs of beer a day, every day. She had the volume on the TV turned down; soap opera characters silently acted out their destinies.

"Well," Scanlon said, standing before Alice for inspection, "how do I look? Like a schoolteacher, or what?"

"It's Johnny," Alice said into the mouthpiece. "Well, don't you look nice.

"But do I look respectable?"

"Well, you could use a trim, and the mustache ... My nephew the hippie," Alice said into the phone. "Althea says hi."

"Hi, Althea," Scanlon said.

"Johnny says hi." After all the years he'd been away, Scanlon wasn't used to hearing himself called Johnny. Only Alice and Ira and those of Alice's relatives who remembered him used this name. As a kid he'd despised it. He established himself as Jack as soon as his family left Groveton. But from Alice and Ira, he could put up with Johnny.

"You need to wish me luck, Alice. I'm off to the faculty bash."

"Will you be back for supper? Johnny's going to a faculty party. Can you imagine?" Alice informed her sister. "Althea says don't drink too much and make a bad first impression."

Althea was probably joking but on the subject of drinking and bad impressions Scanlon was particularly sensitive after losing his job at Consolidated in such dramatic fashion. Alice and Ira knew nothing of his troubles with job and marriage and the fact that he had lost both as well as his little girl. He hadn't been able to bring himself to tell them, and they had been, so far, too gracious to ask questions. But there would come a time when they would need to know. Upstairs, nursing one of Alice's beers while he got dressed for Winship's party, he had seriously considered knocking back a couple of hookers of Alice's Black Velvet for moral support, but Althea's caution ruled that out.

"I believe they're serving dinner," Scanlon said, "so I'm guessing that I'll be expected to stay."

"Just having plain old shepherd's pie," Alice said into the phone. Scanlon wasn't sure she was addressing him or responding to Althea.

"Damn. How could Winship schedule a party on a shepherd's pie night?" As soon as the words were out of his mouth, he realized how presumptuous they sounded. How could he not be wearing thin on this woman whom he referred to glibly as his aunt? She was his uncle's wife and that made him the nephew on his uncle's side. Ever since he could remember them together there had been a feud between Alice and Ira over family loyalty and not always a good-natured one. Since all of Ira's kin had either died or fled Groveton, he was at a clear disadvantage, overwhelmingly outnumbered. Scanlon's abrupt appearance on the scene after an eighteen-year absence must have given Ira some cause for rejoicing.

Alice had always been generous and kind to Johnny Labalm and if there was tension between her and Ira, young Johnny certainly never noticed it. In fact, they both rather spoiled him as a kid. And here he was, back, and being spoiled again. Scanlon did not want to risk turning Alice's generosity into resentment by overstaying his welcome, and by making all kinds of presumptuous statements like the one he had just made. He promised himself to speak to her about the matter first thing in the morning.

"Althea says that just because they're going to feed you that you shouldn't expect a sex orgy or anything. Can you imagine," she said to Althea, "schoolteachers in a sex orgy?"

"Don't go getting my hopes up," Scanlon said. "Listen, I'll see you later and fill you in on the secret lives of schoolteachers."

Ira and Alice rented "dirt cheap" the old house on the bank of the sometimes-turbulent Manoosic River. His uncle had pointed out to him the high-water marks halfway up the kitchen, bedroom, and bathroom walls on the first floor left by the flood and hurricane of 1938. The house had suffered irreparable damage. None of the floors was level; the angles between the ceiling and walls were askew; sills and wall joists rotten; the side porch rotted to the point of imminent collapse. The furnace needed replacing, and it would take more than a few coats of fresh paint to make the place look like anything but a dump, a rundown dilapidated shack. Furthermore, River Road merged with Route 5, the busy thoroughfare to Canada, not far from the house. Scanlon discovered that backing his car out of the driveway could be a harrowing experience as southbound traffic whipped around a blind corner at speeds in excess of the thirty miles an hour that was posted. For an American male his age, Scanlon was not an experienced driver; he'd had his driver's license less than a year and was generally confounded by mechanical objects.

Forget the constant smell of cat urine issuing from the dirt-floor cellar, the cats' virtual litter box. And forget about the two neurotic dogs who whimpered and moaned like abandoned children whenever Alice and Ira left the house together, running from window to window with their plaintive cries until their "mommy" and "daddy" returned. Despite this, and the fact that his ankles had been ravaged by flea bites, Scanlon didn't relish the thought of leaving.

Winship's place was ten minutes west of Fairfield, out on a piece of high ground that commanded a sweeping view of the distant White Mountains of New Hampshire. The principal was waiting for him, glass in hand, on the grassy island in the middle of a circular, crushed stone driveway. Winship had on a heavy Irish fishing sweater. Scanlon marveled at how cool he managed to look in such a sweater in such heat—not a hint of perspiration on his clean-shaved lip.

Winship looked at his watch and said, "I was beginning to wonder if you had gotten lost. Or is this what you city folks call coming fashionably late?" He smiled at Scanlon.

Disarmed, Scanlon managed only to smile back and ask, "Aran Isle?" of Winship's sweater.

Winship looked into his glass. "Gin and tonic. Come on. Everyone's out back. You're the last." Winship led him through the house to the back lawn where the Fairfield High faculty and their spouses were standing around in clusters, talking, and sipping drinks.

"Nice place," Scanlon said as he was taken through the screened porch that connected the main house to the section that Winship told him he had added on two years ago.

"You know what they're asking for weathered barn board these days?" Winship asked Scanlon. Winship shook his head without quoting figures, so Scanlon guessed the price was pretty high. And he was impressed and mildly disappointed that Winship should exhibit such good taste, should live in such agreeable surroundings.

"Madelaine," Winship said to the woman who approached them outside, "this is Jack Scanlon, the new science department. Jack, my wife, Madelaine."

"An entire department. I'm impressed." Madelaine Winship extended her plump hand in greeting.

"How do you do?" Her ankles were thick and her yellow hair was dark at the roots. She had on dark glasses with sequined frames.

"Come with me, Mr. Scanlon." She pulled at his hand. "Let's meet your new colleagues. Well, most of them. The Sorensons don't seem to have arrived yet." Winship had told him he was the last to show. Scanlon wondered if could expect to be needled by this guy all year.

With Scanlon in tow, Madelaine Winship broke into a group standing on the edge of the large lawn, next to a birdbath.

"Stop all your silly chatter and say hello to Jack Scanlon, the new science department. This sturdy gentleman is Lyle Higgins, math, and his better half, Edna. And this is Sophie Metcalf, Fairfield High's librarian, and her husband, Mal." Scanlon shook hands with everyone, promptly forgetting their names. The math teacher had a peculiar way of looking at him with his cold gray eyes that made Scanlon shift his own eyes away immediately. He had the sleeves of his shirt rolled to his muscular biceps; the muscles of his right forearm he flexed menacingly and his handshake was bone-crushing. Scanlon guessed his age as early fifties. He was square-jawed, bifocaled, crew cut. The only man present who wore a jacket besides Scanlon was the librarian's husband. It was a threadbare, ill-fitting gabardine that didn't match his trousers, but his handshake was soft, mushy as overripe fruit.

"Come come, now, Mr. Scanlon. Musn't dawdle. Lots of people to meet." Madelaine tugged at his arm, putting him off balance.

"Pay attention, Jack," said the math teacher, winking, "there might be a quiz later," and laughed heartily.

"Do you intend to introduce me to all these people without giving me a drink?" Scanlon asked as he was led off to another group across the lawn.

"You poor boy. Daryl," she shouted to her husband who was bartending at a white-clothed table near the house, "Mr. Scanlon requires a drink."

Winship shouted back, "What'll it be?"

"Bourbon on the rocks," Scanlon yelled, feeling uneasy to be yelling out drink orders in the company of strangers. Winship raised an arm to acknowledge his order.

Dennis Kitchell, the shop teacher, and his wife, Marion, were chatting with Lillian Bloemer, French and Spanish, and her white-haired mother. Lillian Bloemer's hair was styled in a bee's nest. Her features were coarse, and the lenses of her eyeglasses magnified her pupils to the size of dimes. If Lillian was gross, her mother, dressed in a crisp white dress, was delicate. When Scanlon looked into her eyes, however, he found no one home. She offered him her frail, veiny, liver-spotted hand and a dotty smile.

Dennis Kitchell had been expostulating against the deplorable state of winter heating fuel costs for uninsulated houses, of which his was one, and Scanlon sensed that he was annoyed by Madelaine's intrusion because he greeted Scanlon only perfunctorily, and went back to his argument without missing a beat after the introductions were finished. Lillian pulled Scanlon off to one side and whispered, "Please rescue me from these people." A thin, sullen, teenaged boy in cut-off jeans and T-shirt brought Scanlon his drink and passed around a tray of cheese and crackers.

"Winship's kid?" Scanlon asked Lillian Bloemer.

"Tommy. He'll be a sophomore this year," Lillian said with a sigh, "and you know what pains sophomores can be."

"Afraid I don't. This is my first crack at teaching. I don't think I could have been a pain when I was a sophomore.

"I'll bet. Anyway, you'll find out for yourself soon enough."

"You trying to scare me off?" Lillian Bloemer laughed at Scanlon's remark. She was very short, and her heavy thighs and rear end strained at the fabric of her satin dress. Scanlon thought that she might look more comfortable behind the counter of a delicatessen than in front of a class of French students. "How long have you taught at Fairfield?" he asked.

"Three years. Before that I was in the advertising business. New York. The city got to be too much for mother. It was getting to the point where she was afraid to leave the apartment, even in broad daylight."

"Probably with good reason."

"Nonsense. But it got to be intolerable for both of us so I made up my mind to get out of the city and out of the business. An associate of mine knew a man who owned a house in Vermont he was interested in selling. It seemed like just the thing for mother. I finished the master's degree I'd started twenty years ago at Middlebury, and applied for the job at Fairfield High. It's a five-minute walk from the house. What could be better? I don't mind teaching even if I can't stand the kids. And I have summers off to write."

Scanlon was tempted to ask her how she managed the apparent discrepancy of not minding teaching people she couldn't stand, but Madelaine was yanking him away to more introductions, scolding Lillian for always dominating the good-looking men.

"The cute blond couple over there getting ready to play croquet with the serious-looking young man in the madras shirt are Rachel and Josh Patterson. He's in social studies. Rachel teaches third grade in Burton."

"And the serious-looking young man?"

"Doug Stambaugh. But don't call him Doug. He prefers Douglas because he's been to Yale and he's a Fulbright Scholar. And please don't get him started on the Vietnam War. If he and Lyle get into an argument over war and politics, that will be the end of the party."

Madelaine's hand was moist. Scanlon felt ridiculous being led across the lawn by her. He was introduced to the Pattersons and Douglas Stambaugh who invited him to hit a round with them, but Madelaine insisted that he had a few more people to meet before he would be allowed to enjoy himself.

The Pattersons looked more like siblings than husband and wife. Madelaine explained that they were married right after college—Princeton and Bryn Mawr—and Josh had been teaching at Fairfield for two years. The kids loved him and adored Rachel who picked him up at school every day. Josh Patterson was tall with a self-assurance that Scanlon would ordinarily find offensive but which may have been mitigated by Rachel's smooth, deeply tanned legs. On her bare arms was a soft down bleached by long, idle days in the summer sun. Scanlon would have bet anything that she was a debutante. He made up his mind to see more of Rachel Patterson in the course of the evening, at the same time marveling at the high incidence of Ivy Leaguers in this rural Vermont high school.

He learned from Madelaine that Douglas Stambaugh taught history and would be starting his second year at Fairfield. He struck Scanlon as haughty and correct so he wasn't surprised when Madelaine confided that he was not well-liked by the kids. No, Scanlon would not have minded at all playing around the croquet course in Rachel Patterson's company, but as Madelaine reminded him, there were more of his colleagues to meet.

Winship had started a charcoal fire in the barbecue pit. He had on a red and white striped apron and a chef's hat.

“How’s your drink?” he asked Scanlon. Scanlon handed him his empty glass as Madelaine steered him in the direction of Miriam and Wendell Hawkins who were standing next to the bar talking with Cynthia Sinclair, the other bachelor lady on the faculty besides Lillian Bloemer. Cynthia taught English; Miriam, business and typing. Wendell was Fairfield’s postmaster and therefore privy to everybody’s business. Miriam laughed and said that Wendell had learned a long time ago that nobody in Fairfield had any interesting business. Scanlon noticed that while she said this, Wendell was busy tracing his forefinger along Madelaine Winship’s spine. In his eyes, Scanlon imagined he saw a wicked look. Cynthia Sinclair had on a pleated skirt and a white blouse with a ruffled front. Her hair was done up nineteen fifties style, her rather large lips made to look even larger with a broad swath of bright red lipstick.

She was the only one bold (or obtuse) enough to inquire about Scanlon’s wife, information which Winship evidently had not seen fit to keep confidential.

“We’re divorced.”

Cynthia Sinclair’s hand flew to her mouth. Whether her surprise was genuine or feigned, Scanlon couldn’t be sure.

“I am so sorry. Just leave it to me to always say the wrong thing. I am so absolutely flawless in that respect.” Her hand was on Scanlon’s sleeve; Scanlon, with his new found talent for discovering imperfection, noticed lipstick on her teeth. Tommy Winship arrived with another drink for him.

“Don’t worry about it,” Scanlon said, swirling the contents of his glass, “divorce is in vogue these days.” Cynthia laughed, but it was clear that she had lost her composure. Scanlon was the one who was sorry, now that she looked so forlorn.

“Well, Mr. Scanlon,” said Madelaine, “except for the Sorensons I believe you have met everyone. So now you are one of us.” She raised her glass in a toast. Scanlon gladly drank to himself, looking over the rim of his glass for Rachel Patterson. She was hitting through the final wickets well ahead of her husband and Douglas Stambaugh. She swung the mallet between her legs, the orthodox swing. Her husband and Stambaugh, perhaps thinking it manly, used golf swings.

Chapter Two

On Route 2, Scanlon saw headlights approaching four abreast. Thinking that there was an oncoming car in his lane, passing illegally over a solid yellow line, he steered onto the soft shoulder and stopped, his heart wildly pounding. Only one car passed, and in the proper lane.

Madelaine had been worried about his driving home after all he'd had to drink, so worried that she had insisted he drink down a mug of strong coffee (as if that could nullify the effects of an afternoon and early evening of two-fisted drinking) before he got behind the wheel. Scanlon had drunk her coffee, but she was still not satisfied, peering at him from behind those sequined frames, and he was made to drink a second cup before she would allow him to go. Now he was drunk and wired up from caffeine instead of just drunk. Scanlon was drunk and seeing double but his mind was clear enough to realize that he was in no condition to operate a moving vehicle along snaky Route 2.

Another set of four headlights, again only one car. Scanlon switched his seat to the recline position, lay back and closed his eyes. There had been times in his drinking career when nausea was the constant companion of double vision, when lying down like this would have brought on the "spins." No more. Scanlon couldn't remember the last time he suffered from a case of the spins. It was as if he'd lost amateur status as a drinker.

Had he made a bad first impression on his colleagues as Althea predicted he would if he drank too much? He hadn't been the only one who overindulged. High scores for Winship who maintained an uninterrupted flow beginning with preprandial cocktails, ending with after-dinner beer. And there had been ample quantities of jug wine to go with the steaks. Everyone had been remarkably well behaved. Douglas Stambaugh and Lyle Higgins had refrained from quarreling over Vietnam; Wendell Hawkins made no flagrant passes at Madelaine Winship; and even Winship, to Scanlon's relief, kept his mouth shut on the subject of his mustache and sideburns, satisfying himself with the occasional stare and look of disgust.

Cynthia Sinclair had cornered him after dinner to apologize profusely for her gaff, swearing that she'd heard nothing from Winship about Scanlon's divorce. It just seemed to her that everyone these days was married, except of course for her. She let it slip out that she'd never see forty again, and benumbed as Scanlon was from Winship's booze, he could see how profoundly bothered she was by this fact. Forty years old in Vermont with its harsh winters and no prospects for a husband. The hungry look Scanlon saw in her eyes was *angst*, pure and simple.

The Sorensons had not arrived until dinner was underway. They showed no interest in drinking; Rob Sorenson nursed a beer the whole evening while his energetic little wife, Jackie, left her wine untouched on a side table. Sorenson coached soccer, basketball, and baseball—to Scanlon's surprise no football was played at Fairfield High. Coaching was Sorenson's passion, especially basketball which was the premier sport at Fairfield—capacity crowds at all the home games and a healthy contingent of hometown fans who followed the team on the road. And little Jackie was behind her man one hundred percent, though in winter she was a basketball widow to be sure. They were both very excited over the baby they were expecting in October, although Jackie was concerned that it might take Rob's mind too much off his coaching—Fairfield had its best shot in ten years of bringing home the division title.

It had been Rachel Patterson who struck the one note of asperity. All evening Scanlon had been looking for his chance to get her alone, and after dinner seized his opportunity when he saw her break away from a group and head for the back door. He intercepted her before she could go inside and tried to engage her in small talk. How did she like teaching elementary school? What was it like living in the boondocks? Scanlon found her buoyant, eager to talk about her work, herself, and her husband without the slightest circumspection. So he was taken completely off guard when out of the blue she observed, with a charming toss of her blonde mane, and a guileless laugh, that she thought he was about the most cynical person she'd ever met. Then, as if on cue, Josh Patterson shuffled over to them from across the lawn in all his affable blond bulk. Scanlon had been annoyed to the point of anger, but how could you be angry with Hansel and Gretel? He didn't think they bore him any ill will, even if there was nothing but malice bubbling in Scanlon's gut. What had she meant by that crack and how dare she say such a thing to him? He never had the chance to press her with these questions because she went into the house and that was the last he saw of her the rest of the evening.

Scanlon watched the approach of a single headlight, and when a motorcycle went by he took this as a sign that he was fit to drive.

Scanlon lay wide-awake in his dark room, a tumbler of Alice's Black Velvet resting on his chest. Tomorrow he was supposed to meet again with Winship. The principal had assured him at the party that this time the textbooks would be there. On Tuesday, Scanlon would begin teaching school. That reality hadn't properly sunk in yet. How did one go about teaching school? He remembered how awful his own teachers had been in high school. Would he become stuffy and pompous like Mr. Cutler, hectoring and sarcastic like Miss Perkins? Would he develop a terminal case of bad breath like Mr. Ryder? Would he be despised by his students the way he despised some of his teachers? And if he allowed himself to think about it, having to teach biology, a subject of which he knew precious little, he could have worked himself into a catatonic state without any help whatsoever from Alice's Black Velvet. The physical sciences he could fake well enough, but beyond high school the only course in biology he'd had was one of those freshman surveys where you listened to lectures in the company of five hundred others and your lab experience consisted of dissecting a rubbery fetal pig. There had been a lot of taxonomic gibberish to memorize and, as he recalled, he was grossed out by the pig dissection. Scanlon swallowed some whiskey, trying not to think about it.

Then he began to think about Lucy. He hadn't heard her voice in so long, weeks before he came to Groveton. Katie and her parents did everything in their power to deny him access to his daughter. He should go downstairs now and call them collect, demand to talk to his own daughter. Fat chance of anyone in the Durand household accepting a collect call from him. Something prevented him from charging calls to California on Ira's number. Katie would see to it that Lucy forgot him. There would come a time when he would no longer exist for his little girl the way he no longer existed for his wife. Scanlon drank the last of his whiskey. What was it with him and women? And in the morning he would have to deal with Winship again. He knew how he would feel in the morning, and if he allowed himself to fall asleep there was a better than even chance that he wouldn't hear the alarm clock.

Scanlon fell asleep in spite of himself, just as he had fallen asleep last New Year's Eve. He awakened in a panic thinking that he had overslept, missed his appointment with Winship. But it was predawn light that filtered through the curtains. As he knew it would, his head pounded; the pillow was soaked with sweat and spilled whiskey. If he lay back down he would surely fall back asleep, so he got up and dressed slowly, painfully, his poor head engorged with blood to the point of exploding. He tiptoed downstairs like a sneak thief, carrying his shoes in his hand so as not to wake up his aunt and uncle.

Uncle Ira was already up, of course, as Scanlon should have known he would be.

"Up early this morning," Ira said, standing at the stove brewing the battery acid he called coffee in a chipped, enamel saucepan. "You look a little green around the gills, Johnny boy."

"I wish somebody would have warned me about the drinking habits of schoolteachers. I have an appointment with the man at eight. I didn't want to take the chance of oversleeping."

"Coffee?"

Scanlon's innards turned over at the thought of Ira's coffee.

"This'll kill you or cure you," Ira said, pouring Scanlon a big mug of the murky brew. When his uncle went to the bathroom Scanlon got the Black Velvet down from the cupboard and laced his coffee.

"Top you off?" Ira asked, back from his bathroom routine.

"I'm all right. Hope you don't mind, I helped myself to some of Alice's medicine."

"Hell, no. Got to have some of that hair-of-the-dog. I know the routine."

"I envy you, Ira. It's a nasty, evil habit. Worse than smoking," Scanlon said, lighting up a cigarette. Ira hadn't had a drop to drink in five years, and he had been a varsity drinker in his day. He got fed up with waking up mornings with no memory of what he'd done the night before. So, one morning he woke up and swore off the stuff, just like that. It was a good story, one Alice and her sisters liked to tell, but Scanlon suspected there was more to it than that. At forty-seven Ira looked fit: flat belly, no sagging flesh around the neck, no wrinkles around his clear blue eyes. But he was operating on a single kidney, and was made to follow a strict low-salt, low-fat diet on account of high blood pressure. If he hadn't made the decision to quit drinking on his own, surely the doctors would have insisted. Either way, Ira was better off. Scanlon often wondered what was happening to his own vital organs under siege from alcohol.

"Now if I could give these up," Ira said, lighting up a filter tip. "I can rustle you up some bacon and eggs, if you want. Look like you could use something in your stomach. If you're going to be a drinking man you got to eat if you want to hang on to your liver."

Scanlon refused his uncle's offer of bacon and eggs. He was thinking that a bloody Mary would do nicely but Alice didn't keep any vodka or gin in the house.

Uncle Ira had to be on the job at six, so Scanlon found himself alone in the kitchen giving in to the temptation to open a cold beer of which Alice kept an abundant stock in the refrigerator. The only way to beat a hangover was at its own game. Scanlon chugged half a bottle. This quieted his insides down some. By the time Alice came around at seven, Scanlon had dropped his second empty in the garbage and was feeling a whole lot better.

"Well, don't you look hungover. Want a beer?" Alice said, going to the refrigerator.

"What the hell. You going to have one?"

"Got to have my coffee first." Alice measured out coffee into the electric percolator (she would have none of Ira's evil stovetop brew) while Scanlon went to work on his third beer on top of the whiskey he'd had in his coffee. "Must've been some party last night? What time did you get up?"

"I had coffee with Ira at about dawn, and yes it was some party."

"You drank Ira's coffee? No wonder you look so bad."

Scanlon touched his face to feel what it was about it that looked so bad. He had started finally to feel human, thanks to Alice's whiskey and Alice's beer. How would Winship think he looked?

"Alice," Scanlon began, "I want you to know how much I, you know, appreciate everything you and Ira have done for me, putting up with me. I just want to ..."

"Oh," Alice said, dismissing him with a wave of her hand, "we've always had people in the house. Had my brother's two girls with us all through high school. You never met Jeanette and Judy? Stayed with us all through high school while Armand—you know Armand—was having his troubles with Alice. His wife's name was Alice like mine. You never met Alice, did you? Then we had old man Labonte stay with us for six years, right up where you are now. Died right in that room, in the bed you're sleeping in, poor soul." Alice didn't mention the fact that Johnny Labalm's grandmother spent the last eight months of her life with them. Was it possible that Alice resented the old lady's presence there? She had every right to, but it didn't seem to Scanlon that Alice was capable of resentment. Then, who was he to say that she didn't resent him for freeloading?

"I don't know what to say," Scanlon said.

"Well, you don't have to say anything. Drink your beer. Don't be late for school." Alice laughed.

"You'll at least let me help out with the food. Let me take care of the food, period." Such largesse with beer and whiskey in him. He could barely make alimony and child support payments.

"What for? You eat like a bird. Put a six-pack in the fridge once in a while, let me bum a cigarette now and then."

Scanlon was light-headed when he got up to get ready for Winship, giddy with alcohol and Alice's generosity. The floor moved underfoot like a treadmill. He brushed his teeth three times to scour away the smell of alcohol even though he knew that it did no good. Maybe he would chew a cigarette before he had to face Winship. That used to do the trick when he was a high school kid, or so he believed at the time.

"Smells like my old school," Scanlon said to Winship who sat at his desk shuffling papers around. "Must be the floorwax."

"Be with you in a minute, Jack. Trudy, where in damnation did you put those purchase orders I asked you to type yesterday?" Trudy, a cute young thing with short auburn hair and perky breasts, remembered, distinctly, placing them on top of a stack of packing slips right in the middle of his desk. She glanced at Scanlon and shrugged her thin shoulders. Scanlon offered her a wink but she looked away too soon. Trudy was the one Winship had blamed for screwing up the book order. Fairfield High, class of '66. Scanlon had seen her in her cheerleading outfit in one of the framed photographs downstairs in the trophy case. She stood beside Winship's desk looking exasperated while the principal lifted up piles of papers, flung open drawers in search of the elusive purchase orders.

"Sorry, Jack," Winship said, "everything's topsy-turvy this morning."

You want topsy-turvy, Scanlon thought, peek inside my head and stomach. Trudy produced the missing purchase orders on top of a stack of papers that Winship had just handled. Winship grunted and Trudy raised her head a little in righteous vindication.

"Come on down to the lab. I've got your books. Still in their boxes, I'm afraid," Winship said, looking over at his secretary as if she were the one responsible for the books still being in their boxes. Scanlon tried another wink, and this time Trudy received it and smiled. He'd learned in industry that it paid to make allies of the secretaries.

The lab, as Winship referred to it, was really a combination of laboratory and classroom, a relic with two long lab benches and one soapstone sink in the back of the room, exactly three gas outlets if you counted the one on the lecture desk, and three electrical outlets. No fume hood. The chemicals were stored, in no particular order, in an old oak wall cabinet with dirty glass doors. Between the lab benches and the lecture desk were five neat rows of tablet armchairs. This is where Scanlon would spend seven forty-five minute periods a day.

"Remarkable," Scanlon said.

"How's that?"

"That Fairfield High kids who take science should all be right-handed."

Winship scratched his head in incomprehension. "What?"

"The desks. They're all right-handed."

"So they are," Winship said, shrugging his shoulders. "Nobody's ever complained."

"These the books?" Scanlon asked. Three volumes of hardcover textbooks lay on the lecture desk. Scanlon gave Winship only half his attention as the principal pointed out the big improvements he saw in the new textbooks over the old Dull, Metcalf, and Williams editions they'd been using for centuries. Scanlon was trying instead to imagine what it would be like cooped up in a room like this all day.

"What about these lesson plans I keep hearing about?" Scanlon asked him. "Do I actually have to plan in advance what I'm going to do in class?"

Winship's expression remained deadpan. "I don't check teachers' lesson plans, if that's what you mean. I assume my teachers will maintain a professional attitude. My advice is you start out tough with them. Don't give them an inch unless you want them to take a mile. Later you can ease up on them if you want. The main thing is to let them know who's boss right off the bat."

"Right." Scanlon's dislike for Winship was rekindled. "What about equipment? I don't see any science stuff in here. What about glassware?"

"Well, beakers, flasks, funnels and the like are in those cabinets underneath the student lab stations, but I'm afraid we're short on physics equipment. Perk just used to give them theoretical stuff, problem solving and the like, and when I took over after his death last winter I pretty much did the same thing. Physics was never my strong suit. Anyway, you don't have to worry about that since we're not offering physics this year."

"No physics this year?" Scanlon had looked forward to teaching physics, thought he had understood that physics was the subject Sumner Purnell wanted him mainly to teach. Apparently he had been mistaken.

"Nope. Nobody's complained. Don't worry," Winship said, perhaps sensing Scanlon's dismay. "You'll do just fine. The kids will be too interested in your mustache to notice how nervous you are."

Winship had a talent for reassuring and nettling Scanlon at the same time.

Scanlon thanked him for his advice and back in the principal's office he was given his grade book with a section for written lesson plans.

He said his good-byes to Winship and Trudy, with another wink for Trudy as he backed out the door. This time Trudy turned back to her typewriter without smiling.

The high school occupied two floors in the front of the building. The gymnasium separated the high school from the back of the building where grades one through eight were taught. Under the gym was the cafeteria. The teachers' "lounge" was a small, damp windowless room off the cafeteria that connected by a door with a room used as storage for nonperishables. The kindergarten was a separate, one-story house on a little hillock beside the main building. Sumner Purnell had his office in this house. Behind the school was a dirt playground with swings, jungle-gym, and a carousel-like contraption with metal handbars.

Scanlon went down to the teachers' lounge to have a look at the textbooks. In the middle of the small room was a wooden table with a deeply gouged surface, surrounded by four metal folding chairs. Against the far wall sat an old, mildewy sofa leaking stuffing from its arms and cushions. A folding card table bore a coffee urn, some envelopes of cream substitute, and a jar of sugar cubes. There was no sink in the room, no source of water.

Scanlon dropped his books on the scarred table, collapsed onto the stinking sofa and fell asleep at once. He awoke later with his second hangover of the day—dry mouth, pounding head, roiling stomach. A cracked plastic electric clock hummed on the cement wall above the coffee urn. Ten to one. He'd been asleep for hours.

Instead of driving back to Groveton, Scanlon turned west on Route 2, his eyes smarting in their sockets from the afternoon sunlight. A hot, rainless August had left the pasturelands flanking Route 2 brown. Scanlon drove slowly, in a sort of trance. Traffic backed up on him and began to honk. He waved them around him. The rugged, evergreen landscape merged with the narrow, tortuous road; it was as if he were driving through a forest in some places. When the traffic behind him cleared, Scanlon pulled over his VW and threw up on the soft shoulder. His eyes watered; his nose and throat stung from acid vomit.

There was a decrepit gas station along the road with a Flying A gas pump outside that Scanlon remembered from when he was Johnny Labalm. He and his pals would stop there for cold sodas on their way back from swimming in Goose Pond.

A sign over the door advertised cold beer and ale. Scanlon began to salivate at the thought of a beer. It stank of cooking inside and something like a combination of body odor and disinfectant. It was dark and claustrophobic, exactly as he remembered it, the shelves mostly empty except for sparse rows of dusty canned goods. One entire wall was a beer cooler, the glass opaque with dirt and condensation.

A big-breasted young girl in a sleeveless blouse sat behind a linoleum covered counter reading a magazine. She had on a lot of lipstick, such as the kind worn by Cynthia Sinclair, and her eyebrows were plucked to a pencil line beneath which was a heavy coat of blue eye shadow.

"You old enough to sell me some beer?" Scanlon asked her. She didn't look up from her magazine.

"Dale. Beer," she yelled.

In a little while, Dale appeared from behind a chintz curtain in the rear of the store. He was wall-eyed, even more so than Scanlon, wore a tank-top undershirt, a pair of green work pants that sagged in the crotch; he looked rumpled and cross, as if he'd been taken away from his nap. Dale was maybe thirty years old.

"Do for you?"

"You got Olympia?" Scanlon asked, looking at the girl, then at Dale.

"No."

"Lucky Lager?" Scanlon knew that brand wasn't sold in Vermont or anywhere else in the east that he knew about.

"You can see for yourself what we got," Dale said, motioning toward the beer cooler.

"Forget it. I wanted Olympia. Let me have a pack of smokes. Winstons," Scanlon said to the girl. He could feel Dale's eyes drilling him in the back. He heard the curtain move, Dale leave the room.

"Thirty-five," the girl said, nose still in her magazine. Scanlon dropped a dollar bill on the counter.

"You go to Fairfield High?"

"Quit last year," she said without looking at him.

"Don't like school?" She had on a narrow gold band on her married finger.

"Don't teach you nothin'. Nothin' you can use."

"I see you're a married woman."

"Yeah," she said, looking at Scanlon.

"Dale?"

"Yeah." Her shoulders squared, her voice rose a little.

"How about my change?" Scanlon smiled at her. She gave him his change with an expression like the one he imagined Dale had for him while his back was turned. "Good-bye," Scanlon said.

Scanlon headed east toward Groveton and home.

Chapter Three

That he would be addressed by students as Mr. Scanlon had Scanlon feeling oddly fraudulent. Part of him relished the idea of being the object of such respect even if he knew it to be a formality, an institutional knee jerk. But he had never before been addressed as mister in his life except by clerks and waiters. Still, he wondered if he shouldn't dispense with the mister business with his students, have them call him Jack, or Scanlon. His colleagues would not approve. The impression he got at Winship's party would definitely not support this kind of democratic approach to student / teacher relations. Order, discipline, respect itself would be in jeopardy if he allowed his students this kind of license. He had been surprised at how blatantly cynical some of them had been on the subject of the education of youth. What Lyle Higgins saw in this generation of adolescents was incipient laziness, self-centeredness, and general irresponsibility. How unlike the values of probity, duty, and respect for your elders, imparted to his generation. The social order, in Lyle's mind, was in a state of decay. And Lillian Bloemer, when she had had enough gin to drink, denounced today's youth for their utter lack of discipline, their lack of respect not so much for their elders but for knowledge itself. They had a gift for shirking any kind of academic responsibility. What was most egregious to Lillian, who when she got warmed up marched back and forth waving her silver-plated cigarette holder like a conductor's baton, was their native penchant for seizing upon just about anything that was low, and common, and vulgar in the popular culture, which was to say everything you could name that appeared on TV or in movies emanating from Hollywood. The anti-intellectual movement in America had reached antic proportions with this generation, lamented Lillian Bloemer.

On the drive to Fairfield on this clear, sky-blue September morning, his insides churning from nervousness, Scanlon promised himself to be vigilant against this way of thinking. He'd left the house early to get settled in and calmed down before having to face six separate groups of students who would be looking to him to set their agenda for the day, and for many days to come. The seven miles of Route 2 from Groveton to Fairfield never looked more beautiful, more bucolic than they did today. The oppressive heat wave with its suffocating humidity had yielded to the brisk, cool air that promised autumn. Scanlon counted eight deer grazing among the dairy cows in the sloping pastureland before he reached Fairfield.

The night before, he'd managed to stay sober long enough to work up some reading assignments, write out a rough schedule of topics to cover in each of his classes for the first week. He felt somewhat prepared, not knowing at this point what amounted to preparation. Many questions arose in his mind that had not occurred to him before, as he wrestled with the details of teaching abstract concepts to what he imagined were impressionable kids. Should he lecture to them? Spoon-feed them the way he had been spoon-fed in high school and college? It seemed the wrong way to go about it, but he was at a loss for an alternative.

His sleep had been fitful; he was up several times during the night to check the alarm button for fear of oversleeping. He tossed and he turned and two or three times he'd been tempted to go downstairs to the cupboard, to the Black Velvet. He resisted, exercising a little willpower for a change.

In the school parking lot, three yellow buses were unloading students. The little ones, the lower graders, ran shrieking for the playground. The high schoolers milled around in clusters by the side of the building, talking and laughing, everyone seeming to know everyone else which was no more than he would have expected in a rural school. Scanlon parked his VW and headed for the front door, his arms loaded with books. He had the attention of a few of the kids who watched his every step. He made eye contact with a group of boys and girls near the front door who smiled and said hi. Scanlon smiled back and nodded before pushing through the heavy door. One of the boys held the door open for him.

Inside, he discovered that he was sweating freely and worried that he might sweat clear through the underarms of his jacket.

Scanlon found Winship, Lyle Higgins, and Cynthia Sinclair in the teachers' lounge.

"Like running the gauntlet out there," Scanlon said.

"Want coffee it'll cost you a nickel," said Lyle Higgins.

"Sounds reasonable," Scanlon replied, trying very hard not to wisecrack the math teacher whose face seemed to challenge him to do so.

"How you doing, Jack?" Winship asked. "Nervous?"

"You bet."

"Oh, you'll be over that in no time at all," Cynthia reassured him. She sat at the table blowing into a steaming Styrofoam cup, the rim of which bore a big smear of her scarlet lipstick. Scanlon put his books down on the table, made himself a cup of instant coffee and made sure Higgins was watching when he deposited a nickel in the slot of an ice cream carton labeled "coffee fund."

"So, assembly at eight?" Scanlon asked, for lack of anything else to say in what seemed to him an uncomfortable silence.

"Right," said Winship, preoccupied with a clipboard full of papers.

"Daryl will welcome the students back to school and introduce the faculty," explained Cynthia in her teacher's voice. "You'll be the center of attention, Jack, being the only new teacher this year." She seemed to want to add that his mustache might be another reason for his being the center of attention. Perhaps she held back, thinking that Scanlon would judge her, would get the impression that impropriety came naturally to her, especially after her remarks about his marriage at Winship's party.

"I'm not sure I like the idea of being the center of attention," Scanlon said. Lyle Higgins chuckled.

"After shortened classes I'd like to meet with everyone for a little bit down in Miriam's room. That's down on the first floor, Jack, 104. It's where we have our *ad hoc* faculty meetings. Nothing regular at Fairfield," Winship said. "Well, I've got a few things to do in the office before assembly. See you all there. Good luck this morning, Jack."

"Thanks."

After assembly, in which he was sure he'd received the longest and the most enthusiastic applause of any of the faculty Winship introduced, Scanlon, walking slightly taller than when he'd entered the building, made his way through the crowded halls to his room on the second floor. He would meet first with his homeroomers, thirty-eight freshmen. Classes were shortened to twenty minutes on the first day. The regular schedule began in earnest tomorrow.

There were already quite a few kids in the room when he arrived with his armload of books. They fell silent when he entered. He strode to the lecture desk and made a fuss with his books and papers, conscious of the attention being paid him. He pretended to write meaningfully in his grade and attendance book, buying time, mustering courage for the moment when he must look out and face them. In the meantime, more kids came in and took chairs without fanfare. A bell rang to start the homeroom period. Scanlon sighed and looked out at five rows of upturned faces.

"Welcome to high school," Scanlon began. "This is what you've been waiting to hear all your lives. Right?" A few kids smiled. A girl in the front row, apparently eager to please, laughed out loud as if someone had finally hit upon a profound truism about adolescence. Most of them stared at him, as impassive as the tablet armchairs that held them. "I'm going to have to ask you to write your names on this seating chart I'll be passing around. By June I should have learned all your names." The girl in the front row yelped this time and dropped her eyes in embarrassment when Scanlon looked in her direction.

A small boy with a cowlick and wearing a brown corduroy shirt rolled his eyes. Scanlon laid his seating grid on the tablet arm of the first row chair occupied by a plump girl with a pageboy haircut.

"While you're filling out the chart, what if I just read off your names from my list and you raise your hand when you hear yours. If you don't hear it, it's probably because I've mispronounced it. Please don't let me mutilate your name. What else do you have, if not your good name?" Scanlon glanced at his number one fan in case she found this amusing. This time all he got was a weak little smile.

Scanlon noticed the pungent, if not disagreeable, odor of the barnyard. Some of these kids had no doubt been up since dawn performing their chores. He had time to get through only half the names on his list before the bell rang for the beginning of first period, and his seating grid was stalled in the middle of the second row.

"Be sure to take the same seat tomorrow morning," Scanlon said, his voice drowned out by the scraping of chairs and the racket of exiting bodies.

His homeroom group was replaced by twenty-eight of his biology students, all sophomores. Scanlon looked them over carefully, recalling Lillian Bloemer's observation about what pains sophomores were. He noticed Tommy Winship slouching in a back row chair with something like a sneer on his thin, freckled face. Scanlon's stomach sank. After he finished handing out textbooks, and giving them their first reading assignment, which was met with groans from some of the boys, Scanlon asked them to take out paper and pencil.

"Is this a test, or what?" Tommy Winship asked.

"We don't have any paper," another kid said.

"You got an extra pencil I can borrow, Mr. Scanlon?" an earnest looking kid in the first row asked.

"What is this?" Scanlon said, offering his upturned palms which was supposed to convey exasperation and dismay. "You all look bright enough to know that this is school and schoolwork requires things like pencils and paper and stuff."

"This is the first day," a girl whined. "We never do anything the first day."

"Listen. Those of you who need paper, borrow from a neighbor. Same for you guys without a pencil or pen. Jesus." Scanlon's use of the word Jesus had them tittering and whispering. "All right. Clam up and listen." He shot his cuffs, walked out from behind the lecture desk and folded his arms across his chest. "Are you paying attention?" Several kids nodded their heads, taking him seriously. Two or three of the more perceptive ones smiled.

"In the few minutes remaining in the period, I want you to answer this question: Why study biology? Be sure to sign your name to your paper before you hand it in. Any questions?"

A hand went up. Scanlon nodded. "Is this going to be graded?"

"No." Another hand shot up.

"You take off for spelling?"

"I just told you, this isn't a graded exercise. It's more for my own information than anything. So why don't you get busy. There's not much time left in the period."

"This sucks," he heard someone mutter. Scanlon immediately cast his eye toward Tommy Winship whose head was bent over his paper.

He used the same tack with his chemistry and general science classes. He asked them to write out their reasons for taking the course, knowing that more than likely their reasons had to do with fulfilling the science requirement. The exercise killed some time, filled the void, gave Scanlon a chance to get a grip on himself. He was already beginning to panic; his mind was not operating and he was sweating, sweating, sweating! Drowning in his own sweat, sick to his stomach and wanting a DRINK! What was he doing here? Classes had met for a mere twenty minutes most of which Scanlon had the students writing, but by the time he had met with his last group he was emotionally exhausted, physically spent.

"I would have never guessed that teaching school could be so demanding physically," Scanlon said to Winship down in Miriam Hawkins' room where Fairfield High's *ad hoc* faculty meetings were held. Winship smiled.

"So how did your first day go?"

"Don't ask."

"Rough, huh?" Winship looked concerned.

"No sign of overt hostility yet. A little grumbling over a written exercise, but not a bad start, really. No, not bad at all." God forbid he should worry the principal.

"Good."

Winship's agenda was filled with the minutiae of daily school life, the most significant issue being faculty supervision of the cafeteria at lunchtime. Scanlon was asked if he wouldn't mind taking on the responsibility of adviser to the school newspaper. It had had some problems in the past few years, coming out sporadically at best. One year it came out not at all.

"I won't bring much journalistic expertise to the task," Scanlon said, "but I'll do what I can."

"Hardest part of that job's keeping the mimeograph machine in duplicating fluid," Lyle Higgins said. He was also assigned to help chaperon the dance the first Friday in October. Winship would be on hand to help out.

"Don't let Higgins get under your skin," Josh Patterson counseled Scanlon after the meeting. "He's that way with every new teacher. It's his version of rites of passage. Didn't let up on me till spring my first year. Want to split a sandwich?" He invited Scanlon back to his classroom to share a peanut butter and honey sandwich made with Rachel's own cracked wheat bread.

"Rachel's into baking. She's always got something in the oven. I think she might even be baking lasagna tonight if you'd care to join us." The invitation was off the cuff enough to make Scanlon wonder if he had heard him right. Was Patterson in the habit of inviting people home for dinner without consulting his wife? Whenever he tried to pull that with Katie there would be hell to pay. It may have had something to do with the fact that Katie couldn't cook. She lacked just about everything that Rachel possessed: good genes and a Bryn Mawr education to name two. In any case, Scanlon's instincts told him to decline, although the prospect of spending an evening in Rachel Patterson's company tempted him to accept. Who knew? Maybe he could even convince her that he was not the world's most cynical person.

When Patterson invited him for dinner again a couple of weeks later, however, Scanlon accepted without hesitation.

"Why don't you just follow us out to the house after school. I can show you around Burton. That should take all of five minutes. We can play some badminton, have a drink."

"Sounds great." It did sound great, especially the part about the drink.

Burton was seven or eight gorgeous miles south of Fairfield. The fall foliage was in full color and Scanlon had begun to feel slightly more comfortable in his new life as schoolteacher, even if he improvised from day to day, keeping only one short step ahead of the pack, as it were. But it was a glorious day, full of warmth and color and magnanimity. And soon he would be having drinks with Rachel Patterson. For the moment all was well with the world.

The Pattersons lived in a large, square, yellow house, incongruous among the small capes in affluent Burton, set a hundred feet or so back from the road, shaded by the largest maple Scanlon had ever seen. The land behind the house rose gradually to pasture then gave way to mountainside and its predominance of evergreens.

"Nice backyard," Scanlon said to Patterson, with his eye on Rachel's backside as she fetched something from the trunk of their car. She had on her schoolteaching clothes: black miniskirt, white blouse. She wore no stockings; blonde down stood out on her tanned legs. Scanlon must have been gawking, not paying attention, because he scarcely heard what Patterson said to him.

"What?"

"I said, I wish I could say it belonged to us, but we're only renting. Nineteen rooms. Can you believe it? We only use three of the downstairs rooms and a bedroom upstairs. Place is a bear to heat. No insulation, like most of the houses around here. Come on in."

Rachel went in ahead of them, and when Patterson and Scanlon passed through the shed into the big, old-fashioned farm kitchen she was nowhere in sight. Wide pine floor boards, an old combination oil and wood burning stove such as the kind Johnny Labalm grew up with, and a lead-lined sink with a single cold-water faucet. In the middle of the large room with painted wainscoting was a long tavern table strewn with books, papers, and an old Royal typewriter.

"Rache likes to spread out when she does her schoolwork," Patterson said by way of explaining the condition of the table. Around the table were several painted, unmatched chairs. "Hope you're a kitchen man. This is where we spend most of our time. Come on, I'll show you the other downstairs rooms."

Scanlon knew where he'd spend most of his time if he were married to Rachel. The downstairs was sparsely furnished with makeshift pieces, as if the Pattersons were camping out. In the small room off the living room that

Patterson used as a study was an enormous oak rolltop desk, paper-strewn like the kitchen table.

"This is definitely the biggest desk I've ever seen," Scanlon said, running his hand over the smooth finish as appreciatively as if it were Rachel's behind.

"You'd never believe where I got it."

"Sure I would." He would believe anything Patterson said. Patterson looked altogether too wholesome to stoop to lying.

"The dump."

"I don't believe you."

"Sitting there big as life. All it needed was a little cleaning. You're looking at the finish just as I found it. Who would throw away something like that, can you tell me?"

"Jesus," was all Scanlon could say. "It must weigh a ton and seven eighths." Scanlon felt, all of a sudden, jealous and resentful. Why was it that good fortune followed the Pattersons of the world around like a puppy? He had this magnificent desk, and he had Rachel. And he hadn't offered his guest the drink he'd promised either.

On their way back to the kitchen, they were met by Rachel bouncing down the stairs like a little girl. She'd changed into jeans and a Princeton sweatshirt. She was stunning, and Scanlon was nauseated with jealousy and desire.

"So," she sang in her high, buoyant voice, "how are things going for you at school, Jack?"

"They haven't turned on me yet." Scanlon had to deliberately avert his eyes for fear of being caught staring.

"How about a drink?" Patterson finally asked. "Or is it too early for you, Jack?"

"I guess I'm ready if everyone else is." Patterson must have noticed how he had put it away at Winship's party. Was he trying to be a wise guy?

"Well," Patterson said, rubbing his hands together, "I wouldn't say no to a tall gin and tonic. What about you, Rache?"

"I think I'll wait. Why don't you two play some badminton while I get dinner started."

Scanlon wondered if he should offer to help with dinner even if it went against his instincts to help women in the kitchen.

"All right," Patterson said before he could offer. "Feel like whacking the birdie around for a bit? I can show you Burton another time. What can I fix you to drink, Jack?" Scanlon was not prepared to tell the Pattersons, or any of the others at Fairfield High, that he was already familiar with Burton and all the rest of the Northeast Kingdom. Not yet, if ever.

Patterson rose slightly in Scanlon's estimate when he had bourbon to offer. He had rigged a badminton net on a sloping rectangle of lawn beside the house. Lawn chairs with frayed strapping, a rusty hibachi grill, shuttlecocks and racquets lay carelessly around the grass. It missed being entropic in the way the yards of the poor houses he'd seen on his nostalgic rides through those warrens of back roads around Fairfield and West Fairfield, however. Scanlon felt ill at ease, at a disadvantage. He swallowed some whiskey and prepared to clash with Josh Patterson in a game of badminton on his host's home court. He was no match for Patterson, whose vicious smashes and cunning drop shots had Scanlon lunging and scrambling. When he was lucky enough to get his racquet on the perverse birdie, he would hit long or into the net. In no time his shirt was sweat-soaked and his cigarette-smoke-scorched lungs were on fire. Patterson hadn't broken a sweat, and his breathing was shallow.

"I surrender." Scanlon dropped into a lawn chair and heard the nylon straps rip. He looked at Patterson who inspected his racquet head with a fingernail, frowning.

"I've got winners," Rachel said, coming upon them carrying a tall glass of iced tea with lemon.

"Let me fetch Jack another drink first," Patterson said.

Scanlon handed Patterson his empty glass, conscious of his profuse sweating now that Rachel was near. He need not have worried because instead of sitting down and engaging him in conversation she set about picking up racquets and stray shuttlecocks, straightening out the lawn chairs—conspicuously avoiding him. He asked how school had gone for her today, a fairly dopey thing to ask, but Rachel either didn't hear the question or chose to ignore it. Scanlon was relieved when Patterson returned with his drink but nothing for himself. Scanlon was content to sit and nurse his new drink while Rachel did battle with her husband. He was surprised at the ferocity with which they went at each other. Patterson held nothing back. And if Rachel's moves were delicate, fawn-like, she was able to return her husband's deep smashes with deft flicks of the wrist, and managed to put away a few of her own shots with surprising strength.

"That shot was in, Joshua," she complained, and for a moment Scanlon couldn't be sure if she was serious.

"It was out a mile. Come on."

Rachel stomped her foot. "It was in. Wasn't it, Jack?"

"It looked in from here," Scanlon said, tentatively.

"There. The judge has spoken, and I declare this game officially under protest." Rachel sat down on the ground in mock petulance. Josh slouched in a lawn chair. They were both perspiring.

"All right," Patterson said, "but I want an impartial judge for the rematch." Had Patterson nailed him lusting after his wife? Scanlon looked into his glass, felt his face grow warm.

"How can you expect impartiality after the way you abused me out there?" Scanlon said. To his relief, Patterson laughed.

But Scanlon was nearly finished with his second drink. Patterson had barely touched his first, and it was clear that Rachel would not be drinking alcohol.

"Josh tells me that Lyle Higgins is up to his tricks with you," Rachel said to Scanlon.

"I suppose so. He doesn't bother me." Scanlon rattled the ice cubes around in his glass as if to send a subliminal message to Patterson. "I haven't had much contact with him since the first day, actually." She could be so attentive and cordial with her husband around.

"Jack's getting a reputation as a bit of a radical," Patterson said.

"What do you mean by that?" Scanlon asked quickly.

"Don't misunderstand. The kids love it. You're the first teacher they've had in a long time who doesn't talk down to them. They appreciate it." Patterson spoke as one who also enjoyed a good reputation with the students. Scanlon supposed he should have felt flattered, complimented, but Patterson looked altogether too smug and who knew what he was up to?

No doubt the act that had earned him the "radical" label had to do with last Thursday's meeting. Kids had pegged him, apparently, as a teacher with a sympathetic ear. He had, in fact, in the first few days of school listened to so much muttering about the "repressive" conditions at Fairfield High that he took it upon himself (without consulting Winship) to call a voluntary evening meeting in which anyone who wanted to could air his grievances in a rational, democratic fashion. After all, they were in the cradle of liberty, "town meeting" country. To Scanlon's delight, the meeting was so well attended he had to send kids to other classrooms for extra chairs, and even then, plenty of kids were left standing in the packed room.

The repressive atmosphere they described amounted to what they considered unreasonable homework assignments by some teachers—Lillian Bloemer and Lyle Higgins to be specific—the lack of a Coke machine in the cafeteria (even crummy old Wingate High had a Coke machine). And it wasn't fair the way they were treated like children, either. Imagine having to get a hall pass just to go to the basement! This wasn't the inner city, for crying out loud. Where was the trust? With one or two exceptions, they didn't feel that teachers trusted them at all. And there weren't nearly enough dances. Classes were boring.

Scanlon listened politely though he found most of their concerns trivial at best, downright silly for the most part. They were bored with school routine, and life in the boondocks. They were after a little excitement, a normal enough impulse in Scanlon's opinion.

Nothing was resolved, of course; it was a maverick assembly and Scanlon knew from the start that if Winship had blundered into it he would have been furious. Yet, he felt that something good had come of it. He felt an affinity for these kids, whose names he despaired of ever learning, that had thus far eluded him. He sensed that the feeling was shared. Several kids stayed behind after the meeting adjourned to help return chairs and straighten up the room. Some of his chemistry students even volunteered to inventory and alphabetize the chemical cabinet. They put in a good hour of work and when Scanlon drove back to Groveton that night he felt exhilarated for the first time in he couldn't remember how long.

The next morning, when they were alone in the teacher's lounge, Winship asked him if he belonged to SDS.

"SDS? Are you kidding? Why?" Winship had gotten wind of the meeting, of course. There wasn't much that went on in the place that he didn't know about.

"I'd be careful if I were you, Jack," Winship had cautioned. "Hattie Letourneau's dad is a former FBI agent. He could cause trouble for you if he thought you were trying to stir up the pot."

"You can't be serious," Scanlon had said. Winship's expression had convinced him that he was serious. "It was an innocent little gripe session, for crying out loud. There couldn't have been more than a half-dozen subversives present. Hasn't J. Edgar got anything better for his agents to do than plant them in hick high schools?" Scanlon could see Winship's jaw working, his face take on color.

"A word to the wise, Jack. I'll try to soft-pedal this thing, but I'm advising you to not let this get out of hand. All right?"

"This is insane." Scanlon had taken two handfuls of his hair and pretended to pull.

"I want you to promise me you won't let this snowball."

"I can't promise you anything," Scanlon had said and stalked out of the room. Later, when he had cooled off, he sought out Winship in his office.

"Sorry for acting like that. It really was just an innocent meeting, you know."

"I'm sure. People around here are a little on edge these days, what with the hippie element moving in, and that business in Chicago this summer with the radicals. They're suspicious by nature. Just watch yourself is all I'm asking."

Scanlon recounted his conversation with Winship to the Pattersons.

"My guess is Daryl made up the story about Hattie Letourneau's old man," Patterson said. "Winship's scared to death that any controversy, no matter how trivial, will jeopardize his precious bond issue. He can be such a jackass."

"Josh Patterson!" Rachel said, thrusting back her shoulders, "I can't believe I'm hearing this. He doesn't mean a word of it, Jack. Daryl Winship has been terrific to us, and I think it's to his credit that he's managed to keep everything together as well as he has under the circumstances. You take it back, Joshua, or I'll never speak to you again."

"Circumstances?" Scanlon asked

"That's right," Rachel said. "You would not believe the criticism he's gotten from those PTO ninnies for pushing the bond issue for the new wing. Everyone wants the best education for their kids until it comes time to pay the bills. It makes me so angry." Rachel was passionate in her defense of Winship. To Scanlon, it made her all the more alluring.

"Come on, Rache," Patterson said, looking into his glass, "the man's a yo-yo. You don't deal with him day in, day out."

Scanlon could see from the set of Rachel's jaw that she would have liked to pursue the matter with her husband, but good manners prevailed. She excused herself to go inside to continue dinner preparations. This time Scanlon threw aside caution and offered to go inside with her and lend a hand.

"No thanks, I can manage." Scanlon felt rebuffed.

After dinner—during which Scanlon had drunk too much jug burgundy, much more than his host and hostess combined—as Rachel prepared to wash dishes and Patterson went to the bathroom, Scanlon was emboldened to remove a wisp of hair that had fallen across her cheek. He tucked it behind her ear, excitement coursing through his body like an electric current. Rachel stopped what she was doing to study him.

"What is it, exactly, you want from me, Jack?" Her gaze was steady enough to cause Scanlon to avert his eyes.

"I just want to be friends."

She said nothing. Then to Scanlon's astonishment, she took his head in her soapy hands and kissed him on the mouth. It wasn't a passionate kiss—in truth it was cold and dry—but it was a kiss. He heard the toilet flush. He mopped soap suds off the back of his head with a dish towel. Rachel went back to her dishes. Patterson came into the kitchen carrying *Time* magazine.

Scanlon took leave of the Pattersons, his mind feverish with possibilities. He lay in bed that night on the edge of sleep, his brain full of Rachel Patterson. He tried to put himself to sleep with a scene of the two of them frolicking on the big kitchen table, hoping the image might spill over into his dreams. But in his dreams it was not Rachel Patterson who visited him. It was his five-year-old daughter, Lucy.

Chapter Four

St. Mary's School for Catholic Girls faced the burned-out shell of Our Lady of Fatima from across the narrow pot-holed, dead-end street. Except now St. Mary's was the headquarters of the mental health clinic, whose offices were on the first floor. On the second floor were law offices and a coiffure parlor. Scanlon got out of his car and stood for a while in front of the ponderous brick of St. Mary's. He noticed the year 1884 inscribed in cement over the arched entrance. It was the year his grandmother had been born. The number fascinated him. Eighteen was the number of years he'd been away from Groveton. Grammy would have been eighty-four this year. Maybe there was something to this numerology business. Was crazy Sister Marie, Johnny Labalm's impassioned catechism teacher, still alive? What would she think of her beloved St. Mary's taken over by shrinks, lawyers, and hairdressers?

Scanlon experienced a moment of indecision in which he wasn't sure whether to turn on his heel and flee, or keep the appointment he'd made by phone yesterday, in a mild state of panic.

"Hello there," the receptionist said, too cheerfully, "what can I do for you?" He could have named several things she could do for him. He couldn't help himself from staring at her face, a face that put him in mind of a painting. Modigliani? Long, dark hair fell along both sides of this face from a part down the middle, spilling over the shoulders of her blouse. Scanlon stared, and this Modigliani smiled patiently, no doubt accustomed to odd behavior, working in a place such as this.

"I'm sorry," Scanlon said. "I'm John Scanlon. I think I have an appointment to see a Dr. Kennedy. I called yesterday. I guess I talked to you."

"Yes, Mr. Scanlon. Mr. Kennedy's expecting you. He'll only be a minute. Won't you have a seat?"

Several metal folding chairs were arranged randomly in the middle of the floor, and except for a cheap, Formica-top coffee table on which lay torn and dog-eared magazines, most of them without covers, there was no other furniture. Scanlon sat in one of the chairs and picked through magazines, sweat beginning to course down his sides from his underarms. The receptionist went back to her typing, looking up now and then to smile. In a while a burly man in a dirty seersucker suit appeared through the door to her left, glanced briefly in Scanlon's direction, and said something in a low voice to the receptionist. He went back into his office, closing the door behind him.

"Mr. Kennedy will be with you shortly, Mr. Scanlon."

So that was Robert Kennedy. Not enough he should have such a name, he's got to look like a derelict. He made a more likely patient than a doctor. Or was he, Jack Scanlon, now a "client?" Whatever he was, Scanlon was relieved that he was the only one of his kind in the waiting room today. He crossed his legs and peeked surreptitiously over the top of *Newsweek* at the receptionist. She looked up from her typing, and gave him a big smile. He felt stupid. Kennedy was back in the doorway, beckoning to him with a finger the size of a link sausage.

Scanlon smiled at the receptionist and entered Robert Kennedy's austere office. The walls were military olive drab in contrast to the beige, almost pink walls of the waiting room. Neither room had a picture hanging, no diplomas, nothing. Two wooden straight-back chairs were placed at angles in front of Kennedy's badly scratched and dented gray metal desk.

Kennedy stood behind his desk moving papers around. He motioned for Scanlon to sit down. "I've got a sheet on you somewhere in this mess," Kennedy said, reaching in his breast pocket for a pair of black-framed spectacles. Scanlon had given the receptionist some biographical information over the phone.

"Ah. Here we are." Kennedy perused the sheet of paper, specs pushed down to the end of his big shapeless nose. Irish as a boiled dinner, Scanlon thought, and with a nose like that, probably a boozer. Kennedy's suit looked even dirtier at close quarters; his uncombed hair was dull gray, and curled over his ears and frayed shirt collar. The knot of his tie was pulled away from his throat, and his belly hung amply over the unbelted waistband of his trousers. "What if I call you John?" Kennedy sat down heavily in a wooden swivel chair.

"Everyone else calls me Jack."

"Jack it is." Kennedy still had Scanlon's sheet in his hand. He consulted it again and began to rub his temple with his fat forefinger in a slow, circular motion. The skin around his temple was discolored, like a birthmark, big as a nickel. Then he sighed, raised his wiry eyebrows, and tossed Scanlon's biographical data in with the other scattered papers on top of his desk. He leaned back in his chair. Scanlon held his breath, waiting for it to collapse under Kennedy's mass.

"So?" Kennedy asked, still at his temple.

"So, what?" Scanlon shrugged.

"So why have you come?"

Scanlon hesitated a moment, unprepared for such a question. Then he told Kennedy of his divorce, of his heavy alimony and child support payments, which was why he was seeking help from welfare and not going to a high-priced shrink. Kennedy listened, rubbing his temple with that deliberate, circular pattern that had Scanlon transfixed.

"You sure you shouldn't be talking to a lawyer?"

"Look, I'm new at this. I'm not so sure I buy this psychoanalytic stuff."

"I had a hunch that was the case," Kennedy said. "Why don't you try to give me the real reason you called."

Scanlon looked down at his hands folded in his lap. "I had this terrible dream the other night. That's why I called, I guess. I must have panicked."

"Why don't you tell me about the dream."

"I dreamed I murdered my daughter," Scanlon lied. When Kennedy pressed for details Scanlon made up a dream on the spot in which he had taken aim at a squirrel with a handgun, squeezed off a round which took the top of the animal's head off. Then the animal became transformed into his daughter, Lucy, her brains spilling out of a ragged hole in her forehead, her eyes wide open, incredulous and accusing. It wasn't such a bad improvisation, he thought. Maybe not total improvisation since he had had that kind of dream except instead of his daughter's metamorphosis it had been his half-brother Billy.

Kennedy shifted in his chair several times while Scanlon recounted his dream, and his expression looked pained. "Sorry," Kennedy said, wincing. "Fucking hemorrhoids. Ass feels like a flame-thrower on days like these."

He went into his top drawer for a pack of cigarettes, fished one out for himself and offered the pack to Scanlon. Kennedy lit them up with a wooden match. They sat for a while without saying anything. Cigarette smoke drifted like cirrus to the ceiling, which Scanlon noticed was flaking paint.

"So what do you make of it?" Scanlon asked.

"I leave the dream interpretation stuff to the Freudians and Jungians," Kennedy said. "What do you make of it? How does it make you feel, describing it out loud?"

"What kind of question is that?" Scanlon's voice rose. "How do you think it makes me feel?"

Kennedy, unperturbed, turned to the one window in the room. It looked out over a gully at the backsides of a row of three-story tenement houses with zigzag stairs. Laundry hung on clotheslines strung across porches. Kennedy continued to worry his temple.

"How does it make me feel?" Scanlon's voice went up another octave. "Jesus!"

Kennedy went into his desk drawer again. This time he produced a pint bottle of bourbon and two Styrofoam cups. He poured two generous portions, and handed Scanlon one of them.

"Here. Have a taste. It'll calm you down."

"How do you know I'm not a teetotaler?"

"I can tell a drinker."

"Hey, I like your style, Dr. Kennedy. What, are you one of those Tennessee school of psychiatry types?"

"You should know at the outset, Jack, that I'm not a doctor. Is that going to be a problem for you?"

"I don't know." Scanlon hesitated, "I thought you had to be a doctor, a Ph.D., whatever. There's no law? Anybody can go rooting around in people's psyches? I know this is welfare, but ..."

"So it is a problem."

"I don't know. I told you, I'm new at this. I get a heart attack I don't go to a pharmacist."

"Do you feel that your life is in danger?"

"No, but that doesn't mean I want to spill my guts to some quack. I could talk to a bartender." Scanlon swallowed some whiskey. It was smooth, good quality. Not what he was used to drinking these days.

"Well, Jack, we don't have any Ph.D.s on the staff at present, and the psychiatrist in charge of this unit isn't taking on any more cases. I can try to set you up with someone out of town, in our Barre office, or Montpelier. They might have someone available with the credentials."

"Hey, don't get me wrong. So you're a quack. That doesn't necessarily mean you're incompetent. I told you, I kind of like your style." Scanlon raised his cup. "Besides, I don't think I want to do that kind of driving. Montpelier, Barre, whatever. Sorry if I offended you."

"Suit yourself, Jack. I take no personal offense, even at your feeble attempts at wit."

Scanlon laughed. "That's a fine way to be talking to your patient. How do you know I'm not fragile?"

After some thought, Kennedy said, "What you've experienced is natural enough."

"It's natural to dream about blowing your child's brains out?"

"It's natural to feel lousy about it."

"Then the dream itself is abnormal?"

"I didn't say that."

The whiskey was settling Scanlon down. He was beginning to relax, to feel comfortable with Kennedy.

"Where do we begin?" Scanlon asked, looking at the dregs of his bourbon, wondering if Kennedy would offer a refill. "What, am I harboring some kind of secret wish to destroy the thing I love most in this world? What kind of dark shit is that?"

"Suppose you tell me what happened that day, the day of your dream."

Scanlon described his visit with the Pattersons, leaving out the interlude with Rachel at the kitchen sink.

"Hmm," Kennedy grunted.

"What?"

"You sure you're not leaving something out? It doesn't figure."

"I've told you everything. What do you want?" Scanlon could hear the lie in his voice, and if he could hear it so could Kennedy. "Well, there's one small thing I forgot to add."

Kennedy probed him for his feelings about the stolen kiss, trying perhaps to find a link between infidelity and murder? He asked about Scanlon's wife, the circumstances of the divorce. He asked about Scanlon's mother and his father. He suggested that Scanlon keep a kind of journal or diary in which he should write down his thoughts, and particularly his feelings, about any part of his life, past or present. In Kennedy's opinion, this was a good way to actively engage the subconscious, to bring up memories and associations that might not surface otherwise. It would also allow him to come to weekly sessions prepared to discuss tangible issues instead of spending a better part of the hour dancing around each other.

"A lot of time can get wasted in therapy because of lack of preparation," Kennedy said. "As a teacher, you can appreciate this."

"Hah," Scanlon snorted at the reference to himself as a teacher. "You're sounding a lot like a schoolteacher yourself, Mr. Kennedy."

"I used to do a little teaching. And there's no need to address me as Mr. Kennedy. Bob will do, please not Bobby."

"I'm not so sure about this journal business. I wouldn't know how to begin? How about giving me an assignment?"

"All right, see what you can do with events surrounding your divorce. If something else appeals to you, by all means follow your nose. But if you get hung up, do the divorce thing. OK?"

"You going to want to look at this journal or whatever?"

"If you want me to. It's up to you." Kennedy looked at Scanlon over the top of his bifocals. "You got a problem with the journal? It's only a suggestion. If you don't feel comfortable don't bother with it. I think you should give it a chance, though."

"All right. I'll give it a shot. Listen, about payment ..." Scanlon had explained, not so subtly, how financially embarrassed he was. Kennedy had not brought up the issue of fees, but Scanlon did not want to leave without an understanding.

"Give us what you can. Can you swing five?"

"I can probably handle that." How much hooch could five dollars purchase? He had to balance the therapeutic effects of one against the other.

"Good. This time of day good for you on a regular basis?"

"Sure."

"Good luck, then. See you next week."

"Yeah. Thanks, Bob."

"Don't mention it."

The receptionist was not at her desk when Scanlon left, but in the waiting room was a young couple. The woman was extremely obese with spectacles as thick as Lillian Bloemer's, her hair impossibly tangled and dirty. She wore a thin summer dress with a floral print that accentuated her enormous arms, thighs and bosom. Her companion was thin, and crew cut; his Adam's apple bobbed up and down between the opening of his dungaree shirt. His face was all sharp angles, and his eyes were crazed. They could have been in their teens or in their thirties, it was impossible to tell.

"Dennis, Sheila. You want to come in now?"

Scanlon turned around at the sound of Kennedy's voice. Kennedy didn't acknowledge him. He beckoned to Dennis and Sheila the way he might call in his pets.

That morning, Scanlon had given his chemistry classes their first tests. He would plan to give as many tests as he could on Friday so that he would have the weekend to grade them. There was no desk upstairs, and he couldn't work downstairs with his aunt and uncle watching TV, so he propped himself up in bed with a piece of composition board on his lap. On one side of him lay two stacks of chemistry tests numbering sixty-four in all. The papers looked formidable, so formidable that he decided that grading tests was the last thing he wanted to do tonight.

Scanlon thought about the journal that Kennedy wanted him to keep, the subject that Kennedy wanted him to pursue with his opening entry. He had found an old college spiral notebook with dividers that had some space left in it between his organic chemistry notes and notes for a course in Oriental Philosophy that he had dropped after two weeks. This notebook he placed next to the chemistry tests. He opened it to the second divider and wrote December 31, 1967. Dear Diary, he wrote, feeling stupid and thinking that Kennedy would not approve of such levity in matters as serious as the pursuit of self-awareness. After it became clear to him that he would not get beyond Dear Diary, Scanlon closed the notebook and slid down beneath the covers. He would never be able to write about that night. He closed his eyes and tried to fall asleep, tried not to think about New Year's Eve, 1967.

Chapter Five

"You look like hell. We can forget today's session if you want to."

"I thought you might have a little medicine in your magic drawer."

"What the hell," Kennedy said, furiously massaging his temple, "the sun's over the yardarm." He got out the bourbon and Styrofoam cups. "It's no accident, you know, I schedule you last."

"What about Dennis and Sheila?"

"What?" Kennedy splashed whiskey in each cup. Scanlon watched, conscious of his hands shaking in anticipation.

"The folks who were in the waiting room last week when I left. You said you scheduled me last."

"Oh. That was a one-shot deal."

Those were probably the kind of people Kennedy saw most often; people who were really in need of help, not self-indulgent shits like him. Scanlon sipped his whiskey, resisting with some effort the urge to bang it down in case Kennedy should get the idea he was hard-core, if he didn't have that impression already. What other impression could he have?

"Feel like talking about last night?" Kennedy asked.

"Why last night?" Scanlon looked away from Kennedy's scrutiny, out the window at the gully, at the tenement houses with the ever-present laundry flapping in the breeze.

"For you to get messed up on a work night there must have been a reason. I thought you might want to talk about it."

"For all you know I could get messed up every night. Anyway, I don't see much point in talking about it if that's all right with you." Last night had been anything but routine, but he wasn't in the mood to go into it with Kennedy.

He'd been feeling even more restless than usual, out of sorts, confined in his suffocating room with its slanting walls. He had about four dollars to his name, enough for a few drinks in the downstairs lounge of the Groveton House, Groveton's "fine" hotel. He had stopped by the lounge a few times since he'd been back, gotten chummy with Ruthie the waitress and Leo the night bartender. Ruthie was fiftyish, a widow whose husband had died of cancer of the bowel last year; Leo was a phlegmatic, skinny, little guy, with slicked-back hair and a red bow tie, who liked to give the impression that he was a serious horse player. The management required poor Ruthie to wear a mini-skirted waitress uniform with an embroidered apron. Ruthie with her varicose veins and fat middle in such an outfit. It was undignified. If she minded, she didn't let on.

He found himself ordering up his usual, a shot of Kesslers smooth-as-silk with a beer chaser. It was a little after nine. There were only a handful of the regulars in the place, old men with whom Scanlon had a nodding acquaintance. None of them was familiar to Johnny Labalm, nor did any of them recognize him as the young boy who grew up in their town. To Scanlon, eighteen years seemed like a very long time; to these old geezers it was probably like a weekend. He was frankly surprised that he hadn't run into anyone he knew by now. That streak ended at the jukebox. He was scanning the selections on the rainbowed Wurlitzer, looking for something decent to play, pleased to see that the psychedelic noise hadn't penetrated this far north yet, when he was suddenly conscious of the powerful odor of perfume. He was no perfume connoisseur, but he could tell that this was not the expensive kind. And its source was standing there beside him, peering at him as if he were from another planet. The mustache? Even the regulars, the old *habitués* of the Groveton House lounge had gotten used to it, though for a time Scanlon began to think that he was the only guy in the entire state of Vermont who wore one.

"You're Johnny Labalm. You can't hide behind a mustache. I'd recognize those eyes anywhere," said Laraine McFarland, nee Comstock, a girl whose sweaty hand he'd held in the Palace Theater at Saturday matinees in fifth grade. A precocious fifth grader to say the least, Laraine came to school in soft cashmere sweaters that drove Johnny crazy, and it seemed that sex was the only thing that mattered to her. Not the smelly adult version of sex, but sex all the same. She flirted incessantly, and would render the boys in the class crimson-faced as they walked in perfect innocence to the pencil sharpener only to be accosted by Laraine, who would coyly ask the poor sap if he had a hard-on. They all knew what a hard-on was, but to have the question put to you at the pencil sharpener, and by a girl, especially a girl as alluring as Laraine Comstock, was more than any of them could bear. For some reason unknown to Johnny Labalm, Laraine Comstock had a thing for him. For his part, he was interested in her too, but pathologically shy. No matter, because Laraine made all the moves, and it wasn't long before he was routinely holding hands with her in the dark intimacy of the Palace. Who knew what would have come of that romance had Johnny Labalm remained in Groveton?

What could he do but plead guilty? Laraine McFarland was drunk. She wasn't in the lounge when Scanlon arrived; she must have come in while he was in the men's room. Her serious drinking she had done somewhere else. In the few times he had been in the Groveton House he had not seen an unescorted woman, certainly not an unescorted, married woman. They chatted at the jukebox for a while and then Scanlon found himself at her table, lighting her cigarette and worrying about how he could gracefully avoid buying her a drink. Happily for him, Laraine had not lost her aggressive ways. Before he knew it, Ruthie was at the table with a tray of drinks. Laraine produced a five dollar bill from her purse and placed it on the table. Scanlon did not protest.

"McFarland?" he asked, noticing that her lipstick was on askew and her eyes were glazed. "That name's familiar. Not Chet McFarland?"

"The very same," Laraine said, plumes of smoke issuing from her nostrils. She had on tons of makeup, reminding him of the way Katie used to plaster it on when he first met her. But her bosom was large under her satiny blouse, expanding and contracting with each breath. Scanlon must have been staring.

"You're all alike," she said with a snort-like laugh. "Tits and ass. Men." She said men with more resignation than spite.

Scanlon must have blushed because she put her hand on his sleeve and gave his arm a reassuring squeeze. Chet McFarland, as Scanlon recalled, was about four years older than he was; a triple threat athlete in high school. Was he also the jealous type?

"Tell me about yourself, Johnny. What gives you the right to just up and disappear like that? You married?" She squinted at him, swaying slightly in her chair. As she said, he had, in fact, sort of vanished from Groveton in the summer of 1950. He would have preferred not to at the time, but he was in no position at eleven years old to do anything about it.

"We moved," he said, dodging the question about his marriage, "to New Hampshire. There was nothing I could do about it."

"I thought about you a lot, Johnny," she said, stroking his arm. Scanlon heard chairs moving behind him. The geezers angling for a better view?

"I thought about you, too, Laraine," he lied. Tears welled up in her eyes; mascara ran down her cheeks like spring sap. Her cigarette had fallen out of the ashtray and smoldered on the wooden tabletop. Scanlon picked it up and extinguished it.

"Oh, Johnny, it's so good to see you. You haven't changed at all." Laraine squeezed his arm again with her strong hand. For her part, Laraine had changed enough in eighteen years for him not to recognize her. She filled him in on what he had missed about her and Chet's life in his absence. Married to Chet for twelve of those years; two kids, eleven and twelve, boys. She had good reason to have changed. Chet had knocked her up her senior year and she was forced to drop out of school. He had been the most sought after boy at Groveton Academy. She had dated him her freshman year, when he was a senior. He had gone off to Springfield Teacher's College the next year, lasted one semester, and came back to Groveton to work for his father, who was Groveton's only junk dealer, and to hang around the academy on the prowl for girls like Laraine Comstock. Rumor had it, and in Groveton rumor was always reliable, that Chet had the back seat of his '51 Mercury busy with a different girl every night of the week in warm weather.

"Did you really think about me, Johnny?" She sat back in her chair and looked at Scanlon, her head cocked the way Katie used to do when she was ready to say something nasty to him. "You did not, you stinker. You lie like a rug. I thought about you, Johnny Labalm. A lot."

It could have been the early effects of two shots of whiskey, but Laraine McFarland, nee Comstock, was starting to look good.

"Want to hear some music?" he asked her, raking change off the table.

"Play something nice, Johnny. I want to slow dance."

Scanlon didn't want to dance, slow or fast; he was inhibited by nature, and never so inhibited than when asked to perform on the dance floor. He glanced out at the house on his way to the jukebox. Two old guys playing cribbage at the table near the bar, one old gent staring into space as he drank up his pension check. And Ruthie and Leo, of course, Ruthie engrossed in a magazine, Leo with his nose in the racing form. He and Laraine were hardly the center of attention as he had imagined. What was there to lose?

Scanlon was pleasantly surprised to find "I Apologize" by Billy Eckstein, "The Nearness of You" by Bob Manning, and Peggy Lee's "The Thrill Is Gone." She wanted slow dance, he'd give her slow dance.

Laraine was voluptuous in his arms, her lower body pressed firmly against his. He had the sudden and powerful realization that he hadn't held a woman in this fashion in ... a very long time. He was giddy with Laraine McFarland's pliant body, her cheap fragrance, her warmth. Giddy and very much aroused. They stayed on the floor for all three tunes, and when the last melancholy chords of Peggy Lee's dispiriting song ended, he was left with the problem of getting back to their table without drawing attention to himself. But nobody was paying attention.

"That was nice, Johnny." Laraine had come over all soft and quiet.

"Want to get out of here? Want to go for a walk?"

"I probably should get home."

Don't leave me now, he wanted to say. He was never able to say things like that to women. He wanted more than anything for her to stay with him.

"Come on," Kennedy said, "out with it."

"Out with what?"

"Last night. You're withholding."

"I told you, there's no last night to talk about."

"I see that you didn't take my advice."

"Advice?"

"The diary. The journal, whatever. You forget to bring it, or just didn't do it?"

"Oh," Scanlon said in a low voice, feeling like a kid being chastised by his teacher for not completing an assignment. "That's a familiar line. I'm beginning to use it a lot myself."

Kennedy laughed. "Sorry."

"I tried but I just couldn't get into it. I don't think I'll be able to, if you want the truth."

"Well," Kennedy said, "don't feel like you have to do it. I thought it might be useful, that's all. Maybe later, when we get warmed up. You find the divorce painful to deal with?"

"Yeah. You know, maybe you're right. Maybe we ought to call the game off for today. I feel pretty awful."

"All right, but first tell me what happened last night."

"What are you, a shrink or a gossip? You want to hear about last night you have to pour me a refill." Scanlon offered his empty cup.

"I don't have to do shit," Kennedy said, pouring whiskey for Scanlon, not as much as the first one.

So he held up his end of the bargain and told Kennedy about his meeting with Laraine McFarland in the Groveton House lounge, only he heard himself—and as he got going he couldn't stop—changing the story. He described Laraine McFarland as cheap goods, and loudly abusive of her husband. In this version the house was full, and most of the patrons knew who she was, and they would surely report back to her husband that he was coming on to her when in reality (this new, manufactured reality, not the real thing) it was she who was coming on to him, and now Chet would come looking for him now that his cover was blown, as it were. She was sloppy drunk and loud (he made a point of emphasizing how loud she had been) and at one point, while they were dancing, she accused him of making lewd suggestions to her. She was so loud and theatrical in her indignation that everyone in the place had heard.

The scene so upset him that he left her out on the dance floor on the pretense of going to the men's room and made an escape up the stairs and out the door. What really happened was that he had followed Laraine out of the lounge after she announced that she should be getting home. He caught up with her at the top of the stairs and encircled her waist with his arm in what he thought was a gallant gesture. She was not too steady on her spiked heels. He felt her recoil a little when he touched her. In surprise, he hoped, and not revulsion. Then her head was on his shoulder and she was crying. He could feel her little convulsions under his arm.

"Oh, Johnny, I'm so unhappy."

Scanlon patted her hip, as if this could allay her unhappiness. But it was not her unhappiness that he was interested in.

"My car's in front of the library," he said, his voice husky from drink and ardor, "I'll take you home."

"Please, Johnny," she said, stopping to turn toward him and to take his face between her hands, "don't spoil it. I know what you want. I can't sleep with you. I can walk home. I only live on Webster Street. It was really nice seeing you." Then she reached up and kissed him on the cheek as though he were her little brother, the way Elaine Stacy had kissed him last New Year's Eve. She hurried off, unsteadily, down Main Street.

Now Kennedy was looking hard at him from underneath his wiry eyebrows.

"What are you looking at?" Scanlon asked.

"That's what I'd like to know." Kennedy was working double time on his temple. If he wasn't careful he'd wear a hole in his head and his brains would spill out. "I can't help but wonder why you danced with her if she was ... well, if she was as you describe her."

“You want to know something, Bob?” Scanlon said, having finished his whiskey. “Let me tell you about an experiment with mice I read about in *Scientific American*. They took these white mice, right, and they rubbed their little tails with these glass stirring rods. They rubbed them a lot, Bob, day in day out. What do you think they got for all that rubbing? They got tumors, Bob, malignant tumors, which is what you’re going to get if you keep on with your fucking temple, excuse my Greek. And if you don’t mind my saying so it’s damned distracting.”

“It’s an idiosyncrasy. Let me have it. I’ll allow you yours.” Kennedy continued with his idiosyncrasy.

“I don’t have idiosyncrasies.”

“We’ll see.”

“Don’t forget, you’re the one who asked about last night.”

“You don’t have a high opinion of women, do you, Jack.”

“Is that a question, or what?”

“More an observation.” Kennedy put the bottle back in his desk drawer. Was that gesture, along with his “observation” of Scanlon’s attitude toward women, his cunning way of punishing him? Putting away the hooch, like withholding candy from the naughty child?

“I thought your crowd wasn’t in the business of judging.”

“I was making an observation. You think I’m judging you?”

“You put away the sauce. You got this funny, far away look, as if you’re in the company of a lower life form. What am I supposed to think?”

“It’s the bottle most of all. Right?”

“Another one of your questions slash observations? You’re a shithead in case you didn’t know it.”

“I’ve been told. Listen, we’ve got to talk about this. I’ll see you next week?”

Kennedy was suddenly all business, scooping a fistful of papers from his desk and striding for the door as if he’d been drinking coffee for the last hour instead of straight whiskey. Scanlon got to his feet unsteadily.

“Listen, Bob. Why don’t I try to write something, you know, for next time?”

“That would be good. Give it a whirl. See you next week.”

“Yeah. Next week.” Scanlon watched Kennedy go through the door and he felt like he’d been abandoned.

Chapter Six

Monday morning. Hungover. Scanlon made himself a cup of instant coffee in the teachers' room, put his nickel in the fund and sat down on the smelly sofa to sort out the chemistry tests he'd somehow managed to grade on Sunday before succumbing to heavy drinking, Labalm style. The tests he had avoided for two weeks—the tests kids had even stopped asking about. His first chemistry test; the highest score a sixty-seven, the mean around fifty-two. Who was to blame? He knew the answer.

Danny Picard kicked open the door and came in toting a case of evaporated milk on each shoulder. He was a tall, affable kid with a pockmarked face and an overlapping upper lip. A "shop" type, not one of Scanlon's academic students although he saw Danny every day in his eighth period study hall. Whenever a truckload of supplies for the cafeteria was delivered, Danny hauled boxes to the storage room off the teachers' lounge. For this he was entitled to free lunches. He had no interest in academics, and teachers found him a pain to have in class. Cynthia Sinclair described him as "disruptive." He was probably more exuberant than malicious. Scanlon had developed a friendly, joking rapport with him in study hall. He liked this hick kid who would probably never stray beyond the mountainous borders of the Northeast Kingdom unless the military took a shine to him and decided he needed cultural broadening in some foreign place like Vietnam.

"How's it going, Mr. Scanlon?" Danny rested his load on the corner of the scarred table and unhooked a ring of keys from his belt loop. He gave Scanlon a second look and rolled his eyes.

"Don't rub it in," Scanlon said. Danny unlocked the storeroom door and turned on the light. Scanlon got up to give him a hand with the boxes. His head started to throb again with the effort.

“Thanks, Mr. Scanlon. I got about a dozen more like these if you feel like doing some honest work for a change.” He joked, but Scanlon would have preferred humping boxes of canned milk to facing his chemistry classes this morning with their wretched tests.

Danny was stripped to his T-shirt. He was perspiring, and stank of body odor. His pale arms were sinewy and large-veined, his fingernails chewed to the quick.

“Believe me, I'd like nothing better. See you in study,” Scanlon said, going back to the malodorous sofa to gather up the stinking chemistry tests and his books.

Where had he gone wrong? Scanlon wondered as he climbed the stairs to his classroom like a condemned man. He'd worked so hard—after his fashion—to achieve a rapport with his students, to treat them as individuals, every one of them as if they were worthy of special attention, and this took effort when you were dealing with one-hundred-thirty-eight individuals. In less than a month he'd learned all their names. He surprised himself. What he had apparently failed to do was teach his chemistry students any chemistry. And why should it be any different with the biology kids, the freshman science classes? He felt a cold sense of failure as he hit the second floor landing. Had he been too easy on them, given them too much latitude—allowed that inch Winship had warned him about not giving—not demanded enough homework? Teaching was difficult for him. That was the simple truth of it. In some classes, he had as many as thirty-five students. He allowed himself to get bogged down answering irrelevant questions from the slower kids when he should have been pushing ahead. He was too easily sidetracked, too willing to veer off onto tangents, and before he knew it the period would be over and he would have gotten through only a fraction of what he had intended to accomplish.

Scanlon handed the tests back second period, gave the kids a few minutes to mull over the results, to compare grades, to groan and mutter and shake their heads. He heard several comments of “unfair,” and a few kids said, to no one in particular, that they had studied hours for this test.

How long had he stayed awake last night, even in his alcohol-blunted state of mind, brooding over the implications of this disaster? What should his response be? Should he go to Winship for advice? Lillian Bloemer? He had yet to come up with anything, and there they were with the tests back in their hands. And now they were waiting, faces turned to the front of the room, waiting for him to speak.

Scanlon sat down on the stool behind the lecture desk. He looked out at those faces. If Danny Picard could see that he was hungover was there any doubt that the rest of them could see the same thing? He could only hope that they were too absorbed in their own misery to observe him too carefully.

"So, do you need me to tell you how crummy these tests are?" Scanlon asked, holding up his palms Jack Benny style. Heads nodded, eyes rolled. Kids squirmed in their seats. Scanlon held his nose. A few kids smiled. "The highest grade was a sixty-seven in case you haven't figured that out yet. Sixty-seven," he repeated like one of those loathsome pedagogues from his high school days. "This is unacceptable. This will not do." He got off his stool and moved around to the front of the lecture desk, folded his arms across his chest and bowed his head. The room got suddenly quiet.

"I'm to blame for this, of course," Scanlon said into his chest, head still bowed for melodramatic effect. "It's my job to teach you guys chemistry, and it's all too plain to see from the results of this test that I haven't been doing my job."

"This mean you're going to scale them?" someone asked.

"Shit, I'd forgotten all about the stupid test," Scanlon heard someone in the back of the room say, *sotto voce*.

"No," Scanlon said, "I don't believe in scaling." Where he had come up with this so-called "belief" was anybody's guess, but he heard himself saying the words, and saying them as if he held strong convictions about the scaling of chemistry tests. "I'm not counting this test at all."

This announcement brought the expected cheers, and foot-stomping applause, and Scanlon had to admit, it was gratifying. After awhile, Scanlon raised his hands for silence.

"On Friday I'll be giving you another test on the same material. In the meantime, what I plan to do is come back here, to this room, three evenings a week, after supper, to offer extra help. You are under no obligation to attend these sessions, and I know that many of you live too far away to take advantage of the offer—for you I'll have to make other arrangements—but for you denizens of Fairfield, and those of you with access to the automobile, I'll be here tonight, Tuesday, and Thursday evenings for as long as you need me." More cheering. Scanlon received much the same reaction from his fourth period chemistry class.

Study hall. The last period of a brutally long day. The hangover had subsided, but he was exhausted, thoroughly drained of what little energy he had brought with him to school this morning. Danny Picard, on the other hand, had a surplus of energy. He was restless. He couldn't stay in his seat for more than five minutes, sighing and giving up on his *Practical Economics* textbook. As he was inclined to do in Scanlon's study hall, Danny would come up to the lecture desk to strike up a conversation. Scanlon would oblige most of the time if he didn't have a lot of work to do, but he'd have to frequently shush Danny because Danny spoke in the same loud voice whether he was in study hall, where quiet was supposed to prevail, or in auto shop, where his voice was easily heard over hammers against metal and the screech of compressed air guns. Scanlon didn't know why he bothered to maintain quiet in study hall; half the time the kids used study hall to catch up on sleep or to read comic books. Samantha Burnham was the only one, on the rare occasions she showed up, who read "serious" books.

"Feeling any better?" Danny asked, placing his rough elbows down on the lecture desk, cupping his lantern jaw in his palms.

"Isn't that kind of an impertinent question to be asking an authority figure?"

"What's that mean? Sassy? You're always using them five-dollar words. Can I look at the stuff you got in here?" Danny started to slide open the glass door of the chemical storage cabinet.

"Get out of there, Danny. We spent hours organizing that cupboard. I don't need you fouling it up."

Danny ignored Scanlon and pulled out a can of powdered alum. "I heard stories about this stuff," he said, smiling lewdly.

"What stories?" Scanlon opened his biology text and pretended to be interested in its contents. Danny leaned over the lecture desk and whispered, "Old Levi Caulkins says this stuff'll make a woman's pussy pucker." Danny cackled with delight.

"Put it back." Scanlon didn't look at Danny. He was no prude, but he could feel his ears getting warm and he was afraid he might be in for a full-blown blush. Danny replaced the alum and took out the one-gallon mayonnaise jar in which sodium metal was stored in kerosene.

"What in hell is this? Looks like some kind of brain." Danny sniffed the rusted cover. "Stinks of kerosene. What is this stuff?"

"Sodium metal. And it's very dangerous stuff. You're so interested in everything you should take chemistry."

"How come you got it in kerosene?" Danny turned the jar around on the lecture desk. "How's it dangerous?"

"It's explosive. The moisture in the air can set it off, so put it back before you blow us to kingdom come."

"Yeah?" Danny's eyes shined. "How big an explosion would a chunk this size make?"

"A very big explosion. Now put it back in the cabinet and stop behaving like a little kid."

"Maybe you're right. Maybe I should've took chemistry." Danny put the jar of sodium back and pulled out a glass-stoppered stock bottle with Conc. Sulfuric Acid embossed on it. "I know what this is. Battery acid. Right?"

Scanlon got up and took the acid away from Danny and put it back in the cabinet. He shut the door. "I'd rather you didn't poke around in there. Why don't you go back to your seat and read or something."

"Books are a waste of time. I want to live life, not read about it."

Scanlon knew from previous conversations with this kid that it would be pointless to argue with him about the good that books could do for him in his life. Danny knew, or thought he knew, exactly what he wanted. If his goals weren't ambitious by some standards, they had the advantage of being clear-cut, at least to Danny and his fiancee, Norma Woodruff. Norma had dropped out of school last year and was studying cosmetology in Montpelier. After Danny graduated, they planned to be married. As tempted as Scanlon was to disabuse Danny of the notion of marriage, he kept quiet on the subject. Eventually, perhaps in as few as five years, Danny hoped to start his own auto repair business specializing in foreign cars.

"How do you expect to run a business without having to come in contact with books?" Scanlon asked, realizing at once how stupid the question sounded.

"I'm talking about story books. I can read useful books good enough to get by. I can look up parts in the catalog, read transmission manuals, shit I need. If I want stories I'll look at TV, or go to the show in town."

Winship's voice crackled over the intercom speaker on the wall behind Scanlon's desk. "Can I have a word with you in my office after study hall, Mr. Scanlon?"

"Uh-oh," Danny said, winking, "Your ass is grass now."

"Sit down, wise guy." Scanlon's first thought was that Winship had heard about the poor showing on his chemistry test and would demand an explanation. What explanation? He was a crummy teacher, what could be plainer? Danny was at the back of the room, nosing around the deep sink full of dirty glassware. "Why don't you roll up your sleeves, do a few dishes if you're so interested." Danny grinned. "I'm serious," Scanlon added. The bell rang. Danny shrugged his shoulders.

"I'd a done 'em," he said on his way out the door.

"What have I done now?" Scanlon asked, trying to sound casual. He hadn't had more than a few words in passing with the principal since their little chat about Scanlon's seditious meeting with the kids that night. Poor Winship looked, as always, overwhelmed by the paperwork strewn across his desk; he moved documents by the stack from one place to the other, and he didn't look like a man with a plan.

"Have a seat, Jack. I'll be right with you." He had on his favorite bright green jacket, the one that accented his salt and pepper hair and highlighted his pale blue eyes. His summer tan was only now beginning to fade, and his face was mottled, the lines around his eyes more pronounced.

"I've got an appointment in Groveton at three," Scanlon lied.

Winship pushed back his chair and opened his middle drawer. He poked around in it, and apparently not finding what he was looking for, pushed it shut. He leaned back in his chair and made a steeple with his fingers, and said, without looking directly at Scanlon, "There's talk that you're planning to come in nights to give extra help. Is that right, Jack?"

"That's right. I ..."

"Some people are a little upset," Winship interrupted.

"Upset?"

"Well, yes."

"I don't think I understand."

"Some of the others have the idea that you're trying to make them look bad. You can understand that." Winship kept his eyes on his paperwork, as if that were his main preoccupation and not his talk with Scanlon.

"I'm afraid I'm beginning to understand. What exactly are they afraid of, these 'others'? Do they think I actually want to come back here in my free time?" Since Winship hadn't brought up the subject himself, Scanlon told him about the chemistry test and how coming in after hours was as much to compensate for his own inadequacies as a teacher as it was for the kids' sake. His motive was certainly not anything as devious as to try and make his colleagues look bad.

"I'm sure, Jack. But you've got to realize how this looks to the others."

"You're the principal. Can't you set them straight? Who exactly has complained? I can't believe Josh, or Cynthia, or even Lillian would object. I suppose that leaves my friend, Lyle Higgins, right? Well, maybe I should just have a heart to heart with him myself if you won't."

"All I'm saying, Jack, is you ought to be sensitive to the feelings of your colleagues. That's all I'm saying."

"Then you're not actually forbidding me to come back in the evening?"

"Not in so many words. I would only hope that you'd see this from the broad perspective." Winship looked miserable. Scanlon almost felt sorry for him. On the other hand, Winship seemed to be on the defensive and Scanlon intended to keep him there.

"If you're telling me I should back off just to keep the peace, then I'd have to say to hell with that. What about the kids? What about their needs? I should refrain from teaching them what they're entitled to learn because one or two of my so-called colleagues feels threatened?"

"Why can't you teach your subject during regular hours like everyone else?"

"Believe me, I hope to be able to do that eventually. I'm not an experienced teacher. I've got a lot to learn about technique. As I said, this is as much for my benefit as theirs."

"You've got even more to learn about getting along with people. If you persist on this course, Jack, I can promise you there'll be trouble."

"I've made a promise of my own I can't go back on even if I wanted to." Scanlon could undoubtedly worm out of holding extra sessions if he put his mind to it, but Winship's caution sounded too much like a threat for him to let it pass. What did he have to lose except his job?

"Then I guess there's nothing further to discuss. Don't be late for that important appointment." With that, Winship dismissed him.

Scanlon was boiling mad on the drive to Groveton. He was angry at Winship for being such a jellyfish, for not looking him in the eye, for not backing him up against his spineless colleagues. If, in fact, there were more than one of them involved. He'd bet his anemic week's pay that Lyle Higgins was behind it. He was the senior faculty member, and from what Scanlon had heard from Josh Patterson, and from his own limited dealings with the man, Lyle Higgins was eminently capable of small-mindedness. Scanlon had experienced his share of pettiness, jealousy, and small-time political maneuvering before, but he was apparently naive enough to be taken by surprise to find it in rural Fairfield.

Tomorrow he resolved to talk with Josh Patterson about the matter. In the meantime, he intended to follow through with his plans to return to school after supper and have at it with his chemistry students; Winship and his colleagues could protest all they wanted, then they could kiss his rear.

Chapter Seven

"You got a few minutes to talk?" Scanlon asked Josh Patterson, who was getting ready to eat his lunch at his desk. The classroom where he taught civics and social studies was next door to Scanlon's.

"Sure. Want half an egg salad? Rachel's homemade bread." Scanlon refused the sandwich. He was agitated, right at the edge. A map of eastern Europe was hanging over the blackboard behind Patterson's desk. Beside the map on the board Patterson had written Czechoslovakia in big yellow letters. Patterson unwrapped his egg salad sandwich carefully, as if it were a gift package from Abercrombie and Fitch.

"What's up?"

Scanlon related his conversation with Winship, choosing his words carefully so as not to cast the principal in too unfavorable a light. Patterson listened attentively without changing expression, munching on his sandwich like one of those cows in the pasture above his house. When Scanlon finished, Patterson wiped egg salad from the corner of his mouth with a cloth napkin and sucked on his teeth before he spoke.

"It's like I said when you were out at the house. Winship's got no backbone. He lets Higgins call all the shots. Higgins might as well be principal, if you ask me. No, there's no doubt in my mind that Lyle's behind this. He's afraid that if someone shows initiative, some sign of life, that he'll have to do the same. He's used the same lesson plan for the twenty years he's been teaching here. He's got it cushy, and he doesn't want the boat rocked. I had to find that out for myself my first year."

"Could anyone else be involved? What about Cynthia? Lillian?"

"I'd be really surprised if either of them had a hand in it, but you can never be sure, absolutely sure, about anything, can you?"

"I hadn't even considered Stambaugh. He's so above it all," Scanlon said, and had a moment in which he wondered if Patterson himself might be a part of it. Scanlon smiled.

"What is it?" Patterson asked.

"Nothing. Any suggestions about how I should get to the bottom of this? You got to have heard that I came back last night, against Daryl's wishes."

"Yeah. I heard you were here pretty late, but I wasn't aware that Winship had forbidden you to come back."

"He didn't flat out forbid me."

"Naturally. That would require taking a stand. How was the turnout?"

"Not bad. Maybe a dozen. You think I should confront Higgins, or just let it ride? Maybe I should go back to Winship. I don't know. I'm shooting in the dark."

"I think you should just continue to come back for your extra help sessions, and if anybody's nose gets out of joint, then deal with it." With that advice, thrown out with his usual off-hand nonchalance, Patterson rose and stretched. "Just enough time to move the bowels before fifth period, if you'll excuse me." Scanlon continued to be perplexed at the apparent ease with which Patterson shifted from being open, concerned, even friendly, to utterly impersonal. He wondered if Patterson's secretions were ever as acid as his were at this moment, if his stomach ever turned to concrete with anger and frustration. Probably not. In this respect, Patterson was somewhat like his friend George Stacy. George was on his mind a lot these days. The nauseating stink of egg salad lingered in Patterson's classroom.

Scanlon hated confrontation. He hated it when he was married to Katie. He hated it when he was a kid and was forced to deal with aggressive classmates or neighbors; he hated it when he was in the Navy, and he hated it now with Lyle Higgins seeking to thwart him and cause him grief. He knew he should have it out with the math teacher, approach him with Winship's charges and ask him outright if he was the one behind them. There was a part of him that was afraid of Higgins, afraid of his pure physicalness. He kept seeing those rolled up sleeves, those powerful forearms and biceps. So now he was a physical as well as a moral coward. The idea left a bad taste in his mouth, but by the time eighth period ended, he had mustered enough resolve to face up to Higgins.

"Tell you what, Jack. Why don't you meet me over at my place. I'll build you a drink, and you can get off your chest whatever's weighing so heavy. I live over in East Groveton, not far from where you are, right? River Road?" Lyle Higgins gripped Scanlon's shoulder with his large, strong hand, giving it a squeeze as he invited him to his home. "This is no place for a man-to-man talk."

Scanlon, with great trepidation, had accosted Higgins in his classroom at the end of eighth period. He'd been made to wait, in a state of acute anxiety, while Higgins worked out a derivative on the blackboard for one of his seniors. Ronnie Benoit had actually come to Scanlon with his problem earlier that day, but Scanlon was about as skilled in calculus as he was with women. He had nothing but sympathy for the perplexed Ronnie Benoit.

Scanlon had cooled his heels scrutinizing the classroom bulletin board on which Higgins liked to post aphorisms about the study of mathematics:

While studying pressures and suctions,
Sir Isaac performed some deductions,
"Fill a mug to the brim, it
Will then reach a limit,
So clearly determined by fluxions."

"I understand mathematics, I just can't do proofs."
"The square on the hypothesis right angry is equal to
the hum of the square on the other two aisles."

"A cow has twelve legs—two in the front, two in
the back, two on each side and one on each corner."
"To think logically the logically thinkable—that is
the mathematician's aim."

Like every math teacher Scanlon had ever known, Higgins was pathologically neat and orderly. His desk top was free of extraneous paper, his books, and the way he arranged the tablet armchairs achieved a symmetry not to be found in any other room in the school, not even in Lillian Bloemer's classroom, and she had a Prussian instinct for order herself.

By the time Higgins finished with Ronnie Benoit, Scanlon's meager resolve had all but disappeared. He'd hemmed and he'd hawed and it was Higgins, finally, who had rescued him with his invitation. On the drive to Groveton, Scanlon decided that Higgins knew that he was going to be challenged. So his invitation, friendly enough on the surface, was more than likely a gambit to get Scanlon on his own turf and at a disadvantage. If that was the case it had worked to perfection, for not only had Scanlon's resolve deserted him, he was looking forward to the drink Higgins had promised to "build" him.

The math teacher's house was a neat split-level with no character at all. It rested on a half-acre of scrubby land with a backdoor view of a sand pit.

"Hope gin and tonic's to your liking," Higgins said, handing Scanlon a tall glass as he was admitted to the house through the back door. "Mind the kitchen?"

"Not at all." Scanlon liked kitchens more than gin and tonic, but any port in a storm had always been his motto. Higgins had his sleeves rolled up to the biceps the way he'd had them when Scanlon first met him at Winship's party. Scanlon had to work to keep from staring at those arms. Higgins leaned against the counter and looked over his bifocals at Scanlon.

"And what would be on your mind? Wouldn't have anything to do with mathematics, would it?"

"Not really." Scanlon laughed nervously. He didn't know whether he should remain standing or take a seat at the kitchen table. Since Higgins had not invited him to sit, he decided to stay on his feet. Higgins was looking at him, waiting, a faint smile on his lips, for the parrying to begin. Scanlon described haltingly, and for the second time that day, his conversation with Winship. "What I guess I'd like to know is if you had anything, you know, to say to Daryl, or whatever. He didn't mention any names, so I've been, you know, going around to individuals, asking." It was a stupid lie, easily verified if Higgins chose to bother, but it was out. Now he'd be obliged to follow through on that false pretense.

Higgins smiled and shook his head. "I've been rough on you. That's the way I am with new teachers. You shouldn't take it personal. As for this other thing, I'd be insulted ordinarily, you coming to me with these charges, but I'll allow for you being new. This time. As a matter of fact I think it's a grand idea, you giving up your free time to help these kids. God knows, some of them can use it. Ever occur to you that Daryl's making up the part about the teachers complaining?"

"No. That didn't occur to me at all. What would be his motive?"

"Don't know. Maybe he's jealous of you, your popularity with the youngsters. Maybe he wants to keep you off guard. Daryl can be a funny duck sometimes. Real complicated." Higgins raised his glass to his lips to take a drink, looking at Scanlon over the rim.

Scanlon followed suit, sipping his drink, but he had trouble looking Higgins in the eye. Something told him the man was lying. He scratched his head.

"Now I'm really confused."

"Drink up," Higgins said, raising his glass in the air. Scanlon wondered where his wife was. What was her name? Edna? The kitchen was spotless, the way Katie used to like her kitchen to look. No dishes draining by the sink, the countertop completely clear, no stains or finger marks on the cupboards, stove and refrigerator gleaming. Even the water faucets shone bright, as though recently polished.

Higgins had cleverly sidestepped the issue. There was nowhere else for Scanlon to go with it. He felt cornered. Obediently, he finished his drink, and no sooner had the ice cubes fallen back to the bottom of his glass than Higgins plucked it out of his hand and set about making another.

"You like your booze, don't you? Don't take me wrong. I like a glass myself. Teaching's a tough business. I figure I earn my drink at the end of the day. You?"

"I couldn't agree more. I'd appreciate it if you made this a short one. I've got a ton of papers to grade." Scanlon couldn't believe he heard himself asking for a short drink.

"Yeah. I've heard you've gotten a little behind there. These kids can be pretty insistent when it comes to wanting their tests back. I try to get mine back the day after I collect them."

How much time did it take to correct a math test? Scanlon wondered. Higgins had read his guilt correctly and was busy exploiting it. The best he could hope to do now was get Higgins off the subject.

"You've been teaching for a long time. Did I hear twenty years? Ever feel like trying something else?"

"Not on your life. I've had plenty of offers, too. Industry and what not, but teaching is what I do best, and what I like to do. What about yourself? You planning to stay on board, or are you just testing the waters?"

"I'm not sure yet. Depends on how the rest of this year goes." How the rest of the year went could depend a lot on how his relationship with this man developed. Scanlon watched carefully as Higgins mixed the drinks. He was sure that Higgins had put no gin in his own glass, and the "short" one that Scanlon had asked for was stronger than the first, even if it was mixed in a shorter glass. Scanlon wasn't that upset at getting a strong drink, if the truth was told.

"Well, you seem to have an aptitude for the business, if what the youngsters say can be believed," Higgins said, with that ambiguous smile.

"Thanks. I'm afraid I've still got a lot to learn. If I was any good I wouldn't have to go back nights to give extra sessions, and I wouldn't be having to play cat and mouse games with Daryl Winship and who knows who else."

"Come, now. You're blowing this way out of proportion. Besides, you went ahead and did what you wanted, didn't you? Nobody's the worse for it. Don't take everything so serious."

"Did you know that Daryl asked me if I belonged to SDS?"

"Don't even know what SDS is. That some sort of fraternity?"

"Some people consider it a subversive organization."

"Subversive. Well, well," Higgins said, chuckling, "you look subversive, I'll have to say that, but I understand you've had some military service." Where had Higgins got this information?

"That would rule out subversive?"

"I never met a man who served his country could turn around and do anything to harm her. No man of conscience anyway."

"How can you be sure I have a conscience?" Scanlon felt he had Higgins on the logical ropes. He had to be careful, though. The man did teach calculus.

"You wouldn't be driving seven miles back to Fairfield three nights a week to help out a bunch of lazy kids if you didn't have a conscience. Speaking of driving, you think you're going to be all right behind the wheel after two drinks?"

"I think I can handle two miles, even on your drinks."

"You navy men always did have the reputation for being good drinkers. Served in the army myself. George Patton's Sixth Army."

"I figured you for the Corps."

Higgins ran a hand over his crew cut. "That's what a lot of people think. I was a dogface and proud of it. Serve in Vietnam?" Higgins asked.

"Yeah," Scanlon said, dropping his eyes. He'd spent four days in Saigon once, and long before the war had gotten hot. He hoped Higgins wouldn't press him on his Vietnam experience.

"Then you'll agree with me when I say we should go in there and have done with it. We could have that place cleaned up in no time, we put our minds to it. Look how the Jews handled them Arabs. That's the way we ought to conduct business with the little yellow people. You've been there. You see my point, don't you?"

Scanlon was in no mood to get into this kind of discussion with Higgins. Madelaine Winship's words rang in his ears and he could sense that Higgins was deliberately drawing him into a Vietnam argument. For what purpose, Scanlon couldn't be sure. There was something malevolent about Higgins. Scanlon was growing very uncomfortable in his presence.

"I should be going, Lyle. Those papers are waiting."

"Glad you came by. Feel any better?"

"I suppose so."

"You don't think I had anything to do with it, do you?" There was that smile again. With his close-cropped hair, shiny forehead and square jaw, he looked ferocious, like old blood and guts Patton himself. The smile was diabolical. Scanlon said good-bye and hurried out the door.

Chapter Eight

"Shepherd's pie," Scanlon said, opening the oven door for a peek, "Bless you, Alice."

"Well, I know how much you like shepherd's pie. You and Ira. Why don't you get us another beer, Johnny." Scanlon had every intention of spending an hour before supper grading biology tests, but Alice talked him into having a beer when he came in from visiting Lyle Higgins. Now he would be having his second beer, and on top of the gin he'd drunk earlier, paperwork was out of the question.

Alice had been recounting her day of house cleaning, telephone talking and beer drinking. She had on stretch slacks that were baggy in the knees, and a sleeveless blouse. She looked skinnier than ever, all skin and bones. And lately her dermatitis had been flaring up. It seemed that everything you could name was capable of making her break out. Ira had taken her over to Mary Hitchcock once a week for the past three weeks for patch tests. So far, they hadn't been able to isolate any specific allergens, but Alice was convinced that the fiberglass drapes didn't do her condition any good. In the meantime, she had to apply lotion to the affected areas, lotion by prescription that sold in the drugstore for thirty dollars an eight-ounce bottle. She had the stuff smeared all over her face and bare arms now.

"Your hair looks good," Scanlon said, noticing that it was out of those curlers for a change.

"Gave myself a Toni. All I can afford after I get through paying for the goddamn lotion. I used to be able to get a hairdo at the beauty parlor every couple months."

"Yeah," Scanlon said, "People have been known to support drug habits on less money. What's in that stuff anyway, they want thirty bucks?"

"Don't know. All I know is it works. I have to take pills along with the lotion, you know. That's another thirty dollars every two weeks."

Scanlon felt another tug of free-loader's guilt, particularly now that Alice's medicine seemed to amount to a real financial drain. He offered again to help with groceries. Alice apologized for sounding like they were on the edge of poverty. In fact, the VA paid for most of it. Scanlon didn't feel any less guilty. He'd peeked in the medicine cabinet in the downstairs bathroom. Ira was correct in comparing it to Beady's Drugstore, between her lotion and pills and Ira's medication. If he didn't know better, he'd think it was the kind of medicine cabinet found in the homes of incurable hypochondriacs. Alice's and Ira's afflictions were all too real.

Ira would be coming home from work soon. After his kidney operation Ira had to take the position of shipping clerk, a less demanding job physically than the work he used to do in the foundry. It also paid a lot less. To match the money he made in the foundry, Ira had to work overtime four days a week, and a half-day on Saturdays. He worked too hard, in Scanlon's opinion, for a man in his condition. Scanlon's grandfather, Ira's father, had worked more than fifty years for this company that manufactured machine parts and was Groveton's chief employer, the heart of its economy. He'd been forced to retire in 1944 after a stroke left him speechless and paralyzed on his left side. For his fifty years of faithful service, he had received a gold watch worth maybe a hundred bucks. With any luck, Ira might live long enough to receive a gold watch of his own.

Ira came home from work at six-fifteen and was greeted exuberantly by Lucky and Nanette who had been whimpering and attending the living room windows for the past ten minutes in anticipation of their "father's" arrival.

"Something smells good, Mother," Ira said, winking at Scanlon, for he knew exactly what it was that smelled so good. Alice's menu didn't vary much from one week to the next. This was all right with Ira, and Scanlon had no complaints. Alice described her own cooking as just plain old Yankee, but there was nothing plain about it in Scanlon's opinion. And Ira had always loved her cooking. Scanlon supposed Ira loved his wife, too, despite the almost constant bickering that went on between them.

They sat down to eat at the kitchen table. Alice set the dining room table only when they had people over.

"Fantastic," Scanlon said of the shepherd's pie. He and Alice drank beer from the bottle with their meal; Ira drank skim milk. Ira drowned his salad with bottled Italian garlic dressing and went to work on his first plateful of casserole with a vengeance. Scanlon remembered Ira as always having a workingman's appetite. He finished his first helping without lifting his eyes from his plate. Alice served him seconds without a word, then pushed the casserole toward Scanlon.

"Have some more," she said, "Eat it up, or it'll only go to waste."

"Maybe just a little." Scanlon served himself, conscious all of a sudden of tension between his aunt and uncle. Ira hadn't had much to say since he'd come home, and Alice had been uncommonly quiet. From her, Scanlon was used to hearing incessant chatter to which he only half listened. Ira sometimes tuned out altogether. For all he knew, Scanlon thought, he could be at the bottom of the silence.

"Want to come over to Althea's with us after supper, Johnny?" Alice asked. Scanlon hadn't been lying to Higgins about his paperwork. If he let it go one more night, there would be one more set to add to it tomorrow. And a visit to the Goodwins meant serious drinking.

"I should stay home and get caught up on paperwork. Thanks anyway."

"It won't hurt to take one night off. Besides, we won't stay late. Your uncle has to get his beauty sleep," Alice zinged Ira. Scanlon thought this was unfair of her considering that Ira had to be up at five o'clock every morning and didn't get home until after six most evenings.

"That's right, Mother," Ira said, matching her sarcasm, his mouth full of food, "so try not to yak all night for once. Jesus." He said to Scanlon, "Them women get together, they never take a breath."

"Well," Scanlon said, weakening, "if you're not going to be late."

"I'll zip through these dishes, and we'll be on our way." Alice got up to start clearing away the supper dishes. She had hardly touched any of her food. Scanlon helped her clear the table; Ira got the Groveton Record and went to the bathroom.

"Let me help with the dishes for a change," Scanlon said. "Let me dry."

"Don't be silly." Alice ran hot water and squirted green liquid detergent into the dishpan. What if she's allergic to dishwashing detergent? Scanlon thought. Her hands were raw and chapped from having them in hot water practically every day of her life. Scanlon had washed his share of dishes when he lived with his mother and bad Bill Scanlon. While he was married to Katie he didn't do dish one. Even if he had wanted to, Katie wouldn't let him near the sink. The kitchen was the woman's bailiwick. Alice was of the same mind.

They drove to the Goodwins' house in Ira's 1957 Ford Fairlane. The door on the driver's side had been known to fly open on its own account without warning, as if infected with poltergeists. The engine was temperamental as well, sometimes refusing to start for as trivial a reason as high humidity. Ira was under the hood as often as he was behind the wheel. In all the years he had been driving used cars, who could calculate the money he had saved on repairs because of his mechanical aptitude? It was no more than a five-minute drive to the Goodwins, but Alice never went anywhere in the car without her beer. Scanlon brought one along, too, to be polite.

Willie Goodwin's black lab, Duke, was dozing on the front porch when Ira pulled up in front of the house. He started barking as soon as the car door opened. The porch light went on, and Scanlon could see Althea's silhouette through the curtained front window.

Ira grabbed hold of Duke's muzzle and yanked it back and forth. Alice went straight in the house, followed closely by Scanlon, who wasn't sure about dogs. Willie Goodwin was lying on the sofa in the darkened living room watching hockey on the twenty-one inch floor model color TV, one of the first of its kind in Groveton, according to Alice. On the floor beside him was a bottle of beer and an empty shot glass. The only light came from the TV. Alice and Althea went into the kitchen.

"How's it going, Willie?" Scanlon sat down in the chair next to the sofa. On the porch, he could hear Duke's low growl as Ira roughhoused with the beast. Eddie, Willie's ten-year-old son, his youngest, was lying on his stomach on the floor, inches from the TV screen.

"Fair to middlin'," Willie said. "Help yourself to a beer. There's a bottle of V.O. on the kitchen table. You can bring that back with you, too. Get yourself a glass."

Scanlon was thinking that it couldn't be good for Eddie's eyes, being so close to the tube, not to mention the radiation effects. He wouldn't dream of saying anything to Willie about how to raise his kid. Willie worked seasonally as a construction crew foreman, and in the off-season he spent most of his time drinking at the American Legion or the VFW. His appetite for liquor and women was once again the issue between him and Althea. In the past three years they'd split up three times, in each instance only briefly. A fourth breakup appeared imminent. Their relationship, or as much of it as Scanlon had been able to glean from overheard conversations between Alice and Ira, had similarities to his mother's and Bill Scanlon's, although Bill Scanlon never kept anything as remotely steady as a seasonal job. Willie provided for his family's physical if not their emotional needs.

"How's that piece of shit running?" Willie asked Ira when he came in the house.

"Runs like a top, long's it don't get too muggy."

Scanlon asked his uncle if he wanted anything to drink. Ira wanted ice water. Scanlon drained the beer he had brought with him and went into the kitchen.

Alice and her sister were at the kitchen table drinking beer. Althea's face was puffy and her eyes were red-rimmed and damp, as if she'd been crying. After greeting Althea, Scanlon poured himself a shot of V.O., Willie Goodwin's idea of quality whiskey, and tucked the bottle under his arm. He managed somehow to handle the bottle, his shot, two bottles of beer and Ira's ice water in one trip. He didn't want to have to come back in the kitchen with Althea feeling the way she did.

The TV cameraman was having trouble following the puck; players swirled around the rink in pursuit of the elusive disc, but they might have been chasing phantoms for all Scanlon could tell.

"My old lady saying nice things about me out there?" Willie asked, not sounding very concerned. Scanlon was put in mind of last New Year's Eve when he was in a somewhat similar relationship with his own wife.

"Don't know, Willie. I was always taught that it was impolite to eaves-drop," Scanlon said. He put his shot away in one swallow and quickly chased it with cold beer. His stomach recoiled, his eyes watered. Eddie, lying on his stomach, chin resting in his hands, kicked at the floor with the toes of his shoes.

"Cut that shit out," Willie said, and Eddie stopped immediately. Willie hadn't raised his voice, but even Scanlon could hear the menace in it. He was tall and big-boned, with hard, sinewy arms like Danny Picard. Scanlon studied Willie lying there on the long sofa, the TV light flickering eerily over his recumbent body clad in tank-top undershirt and blue jeans worn through at both knees. He wore his hair short, almost crew cut length. His ears were long with detached lobes, and he had a prominent lantern jaw. Scanlon couldn't remember if his eyes were blue or gray, only that they were pale and very cold. Had he ever seen Willie smile? He laughed a lot, but his laugh was mirthless, on the edge of bitter.

"She's up to something," Willie said, bringing the whiskey bottle to his lips, not bothering with the amenity of his shot glass. He took a couple of short tugs and put the bottle back down on the floor. "Been stomping around here all goddamn day, pissing and moaning and cleaning house like the priest was coming to supper. She's up to something." Willie reached for the whiskey, this time pouring himself a shot to the brim in his glass.

"Well you know them Royer girls," Ira said, "Yakking and house cleaning's what they like to do."

"They got nothing against drinking a beer neither," Willie said with one of his hoarse laughs. "She been givin' me shit all day."

Scanlon had overheard Alice talking on the phone to Althea a few days ago. From what he could gather from Alice's end of the conversation, the subject had to do with whether Althea moved out of the house herself this time instead of throwing Willie out the way she had done the previous three times. Maybe if she left, she would be less inclined to take him back. Alice was impatient with her sister's tendency to give in too easily and take Willie back only to experience the same grief again. She told Althea it was like a vicious circle, their breaking up and coming back together. Nothing had really changed between them. All her married life Althea had been bringing her troubles with Willie to Alice, and by extension to Ira, upsetting their lives and then going her merry way. Alice had had enough, or so she'd said to Althea. Scanlon had the sense that Ira certainly had had his fill of the Goodwins and their marital problems. Ira was a longtime acquaintance of Willie Goodwin. When Ira was a serious drinker, Willie was his constant companion. Scanlon guessed that he must be torn between his friendship with Willie and his allegiance to Alice's sister. Whatever his true feelings, he refused to discuss the Goodwins with Alice any longer, and that, no doubt, was at the bottom of the tension between them. Maybe he'd been invited along tonight to act as a buffer.

"Where're the rest of the troops tonight?" Ira asked Willie. The "troops" consisted of the Goodwin's three other sons. Billy, the oldest, was fourteen; Donny and Dave were thirteen and twelve respectively. Scanlon wondered what could have caused the two-year hiatus between Dave and Eddie. Donny was mildly retarded and somewhat more than mildly hyperactive. He was now at the single-minded stage, fixated at present on bowling. Scanlon had taken him to the alleys once, not long after he had moved in with Alice and Ira, and ever since that time, whenever he had occasion to run into Scanlon, Donny hounded him to take him bowling again. Bowling, bowling. That was all the kid could think about. The thought of Donny and bowling, and Althea and Willie's impending breakup filled him with gloom. And there was Dave, the quietest of the three Goodwin boys, who had little to say to Scanlon since the time he'd accidentally slammed the kid's finger in Ira's car door.

"Be goddamned if I know," Willie said. "They're in and out of here a hundred times a day."

"Billy's over to Pam's," Eddie piped in, making Scanlon wonder just how absorbed he was in the game. Kids heard everything, and there was plenty to listen to in the Goodwin household.

"That's nothing new. Spends all his time over there," Willie said, reaching for his beer, finishing it off in one long, gurgling swallow. Then he took the whiskey he'd poured earlier and quaffed that. This was not the way Willie usually did his drinking. Scanlon remembered him as a slow, deliberate, efficient sipper, a man who was at it for the duration. "Have her knocked up, next thing you know."

"What's Billy, a freshman this year?" Scanlon asked.

"I guess so. Wasting his time at the goddamn Academy. Should've went to trade school. I tried to tell him. Kid don't listen to nobody. Knows it all; thinks he can do anything he damn wants. You wait; soon's he turns sixteen, he'll quit and go to work for Pam's old man." Willie hadn't gone past eighth grade himself. For that matter neither had Ira, nor Scanlon's mother. Among his relatives Scanlon was vastly over educated, not that anybody deferred to his superior schooling, and certainly not to his superior wisdom. To these people he was simply little Johnny Labalm, and wasn't it cute that he was teaching high school in Fairfield.

"You want me to have a talk with him?" Scanlon asked.

"Be wasting your breath. Can't tell that kid shit. Probably run into that all the time over at Fairfield, don't you? Kids these days think they got the world by the balls."

"They're not so bad," Scanlon said.

"You keeping your hands off that high school poon tang? Can't be easy. That's eatin' stuff, high school girls."

"I don't notice those things, Willie. I got my mind on academic, not country matters," Scanlon said, feeling instantly like a jerk for alluding to Shakespeare with Willie Goodwin.

"There's a pile of horseshit if I ever smelled it." Willie's laugh made Scanlon angry this time. Ira laughed, too. Scanlon left the room to get another beer and to cool off. "Bring me another beer, Johnny," Willie ordered.

By now, Scanlon was oiled enough to put a consoling arm around Althea's shoulders. Her face was bloated, leathery and coarse from her habit of lying around in the chaise lounge and soaking up the hot afternoon summer sun.

"How you doing, Althea?"

"I'm doing fine, Johnny. Yourself?" Althea looked up into Scanlon's face and smiled, her eyes watery and full of sorrow.

"Can't complain."

"What's that shithead been telling you in there? The bastard. I hope he burns in hell." Althea's face screwed up. She started to cry. Scanlon patted her shoulder and looked at Alice, shaking his head, thinking he had to be the world's biggest hypocrite. "He's a no good cocksucker," Althea moaned. Scanlon's hand recoiled from her shoulder. He was embarrassed to hear this kind of language from Althea in front of Alice. He shouldn't have been surprised. Althea had a mouth like the sailors he'd served with in the Far East, and it didn't matter who was listening. She talked the same way whether the kids were around or not.

"Nice talk," Alice said. "The priest ought to be here to listen to your mouth."

"Anyone need a beer?" Scanlon opened the refrigerator.

"Thanks, Johnny," Althea said.

He rummaged in the refrigerator looking for three bottles of beer among the junk in there: the Cheeze Whiz, the half used jars of jams, and spreads, and mustards; the foiled leftovers, wilting lettuce, and open bowls of spaghetti sauce and mashed potatoes—the flotsam of Willie and Althea's, Billy, Dave, Donny, and Eddie's common life.

"So how's everything, Johnny?" Althea asked him, smiling wanly. He opened a beer for her and one for himself. Willie's he put aside on the drainboard beside the sink. "Getting much?"

Scanlon noticed that she had plucked her eyebrows, and it was this that made her nose seem fleshier, her eyes too far apart.

"Not much to get in these parts, I'm afraid."

"Just got to know where to look. Follow Willie Goodwin around sometime. He'll lead you to pussy like one of them dowsers. Gets more ass than a toilet seat." Althea laughed and lit a cigarette. Alice looked disapproving, her lips pressed in a thin straight line. She didn't look at her sister, and she didn't look at Scanlon. Scanlon stared down at his beer bottle, which he dangled from two fingers at his side.

"Johnny's getting quite the reputation over in Fairfield," Alice said. Scanlon looked at Alice, surprised at her out-of-the-blue remark.

"What reputation?" he asked.

"Come on, Johnny, don't act modest. Everyone's heard how good you are with the kids. They call him The Prince, the kids do. Can you imagine?" Alice said to Althea.

"Where did you hear that?" Scanlon tried not to sound too interested.

"Oh, Judy Letourneau keeps me up to date on you, Johnny. We talk on the phone once or twice a week. Used to see her more often when I went to beano." Alice (and everyone else he knew around here) pronounced Letourneau with the accent on the first syllable so that it came out sounding like "Let No." Scanlon knew exactly who she was talking about.

"Hattie's mother?"

"Well, yes, and Hattie's one of your biggest fans. She's such a sweet kid. What a beautiful baby she was."

"What's Mr. Letourneau do for a living?"

"Works for the government or something. Doing what, I don't know. He's hardly ever home."

"What else did she tell you about me?"

"Johnny sounds kind of nervous, if you ask me," Althea said. "Must be getting into some little girl's drawers over there."

Winship could have been telling the truth about Hattie Letourneau's old man being a fed. But didn't he say "former" FBI agent?

"What do you take me for, Althea?" Scanlon tried to make light of Althea's remark, to treat the idea as too implausible to be taken seriously. He supposed it was. But what man with two eyes in his head could not notice the flash of underpants on those mini-skirted front row girls? He'd been disarmed at first; now he was no longer distracted, and as far as he could tell none of the Fairfield High girls possessed enough sexual guile to seek to gain favor with him. He wanted badly to press Alice for more information. Now that Althea had gotten the conversation turned in this direction he was afraid of appearing too eager to change the subject. Before he could say anything, Ira came in the kitchen to remind Alice that he was a workingman and needed his sleep.

Scanlon had drunk only one shot and one beer at the Goodwins, and for once he didn't feel the need to drink any more. He was eager for it to be tomorrow, to get to school, to have it out with a few people, to get to the bottom of this "reputation" business. The Prince, indeed.

Chapter Nine

"I don't pretend to be an expert in the life sciences, Daryl, but it strikes me as odd that the text we're using doesn't include a unit on evolution."

"It's not so odd, Jack," Winship replied, "I chose the text for that reason. That was one good reason anyway. The other had to do with the illustrations. You'll have to admit, they're a damn sight better than the old Dull, Metcalf, and Williams."

"To be sure." Scanlon had no idea whatsoever about the Dull, Metcalf, and Williams texts that Winship kept alluding to. "But don't you think that not having a unit on evolution is a serious omission?" Scanlon was goading the principal, and he wanted Winship to know it. "I mean, it is one of the great unifying themes in biology, isn't it?"

"Folks around here aren't all that comfortable with the notion of evolution, Jack. People feel pretty strongly about the issue, as a matter of fact. I tried teaching it once and there was hell to pay from the PTO."

"What state am I in? Tennessee?"

"I wouldn't advise you to do anything on your own, either, Jack."

"I can't believe this," Scanlon said, shaking his head on his way out of Winship's office. He'd gone to see Winship on a fishing expedition, using the evolution issue as an excuse to engage the principal in conversation. What he really wanted to find out was whether Winship had anything to say about his coming back to give extra help the other night. Scanlon hadn't anticipated Winship's position on the teaching of evolution, and it had him so agitated he walked right past Douglas Stambaugh in the corridor without returning Stambaugh's greeting. Stambaugh, apparently insulted, followed Scanlon into his classroom.

"Have we dispensed with the courtesy of returning greetings from our colleagues?"

"I beg your pardon?"

"I'm talking about being snubbed in the hall. I thought we were at least observing the pretense of civility."

"I'm sorry, Douglas, I didn't see you in the hall. I'm sorry."

Stambaugh held three hardcover books against his chest. In Scanlon's opinion, it was a fairly effeminate way to carry books. The history teacher had on a brown corduroy jacket with leather elbow patches, a plaid shirt underneath with a yellow knit tie.

"Well, you did look preoccupied. I suppose I'm just growing weary of the masks everybody wears around here. Apology accepted." Stambaugh held out his hand. Scanlon shook hands with him although he found it a silly gesture. Stambaugh was a strange bird. Then, before thinking first, Scanlon heard himself telling Stambaugh about his conversation with Winship on the extra help issue. He was careful not to suggest that he suspected Stambaugh himself of being involved in so pedestrian a conspiracy, if it could be called such a thing. In truth, he couldn't imagine Stambaugh plotting with Winship or anybody else, or even caring what Scanlon or any of the other Fairfield teachers did in their free time. He read Stambaugh as politically and socially aloof. The furtive concerns of the Winships and Higgins would interest him not at all. Wasn't he, after all, a Fulbright Fellow?

As Scanlon related his story, Stambaugh listened attentively, stroking his dimpled jaw from time to time. He had a long, patrician nose, a high forehead and straight silky brown hair that spoke of good nutrition and good heredity, like Josh Patterson and his winsome Rachel.

"I'm not at all surprised to hear this," Stambaugh said when Scanlon finished. "I've had similar experiences with him. I wouldn't place too much importance on it if I were you. He's a typical civil servant, afraid of controversy."

Scanlon, encouraged by Stambaugh's position, went on to recount his run-in with Winship over evolution.

Stambaugh laughed. "That doesn't surprise me either. Last year he chastised me for teaching what he termed "revisionist" history. It had got back to him that I had attributed to Lincoln motives for engaging in the Civil War that were less than altruistic with respect to the fate of Negro slaves."

"What do you make of it?" Scanlon asked, shaking his head, "Is he blowing smoke, or do you really think some of our colleagues are going behind my back."

"Impossible to say. We perhaps should talk about this some more. What are your plans for this evening?" Scanlon was scheduled for an extra help session after supper.

"Tomorrow would be better for me. You know the Groveton House?"

"I wouldn't blame you if you never wanted to see me again, Ruthie," Scanlon said, trying on his sheepish, little boy look which used to endear him to adults when he was really a little boy.

"You were out of line the other night, Jack. Way out of line." Ruthie stood over him in her absurd mini-skirt and lace apron. She was tight-lipped, her eyes unblinking. Beyond her big hip Scanlon could see Leo's head and shoulders behind the bar. Leo also had a hard eye on him as he did something with his hands under the bar. Scanlon winked at the skinny bartender but Leo didn't look in the mood to play. Scanlon had overestimated his power to charm Ruthie. He began to sweat under her scrutiny.

"I was a real A-hole the other night, wasn't I? I'm really sorry, Ruthie. I don't know what got into me."

"What got into you was too much bourbon and too much beer."

"What I said to you. You know I didn't mean it, don't you?" Scanlon knew only that he had said something that had hurt Ruthie's feelings and caused Leo to throw him out. He had no memory of his actual words.

"I know what I am, sonny. I don't need your kind to remind me."

"I'm really sorry. What can I say?" All of a sudden he was a "kind." He didn't have to ask what kind either. He was sick to death of being judged, sick of being misunderstood, sick of the turn his life had taken. He started to get up. He would wait outside for Stambaugh, take him somewhere else.

"Sit down, you ninny," Ruthie said. "You're not sorry you hurt my feelings. All you're worried about is that I might not forgive you. Just like a man." Ruthie let out a harsh laugh. "Lucky for you I think you're cute." Ruthie glanced over her shoulder at the bar. "I doubt if Leo thinks you're so cute. It might be a good idea if you had a talk with him."

"Thanks, Ruthie," Scanlon said, feeling like her moral inferior, "but I really am sorry I hurt your feelings. I wish you'd believe that."

"OK, so I believe you. Now go tell Leo you're sorry for acting like a horse's ass."

Leo allowed him to bow and scrape and wax contrite. If that wasn't enough, he was made to listen to a lecture on barroom decorum, and finally given a warning that if he caused another scene like the one the other night, he could expect to do his drinking someplace else. Permanently.

"I'll be a good boy, Leo," Scanlon said, instead of telling the little twerp what he could do with his tacky lounge. But there really wasn't another place in town, unless he wanted to drink in the company of American Legionnaires or Veterans of Foreign Wars.

Ruthie brought him his usual, and before Stambaugh showed up Scanlon put away two more shots.

Stambaugh hesitated at the bottom of the stairs, squinting in the dim light. Scanlon waved to get his attention. Stambaugh looked awkward, as if he wasn't used to being in cocktail lounges. When he spotted Scanlon, he wove a course between the close together tables instead of taking the clear route along the periphery.

"Ah. You made it. The hard way, though. What're you drinking?"

Stambaugh appraised the room carefully before he sat down, his forehead wrinkled in a frown.

"Something wrong with the joint, Douglas?" Scanlon lit up a cigarette and offered one to Stambaugh. He shook his head and reached inside his sports jacket for a curved stem pipe with a rough-hewn bowl. More searching in his inside pocket turned up a leather tobacco pouch. He knocked dead ashes into the ashtray, as Ruthie appeared to take his order. Scanlon didn't introduce Stambaugh to Ruthie, and Ruthie, perhaps sensing that Scanlon didn't want his elegant friend knowing that he was acquainted with the likes of her, maintained a professional distance. Stambaugh asked for Campari and soda. When Ruthie told him they didn't have anything that sounded like that, he ordered up the only foreign beer the Groveton House carried, Lowenbrau, which Stambaugh pronounced the German way causing Ruthie to roll her eyes and ask him what the hell that was.

"Do you come here often, Jack?"

"Not really. I like the jukebox." Stambaugh looked over his shoulder in the direction of the jukebox, and set about refilling his pipe.

"It's really quite charming in here. What is it about the jukebox you like?"

"Oh, I don't know. Some old big band tunes that get the nostalgic juices flowing." Scanlon made rings on the table with his glass, feeling all at once uncomfortable in Stambaugh's company.

"I see." Stambaugh pulled a lighter from his pocket, and directed a blowtorch-like flame down at an angle into the pipe bowl. Scanlon had never seen a pipe lighter in action before.

"I've been thinking a lot about this thing with Winship," Scanlon said. "It doesn't make any sense. He's supposed to be such a tiger in his dealings with the PTO and the school board over bond issues and all that. You'd think he'd be more concerned about those things than what people might think about what his teachers are doing in the classroom."

Stambaugh sucked on his pipe and looked up at the ceiling, as if pondering Scanlon's remarks in utter seriousness. In the meantime, Ruthie brought Stambaugh his beer, and another shot and a beer for Scanlon, leaving the drinks without a word. Scanlon made a mental note to talk to Ruthie before he left, to explain himself. What was there to explain? That he was ashamed to admit to his snotty friends that he had dealings with real people?

"I doubt that one thing has very much to do with the other. Winship feels more comfortable arguing for bond issues because in his mind that signifies progress. The important point is that the citizens of Fairfield share this view. Money and commerce are values Winship and the Fairfield community share implicitly. If they disagree on particulars it's not in principle but in kind. To Winship and the school board, and the PTO, the public education of their children has a fundamental purpose." Stambaugh paused to take a sip of beer. Scanlon was irritated because Stambaugh left the obvious question hanging for effect. "To maintain the status quo," Stambaugh continued when he apparently realized that Scanlon was not biting.

"I was never under the illusion that he was the champion of truth and beauty, Douglas. Maybe what you say is true. So what? What I fail to understand is why he's oblique with me one day and down my throat the next. I never know what to expect from the guy." Lyle Higgins, Scanlon recalled, had said that Winship was "complicated."

"He wants to keep you off balance," Stambaugh said, as if this should be obvious. "It's his way of keeping you in line. Don't make the mistake of thinking that just because he behaves like a buffoon most of the time that he's a fool as well."

"Buffoon, fool. Screw him, anyway. I'm going to teach evolution and if he doesn't like it he can fire me. What do I care?"

"Go, Mr. Scopes." Stambaugh threw his arm over the back of a chair and smiled at Scanlon. Scanlon, for his part, searched his sharp features for a sign of condescension but saw only a good-natured smile that revealed interesting lines around his eyes and mouth.

"Thanks."

"Frankly, I'm envious of you."

"Sure you are. A lot you have to be envious." Stambaugh packed some more tobacco in his pipe. He had taken only that one sip of beer. He had this inside joke smile on his face. Scanlon didn't quite know what to make of it. Perhaps he was being condescending after all. At this point it hardly mattered; he was on his third shot and feeling absolutely no pain.

"You must be aware of how highly regarded you are by the students. I'm envious of this effect you have on them, apparently without even trying."

"You're exaggerating. Anyway, this isn't a thing you can achieve by trying, and let me tell you, nothing comes easily to me."

"I don't think I meant it quite that way."

"Besides, how well I get along with the kids doesn't seem to cut it with the boss." Could Higgins have been right in suggesting that Winship might be jealous of his popularity with the students? He decided not to share this information with Stambaugh. "We could go around and around with this all night, but I'm getting bored with the subject."

"Right. Winship is hardly worth the effort."

"So tell me. What did you do for your Fulbright?" Scanlon asked, signaling Ruthie for another round. "Get busy with your beer. You don't want to fall behind."

"I studied for a year in Vienna."

"Studied what?"

"German history in general, Germany's involvement in World War I in particular. It's my special interest, along with the American ante-bellum South."

"Quite a range of interests," Scanlon said, not terribly interested. "Great preparation for teaching high school." Stambaugh laughed and sucked on his pipe, which had gone out.

"What brought you to Fairfield, Jack?"

"Shirking larger responsibilities," Scanlon said, wondering how much Stambaugh knew about his circumstances.

"Speaking of larger responsibilities," Stambaugh said in low, conspiratorial voice, a deep furrow suddenly appearing on his smooth forehead, "what's your draft status?"

"I doubt that my draft board has any interest in me at my advanced age. I've also got four years active duty to my credit."

"You're very fortunate." Stambaugh relit his pipe with his marvelous lighter.

"I know. Timing's important. I take it your draft board's gaining on you."

"Yes. I'm close to the bottom of my bag of deferment tricks. I'll go to Canada before I submit to the military." An edge had crept into Stambaugh's voice.

"Is that why you came to Fairfield? To be close to the border?"

"That wasn't my reason for coming, but now that you bring it up I confess that its proximity gives me some comfort."

"Is all this aversion to the military your conscience talking or are you just plain yellow?" Scanlon asked with a smile.

"I don't believe in murder," Stambaugh said, unfazed by Scanlon's taunt, "by individuals or by governments."

"So, it'll be your highly developed conscience that sends you running for the border? Very interesting."

"I choose to believe that it is. My conscience, that is. How can anyone ever be absolutely certain?"

"By looking down deep. But I suppose you've been through all that often enough. What are you going to tell me, that resisting the draft is a morally courageous act?"

"Yes. In many cases I think it is precisely that."

"But not in every case, of course."

"Of course."

Talk of draft dodging, cowardice and courage had created a gulf between them, a palpable tension. Scanlon thought he saw Stambaugh's eye twitch at one point, and now he was busy disposing of unburned tobacco in the ashtray. He agreed with Stambaugh in principle. It was Stambaugh's smugness that irritated him, that had him sounding off like a flag-waving hawk.

"When do you think you'll be receiving your greetings?"

"I'm not sure. I have a high number, so that might buy me some time."

"They wouldn't jerk you in the middle of the school year."

"Nothing this government did in the name of warmongering would surprise me."

"Spare me, Douglas. You can't be serious." Ruthie delivered Scanlon another whiskey and a fresh bottle of beer. "Your beer's probably flat, pal. Better bring him a new one, Ruthie." Scanlon caught himself too late addressing her in familiar terms. Stambaugh registered no sign that he'd noticed anything out of the ordinary.

"I don't care for another, thank you," Stambaugh said, and Ruthie shrugged her shoulders and went back to the bar to chat with Leo. It was a slow night. Only two of the old regulars, besides themselves, drinking quietly over their cribbage board.

Stambaugh stared down at the table, a cuff of muscle working in his jaw. "I had the sense from the very first time we met at Winship's party that you resented me. I know I haven't mentioned it, but it's bothered me. Bothered me a lot. You do have a way of forcing confrontation, don't you."

"What are you talking about?" Scanlon's voice rose. "I don't resent you. I don't think about you at all. And what if I did? What difference should that make to you?"

Stambaugh laughed. "What difference would it make to me? I don't happen to feel comfortable with your animus, particularly since I'm not aware of the reason."

"Animus? You spent too much time in Vienna, Douglas." Scanlon lit a cigarette, sipped some whiskey. "No, Douglas, I don't resent you. Your attitude toward the draft pisses me off a little, but I wouldn't call it resentment."

"You're sympathetic to the government's involvement in Vietnam?"

"Did I say that? I didn't say that." Scanlon turned away slightly from Stambaugh so that he wouldn't have to look directly at him.

"What would you do in my place, Jack?"

"I don't really know," Scanlon said after a long pause, while he examined the bottom of his shot glass as if the answer were to be found in there. "I suppose I'd go. Yes, I guess that's what I'd do. Not out of patriotism or anything like that. I'd go out of inertia. I come from the inertia generation, Douglas. When I was in high school, I remember we used to have serious discussions over beers in parked cars about the necessity of war. We used to say in all earnestness that war was the only way a young man could discover for sure whether or not he was a coward."

Stambaugh laughed.

"In those days it had the ring of truth, Douglas. I'm not sure where I am on the question nowadays."

"I sense that you see the fallacy in that way of thinking."

"You're very sure of yourself, Douglas. That's another thing about you that bites me." Scanlon slapped his open hand hard on the tabletop. This got Ruthie's attention. She wandered over to their table with that don't-you-think-you've-had-enough-for-one-night-Jack expression. She gave him the palms down sign to cool it, and looked over her shoulder in Leo's direction. Leo was on the phone, his back to the room. Scanlon tried for meaningful eye contact with her, to let her know how much he appreciated her discretion.

"Forgive me," Stambaugh said, "but until someone convinces me otherwise, I'll continue to look upon this war as illegal and immoral."

"You wouldn't be the first coward to hide behind morality," Scanlon said without thinking. Out of the corner of his eye he thought he saw Stambaugh wince. "I'm sorry I said that, Douglas," Scanlon said after a long, awkward silence. "Really, I'm sorry I said such a thing. I've had too much to drink. I'm in no position to be judging you."

"Apology accepted. If you were trying to get to me you succeeded. It really bothers me that you think I'm insincere."

"Hah," Scanlon said, embarrassed. "You shouldn't let what I say, and less what I think, bother you. You got enough grief without worrying about small things like that."

"Well, I respect you, Jack. What you think is important to me."

Scanlon, trapped by Stambaugh's candor, said, "Listen, cut the crap, all right? Why don't you drink some beer? If I didn't think you were OK, would I be down here risking my reputation drinking with you, the way you're dressed?"

"The way I'm dressed?" Stambaugh asked in all seriousness.

"Yeah. Where do you think you are, the Harvard Club? This is Groveton, Vermont, pal, in case you hadn't noticed."

"I went to Yale."

"So I've heard. Begging your fucking pardon."

"I'm not much of a drinker, I'm afraid." Stambaugh sounded almost apologetic.

"There you go. There had to be a reason I took a dislike to you. Never trust a man who doesn't drink," Scanlon said, raising his bottle in a toast and taking a long swallow. "You got any vices, Douglas?"

Stambaugh smiled like a little boy with a wicked secret he was dying to share.

"I confess to a mild weakness for hashish. In fact, I'm going to Cambridge this weekend. I've heard there'll be some quality product around. Maybe you'd like to share some with me."

"I told you before, Douglas, I come from a different generation. We never fooled with pot in my day. Marijuana is the first step down in the journey to heroin addiction and damnation."

"How enlightened."

"Go ahead, laugh. I tried it once or twice on the West Coast. Highly overrated. I got nothing out of it except an upset stomach."

"I think I can guarantee that what I bring back this weekend will change your mind."

Scanlon laughed. "I've heard that song before, Douglas."

"Do you call me Douglas all the time to mock me?" Stambaugh asked.

"What do you mean? I ... Well, I was under the impression that was how you preferred to be addressed. I was told. You ... Well, you seemed like the type. You don't like Douglas? I'll be damned."

"My friends call me Doug. I'd like to count you as my friend, Jack."

"Hey, Doug, I'm flattered. What can I say?" Scanlon finished off his beer in honor of their new friendship and hoisted his empty for Ruthie to see. When Ruthie was beside him with a hand on his shoulder, he could tell from her touch that he was shut off. Ruthie whispered tactfully in his ear, though Stambaugh would have to be stupid not to know what she said.

Stambaugh, exhibiting a little tact of his own, looked at his wristwatch and said, "I really must get to my devotions, Jack. I'm glad we had this talk. I hope it's been as useful for you as it has for me. It's nice to know that one has an ally in the cold war with the Winships and Higgins."

"Yeah. Thanks, Doug. Be seeing you." Stambaugh left Scanlon at the table. Scanlon thanked Ruthie for the gentle handling, and left the Groveton House, none too steady on his feet.

That night, Scanlon dreamed of air raids, exploding bombs, attacking fighter planes with machine guns blazing, firestorms. He awoke in a sweat, with a palpitant heart, and couldn't get back to sleep. He tiptoed downstairs for a beer, something to settle him down, to help him back to sleep.

As a kid he'd had such dreams, especially after a visit from the air raid warden with his hard-hat and flashlight, and his earnest instructions on the dowsing of lights and the pulling of shades. In Johnny Labalm's mind, this was the real thing. All his imagination needed to complete the nightmare was the image of a Saturday matinee war flick, a John Wayne-against-the-Japs-in-the-jungle movie—with air support. He got closer to the real thing in the Navy during weapons demonstrations in the Western Pacific where real jets fired their rockets at sleds towed by destroyers. Polaris missiles came out of the sea like phalluses launched from invisible submarines, heading purposefully into the cloudless blue sky toward an unknown target. Scanlon had awakened from dreams like these, off and on, for years. They were preferable to dreams about his daughter, dreams that sent him running for the psychiatric couch, as it were.

The beer was no help. He drank two down quickly and was still wide-awake. He tried to read, but he couldn't concentrate. He tried to write in the journal as Kennedy had asked him to do but got nowhere with the blank page.

He turned off the light and tried to force himself to sleep, knowing that this would be futile.

Chapter Ten

"Oh dear," Janet said to Scanlon in the waiting room. "I tried all morning to get you at home, but the line was busy."

"What's up?"

"I'm afraid Mr. Kennedy won't be able to see you today. If you want to, he can see you early next week." Janet had been crying, and her lower lip began to tremble.

"What is it? What's wrong?"

"I shouldn't say anything." But now the tears started again, and were overflowing, cascading down her cheeks. In the early years of his marriage to Katie, when he still had the power to make her cry, her tears always left a trail of mascara down her cheeks. Janet's tears seemed less dramatic for lack of makeup. "He obviously hasn't said anything to you," she said, her voice on the verge of failing her.

"Maybe you should tell me. I won't say anything to Bob. Maybe I can help."

"Sara's not going to make it, I'm afraid," Janet managed to say before her voice gave up. Scanlon placed a hand carefully on her shoulder, on her soft sweater. When she got back in control she told Scanlon that Sara was not Kennedy's wife. She was his thirteen-year-old daughter, succumbing to leukemia after six months of chemotherapy.

Scanlon sat down on one of the metal folding chairs. "He never said anything to me."

"It's so unfair. Mr. Kennedy is so sweet, and Sara is an absolute angel. It's just not fair." This time Janet sounded angry. Scanlon sat and stared at his hands.

"Is there anything I can get you?" he asked Janet.

"No, thank you." Janet pulled several tissues from the box she kept on her desk. "Do you want me to reschedule you?" She blew her nose and wiped her eyes.

"No, no. The regular time's all right. That is ..."

"I'll call you if there's a problem," Janet interjected.

"Yeah. Are you sure you're all right?"

"I'll be fine."

"Well, see you next week, I guess." Scanlon made no move to leave, however, as Janet looked to him about to have a relapse. He stood in the middle of the bleak room and watched poor Janet fall once again into tears and sobbing. He went over and put his hand on her shoulder again, feeling her bucking sobs move along his arm like a current.

"It really is so unfair," she sobbed. Scanlon patted her arm. He felt inept in this role of comforter. All he could seem to do was pat her soft arm while she cried. If he didn't think she would have taken it the wrong way, he would have embraced her. She would have been correct to take it the wrong way; partly correct, because he found her powerfully alluring in her grief. After a while, her crying yielded to sniffling and the occasional spasmodic sob.

"Thank you, Jack," she said, after she'd cried herself out.

"That's all right."

"Thanks anyway." Janet gave him a brave smile.

"You want some water or something? Some aspirin?"

"No. Honestly, I'll be all right now. It's just so ... sad." Janet's tear-stained face screwed up into crying again. This time Scanlon pulled a handful of tissues from the box and without stopping to think, took her chin in his hand and began to dab the tears from her cheeks. She took the tissues away from him, and he knew instantly that he had stepped over some line, that he had done something wrong. "Thanks again, Jack. I'm sorry to put you through this. I promise I'll be all right this time."

Scanlon took this as his cue to exit.

"Well, I'll be going then. You sure you're all right?"

"I'll be fine. Thank you for being so kind."

"Evolution is a fact," Scanlon said to his first period biology class ten minutes before the period ended. He paused for dramatic effect, feeling much more nervous than he thought he would in defying Winship. "There is simply no question that life-forms have changed over time, long periods of time, unimaginably long periods of time. So, now is the time to get out of your heads once and for all that there's a real dispute between the theory of evolution and the Book of Genesis."

Junior Darling's hand went up instantly, and without waiting to be acknowledged, he said, "My father says they can't prove evolution, and it's the Communists who want us to believe in it so we'll stop believing in God." Holly Bean, one of Scanlon's biggest fans, giggled. Junior Darling was considered by the girls to be the leading weirdo in bio class if not the whole sophomore class, maybe even the whole school. He was forever offering, unsolicited, the opinions of his crackpot, Free Will Baptist family. Junior was quite a gifted student, and Scanlon felt he would go places if he could get away from his family's influence.

Donald Dubois, whose name everyone pronounced "dew boys," rallied behind Junior by submitting, without raising his hand, that evolution could not actually be proved. Therefore, the theory was invalid. Donald was considered by his classmates to be a prodigious logician. He was a good math student according to Lyle Higgins, and anybody who was good in math was looked upon with awe by most students. The truth was that Scanlon was not that well prepared on the subject of evolution. He'd had to travel all the way to Burlington, to the university library, to find anything informative on the subject, and had spent all one Saturday afternoon reading and taking notes instead of drinking, which was what he really felt like doing. He thought the Darwinian and Lamarckian versions of evolution would be something sophomores could handle. Of course he had no precedent for such an assumption, no experience. The Lamarckian argument—the use and disuse thing, and the inheritance of acquired characteristics—would no doubt appeal to kids more than Darwin's principles of variation and natural selection. But Scanlon was hardly an expert, and he knew it. At best, he would be teaching with only two or three steps head start on his students.

"Who's got a Bible?" Scanlon asked facetiously, not expecting to be taken seriously, and was therefore disarmed when Clara Delaney produced a pocket version from her plastic book bag, and solemnly delivered it to the lecture desk.

"Gee, thanks a lot, Clara," he said with feigned annoyance, wondering what he had got himself into. He turned to the Book of Genesis and began to read aloud. Then he stopped and asked the class if they knew what the word genesis meant.

"It means beginning," Donald Dubois said impatiently.

"Just making sure. No need to take offense." Scanlon skipped to the passage where God invoked the waters to bring forth "the moving creature that hath life, and fowl that may fly above the earth in the open firmament of heaven." Scanlon asked if anyone had a problem with that passage. His question was met with silence. "I know that most of you consider the words in the Bible as literal, revealed truth, and completely unimpeachable, but try to imagine for the sake of argument that there could be another way of looking at the beginning. For example, who knows anything about fossils?" Scanlon was not surprised to see the hands of Junior Darling and Donald Dubois shoot up simultaneously. "Come on. There must be someone else who's heard about fossils."

Loretta Small, who never had anything to say in class, took a chance and asked if fossils weren't somehow involved in the evolution business.

"Well, what about it, Donald? What do fossils tell us?" Scanlon pointed at Dubois, hoping to gain some measure of control.

"Extinct life forms," said Donald Dubois.

"And what does the idea of extinct life forms suggest to you? Anybody?" The bell rang before Donald or anybody else had the chance to answer, and Scanlon realized that he was sweating profusely and his mouth was dry. All he had wanted to accomplish in the ten minutes was to leave the class with something to think about overnight, as if they would think about anything except what early evening television had to offer in the way of intellectual stimulation.

In his fourth period class, there was no one of Donald Dubois' caliber to provide the give and take of discussion. All Scanlon's attempts at Socratic midwifery resulted in silence and blank stares, his thought provoking statements left hanging in the air like stale cooking. If Winship found out he was teaching the forbidden subject it wouldn't come from his son, because Tommy Winship had all he could do to keep his chin off his chest in his backrow seat. Scanlon would have to approach the subject from a different angle with this class, which meant he would have to spoon-feed them, lecture them to sleep.

Winship summoned him to his office seventh period, his only free period of the day. News had traveled faster than he thought it would.

"I see that you've gone ahead and done what you want, despite my feelings. I guess I shouldn't be surprised," Winship said, sitting on the edge of his desk, legs crossed, both hands clasping his knee. "I've made an appointment for you to talk to Sumner, eighth period. I'll cover your study hall. That will be all, Jack."

Scanlon had not talked with Sumner Purnell since his interview in April. He remembered the superintendent as a gentle man, quiet and rustic in speech and manner. Cynthia Sinclair referred to him as a Teddy Bear, and from what Scanlon could gather from casual talk, he was well-liked and respected by all the teachers and principals in his district. His office was in the building where kindergarten was taught, on the hill beside the high school. Scanlon was told by Purnell's secretary to go right in, that he was expected.

"Have a seat, Jack. It's nice to see you. Been a long time. Fall's a busy time for me. On the road most days," Sumner Purnell said from behind his desk, dwarfed by the size of it. He had on a plaid shirt, which clashed with his checkered jacket, and he wore a black string tie.

"Good to see you, too, Mr. Purnell."

"You obviously know why you're over here, Jack, so we won't waste time with small talk. Daryl's got the notion that you're trying to undermine him. What have you got to say about that?" Purnell's bushy eyebrows met over his nose. He removed his wire-rimmed glasses and busied himself wiping them with his big, plaid handkerchief while he waited for Scanlon to reply. Scanlon breathed deeply before responding.

"It's not true." Despite the superintendent's easy manner, Scanlon was nervous. "I've apparently done a few things that haven't pleased him, but whatever I've done, it hasn't been to undermine him. Besides, I'm pretty sure I told him I was going to teach the evolution unit, and I don't remember that he told me outright not to. This is 1968, for crying out loud. Every school teaches evolution. If they don't, they ought to." Scanlon was shaking.

"You may be right. But you've got to understand that there are some fundamental differences between what city folks consider acceptable curriculum and what's agreeable to folks around here. You'd really have to have been raised in these parts to appreciate what I'm saying, Jack." Sumner Purnell knew nothing of Scanlon's Groveton roots and Scanlon had no intention of revealing them. To Purnell, Scanlon was just another city slicker railing against provincialism without a deep understanding of the concerns of the locals.

"I don't really see what the region has to do with it. The truth is the truth, and rural kids are just as entitled to it as anybody else. I mean, some of them are going to be in for a rude awakening when they go off to college and bump into new ideas. What's going to happen to them? They should be prepared. That's how I feel, for what it's worth." The superintendent maintained his kindly smile, yet managed not to look directly at Scanlon.

"You could be right. Well, if you can persuade Daryl, I certainly don't have any objections to your teaching the subject. You should be warned, though. There are going to be some ruffled feathers among the parents out there. Do you think you're prepared to deal with them? Some of these folks can be cantankerous."

"I'll get myself prepared."

"Why don't we leave it like this, then. You have a talk with Daryl. Whatever meeting of the minds you two come up with will be all right with me. Fair?"

"I guess so." Scanlon shook hands with the superintendent and left his office feeling outwitted. Winship was not likely to come around to his argument easily, if he came around at all, and Purnell no doubt knew this. Tonight was Scanlon's night to chaperon the dance. Winship would be there, too.

Scanlon arrived at school a half hour before the dance was scheduled to start. He went to the teachers' lounge to leave his coat and to have a smoke before going up to the gym. The prospect of chaperoning a high school dance left him nervous at the last minute; he'd picked up a six-pack of beer in Groveton and drank two of them in the time it took him to drive the seven miles to Fairfield. Now he worried that Winship might smell it on him.

He hoped the kids would be better behaved tonight than he had ever been at his high school dances. Had he ever actually danced at one of those awful affairs? He never learned to jitterbug, and he'd been so self-conscious around girls at that age he never dared ask a girl to slow dance. What he, and many boys like him, did was to show up half drunk and lurk around the edge of the dance floor in the shadows, in a small group, watching with secret envy as the guys who knew all the dance moves held those soft girls in their arms. And one always had to be on the lookout for the approach of a chaperone. For him, high school had been no fun.

Scanlon finished his cigarette and wandered into the cafeteria where Maureen Goff and Tammy Beaulieu were busy organizing the refreshments. He poked his head through the serving line window.

"Need any help in there?" he asked. The stainless steel inserts in the steam table were rimmed with grease and crumbs; the smell of high school cafeteria was still powerful.

"Oh, hi, Mr. Scanlon," Tammy Beaulieu said. "No, I think we got everything pretty much under control. Save me a dance tonight?" Tammy was a sophomore with short, dark hair, and with what kids described as a "personality." She was struggling in his biology class, more from lack of native ability than lack of effort. She had a cute, turned up nose and a good enough figure to make the varsity cheerleading squad. Sometimes he thought she flirted with him, but he had never had the knack for knowing for sure when he was being flirted with.

"I'm not much of a dancer, I'm afraid. Tell you what. If they play the Bunny Hop I'll get in line with you."

"What's your favorite group?" Maureen Goff asked him as she stretched cellophane wrap over a platter of brownies. Maureen was also one of his biology students, but unlike Tammy, quite gifted, almost the caliber of Junior Darling. She was dark, long-haired, and her bone-framed glasses gave her an air of sophistication. She was anything but sophisticated, even if she did possess an impressive intellect. She was also a cheerleader, JV.

"Name some groups and I'll tell you if they're among my favorites." Scanlon wasn't up on the current music scene. He'd heard of the Beatles, of course, and the Rolling Stones. Except for the most popular names he was ignorant of the purveyors of rock and roll.

"You like Big Brother and the Holding Company? Strawberry Alarm Clock? Spanky and Our Gang?"

"Never heard of any of those. Sorry."

"They're great. Bet Mr. Scanlon's a big Beatles fan, right, Tammy?"

"Beatles or Stones," Tammy said.

"You read me like a book. How about I test one of those brownies? You didn't juice them with illicit drugs, did you?"

"All right, Mr. Scanlon, but just one." Maureen handed him a brownie. It was still warm.

"Thanks," Scanlon said, winking at the girls.

Upstairs in the gym, the decorating committee was working frantically to put on the finishing touches. Tommy Winship was high on a ladder in the jump ball circle attaching crepe paper streamers to a *papier mache* replica of a crystal ball. More crepe paper: yellow, blue, red, and orange festooned the open girders above the floor. All the bleachers were folded up to make more room for dancing. Posters on the wall advertised the fact that this dance was sponsored by the sophomore class, clearly the most gifted, the most energetic, and by far the best looking class at Fairfield High.

Scanlon found a metal folding chair against the wrestling mat under the north basket and sat down to admire the crew in action. They should be so purposeful and efficient in their schoolwork. If he could find things for them to do in class that could generate half this enthusiasm, he would have something. This kind of thinking drew him into a dark mood, as he considered his real shortcomings as a teacher. In his self-absorption, he didn't notice Winship come up and open a folding chair beside him.

"Did I wake you?" Winship sat down.

"I was hypnotized by all the meaningful activity," Scanlon said, not rising to Winship's remark.

"They do seem to have things under control." No sooner had Winship said this than the room was filled with an abrasive electronic screech.

On the stage, Scott Pettingill held his hands over his ears. Winship got up and walked over to the stage. The noise continued for a few moments more. Winship hoisted himself on stage, and the noise stopped. He conferred with Scott Pettingill over the placement of speaker wires, fiddled with the controls on the console that was set up on stage, looking quite competent and authoritative. Scott Pettingill's head nodded in affirmation of whatever it was that Winship said to him.

Kids were already starting to drift into the gym, having the backs of their hands stamped at the door when they paid their fifty cents for admission. Suddenly the main lights went off and were replaced by stage spots with colored gels. Mirrors attached to the *papier mache* ball sprayed reflected light on the floor and walls when it rotated. The gym was thrown into a gauzy, pinkish hue. Then the music started, loud and muddied; it ricocheted in the poor acoustics of this cavernous room designed for basketball contests.

Winship was back. "Think you can put up with this for three hours?" he shouted. More kids appeared. Boys migrated to the east side, girls to the west. Nobody had taken to the dance floor yet. Scott Pettingill, who disc-jockeyed all the dances, was speaking into a microphone. His voice was distorted. The only words Scanlon could make out were welcome and sophomore. A few uninhibited couples skipped out onto the floor after Scott had finished his greeting, and the floor was crowded for nearly every dance for the next thirty minutes. So far, every tune played had been a fast one. Scanlon observed that kids danced the same way out here in the boondocks as they did in the city, if you could call what they were doing on the floor dancing. To him it was more like masturbation. What one partner did had little to do with the other. It was not until the evening was half over that a slow number was played, and boys and girls clung meaningfully to each other, not dancing so much as holding and shuffling, the girls with both arms wrapped around the boys' necks.

Several girls had come over to ask Scanlon to dance. He'd tried, as gracefully as he knew how, to decline, claiming everything from ineptitude to a sore ankle. Winship, on the other hand, oblivious it seemed of his total lack of rhythm or coordination, danced with every girl who asked him. Scanlon thought, uncharitably, that the girls only got the principal on the floor so that he could be made fun of. And he did look comical out there, his arms churning in stiff, piston-like, up-and-down motions, his upper body bent at the waist in a posture that suggested to Scanlon someone filling his pants. But he got up every time he was asked.

Hattie Letourneau, however, was not to be denied. She dragged Scanlon out of his chair onto the floor, and to his horror, kids began immediately to form a circle around them and to clap their hands to a song, the rhythm of which Scanlon could not locate with his body.

Then the music stopped abruptly. Scott Pettingill's eerie, sepulchral voice filled the gym. A song was being dedicated to Scanlon: "Light My Fire," by the Doors. What would Winship make of that? Scanlon wished he could make himself disappear. The song no doubt referred to the Bunsen burner mishap he'd had in chemistry class recently. He'd been demonstrating its proper use and sent a yellow, three-foot high flame toward the ceiling. He'd been embarrassed, the kids, of course, delighted.

Dancing with the slender and graceful Hattie Letourneau made him feel heavy and uncoordinated, and unlike Winship, painfully self-conscious with all eyes on him.

"Thanks, Mr. Scanlon," Hattie said when the song finally ended, "Save me one for later."

"Oh, sure."

"You're a good sport to get up there, Jack," Winship said to him when he returned to his chair. "Damned songs go on forever, don't they? Can't hear yourself think in here. Come on out in the other room. I'd like a word with you."

"What's on your mind, Daryl?" Scanlon asked in the entryway outside the gym.

"Can I bum a cigarette?" Winship asked.

"Sure." Scanlon shook out a cigarette for each of them.

"I had a chat with Sumner after school today. He told me about your conversation. I just want you to know that if you're still determined to go ahead with this, I won't stand in your way. I want you to understand that there are likely to be repercussions though."

"Mr. Purnell mentioned that some parents might object."

"Object! If that's all they'd do, I would have put evolution in the curriculum years ago. It wouldn't surprise me if they pull their kids out of school when they hear about it."

"They can't do that, can they? Legally?"

Winship laughed. "Watch and see what they can do. Some of these people have their own legal system. You'll see."

So Winship and Purnell were setting him up for a lesson in how the real world operated in the Green Mountain state. He could teach what he wanted, what he believed should be taught, but shouldn't expect any support from his principal or his superintendent. That would be all right with him.

"Thanks for the encouraging words," Scanlon said.

"Don't mention it." Winship snubbed his cigarette out in a pail of sand. "We'd better get back inside before the natives get too restless."

In the course of the evening, most of the kids made a point of coming over to where he was sitting to say hello and pass a few moments in hard-to-hear conversation. The next song they dedicated to him was "Revolution" by the Beatles. Winship would have a field day with that one. This time he danced with Grace Ouimette, which had the advantage of drawing at least the boys' attention away from him. Grace was a well-built senior, wearing the miniest of mini-skirts, and a satiny blouse (like the one worn by Laraine McFarland that night) that played up every contour of her large, quivering breasts. To Scanlon she was a cow; to the Fairfield High boys who ogled her shamelessly, she was a goddess.

Toward the end of the evening, Samantha Burnham arrived with two boys with long hair and denim jackets who were not Fairfield High students. Samantha was a senior and what Cynthia Sinclair described as a "free spirit," not meaning the phrase to be flattering. Tonight she had on a long, filmy skirt and a white peasant blouse with embroidery down the front. She was barefoot. Winship spotted them right away and hurried over to the three of them before they got beyond the door.

Scanlon watched from his chair under the north basket. Winship's back was to him. He leaned toward the trio, turned more toward Samantha than the boys, gesticulating excitedly. He was all hands, and his head went back and forth as if he were saying no, no, no. The boys looked at each other with insolent smirks, as if to say, who's this joker? Samantha put her hands on her hips and thrust her jaw at Winship. Curiosity got Scanlon up from his chair just as she turned on her bare heel and stalked out, the boys, heads bobbing, following in her wake.

"What was that all about?" Scanlon asked Winship.

"Damn that Samantha Burnham. She's been nothing but trouble ever since she came here. She knows damn well that we don't allow outsiders to these dances. She brought those hippies here to defy me. It does no good to talk to her father, either. He's worse than she is. Completely permissive. Lets her do anything she damn pleases. If he's so damned set on her being free, he should have sent her to Summerhill or some such place. I almost feel sorry for her, having a man like that for a father."

"What kind of student is she?"

"Oh, she's very bright. Very bright indeed. Too smart for her own good. Thinks she knows more than her teachers. When she bothers to come to school at all, she spends more time in my office than she does in class. Nobody can stand her."

"Interesting. She shows up for my eighth period study hall occasionally."

"Be happy you don't have to teach her."

After the dance Scanlon offered to stay and supervise cleanup by himself, but Winship was adamant that Scanlon go home. He would look after the cleanup. Samantha Burnham had put Winship in a bad mood, and he was taking it out on Scanlon, was the way Scanlon saw it. Had the principal interpreted his interest in Samantha as taking sides against him? Scanlon left in a state of agitation, as he had done so many times in his association with Winship.

Scanlon drove back to Groveton by way of North Fairfield, along the dirt road that followed a fast moving brook, which emptied into the Manoosic River. He drove slowly, a bottle of beer between his legs, keeping a sharp eye for deer. He had been surprised on this road at night before by three of the creatures cutting so closely in front of him that he'd had to slam on his brakes to avoid colliding with a fawn.

Some of his students lived out in North Fairfield, in poor houses with yards littered with junk, with the husks of old cars abandoned in fields, rubber tires hanging by ropes from the limbs of trees. One could be misled by the neat farms and tidy houses along Route 2 into thinking that all was well and prosperous in the exquisite beauty of rural Vermont.

Scanlon slowed down for a hairpin turn by an abandoned sawmill gone to weed, the brook running loudly past it. On the other side of the road was one of those poor houses. Lopsided, like the one Alice and Ira lived in, it had curtainless windows, detritus all over the sagging front porch—an old refrigerator with the cooling unit, like a stack of coins, on top; a rusty bike with the front wheel missing; stacks of newspapers, loose bottles, a baby bassinet. Next door was a crumbling barn with a sway-backed roof. A hand-lettered sign in the window of the house read NIXSONS THE ONE. Scanlon finished a beer and reached into the paper bag on the seat beside him for another.

In Groveton, he drove down steep Western Avenue looking for signs of life at eleven-forty-five on a Friday night. Not a living thing on the street; nothing open, not even Guyette's Pressure Fried Chicken and Pizza. This is no town for a grownup to live in, Scanlon thought. He turned right on Lower Main, surprised to find the new Hackett's Diner open. He had vivid memories of the old Hackett's Diner when he was a kid, before the shiny aluminum siding had been put on the outside, the glass and chrome on the inside. The smell of real hamburgers sizzling in their ample fat on the black grill, up front, where customers could see them and smell them cooking. The white enamel flip-top sugar bowls, the black felt menu board with plastic letters spelling out the day's specials. The plastic pastry safe on the counter; stools without backrests. The counterman punched out your check with a metal gizmo, and you paid at the register next to the door.

Now everything was clean. Everything gleamed, reflected light, conformed to board of health standards. Scanlon squeezed onto a stool at the counter, a stool with a backrest. All the other stools were unoccupied. He pulled a menu from between a pour-type sugar dispenser and a highly polished napkin holder. The menu was heavy, bound in rigid clear plastic, Hackett's Diner printed in big, black letters across the front; very professional. Fresh looking pastries—pies, slices of cake, turnovers—were displayed on immaculate, chrome-plated shelves behind the counter, mirrored from above giving the illusion of twice as many objects. Scanlon wasn't hungry. He didn't know why he had come into this place. He flipped the pages of the jukebox selections, but didn't bother to read them. There was no sign of a counterman or a waitress.

He turned on his stool, intending to leave, and caught the reflection of Danny Picard and Norma Woodruff in the mirror behind the counter. They were cuddled up in a leatherette booth at the far end of the diner, apparently oblivious of Scanlon. All four of their hands were clasped together on the tabletop. Their heads were close enough together to be kissing, but they were not actually kissing. Just looking at each other like people in love. They hadn't attended the dance. Danny had little to do with school activities, and Norma had quit school a year ago. Scanlon had seen her in the school parking lot once or twice. Once, Danny had introduced them. Norma was plain—lustreless hair, pale complexion, eyeglasses too big for her small face. Tonight she had on a pink cardigan sweater, and Danny wore a tight-fitting plaid sports jacket. The sleeves were too short, and his hands looked enormous. Norma had been Danny's girl since she was a freshman, and as soon as he graduated they would be married. Danny had told him once where she worked, but he'd forgotten. Kids at school made fun of Danny's devotion to Norma, but not when he could hear them. Should he go over and say hello? No. They were far too absorbed in each other. He would be an unwelcome intrusion. He slipped off the stool and out the door.

Chapter Eleven

Scanlon's anxiety mounted as the day of his regularly scheduled appointment with Kennedy approached. He should have called Janet to find out if Kennedy would be able to keep the appointment. If she had tried Alice's number and continued to find it busy, there was no way she could contact him unless she tried to reach him at school, and he doubted that she'd be so indiscreet as to do that. Scanlon wasn't sure he was ready to face Kennedy under the circumstances, but he was feeling increasingly unsettled. He couldn't seem to concentrate; he was falling way behind in his paperwork, so far behind he was afraid he would never catch up. How long before the kids' indulgence and goodwill would stretch to the limit, if they weren't already?

As he feared it would, winter came calling early, leaving six and a half inches of fresh snow on the ground, catching him without snow tires. Higgins had insinuated that it was unmanly to put snow tires on any vehicle operating on fewer than six cylinders.

Tonight, as he got into his car to drive to Fairfield for the extra help session that students had come to depend upon and expect, he was seized with fear, fear of losing control of his little car on icy Route 2 and plunging to his death on Crow Hill. But Route 2 was in better condition than it had been that morning, and though his body was tense and his heart thumped palpably beneath his shirt, he drove the seven miles without incident.

There were already a half dozen kids in the room when he arrived. A light was on in Winship's office, so he assumed that the principal had let the kids in. On the other hand, he could have forgotten to lock his door when he left that afternoon, in which case Winship would blow his top, he was such a security fanatic.

"How'd you guys get in?" Scanlon asked, taking off his coat.

"Door was open, and the lights were on. I just walked right in, sat right down, and baby let my mind run free," said Robbie Trishman, who probably needed extra help least of anyone in either of his chemistry classes. Nevertheless, he'd appeared for every session, which may have had more to do with the fact that Hattie Letourneau attended all the sessions, too. Hattie didn't seem to have the time of day for Robbie or any other of the Fairfield High boys who were struck by her slender figure, her dark, lustrous hair, deep-set eyes, and flawless complexion, which Scanlon compared to porcelain. She was just friendly enough to provide the encouragement to keep the boys in pursuit, and aloof enough that they had to think she was unapproachable. Robbie Trishman no doubt hoped to impress her with his chemistry acumen, for chemistry was Hattie's nemesis and threatened to blemish her straight-A report card with a C, a fate worse to her, Scanlon imagined, than a pimple on her chin. Robbie wasn't a bad looking kid, tall and blond, if a little overweight and near-sighted. He looked the intellectual with his heavy black-framed glasses, but if he was as intelligent as they came at Fairfield High, he was not that interested in intellectual matters. For that reason, he would probably never get anywhere with Hattie Letourneau.

"Mr. Winship been around?" Scanlon asked. Hattie told him that the principal had poked his head in the door a few minutes before Scanlon arrived. He had not asked where Scanlon was.

Besides Hattie and Robbie, present were Lloyd Rumsey, Paula Gallant, Larry Hart, and Scott Pettingill, the Friday night dance DJ. Odd that six of his better students were habitually at evening session, while the ones who could really use the help seldom attended.

"So what's on your little minds this evening?" Scanlon reached in his top drawer for the evaporating dish he used as an ashtray. Winship would not be pleased if he found out that Scanlon smoked during these meetings. He did it partly to create a more casual atmosphere in the evening than during regular hours, and partly because it relaxed him. He didn't allow any of the kids to smoke, however, and so far none of them, not even Scott Pettingill, who liked to question authority almost as much as Samantha Burnham did, had challenged him for practicing the old double standard.

"I simply cannot," Hattie Letourneau lamented, grinding the eraser on her pencil into the tablet arm of her chair in utter frustration, "comprehend gram-molecular weight! It's so stupid and pointless, and who on earth cares?"

"My sentiments exactly," said Scott Pettingill. "Who'd ever use the stuff except for a chemist? None of us wants to be a chemist. At least I don't. What about you guys? You want to be a chemist, Hattie? Paula? Larry? I didn't think so. Then it's settled. Nobody at Fairfield High is interested in a career in chemistry, therefore there is no need, and no point in studying gram-molecular weight junk. Case closed. Let's go to the gym and shoot some hoops."

"Oh, shut up, Scott. We've got a test coming next Friday, and if I don't get at least a B on this one, I will absolutely die," Hattie said.

"Gram-molecular weights aren't that hard to understand," Robbie Trishman said, his eyes on Hattie.

"Well, suppose you get up here and explain it, Robbie," Scanlon said, taking a chair in the front row. "You can't do any worse than I have." Without hesitating, Robbie Trishman hoisted himself out of his chair and headed for the blackboard.

"The subject today, boys and girls," he began, in his parody of Scanlon, "is the concept of the gram-molecular weight. " He went on to make what Scanlon believed was a credible analogy with coffee beans, using a Colombian coffee TV commercial apparently known to everyone in the room. Scanlon was impressed with the boy's skill at making the slippery concept come to life; he had certainly done a better job than Scanlon had. Hattie Letourneau was not as impressed.

"I'm going to flunk chemistry," she moaned. "I just know I'm going to flunk chemistry." To Hattie, any grade below a B was equivalent to a failure.

"No one is going to flunk chemistry," Scanlon said. "You'd have to do zero work to flunk. This stuff really isn't as difficult as you're building it up to be. If Robbie and Scott can get it, is there any doubt that you can, too?"

"But Robbie is such a brain," Hattie said, not looking encouraged by Scanlon's encouraging words. Robbie Trishman's eyes shined and his breathing deepened.

"Let's try to apply Robbie's analogy," Scanlon said, and worked a few problems out on the board. In a way, Pettingill was correct: The topic was essentially pointless, a lot of number crunching for its own sake unless a kid had some insight into the larger significance of the idea, the insight possessed apparently by Robbie Trishman and Scott Pettingill. How much of what he and his colleagues taught these kids was really worth knowing? To raise such a question with his colleagues would be equivalent to blasphemy.

"That was a decent job you did tonight, Robbie," Scanlon said to Trishman, who lingered behind after the others had gone, ostensibly to check on the progress of a chemical reaction he had going in a beaker in his lab locker.

"Thanks. It was fun."

"Mind if I steal it and use it on the whole class? I'll give you the credit."

"Sure, why not? But I'll probably be in for more blame than credit when nobody understands what you're talking about. Like tonight."

"I'll risk it. See you tomorrow, Robbie."

Scanlon remembered to lock the classroom door before he left. Winship's office door was open; the principal sat behind his desk, shirtsleeves rolled to the elbow. It was too late for Scanlon to turn around. It would look like he was trying to avoid him.

"How'd it go tonight, Jack?" Winship looked up from the papers strewn over his desktop. Scanlon had the uneasy feeling that Winship had been waiting for him.

"Not too bad. What brings you here at this hour?"

"What else is there in my life these days? The bond issue. I've got to have a revised proposal for the school committee by tomorrow, and I was checking old purchase orders for capital items expenditures. Pretty mundane stuff to you." Here we go, Scanlon thought. "Thought I smelled smoke a while ago. You run any burners tonight?"

"No." Scanlon remembered that he'd left his ashtray on the lecture desk and hadn't emptied the dead butts.

"Must be my imagination. By the way, your classroom door was open when I got here tonight, and I didn't see your car in the parking lot. Luckily no kids had shown up yet. I made sure they knew I was around when they came, though. You should probably be more careful about locking up in the future, Jack. There are some pretty dangerous chemicals in that room, and you know how kids are."

"I was coming back tonight anyway. I didn't see any harm in leaving it open." Scanlon barely remembered leaving the building that afternoon, let alone thinking about what little harm there would be in leaving his classroom door unlocked.

"I'd feel better if you'd take the time to lock whenever you're going to be away from the building"

"Sure. Sorry. I'd better go back and double-check the door before I leave, right now. See you in the morning."

"Good night, Jack."

Scanlon went back to his room. He emptied the butts into a paper towel and stuffed it into his pocket. He washed out the evaporating dish and put it back in the drawer. Pausing at the door, Scanlon sniffed the air in the room in case Winship took it in his head to snoop around before he left. He smelled nothing, but his sense of smell had never been very acute, so he got out the disinfectant and sprayed liberally just to be on the safe side. He locked the door behind him and left the building by the south stairs, walking quietly, like a thief.

Scanlon managed to put off calling Janet until an hour before his scheduled appointment. Janet informed him that Sara, Kennedy's daughter, had died the previous Saturday, but that Kennedy was keeping his appointments. She asked Scanlon if he felt up to keeping his.

"What do you think, Janet?" Scanlon asked. "How is he?"

Janet assured him that Kennedy would be all right and he shouldn't worry about being made to feel uncomfortable. Mr. Kennedy was a professional.

What professionalism had to do with it, Scanlon didn't ask. He knew that he wouldn't be all right in Kennedy's place. He wasn't eager to be in Kennedy's presence while the man was grieving; he'd been all but paralyzed by Janet's mild display last week. "If you're sure he feels up to it, then I guess I might as well come in."

Scanlon stopped by the liquor store to buy a pint of Kennedy's brand of whiskey for his counselor's desk drawer. In order to avoid having to make conversation with Janet in the waiting room, Scanlon waited in his car until he heard the Town Hall clock strike four. While he waited, he was acutely conscious of the brown-wrappered pint on the seat beside him, and he doubted he would have been able to spend another five minutes alone with it.

"Brought you a little gift," Scanlon said, holding out the bottle to Kennedy. Without a word, Kennedy produced two cups from his desk drawer and proceeded to unwrap the bottle and pour their drinks.

"*Salud*," Kennedy said.

"I don't know what to say," Scanlon mumbled, after his whiskey had hit bottom.

"Don't say anything. Drink up." Kennedy emptied his cup and poured himself another. He pushed the bottle across his desk to Scanlon.

"I don't feel much like talking about myself today, if that's all right with you." Kennedy looked pale, and his eyes were bloodshot and dark around the sockets. He hadn't shaved in a couple of days; and his suit was so wrinkled that Scanlon just knew Kennedy had slept in it.

"Talk about anything you like, or don't talk at all. Just sit, if you feel like it. Drink and be quiet. Whatever suits you."

“Anything I had to say would be so ludicrous. I don’t follow football. The World Series is history. It’s too late to cry over Nixon’s election, and we’re going to have to learn to live with the hippies and Hell’s Angels buying up all the prime real estate.” Scanlon took a deep breath. “I’m really sorry, Bob. I don’t know what else to say.”

“You don’t have to say anything, Jack.” Kennedy knocked down his whiskey in one swallow and poured more in his cup. He offered Scanlon the bottle, and Scanlon filled his own cup.

“I don’t think I can do this today. Is that all right with you?” Scanlon said after a long silence.

“Whatever you want. Thanks for the hooch. See you next week.” Kennedy poured more whiskey in his cup.

At the door, Scanlon paused, his hand on the knob. “No shit, Bob. I’m really sorry. What can I say?” Kennedy had no answer. Scanlon shut the door quietly behind him. He was glad not to find Janet behind her desk.

Chapter Twelve

After a half hour, it was clear to Scanlon that no girls were going to show up for extra help. It was also clear that the boys who were present had come not so much for chemistry tutoring as in the expectation of seeing the girls.

"All right, Scott," Scanlon said, "we'll go down to the gym and shoot some hoops. Why even bother with the pretense of coming for chemistry help? Why don't you just get Coach Sorenson to open the gym for you every night?"

"Coach has got no use for anybody who hasn't come out for varsity. Besides, he's a daddy now. He's got to stay home and warm up formula and change diapers," Scott said. The other boys laughed the way one would laugh at a private joke. Was Sorenson the butt of private jokes? Was he in the same company with Lyle Higgins and Lillian Bloemer? Scanlon would have been surprised to find that it was true. He thought Rob Sorenson was popular with the kids the way Dennis Kitchell was. "Shall we head for the hardwood? There're six of us. We can play half-court. Maybe someone else will show up. I'll take Roy and Mr. Scanlon. We'll be skins."

Scanlon followed the boys to the gym feeling uneasy about being there after school hours. Now he was in the building practically under false pretenses. Next week, the varsity and JV basketball teams would begin night practices. That would be all right with him. And he didn't like having to remove his shirt. Alice's cooking had packed close to twenty new pounds on him; and she accused him of eating like a bird. The booze he consumed didn't burn any calories, either. Ten of those pounds, in fact, could probably be attributed to beer. No, he wasn't eager to run up and down the court with his flabby chest and gut. He suggested to Pettingill that the other team be skins, using an incipient cold as an excuse.

"All right. You guys be skins. Mr. Scanlon doesn't want to show off his physique," Pettingill announced. Scanlon winced.

"Take your shoes off if you don't have on sneakers," Scanlon said quickly, "I don't need Mr. Sorenson yelling at me." Pettingill found a ball on the floor and put up a pretty good jump shot. Scanlon had never mastered the jump shot. One of the reasons was that he couldn't jump well, the other had to do with his lack of strength in the wrists. Jump shooting required good wrist strength in addition to jumping ability. He'd been bitterly disappointed at having to warm the bench on his high school freshman team. His Uncle Mitch had high hopes for him as a basketball player; he even had the illusion himself that he might one day make a decent guard. In high school he was too short, and if he had quick hands on defense, they were also small hands. He quit in the middle of the season, after getting a total of three minutes playing time in nine games. After that he stayed away from all school activities that were even remotely organized.

Scanlon stripped down to his T-shirt and took off his shoes. He retrieved a ball from under the bleachers and put up a two-handed set shot from fifteen feet that fell short of the basket.

"What kind of shot is that, Mr. Scanlon?" Roy Perkins, his teammate along with Scott Pettingill, asked.

"You've never seen the two-handed set shot? " Scanlon asked. "Where you been, boy?"

"Here you go, Mr. Scanlon," Scott yelled, "Drive the basket. I'll feed you." Scanlon ran toward the basket, his stockinged feet slipping on the highly polished court. He took a bounce pass from Pettingill but his lay-up sailed high off the backboard, missing the rim. "Try it from the other side." Pettingill fed him another bounce pass, and this time he concentrated and laid the ball in off the glass.

"Let me try a couple more outside shots before we get started," Scanlon said. He sank two out of three twelve-footers, was beginning to get the feel of the ball, the range of the basket, and he remembered how much he loved basketball.

"You guys've warmed up enough," Charlie Tibbetts of the skins team said. "Now it's time to get your asses whipped." In the meantime, several more boys and three girls, one of them Hattie Letourneau, had appeared. Scott recruited the new boys and decided that the game could be played full court now that there were four on a side. Scanlon wasn't so sure he was up for full court; he was already winded from the short warm up. Without him there would be an odd number, so he felt obliged to stay on the shirts team until another boy showed up. And he wasn't too keen about having the girls watch from the bleachers. At the dance, it had been dark and there had been a lot of people on the floor.

Two trips up and down the court left Scanlon on the sideline choking for air. His chest and side ached, his T-shirt was sweat-soaked.

"You going to make it, Mr. Scanlon?"

"No, Scott," he gasped, "I am not going to make it. Get one of the girls to sub for me while I catch my breath. And never take up smoking."

"You're kidding. We can't let a girl sub for you. We'll wait for you to recover. Don't take all night."

Scanlon loafed on defense after that, and whenever he got his hands on the ball on a turnover or a rebound, he deliberately slowed down to a half court offense, ignoring Scott Pettingill's exhortations to push the ball up. He was involved in only one fast break, and it left him so winded that he had to check out to the sidelines again. But he had executed well, remembering to take the ball into the middle, and to hold onto it until the defense committed before he passed off. He'd dished off a perfect lead pass to Pettingill on the wing, who'd laid it up for two easy points. Despite being in danger of expiring for lack of air, Scanlon was experiencing enormous physical pleasure. He hadn't had this good a workout since the Navy.

While the game was going on, several more of his chemistry students had come into the gym. They sat as a group in the bleachers and watched the play on court. Scanlon wasn't accustomed to having kids show up late for his evening sessions; nevertheless he felt a tug of guilt for being in the gym, romping on the basketball court.

"I really ought to get back upstairs," Scanlon said to his teammates. "They're starting to come out of the woodwork. Let's call it a night," he announced.

"Ah, come on, Mr. Scanlon. It's not your problem they're late. Anyway, you're all pitted out. You don't want to gross the girls out, do you, Mr. Scanlon?" Pettingill winked. Scanlon wondered what he was thinking.

"We probably shouldn't be in the gym in the first place."

"Why not? You're a teacher. You can do what you want."

"That's it, boys and girls," Scanlon reminded them, as no one was making a move to leave the floor. "Somebody get the lights. Now let's go." Scanlon clapped his hands to get them moving. He struggled to get his shirt on over his sweaty T-shirt, and as he sat down on the bleachers to put on his shoes, Hattie Letourneau and Paula Gallant swooped down from the upper tiers and plunked themselves down beside him, one girl on each side.

"I knew it was only a matter of time before he gave up on us, Paula," Hattie said, bending forward to talk to Paula across Scanlon's front.

"Me, too," Paula Gallant said with an exaggerated deep sigh. "I guess he doesn't like us."

"Where were you guys tonight?" Scanlon worried that he might "gross them out" at this distance, but they showed no signs of moving away from him. In fact, they were so close he could feel their body heat. A shiver moved along his backbone.

"I'm sorry, Mr. Scanlon. We should have told you this morning that we'd be late. My mother gave me a birthday party and invited a lot of the kids who usually show up for extra help."

"That's all right, Hattie. Happy birthday. I won't ask how old you are. How old is she, Paula?"

"Thirty," Paula whispered, reminding him that thirty was how old he would be on his next birthday.

"Well, if you guys have any questions, I guess I can give you a few minutes. That is, if you don't mind being tutored by a jock."

"Hey, you were great out there, Mr. Scanlon," Hattie said. "Did you play in college?" He didn't think he'd performed that badly, certainly not badly enough to deserve a teasing from Hattie Letourneau, if she was indeed teasing.

"Yeah. Made All-American four years. I'm surprised you haven't heard of me. Sportscasters compared me to Bob Cousy enough."

"You're kidding. Right?"

"Right. What about it? Want to grind out a couple of problems on the board?" Scanlon said, putting on his jacket.

"I don't think we can do ourselves any good going over more problems. I mean, I've studied and studied until I'm starting to have dreams about Avogadro's number." Paula agreed. They had reached a point in their studies where, they felt, more of it would work against them. They would come into the test on Friday and just do the best they could, come what may. Hattie reminded him that if she didn't get a B on this test that her life would be ruined, but not to let that influence him in any way. How much subconscious influence would it have? he wondered, the joke aside.

Part of him wanted to tell them not to take a chemistry test so seriously. He never had in high school or college. To take such an attitude about his own tests would no doubt invite catastrophe. As he watched the girls walk across the gym floor, talking animatedly with each other, their steps buoyant and carefree despite the prospect of the dreaded chemistry test, Scanlon was more convinced than ever that he was not cut out to be a teacher.

He got home at ten-fifteen. Alice was nested on the sofa with Lucky and Nanette. She was in her favorite pink housecoat, an afghan blanket pulled up to her chest. The temperature in the house must have been eighty degrees. The TV was on with the volume turned low so Ira, who was asleep in the next room, wouldn't be disturbed.

"Mind getting me a beer, Johnny?" she whispered, checking out the foamy dregs of the bottle she held in her hand. "Get yourself one, too." Scanlon went into the kitchen to fetch their beers.

"What're you watching, Alice?" Scanlon seldom watched television. Unless it was in a bar, Scanlon couldn't sit for very long in one place. Alice was involved in a movie thriller with Jack Palance and Joan Crawford. In the scene, Joan Crawford had on a pointy-shouldered suit that reminded Scanlon of one his mother used to wear when he was Johnny Labalm. He was turned off by Joan Crawford's thick eyebrows. Her lips turned him off, her hair-do, and her voice, and just about everything else about her he could name. Jack Palance, always the heavy, was wooing an unsuspecting Joan Crawford into marrying him but only so that he could murder her for her inheritance and then run off with his blonde co-conspirator played by Gloria Grahame. Scanlon used to enjoy movies before he married Katie, but Johnny Labalm was a fanatic moviegoer. He would be constantly after his grandmother or Aunt Lilly to take him to evening shows, and he never missed a Saturday matinee. His tastes had changed only slightly over the years, and if he were pressed to choose his favorite kind of movie, he'd have to admit to a preference for adventure flicks, even today. Serious movies, the kind Elaine Stacy called "films," generally bored him. Only under extreme pressure from his intellectual friends, who insisted he had a cultural obligation, would he sit through a foreign movie with subtitles. In the years he lived with Katie, he saw maybe a half-dozen movies. Katie liked romantic farce, such as the kind made with Rock Hudson and Doris day, movies which would have Scanlon asleep before the end of the first reel. Katie had no use for adventure movies, so on the infrequent occasions they went out together, it was seldom to the movies.

Since he'd been back in Groveton he'd gone to one movie, *The Fox*, adapted from the D. H. Lawrence story. When he was a kid, Groveton supported two movie theaters. Now there was only the Palace with its rococo interior, its horsehair seats. He'd left before *The Fox* ended, fed up with the characters and their sweaty perversions. Sandy Dennis alone was more than he could bear to watch. He hadn't been able to stand her when Elaine Stacy talked him into going with her to see *Who's Afraid of Virginia Wolf* and he couldn't stand to look at her or listen to her in *The Fox.* She looked always on the verge of throwing up, and her adenoids should have been taken care of years ago. So she was married to Gerry Mulligan. Jeru must have been high on smack when he hooked up with her.

Jack Palance's murder plot was foiled by Joan Crawford's cunning; she would live to wear her pointy-shouldered suits and too much lipstick. The worst she had suffered in this script was a little disillusionment over the intentions of men. Alice had been so transported into the world of the movie that on a few occasions she had actually cried out warnings to poor Joan Crawford, when her death at the hand of the maniacal Jack Palance seemed imminent. Toward the end of her life, Johnny Labalm's grandmother had crossed over into that strange region where television and movie life became indistinguishable from the real thing.

"Pretty good flick," Scanlon said. "Too bad Joan Crawford didn't get what was coming to her."

"Oh, I like Joan Crawford." Alice stroked Lucky with one hand, Nanette simultaneously with the other. Two of her cats had taken up positions, sphinx-like, on the arms of the sofa. Alice's cats (were there five or six?) moved through the house like wraiths. Scanlon had been startled a number of times when he'd blundered into one of their hiding places. They could be found anywhere: in closets, on or under chairs, in cupboards. There was no place in the house that they were forbidden to go. With the onset of cold weather had come a decline in the flea population. His ravaged ankles were finally on the mend, and he didn't mind so much the fact that Ira gave the dogs their baths in the tub Scanlon used upstairs. He used to believe that the fleas bred in the tub after one of the dogs had been in it, and whenever Scanlon took a bath his skin crawled. He didn't like baths, didn't think it was any way to get clean. He'd have given a lot to have a shower tonight to clean away the sweat he'd worked up playing ball.

"You going to watch the Carson show?" he asked Alice.

"Yes. Buddy Hackett's on tonight. He's such a riot."

"You think it would be all right if I ran a bath? I mean, it won't bother Ira will it?"

"Oh, no. He's dead to the world by now. Couldn't wake him up with a bomb. There should be plenty of hot water."

"Thanks." Scanlon made no move to get up. The eleven o'clock news was coming on. He stared at the screen, not listening to the newscaster's words, his mind on Alice. Should he ask her about his father? Ira must have talked to her about the matter at some point in their marriage.

News footage of the war came on the screen: A helicopter hovered a few feet over an open field at the edge of the jungle. The air turbulence from the rotor blades beat the tall grass flat against the ground. A civilian reporter in fatigues was talking into a mike. Two Marine medics ran crouched over toward the helicopter, bearing a wounded GI on a stretcher; their dog tags slapped against their chests. They had on Red Cross helmets and khaki T-shirts. Several Marines stood around, shouting and gesticulating, giving the impression that confusion reigned.

The camera moved in for a close-up of the wounded Marine. He was still conscious, bewildered, looking not so much in pain as in shock. One side of his face was covered with so much blood it was impossible to make out his wound. What could be seen was that his left arm was missing below the elbow. There was no visible sign of the enemy, but from the expressions on the faces of the Marines, there was little doubt that "Charlie" was a real presence. Then there was an abrupt cut to a commercial for two-ply toilet paper.

"How're Willie and Althea doing?" Scanlon asked.

"Well, my God. Those two. Like something out of *Peyton Place*. That girl doesn't know what she wants. One day she's telling everybody what a bum he is and how she's going to leave him for good this time; next day they're like lovebirds. I don't dare bring up the subject with Ira anymore. He'll bite my head off. Now they're talking about going to Sherbrook for the weekend, just the two of them, like a second honeymoon or something. If they do, Donny and Eddie will probably stay here with us. They shouldn't be any bother. I'll put them up in the front bedroom."

"What about the other two?"

"They'll stay at Cecile's." Cecile was Alice's older sister.

"Maybe I can take Donny bowling this weekend and redeem myself with him."

"Oh, that Donny can't think about anything else since you took him. Willie would never take him anywhere, and Althea wouldn't be caught dead in a bowling alley. To hear her talk, you'd think she was from society or something. Donny's a little hyper, you know. His parents don't help matters, the way they talk to that kid." Alice shook her head. Scanlon had heard her and Althea refer to Donny's hyperactivity many, many times before, but Alice still talked as if this were brand new information. And he had become so used to her non sequiturs that he gave up asking her to explain. The question he'd wanted to ask, had intended to ask, was left, as it had been all his life, unasked. He said goodnight to Alice and went upstairs to soak in the tub, his long neglected muscles already feeling the effects of playing basketball.

Chapter Thirteen

"I couldn't have held out much longer," Scanlon said as Stambaugh got him a bottle of German beer out of his little apartment-sized refrigerator. His apartment was also small but had the advantage of being close to the school, if that could be thought of as an advantage. Out of politeness, Scanlon imagined, Stambaugh opened a beer for himself. He had removed his jacket, and rolled the cuffs of his tattersall shirt to the wrist; his blue knit necktie was loosened as well. This was as casual as Scanlon had ever seen him.

"Sorry if I sounded so conspiratorial yesterday. I hope it didn't cause you any loss of sleep." Stambaugh invited Scanlon to sit on the oversized red leather sofa with its scuffed arms and worn cushions. Stambaugh sat at the cushioned window seat in front of a bay of windows that looked out on the sloping hills behind the house, hills covered by last night's fresh snowfall.

"This is very cozy," Scanlon said, sitting on the big sofa, feeling its cushion yield to his weight like something hydraulic. He liked the way the walls slanted to the ceiling, and the window seat added to the room's charm. The door to Stambaugh's bedroom was open a crack, wide enough to see that his host's bed was neatly made. Stambaugh had told him that the apartment came furnished as well as heated, but even the furniture, as if by his very presence, had Stambaugh's signature of elegance. "Yeah, you must be very comfortable here. A private entrance, that's important."

"Especially with the ever vigilant Mrs. Mackenzie. She has bizarre rules of conduct for her tenants, of which, by the way, I am the only one. She's always rented exclusively to Fairfield High teachers. Had you heard?"

"I've heard she's a little eccentric." Scanlon was envious of Stambaugh's apartment, Stambaugh's independence. How much rent did he pay for this? Scanlon wondered.

"When I arrived in September with my fifty-odd cartons of books, she was appalled that there wouldn't be enough shelf space for them all. So she immediately called the man who does work for her around the house and had him build me those shelves. The brick-and-board's my doing." Stambaugh referred to the chest high tier of bookshelves along one wall. Mrs. Mackenzie's handyman had even built a cabinet at the end of the bookshelves to hold Stambaugh's hi-fi and record albums. Scanlon had declined Stambaugh's offer of a beer stein he'd brought back with him from Austria. Stambaugh, however, poured his own beer carefully into one. Scanlon waited for him to take the first drink.

"According to Mrs. Mackenzie, her husband was an inventor. Just before he died, he invented the electric can opener. Unfortunately, he was unable to patent it before the idea was stolen from him. Same thing with the garage door opener remote control device. Stolen."

"Man sounds like a regular wizard. When did he pass on?"

"Last year. Cancer of the rectum, of all places. After she finished telling me about her late husband, she laid down her rules for tenants. No loud music after 8:00 P.M., and no visitors of the opposite sex after that hour. Her living room is directly below my bedroom," Stambaugh said, pointing to the floor, "and her TV is on until eleven, twelve o'clock every night so loud it could be in the room with me. That's the only drawback to the place, I'm happy to say."

"I'm sure, but at the risk of sounding impatient ..."

"Oh, sure. I suppose I was stalling. Now that I've had time to sleep on it, I realize I may have been hasty. I should never have said anything to you."

"Don't do this to me, Doug."

"I suppose I have no choice, now that I've got you in such a state." Stambaugh sighed and got up from the window seat to lean against the door jamb leading to the kitchenette. He looked into his beer stein. "I overheard Rob Sorenson talking with Winship as I was passing by his office yesterday afternoon, just before eighth period. He was talking loudly enough for me to hear him through the closed door. Naturally I stopped to eavesdrop." Stambaugh looked up with a bashful smile.

"Naturally."

"The hall was empty, so I was able to listen for a while. It's so uncharacteristic of Rob Sorenson to raise his voice. He was shrill, to put it mildly. Otherwise I would never have stopped to listen."

"I understand. Would you mind getting to the point?"

"I heard him shout your name. I actually put my ear against the door. Can you picture that? It seems that Rob is upset with you for allowing kids to use the gym in the evening. He went on to complain that you were using the evening help sessions as a ruse to get into his gym to—and I'm paraphrasing here—ingratiate yourself with the students. He said the condition of the floor was a disgrace when you and the kids got through with it; it would have to be stripped and refinished before the first home game. He was incensed; he demanded that Winship take some action. That's why I thought I ought to warn you, though I realize now that I'm a little late with the information for you to be forewarned. I was ambivalent, under the circumstances. But it's my guess that Winship hasn't said anything to you yet."

"No." Scanlon felt light-headed.

"Are you all right, Jack? I shouldn't have said anything. I knew it."

"No. It's all right, I'm glad you did. I'm just so, I don't know, flabbergasted. The asshole couldn't have come to me?" Scanlon had thought, apparently mistakenly, that he was on pretty good terms with the coach. They talked easily enough with each other, mostly innocuous conversations about sports, or how so and so, who was a good basketball prospect, was doing in chemistry. Sorenson worried about his players' academic standings only as it affected their eligibility. Sorenson appeared to him as straight, uncomplicated to the point of even being on the dumb side, certainly ingenuous. So much for trusting in appearances.

"I agree with you, Jack. Going behind a colleague's back like that. It's unprofessional, reprehensible. If I were Winship, I'd lecture him on professional ethics." Stambaugh examined the contents of his beer stein with a frown. "I should have confronted him myself after what I heard. Believe me, he wasn't trying to keep it confidential. But I said nothing." Stambaugh looked down at the floor this time. Scanlon wasn't sure whether Stambaugh meant he felt he should have said something to Sorenson or to Winship. What did it matter?

"Well, you can be sure I'll have something to say to the ..." Scanlon's hands were shaking.

"Maybe you ought to consider the wisdom of doing that."

"What wisdom? You said you heard him. Don't worry, I won't bring you into it."

"It's not that. Listen, I'm almost positive that Daryl must have said something to Sorenson. Otherwise you would have heard from him by now. Rob was so patently wrong in what he did that what other choice would Winship have but to remind him of the ethics involved? Give the devil his due."

“The self-righteous creep,” Scanlon said, referring to Sorenson, because he couldn’t get his mind around what he had been accused of by the coach. “We left that floor in the same condition we found it. I personally saw to it that everybody who didn’t have on sneakers took off his shoes. Goddamn!” Scanlon brought his fist down hard on the sofa cushion sending up a little cloud of dust. “I don’t have to ingratiate myself with these kids. He ought to hear the way they talk about him, the jerk.”

Scanlon would be hard put to explain to Winship, if the principal decided to ask, why he was frolicking in the gym the other night instead of pounding chemistry into his students’ thick skulls, particularly after the righteous indignation he’d laid on Winship when he’d objected to the extra help sessions. It didn’t justify Sorenson’s actions, but Scanlon was on pretty thin moral ice himself.

“Are you sure you’re all right?” Stambaugh asked him, his voice full of concern.

“Yeah, I’m all right. I just have to cool down. I’m really naive, not to mention a slow learner.”

“Don’t place too much importance on this, Jack. I wouldn’t be surprised if Rob had second thoughts and went back to apologize to Daryl. Think about it. Does Rob Sorenson strike you as the kind who could bring off a conspiracy?”

“I doubt that conspiracy’s his motive.” Scanlon laughed harshly. “Ten minutes ago I wouldn’t have thought he was capable of stabbing me in the back either.”

“If you want my advice I’d tell you to not say anything to Rob just yet. Let a little time pass before you confront him. There has to be more to this than meets the eye.”

“I’m not sure I’m capable of waiting. I hate this shit, these accusations. It drives me nuts. It’s so fucking stupid. I don’t think I can look Sorenson in the eye knowing what I know and keep my mouth shut. You understand?”

“Tomorrow you may feel differently.”

“Yeah, tomorrow I’ll be even more pissed off than I am today because I’ll have a whole night for it to fester. It’s not that I care so much what a meatball like Sorenson thinks about me, you understand? It’s the injustice. That’s really all it is.”

“I understand. I had another reason for asking you over this afternoon,” Stambaugh said, a boyish smile replacing the frown.

“Oh, yeah. What now? Cynthia accusing me of rape?”

"I wondered if you had plans for Thanksgiving break. My parents have a place on Martha's Vineyard, and I'm joining them for Thanksgiving dinner. They have to get back to the city, but I plan to stay on through the weekend. How would you like to come down and join me for any part of the weekend that suits you?"

"I don't know, Doug. I'm not sure what my aunt and uncle have planned. It's good of you to invite me, though." Scanlon would have liked nothing better than to get away from Groveton, and Fairfield, even for a weekend, but he wasn't prepared to admit to Stambaugh that he couldn't afford the trip to the island.

"Well, in case you do find the time, I'll leave our phone number with you. Just give me a call if you decide to come. The island is really very pleasant in the off-season."

"I've heard it's not so bad in the on-season. I've never been." It was a place Scanlon had always associated with the privileged class, a class of which he was not a member. Was he being patronized? He'd expect this kind of treatment from Patterson but not from the earnest Mr. Stambaugh.

"In that case, it's time you had a visit. I can promise you a nice time. Besides, it would be tonic for you to get away from here for awhile, away from these petty concerns." Stambaugh ran a hand through his hair. "God, if I didn't have my occasional weekends in Cambridge, I don't know what would become of me."

"Have any luck with the stuff you told me about last time you were there?"

"Excellent luck, as a matter of fact. Can I interest you? Not here, of course. The widow Mackenzie would suffer apoplexy if she thought drugs were being abused on the premises."

"I'll pass. I wasn't jerking you about my being a non-user. If you can't fire up in here, where then?"

"I've done a little with Josh and Rachel at their place. Sometimes I just take the car out on a back road. I hardly use it at all during the week." Scanlon was surprised to hear that Stambaugh met socially with the Pattersons, even more surprised to learn that they smoked marijuana together. There was no real reason for him to be surprised, if he thought about it. They were social birds of the same feather.

"What's Rachel like under the influence?" Scanlon asked, hoping that he sounded casual in case Stambaugh should perceive more than casual interest in the question.

"Very cute. She gets silly, like a little girl, and she becomes very affectionate." Stambaugh smiled paternally. If he knew Stambaugh better, if he were more sure of him, Scanlon would have pursued the details of Rachel Patterson's drug-induced affections.

"When you asked me here yesterday, I was almost positive that it had to do with you and your draft board. I'm glad you're still a free man."

"I doubt I will be for long." Stambaugh sighed. "Yesterday I heard from one of my college roommates. He received his notice last week. In fact, he's coming up for a visit on Friday. You ought to meet him. He'd be interested in your point of view."

"Meaning that he's getting ready to bolt?"

"He's given it serious thought."

"Then I doubt he'd have any interest in what I had to say."

"On the contrary. Why don't you plan to come over after school on Friday and see for yourself."

"I don't know. I'll have to see." Scanlon didn't know if he was ready to get into the fire again on the subjects of duty, honor, and draft evasion. It had gotten dark outside since he'd been in Stambaugh's apartment, and his beer had gone warm. He considered driving over to Sorenson's house, halfway between Fairfield and Burton, to have it out with the coach. Stambaugh thought he should sit on it. For some things he had no patience. "I should be going, Doug. Thanks for tipping me off on this thing. I appreciate it."

"Give some thought to my suggestion, Jack. At least wait for one day."

"I'll think about it."

Chapter Fourteen

Scanlon left for school the next morning with an eagerness bordering on frenzy. He hadn't slept well, keeping himself awake weighing the merits of Stambaugh's counsel against what his gut was telling him, which was to have it out jaw to jaw with Sorenson first thing in the morning. As it happened, Sorenson had called in sick. Scanlon hoped that it was the swine's conscience that made him sick. He made up his mind about one thing and that was to stay more alert from now on to signs of what looked like a growing conspiracy to discredit him. First there was Winship and then Higgins, and now the All-American boy coach wanted a piece of the action. Kennedy would write "paranoid" in his notes if he knew what Scanlon was thinking.

So he was all energized this morning for nothing. Sorenson was out of the picture, and the only contact he had with Winship all day was when his voice came over the intercom in Scanlon's room to ask him if he would mind taking over detention this afternoon for Sophie Metcalf, who had gone home with a migraine. A pestilence apparently was sweeping through Fairfield High.

All day he was on edge; he couldn't concentrate, he couldn't finish the chicken salad roll Alice had put up for him from last night's leftovers. They had him crazy around here.

Samantha Burnham didn't show up for study hall. Got a sick excuse from the school nurse after lunch. Probably out smoking pot and fornicating with those hippies from the college of freaks. He remembered Winship telling him that she was no paragon of good attendance. He hoped she never showed up for study hall.

Scanlon had become so self-absorbed by the end of the day that he left the building forgetting that he was supposed to take Sophie's detention. He actually drove half way to Groveton before it dawned on him. He rushed back and panicked when he found only one kid in the room, Denise Marcotte, a plump little red-head, a sophomore from his biology class. Then he saw that Denise's name was the only one on the detention list. She was there for gum chewing in Frau Bloemer's class. She chewed gum all the time in his class. He didn't care if kids chewed gum, as long as they didn't stick it under the chairs or the lab benches; actually he didn't even care if they did that.

Denise brought a garter snake to class one day. Had the thing slithering up her fat little arm, stroking its chin. She had the idea Scanlon might want to dissect it for the class. He was scared of snakes, always had been, and it took everything he had to hide the fact from her and the rest of the kids. He thought it odd at the time that she should display such gentleness and affection for the thing and yet be willing to sacrifice it to dissection. Then, he'd learned that farm kids weren't all that sentimental about animals, except maybe farm girls for their horses. One time a girl in his class cried for a whole day because her horse had a cold.

Denise had plenty of homework to do, and Scanlon had enough fantasies involving Rachel Patterson to occupy his dirty mind for the half hour left in the detention period, when out of nowhere little Denise Marcotte, the snake lady of Fairfield High, was asking him if he didn't think monogamy had run its course in Western civilization. Taken by surprise, of course, Scanlon facetiously asked her if she saw similar trends among the barnyard animals at home. Denise was in no mood for jokes. She pressed him for an answer. He wondered what on earth had inspired the question. Had she heard something about him that made her think he was sympathetic to this notion of monogamy?

Denise had her unblinking eyes on him, waiting for an intelligent response. He told her he thought monogamy still had a few miles left as a means of maintaining the social order, even if he didn't approve of the idea personally. The last statement he meant as a joke. He couldn't seem to remember that Denise had no sense of humor. She nodded her head as if this was very important stuff to hear from her bio teacher. She had her own views on the issue. Denise thought monogamy was on its way out; from now on society would be organized around different sexual and familial mores. She couldn't imagine herself spending life with only one sexual partner, and anyone who claimed otherwise was probably lying, or kidding himself. In class he never heard a peep out of this kid, and now here she was laying this radical stuff on him. Where had she got ideas like that in her homely little head? Then he heard a note of bitterness in her voice. He began to think that there was probably trouble at home, and she was using this off-the-wall monogamy stuff as a way of coping. He didn't know. He really didn't know how to deal with girls and their problems. If she was sending out an SOS, he was incapable of answering. A fine father of a young daughter he would make. It's not that he didn't feel for the kid; he just had no talent, maybe no inclination, for drawing people into his confidence.

He sat there with Denise for the last ten minutes without saying a word. When it was time to go she gathered up her books, said good-bye, and that was the end of it. Cynthia Sinclair was more or less in charge of the kids' emotional life. Tomorrow he guessed he should have a word with her about Denise. It could be that Cynthia knew something. Maybe the kid's old man was having a fling with another woman (or spending too much time with the livestock). Mom could be playing with the RFD mailman, who knew? Cynthia might be able to clue him in. That is, if she wasn't still embarrassed about letting it all hang out for him at Winship's party. That was a long time ago. Light years ago. Cynthia was a fool, but he liked her in spite of it. Anyone that unself-consciously ridiculous couldn't be all bad.

Friday morning arrived and Scanlon had heard nothing further concerning Sorenson's complaint against him. Perhaps Stambaugh was right about the coach having second thoughts. Friday was also the day Stambaugh was expecting a visit from his former college roommate, and before homeroom period Stambaugh stuck his head through the door of Scanlon's room to remind him of his friend's visit. Scanlon had forgotten.

"So, about two-forty-five?" Stambaugh said, his eyes darting around the room to survey the chaos on the lab benches, his nose wrinkling involuntarily at the acrid smell of formaldehyde. Dissecting pans with the hacked remains of frogs, fetal pigs, rats, dogfish, lay strewn among the dirty glassware of completed chemistry experiments that Scanlon hadn't gotten around to having the kids clean up. He had tried himself, half-heartedly, to break down the reflux columns, clear away the flasks and beakers and rubber tubing and test tubes, but gave up, thoroughly demoralized by the task. There never seemed to be time enough to have kids do it themselves at the end of a period. He knew it was only a matter of time before Winship got on his back about it.

"Yeah, I guess so," Scanlon said, picking up on Stambaugh's disapproval of the condition of the room. "I really should spend the time getting this pit squared away." He wasn't in the mood to meet Stambaugh's friend.

Something heavy seemed lodged in the pit of his stomach. He felt like lying down, going to sleep.

"Stewart's expecting to meet you, Jack. You can spare a few minutes."

"Yeah, all right. I can't stay long." Friday was the day he saw Kennedy, so he wouldn't feel too much like a liar telling Stambaugh he had a doctor's appointment in Groveton at four.

Stambaugh couldn't have had a worse effect on him if he had come right out and scolded him for the way the lab looked. Unknowingly, Stambaugh had activated the guilt that had been lying dormant in his gut all week, and the rest of the day would only get worse.

First period chemistry: While Scanlon struggled to explain the significance of the sp^3 hybrid orbital to the chemistry of the carbon atom, Llewellyn Clark and Sylvia Childs whispered and giggled in the back row. Scanlon stopped his lecture for dramatic effect. Llewellyn and Sylvia continued their whispering and giggling, unaware that he had stopped talking. The rest of the class tittered and shuffled and twisted around in their chairs to get a look at the oblivious couple. Scanlon felt them all slipping out of his control, and before he was fully aware of what he was doing, had picked up an eraser and hurled it in the direction of Llewellyn and Sylvia. The eraser glanced off Llewellyn's shoulder, bounced onto the cluttered lab bench behind him and knocked an Erlenmeyer flask off an iron ring. The flask shattered on the lab bench. Llewellyn Clark was not the only one in the room who looked astonished.

Second period biology: Scanlon, still rattled from the eraser incident in his chemistry class, tried to conduct a class discussion on the relative contributions of heredity and environment to animal development.

"It's sometimes described as the nature-nurture issue," Scanlon said, hoping that a catch phrase would appeal to kids raised on television. But little Romeo Boudreau, the youngest of a family of fourteen children who lived on a poor farm in West Fairfield, and who was marking time until his sixteenth birthday when he could legally declare an end to his formal education, had other plans. He was small with a head too big for the rest of his body, and he came to school with manure caked boots and talked like a little old man in his hick Vermont accent, and was even more opinionated than Junior Darling but not nearly as bright.

"The reason niggers have lower intelligence than whites is because their brains are smaller. This is what you call nature, right?" Romeo said, and looked around the room for his classmates' approval, a wide grin on his face. Scanlon was so angry he couldn't think of anything to say. Finally, working hard to keep himself in control, Scanlon asked Romeo where he had obtained that information, in *The Farmer's Almanac*?

"Nope. *The Enquirer*," Romeo said with not the slightest hesitation. Holly Bean said she had read that too and that her parents had confirmed the fact. And the inferiority of Negroes was well documented in the Bible, she added. Most of the class was behind Romeo and Holly; if there were any who were not, they kept their opinions to themselves. Scanlon had asked Romeo what gave him the right to use terms like "nigger" to describe human beings.

"A bigger brain than your average nigger," Romeo had replied as if he'd rehearsed the comeback, leaving Scanlon hot-faced and mute in front of a class of howling sophomores.

In the second floor hall between periods: Grace Ouemette accosted Scanlon at the drinking fountain.

"What's got into you today, Mr. Scanlon? Everybody says you're acting like a poop." Scanlon caught a whiff of her strong perfume and looked up from the waterspout into Grace's serious blue eyes, shadowed with a heavy layer of blue eye goop. She came to school every day made up like a streetwalker, with her teased hair and spiked heels. She looked thirty and acted at times like a ten-year-old. She held her books against her chest pushing her big round breasts out like water wings. Her voice was as brassy as her hair and she had no qualms about speaking her mind. Scanlon averted his eyes to the floor only to notice that Grace had a run in her right, black mesh nylon.

"I haven't any idea what you're talking about, Grace. Don't you have a class to go to?"

"Well, I guess everybody's right," Grace said, and walked off down the hall in indignation, her spiked heels striking the dark oak floor like pistol shots, her big rear end undulating beneath her tight-fitting, black mini-skirt.

Lunchtime in the cafeteria: Scanlon observed Junior Darling stuffing oatmeal cookies into his jacket pocket on his way out of the cafeteria. Scanlon followed him.

"Junior," Scanlon said when he caught up with the boy, "what did you put in your pocket back in the cafeteria?"

"Cookies," replied Junior, looking up at Scanlon through his thick spectacles in perfect innocence. There was a rule against removing food from the cafeteria, one the kids totally ignored and which was even winked at by such hard-noses as Lyle Higgins and Lillian Bloemer.

"You haven't heard about the rule about not removing food from the cafeteria, Junior?" Scanlon watched Junior Darling's brow wrinkle in confusion. "Why do you think we have rules? So selfish little snots like you can do anything they feel like doing whenever they want? Answer me!"

Junior stammered for an answer, tears starting in his myopic eyes. Scanlon sent him back to the cafeteria to return the cookies. For good measure, he assigned Lisa Perreault and Debbie Coutreau to afternoon detention for gossiping in the hall by Debbie's locker when they should have been in typing class. It was the first time he had ever assigned a kid to detention. By the time last period came around, kids were walking past him in the halls as if they didn't see him.

Eighth period study hall: On Friday, there were only a dozen kids assigned to eighth period study hall. Today only eight were present. Scanlon knew he had seen the absentees earlier in the day. He made a note of their names and with grim satisfaction resolved to find out why they had not attended.

Samantha Burnham arrived after the bell had rung and took her seat without so much as looking in his direction. She got a pair of reading glasses and a paperback book out of her cloth handbag and settled down to read. Scanlon walked toward her desk intending to challenge her for being late but kept on walking through the maze of tablet armchairs to the back of the room. He glanced at the cover of the book she was reading when he passed her, not surprised to see that it was *Siddhartha* by Hermann Hesse. Hesse and Tolkien were the darlings of the hippie crowd. They particularly liked Tolkien after a snootful of hallucinogens. Scanlon had read neither Hesse nor Tolkien. With his truncated attention span, it wasn't likely that he would any time soon.

Samantha was very pale; unlike many Fairfield High girls, she wore no makeup. She had a Cupid's bow mouth and a small mole on the right side of her fine, dimpled chin. Samantha reminded him of a movie actress whose name he couldn't summon. Back behind his lecture desk, Scanlon studied her over the top of his chemistry text, watching her light blue eyes, made to seem lighter by her long, pale lashes, move swiftly over the pages of *Siddhartha.* She appeared to be so totally absorbed in the book that nothing else existed for her, certainly not his scrutiny, not even Danny Picard's incessant drumming on the tablet arm of his chair in restlessness and boredom. Scanlon put a finger to his lips when he made eye contact with Danny. Danny grinned, shrugged his shoulders and continued drumming. Scanlon motioned with his head for Danny to come to the lecture desk. Danny eagerly obliged.

"What's with the paradiddles? Some people are trying to study," Scanlon said.

"Yeah, right," Danny said, rolling his eyes. Samantha Burnham was the only one present who seemed remotely interested in studying. Scanlon wasn't aware that Cynthia had assigned *Siddhartha* in her senior English class, however.

"Why don't you bring something with you to read once in awhile?" Danny planted his elbows on the desk and laid his chin in his hands. "Don't get comfortable. I want you back in your seat, and no drum rolls. Understand?"

"You really do have a hair acrost your ass today, like everybody says," Danny said, standing up straight, and smiling with what Scanlon on this day characterized as insolence. "What's the matter, not gettin' enough?"

"That'll do." Scanlon stared coldly at Danny Picard. The boy held his smile. "Take your seat before you say something you'll be sorry for."

"Whatever you say, Prince." Danny started for his chair.

"Come back here," Scanlon said, loudly enough to raise everyone's, including Samantha Burnham's, head. Kids were used to having Danny up at Scanlon's desk talking with him during study hall.

"Come on, Mr. Scanlon," Danny said, his eyes dodging around the room, "take it easy."

"Step out into the hall. I want a word with you." Scanlon addressed the others, "Try and force yourselves to not run amuck for the minute and a half I'll be out of the room." Scanlon followed Danny Picard out of the room and closed the door quietly behind him. Danny, hands thrust deep in his pockets, leaned with his back against the bank of gray lockers across the hall.

"You trying to provoke me?" Scanlon asked in a low voice.

"What the hell are you talking about? I'm not trying to do anything. What's got into you?" Danny was beginning to look concerned, as if he had misjudged Scanlon's intentions. He was no longer smiling.

"You make a nuisance of yourself in study hall and you want to know what's got into me? I'm getting a little tired of watching you waste your time every day of the week. All right, it's your time, but that doesn't give you the right to waste someone else's." Danny's eyes narrowed and had taken on a hard look. His pockmarked complexion was starting to look menacing to Scanlon, and when the boy's hands came out of his pockets to hang loosely by his sides at the ready, Scanlon felt his stomach muscles tighten.

"What, are you going to put me in detention?" Danny sneered.

"So you can disrupt that group, too? Don't worry. If you'd just bring something with you to read, or some homework, we wouldn't be having this discussion." Scanlon stepped back, giving Danny more room.

"You know how I feel about reading, and when have you ever seen me do homework?" Danny relaxed and leaned against the lockers again, folding his arms across his chest.

"You've got to find something to do with yourself in study hall so you won't interfere with people who want to study."

"Nobody wants to study in study hall. Why don't you just let people shoot the shit. Study hall's a joke."

A door opened down the hall. Scanlon saw Winship's head sticking out of his office door. Scanlon waved to indicate that he was in control. Winship retracted his head and closed the door. Danny stared at the floor, smiling.

"You know I can't allow that, Danny. Don't be a wise guy."

"I was just kidding around like I usually do. I thought that's what you were up to, too. Excuse the shit out of me."

Scanlon sighed. "You're right. It's my fault. Suppose we forget the whole thing. Come on, let's go back in."

Scanlon returned to find all the kids except Samantha Burnham in a huddle, whispering and giggling. They broke and fell silent when he came in the room.

"I'm pleased to see that at least one of you is above the lure of gossip," Scanlon said, looking at Samantha, who looked up from her book long enough to crush his spirit with a look of disdain. He sagged onto his stool behind the lecture desk and hid behind his chemistry text until the bell, ending Jack Scanlon's worst day at Fairfield High, finally rang. Samantha hung behind after the others had left to inform Scanlon that she was surprised to hear such a jejune remark from him, and marched briskly out of the room before he had a chance to reply.

He was standing in a daze, his mouth half open, when Winship appeared in the doorway, looked over his shoulder as if he were being followed, and entered the room, closing the door behind him.

"What was all that about in the hall?" Winship asked, his eyebrows rising. "My God, Jack! Look at this room! No, smell this room!" He walked rapidly to the windows and began to lift them open.

"If we had a fume hood like any normal lab, we wouldn't have to do that," Scanlon said, sitting in one of the armchairs that were strewn helter-skelter around the room.

"You could have opened the windows," Winship said. "I'm surprised kids haven't complained. This is a disgrace."

"If you forget to close the windows you run the risk of radiators freezing up overnight and bursting. How would you like to deal with that kind of mess?" Scanlon spoke like someone in a trance.

"The trick is not to forget to close the windows before you leave." Winship stood in front of Scanlon, putting a foot up on the seat of a chair. Cold air moved into the room from the open windows, and Scanlon was quickly chilled to the bone.

"There hasn't been time to clean up," Scanlon said, sweeping his arm to include the mess on the lab benches. "There's never enough time."

"You've got to make time. Stop what you're doing five minutes before the end of the period and insist that the kids do a thorough cleanup. Get them into the habit, if it isn't too late by now." Winship sounded disgusted. Scanlon felt very tired; he could have curled up on the filthy floor and gone instantly to sleep. "I want this place cleaned up by the end of classes on Monday. Use the whole class period if you have to, but get it done."

"Aye aye, sir," Scanlon said, and saluted.

"Now what was going on with Danny Picard out in the hall?"

"Nothing. It was a misunderstanding."

"Are you sure? My patience with him is wearing thin. I've had complaints about him from every one of his teachers this week. He's getting a little too big for his breeches, so if he's been giving you a hard time I want to know about it."

"If anything, I'm the one giving him the hard time." Scanlon got up and started to gather his books from the lecture desk.

"There's something else I want to discuss with you, if you can spare a minute or two." Winship looked over his shoulder at the closed door. Scanlon tightened, expecting to be finally confronted with Sorenson's accusations. "I'd like it understood that what we talk about here is to be considered confidential. All right, Jack?"

"Sure." Scanlon turned to face Winship who was rubbing his hands together, looking at the floor. His hair was flattened on one side, as if he'd been sleeping on it, and a cowlick had sprung up in the back looking incongruous on the ordinarily suave principal.

"I have to ask you about Doug," Winship said, tracing his finger along the edge of the tablet arm.

"Doug who?"

"Stambaugh, of course."

"You could have been referring to Doug Leclair for all I know."

"All right, I mean Doug Stambaugh." Winship removed his foot from the chair, shook out his pant leg and sat down in another chair. "Why don't you sit down."

"I can't stay long. I've got a three o'clock appointment."

"This won't take long. I have some concerns about his conduct in history classes. He's a very bright fellow, as you know; way over the heads of these kids, I'm afraid. What concerns me is that he's using his position to fill kids' heads with political propaganda. I've received a number of phone calls from parents."

"Why talk to me?" Scanlon squeezed into a chair with his arms full of books and papers, his curiosity piqued.

"I thought since you and Doug seem to be on friendly terms that you'd be the logical one to talk to."

"If we were on the friendly terms you think we are, what makes you think I'd want to discuss something like this behind his back?"

Winship lowered his voice. "I don't think of this as going behind his back, as you put it. This is a professional matter, nothing at all personal."

"Whatever. Anyway, I think you're off the track as far as our friendship is concerned, and I assure you I know nothing about him using his classroom to spread propaganda. Doesn't sound like him, if you ask me. What can I say?" He should have sent Winship to see Josh Patterson, Stambaugh's pot-smoking companion.

"And I suppose you haven't heard about the stink he's making over my decision to take last week's *Time* out of the library."

"No, I haven't." He was telling the truth. But why hadn't he heard? What was Winship up to now?

"Were you aware that he's filed for conscientious objector status?" Winship was not one to look you in the eye, but his eyes, slightly bloodshot today, were honed in on Scanlon now.

"As a matter of fact I'm not aware of that. I would think that was his business."

"It all adds up."

"I don't think I know what you mean."

"He'd be just the type to try to use his position to brainwash impressionable kids. I hope you're not holding back something from me. This is serious."

"I'm the guy you didn't want teaching evolution. You thought that was radical. You sure I'm the one you want to be talking to about this? Why not go straight to Doug?"

"Don't be naive." Winship scratched his scalp and checked his fingernails. He looked puzzled and agitated. Scanlon struggled out of the chair with his armful of books and papers.

"I've got to be going. Sorry I couldn't be of help."

"I'll bet you are. I mean it, Jack. I want this lab cleaned up by Monday morning. This is a disgrace." So now it was Monday morning. Winship got out of his chair, gave the lab the once over, and left, shaking his head.

Scanlon dumped his books in the back seat of his car and walked across Route 2 to Stambaugh's apartment. He waved to the eccentric Mrs. Mackenzie, who was at work clearing a path to her front porch with a long-handled snow shovel. She had on a Navy pea coat over her bathrobe, a black knit Navy watch cap on her head. Stambaugh, or one of the high school kids, should have been shoveling her snow. Just because she was daffy was no reason she should be tempting a heart attack. Scanlon would have offered to do the job himself if he hadn't been so anxious to hear about Winship's *Time* magazine caper.

"Doug's talked a lot about you, Jack. Nice to meet you at last," said Stewart Benjamin, Stambaugh's former college roommate.

"Good to meet you, too, Stewart." Scanlon responded in kind to Benjamin's surprisingly strong handshake. Surprising because Stewart Benjamin was tall, perhaps six-foot-four, and looked frail. He wore round-framed glasses and his absolutely straight brown hair was as fine as corn silk. The glasses made his small, thin face look spiritual. "Doug tells me you're about to experience a change in your way of life."

"Yes. One I hope will be of my own choosing." Benjamin grinned and sat back down on Stambaugh's enormous leather sofa. Scanlon took a seat at the other end; Stambaugh remained standing, and seemed nervous. He had removed his jacket and tie in favor of a cardigan sweater. Even in a casual sweater, he looked altogether too formal. Stambaugh and Benjamin were not drinking when Scanlon arrived but joined him for beer, pouring theirs into Austrian steins while Scanlon drank from the bottle. He had on expensive pleated, wool trousers, the kind you see on guys used to spending time in ski lodges, and a bulky white sweater with a rope pattern down the front, probably knit by hand. He extended one long leg on the sofa (his loafered foot resting inches away from Scanlon's pant leg) and slung his arm over the back. He was a study in casual.

Stambaugh, on the other hand, continued to look ill at ease. He tried leaning his weight against his bookcase until it started to buckle; he stood in the middle of the floor but couldn't find anything to do with his free hand—it found its way to his pocket, through his hair, under the belt of his trousers, back to his pocket. Scanlon was getting nervous watching him. Benjamin, who seemed to have a kind of power over his former roommate, finally suggested that he sit down and relax. Stambaugh reacted as if that were a terribly creative suggestion and sat down across from them in his upholstered rocker. Scanlon wanted to get straight to the *Time* magazine issue. He was impatient with all these tedious, Ivy League amenities.

"You here for the weekend, Stewart?"

"I'm on my way to Stowe, actually. I'm trying to talk Doug into coming along, even if he doesn't ski. The change in venue will do him good."

"Stewart teaches English at a private day school in Cambridge," Stambaugh said, like a stage mother. Even in the sitting position, Stambaugh was having difficulty relaxing. He sat on the very edge of his chair, drumming his fingers on his beer stein. Does he think I'm going to embarrass him in front of his upper-middle-class friend? Scanlon wondered.

"You must get a different caliber of student in a private school than we do here," Scanlon said.

"Oh, I'm sure. Doug tells me the students at Fairfield High aren't too terribly motivated," Benjamin said, glancing at his wristwatch. "Doug, we should plan to leave soon. I want to get a few shots behind the house before the light quits, and we shouldn't be on these roads too long after dark."

"I can't stay long anyway. Got an appointment in Groveton at four," Scanlon said, to reassure Stambaugh. He was more than a little annoyed that he'd been led to believe that his visit was welcome. Benjamin couldn't have been less interested in meeting him if he tried. Maybe he was actually trying to be aloof. Scanlon swallowed some beer and rose.

"You don't have to go so soon, Jack," Stambaugh said, getting up himself.

"Suppose I choose to?" Scanlon said, looking over his shoulder at Benjamin who was preoccupied with something on the front of his sweater.

"Please. Stewart didn't mean to imply that we were in that much of a hurry to go, did you, Stewart?"

"No, of course not." Benjamin didn't look up from his sweater. Stambaugh touched Scanlon lightly and gestured for him to sit back down.

"Let me get you another beer." Stambaugh hurried to the kitchen leaving Scanlon to wonder what the hell was going on.

"I don't see last week's issue of *Time* magazine among your coffee table reading, Doug," Scanlon said to Stambaugh when he returned with another green bottle of German beer. "Winship been around visiting?" This coaxed a little smile out of Stambaugh.

"It's almost too good to be true," Stambaugh said, sitting back down in the rocker.

"What is?" Benjamin said, not sounding that interested.

"I'm not sure myself," said Scanlon. "Winship mentioned it while I was talking to him just before I came over here. I didn't press him for details. I got the impression that it's pretty generally known, though. As usual, I'm the last to hear anything."

"You've heard all that's important to hear," Stambaugh said. "Winship—he's the principal," Stambaugh said for Stewart Benjamin's information, "didn't like *Time's* review of *Che*. Thought it was unsuitable for tender minds. There was a reference to simulated copulation on stage, in Winship's mind enough justification to have it removed from the shelf. Now the kids will head for Groveton and stampede the newsstand for the thing."

Scanlon watched Benjamin out of the corner of his eye. Benjamin continued to finger the sweater, not seeming to pay attention to his friend's account of the *Time* story.

"How did Sophie react?" Scanlon asked Stambaugh.

"Sophie's the librarian," Stambaugh explained to the uninterested Benjamin. "I doubt that Sophie cares one way or the other. Her mission is to keep kids quiet in the library. What is on the shelves or not on the shelves is not her concern. In any case, she would never challenge Daryl's authority."

"Where do you figure in this?" Scanlon asked.

"As you know, I occasionally ask students to read articles from the popular press and give brief oral reports. I think it was Samantha Burnham who stood up in class and accused Winship of having *Time* taken out of the library, and demanded that I take action. I thought she was just making waves the way she likes to do. I forgot about it until next period when a student I had asked specifically to do a report from *Time* claimed he wasn't able to do it because the magazine was no longer in the library. That's when I decided to talk to Winship."

"What I wouldn't have given to be in on that conversation," Scanlon said.

"When he gave me his reason for pulling it, I made the mistake of suggesting that he was joking. Wouldn't you have thought he was joking, Stewart?"

"Sick joking," Benjamin said immediately, belying Scanlon's suspicion that he had tuned out.

"You'd have to know Winship," Scanlon said.

"What more can you expect in a place like this?" Benjamin said, done examining his sweater at last. Scanlon bridled at his remark. If he hadn't been Stambaugh's friend, Scanlon would have gone after him.

"Whether or not I expect it, Stewart, has nothing to do with my reaction. This is a blatant act of censorship and it's wrong. I don't care where it occurs."

"It just seems like such a waste of time," Benjamin said, taking no offense at Stambaugh's chastening, and apparently not deliberately punning *Time* magazine.

Scanlon wanted to know how Doug had responded to Winship after that.

"My next mistake was to ask him if he understood the implications of what he had done. As if censorship were not bad enough, he has to be high-handed about it and act without consulting anyone. He may have spoken to Higgins, but I'm reasonably sure no one else knew in advance what he planned to do. Which raises the question of professional courtesy if not ethics."

"It must have pleased him to hear that from you," Scanlon said. Stambaugh smiled mischievously, pleased with himself that Scanlon approved.

"You have never understood the true meaning of the word livid until you have seen Daryl Winship challenged." Stambaugh was delighted to be able to gossip in this fashion, something Scanlon imagined he didn't indulge in as a rule.

"More, Douglas, more!" Scanlon urged, intending to elicit everything about the exchange that he could from Stambaugh. He had moved forward on the sofa, positioning his back so that Benjamin was partially blocked from Stambaugh's view, and this he did deliberately.

"He sputtered about my fuzzy-headed, liberal ideas," Stambaugh quoted the principal with his fingers, "and reminded me of my over privileged status. I'm overeducated and spoiled, in case that had escaped your notice. I tried to reason with him, but he told me he had more important things to do than deal in abstractions with me." In part because of Benjamin's presence,

Scanlon decided against sharing with Stambaugh the conversation he'd had with Winship about him. Stambaugh needed to be told, but he wanted to tell him in private; he wanted Benjamin excluded.

"What if we called an *ad hoc* faculty meeting?" Scanlon said. "How many of our colleagues do you think would be behind you?"

"Listen, Doug," Stewart Benjamin said, rising from the sofa, "I'd really like to get started before dark."

Allowing the devil his due, Scanlon supposed the censorship flap was trivial considered alongside the choices Benjamin was faced with. Something in Benjamin's demeanor, however, made Scanlon doubt that his decision was as morally significant as Doug Stambaugh's. Scanlon had been invited to meet this fellow, ostensibly to discuss that very issue. So far, there had been only oblique reference to draft dodging.

"All right, Stewart," Stambaugh sighed. "I'll have to take some work with me. Give me half an hour."

"Planning on skiing all the way over the border, Stewart?" Scanlon taunted.

Benjamin stood in Stambaugh's bedroom doorway, his head barely clearing the lintel. He reached up with both hands as if he intended to chin himself.

"Canada's not for me. I prefer Sweden," he said, turning on his heel and going into Stambaugh's bedroom, closing the door behind him. Scanlon looked to Stambaugh for his impression, but he was down on one knee in front of his bookcase, his back to Scanlon.

"He makes it sound like he's choosing a vacation spot," Scanlon said. Stambaugh didn't reply. "So this is the guy you were so anxious for me to meet?"

"He's not himself since he received his letter. He's distracted. To someone who doesn't know him, it might appear as rudeness."

"Canada's not good enough for him. What does that make you for choosing Canada?"

"I haven't made up my mind where, or even if, I'm going. I think the choice of Sweden is based on Stewart's knowledge of the language. It's not what you think." Stambaugh was still on his haunches in front of the bookcase, his back to Scanlon.

"So now you know what I'm thinking. You Yale people are full of surprises." Stambaugh turned to look at Scanlon.

"You really should have that inferiority complex looked at, Jack."

"You invited me here for this?"

"I thought you might enjoy Stewart. I'm sorry." Stambaugh had pulled several hardcover books from the shelves and had set them down on the table next to the sofa. He looked around the room, finger pressed to his chin, as if trying to remember where he had put something. Scanlon chose to read this gesture as a snub, and a not very subtle one at that.

"Well, you're busy getting ready for your ski trip. I'll be on my way. Thanks for having me up to meet your pal." Let him deal with Winship by himself, Scanlon thought, getting into his coat.

"What's gotten into you, Jack?" Stambaugh said. Stewart Benjamin reappeared having changed into wide wale corduroys and a yellow chamois shirt. He carried an expensive camera, which he tossed carelessly on the sofa.

"I really would like to get some shots from the hill in back of the house before we leave," he announced to Stambaugh, as if Scanlon were invisible. Scanlon left without another word and descended the steep flight of stairs half-expecting Stambaugh to call him back.

Stewart Benjamin's road-salt encrusted, green Volvo was parked in the driveway. There were two pairs of skis and poles in the roof rack. It had blue Connecticut plates. Scanlon peeked inside. There was an old-fashioned Navy duffel bag with drawstring in the back seat, bulging with clothes, the heel of one hiking boot sticking out of the puckered opening. There were loose articles on the seat as well: more chamois shirts, a balled-up pair of wool trousers, a down vest, another camera in black leather case, some empty soda cans. The doors were unlocked; anyone could help himself to Stewart Benjamin's possessions, and Scanlon imagined that no one was less concerned about it than Stewart Benjamin.

Scanlon felt heavy and cold as he looked east and west for oncoming traffic before crossing Route 2. He got into his little VW with its contents of textbooks, uncorrected test papers and lab reports, and drove the seven miles to Groveton.

Chapter Fifteen

The little L-shaped white house with black shutters, where Lillian Bloemer lived with her dotty mother, was down in a sort of hollow bounded by three giant maples and scattered young pines. Bare vines ran up the side of the house that faced the road and seemed to hold the structure in their grip. Scanlon brought his car to a stop on the snowy road in front of the house, wondering if any of his colleagues had been invited, too. Lillian's invitation for drinks had taken him by surprise. She had said often enough that she should have him over, but he never really believed she would follow through.

He got out of the car and looked up at the low sky. A light snow was beginning to fall. There was already more snow on the ground than he ever remembered seeing before Thanksgiving. He must be prepared to find Doug Stambaugh there, or just about anybody except for possibly Dennis Kitchell, or Coach Sorenson, whom Lillian had once told him were two of the most boorish people she'd ever met, which made him wonder how she described him to other people. He'd be civil to Stambaugh, but aloof. He'd watch his drinks and act with utmost dignity. Scanlon sighed and held onto a wooden handrail as he stepped down the three slippery steps to the neatly shoveled S-shaped path leading to Lillian Bloemer's front porch.

Three ears of Indian corn were hung on the black front door. Before he could use the brass knocker Lillian had the door open.

"Hello there. Nice you could come. Step in. Let me have your coat," Lillian said, a highball glass in her hand. She had on the same dress she'd worn at school that day, but she looked lumpier in it than she had earlier, and Scanlon realized with distress that she had probably removed her girdle. As he got out of his overcoat, his eyes fell on his hostess's pudgy feet spilling over the sides of an expensive looking pair of brocade slippers. She took his coat and hung it in a closet off the vestibule. "What can I offer you to drink?"

"What you've got looks good." Scanlon rubbed the cold from his hands. "This is very cozy." Lillian Bloemer, he discovered instantly, kept her house hot, the way Alice kept her house and Kennedy his office. He stood on highly varnished, wide, pine boards on which lay a threadbare oriental runner. Standing in a corner was an heirloom grandfather clock. He was startled by his own reflection in a gilt-framed mirror hanging on the wall facing the front door. His hand went instinctively to the knot of his tie. There was the smell of something freshly baked.

"Scotch and soda, then?"

"How about just Scotch."

"Fine. Come into the living room. Mother's there." Lillian escorted him into an opulently overfurnished living room, which perhaps only seemed so because of the presence of a baby grand piano. A fire was dying in a raised hearth fireplace. Scanlon would have offered to rebuild it if the room wasn't already so oppressively hot. And everywhere there were plants. Plants in hanging baskets in the big, many-paned window that looked out upon the dark trunks of the giant maples; plants that bore flowers of pink, and lavender, and orange, shaped like brandy snifters with protruding stamens and pistils. Along an entire wall, potted plants grew under the violet hue of fluorescent lights. Everywhere exotic blossoms such as he'd never seen before, not even in the jungles of Guam or the Philippines.

Mrs. Bloemer sat in a Victorian love seat upholstered in material like Lillian's slippers, her lap full of crochet work. She had on a crisp white dress, perhaps the same dress she'd worn when Scanlon met her at Winship's party in September. She was still as strikingly handsome as he remembered her. What must Lillian's father have looked like? Mrs. Bloemer's crochet hook dipped and flashed with astonishing speed. No one else had arrived yet.

"Do you remember Mr. Scanlon, dear?" Lillian asked her mother in falsetto voice. Mrs. Bloemer smiled faintly, but she didn't look up from her work. Scanlon thought her eyelids flickered. "It was quite some time ago that you met." Lillian turned to Scanlon. "Don't be hurt if she doesn't remember."

"Of course not."

"Make yourself comfortable while I fix your drink." Lillian left him in her mother's company. Scanlon sat down carefully in a wing chair and fingered its nubby fabric.

"It's nice to see you again, Mrs. Bloemer. Your plants are very impressive," Scanlon said, remembering suddenly that Lillian had once told him that her mother had been a horticulturist of considerable reputation. "I've never seen anything like them."

"The blue jays, how they torment the kitties," Mrs. Bloemer replied, in a high-pitched voice.

"I know what you mean," Scanlon said, looking over his shoulder for Lillian. "Blue jays are always after my aunt's cats."

Mrs. Bloemer didn't answer. Her eyebrows rose and fell as if she were carrying on an internal conversation. Lillian was taking a long time to make a simple drink. Probably fixing me an arsenic cocktail, Scanlon thought, looking at Mrs. Bloemer whose perfectly groomed hair seemed to have a blue tint, or it could have been the fluorescent plant lights playing tricks. Scanlon loosened his tie and wondered if it would be impolite to remove his jacket. Lillian arrived with his drink.

"Try this." Lillian handed him a thin, cold, monogrammed glass and took a seat next to her mother.

"I was just telling your mother how impressed I am with her plants."

"Really?"

"Yeah." Scanlon sipped his drink.

"You don't have to pretend to be interested in Mother's plants. I won't think you're impolite."

"I'm not pretending," Scanlon said, perhaps too quickly. Lillian laughed and offered him a cigarette from a silverplated case. She took one for herself and inserted it in a silver cigarette holder. He hadn't drunk much Scotch in his life, but he could tell what Lillian served him was high quality. He must remind himself not to swill it the way he did the whiskey he was used to drinking.

"So, how do you like the teaching business so far?" Lillian leaned back and put her arm up on the back of the love seat. Her slippered feet barely reached the floor, and Scanlon couldn't help noticing that she'd rolled her stockings down below her fat, dimpled knees. He averted his eyes quickly. Scanlon hesitated in response to her question, his mind tangled with too many ways to answer her. "Is that such a hard question, Jack?"

"The question's easy enough. It's the answer that's giving me trouble."

"Well, from all reports you seem to be doing famously," Lillian swirled Scotch whisky around in her glass like a seasoned drinker.

"Depends on who's doing the reporting." Scanlon kept his eyes lowered in case Lillian had something else to show him that he wasn't eager to see.

"The kids adore you. Don't expect to hear anything positive from your colleagues. It's the lack of negative criticism that you have to interpret as approval."

"Speaking of colleagues ..."

"I haven't invited anyone else, if you're wondering."

"Oh." Scanlon looked up and smiled. "I'm flattered."

"Don't be. I never have more than one guest over at a time."

"Oops." They laughed. Mrs. Bloemer looked up from her crocheting to smile, as if she shared the humor. "As for the kids' adoration," Scanlon added, "you obviously haven't heard from them lately."

"Oh, I heard all about the other day. No one took that seriously. Just poor Mr. Scanlon having a bad day. You're as entitled as the rest of us to a bad day, dear boy. Besides, in their eyes you can do no wrong." How much condescension could he be expected to endure? From Lillian he hadn't expected it. "If you'd care to hear my opinion, though," Lillian continued, "I think you're much too lenient with them. It's not uncommon with popular teachers who haven't had much experience. Before you get hurt feelings, remember this is well-intentioned criticism."

"I don't doubt it. The truth is, I don't believe I'll be sticking with the teaching business, as you call it, after this year." Scanlon surprised himself with this declaration, not having consciously formulated any such decision beforehand.

"That would be the teaching business's loss." Lillian smiled. In repose she looked utterly relaxed, soft around her ordinarily hard edges. If only those kids who loved to despise her for demanding more of them than they thought they could deliver could see her now.

"If I were half the teacher you are, I might reconsider."

"My, aren't we sickening this afternoon."

"I mean it. Anyway, I don't find the work much fun lately, especially the paperwork." Scanlon took a good drink of Scotch. The grandfather clock in the vestibule struck the half hour Westminster fashion. Outside, the snow fell harder. The overheated room had Scanlon sweating, and the alcohol didn't make it any better. If he removed his jacket now, he'd be embarrassed by his sweat-stained underarms. He tugged at his collar.

Lillian wanted to know what he intended to do next with his life. He told her he'd considered going back into industrial engineering, but he'd considered no such thing. He had sealed his fate in that profession by his antics at Consolidated after Katie left.

"Why did you leave the field in the first place, if that's not too personal a question?"

"Not too personal, just too complicated. I'm surprised Daryl hasn't brought you up to date on my personal life." It was too late to take it back. Lillian's pencil-line eyebrows rose perceptibly.

"Daryl has said nothing to me about your personal life, I assure you." Lillian turned to her mother. "Maybe Mr. Scanlon will fetch another log for the fireplace. Are you warm enough, dear?"

"Clytemnestra brought home a chipmunk this morning," Mrs. Bloemer replied.

"That naughty kitty. Jack, would you mind? The wood is in the shed, just off the kitchen. I'd better show you." Lillian hoisted herself out of the love seat and smoothed the wrinkles out of her skirt with both hands. "Come. I'll freshen our drinks while you're getting the wood." Scanlon went to get wood to add to the inferno, his shirt and underwear clinging to his skin like plastic wrap.

It was deliciously cool in the shed. Scanlon lingered there to mop his face and pick his shorts away from his crotch before returning to the living room with the smallest birch logs he could find. He placed two on the embers where they instantly ignited.

"That's nice dry wood you've got there," he said to Lillian.

"What makes you think Daryl Winship would confide in me about your private life?"

"It didn't come out exactly the way I meant it. I shouldn't have said anything." Scanlon stared into his glass.

"I can't imagine how else you could have meant it, but there's no need to act contrite. I'm only trying to generate a little cold-weather gossip. You are in favor of gossip, I hope."

"Sure, but I'm afraid I don't have much to offer."

"Come, now. Don't tell me it's all business at those evening sessions. If I know these kids, they have plenty to say about us." Lillian was enjoying herself, color coming into her puffy face, her magnified pupils dancing behind the powerful lenses of her eyeglasses. She crossed one leg over the other and held her slender cigarette holder at her fingertips like a starlet, her pudgy elbow propped on her meaty thigh.

"I don't gossip with students," Scanlon said, hearing indignation in his voice.

"That's really admirable, but don't tell me you haven't overheard things." He wondered if Lillian really wanted to know what he'd overheard the kids say about her.

"I don't listen to their talk, Lillian."

"You don't have to be coy. I know what they say about me. It's what they have to say about the others that intrigues me. What do they think of Dennis Kitchell, or that ass Rob Sorenson? I don't begrudge you your popularity, Jack, but it galls me that kids are taken in by the Dennis Kitchells and Rob Sorensons." Lillian flicked ashes in the clean glass ashtray at her side. "It only serves to confirm what I already know about their inability at this age to judge character."

"Don't you think we ought to be more concerned about this censorship thing?" Scanlon wanted to get Lillian off the subject of his supposed confidential relationship with the students.

"You mean *Time* magazine? I've expressed my views to Daryl. We have an understanding." Had the playfulness gone out of Lillian? Scanlon sensed that he had led himself into thorny territory.

"Doug told me he had quite a go-around with Daryl. What's your read?"

"I'm not in favor of censorship, of course," Lillian said, with a wide arm gesture that she must have imagined produced cigarette ashes on her dress because she brushed the nonexistent ashes away with short, agitated strokes. She smiled quickly to inform Scanlon that she hadn't lost her composure. Could she also have had an encounter with Winship? "Daryl and I have a polite, impersonal, thoroughly professional relationship. I do my work the way I see fit, and he doesn't interfere. He expects the same consideration from me. And I suggest that if you really want to have as little to do with him as possible that you assume the same attitude." The finality of her statement left an awkward void in the conversation. For what seemed to Scanlon a long time, the only sound was the steady cadence of the grandfather clock ticking away the long seconds. In desperation, he remembered finally that Lillian had authored four children's books. When he mentioned the fact, she once more became animated. She sat up straight and smiled.

"I don't think authors of children's books are taken seriously enough," Scanlon said.

"Are you serious, or just being hyper-complimentary again? In any case, I happen to agree. They aren't taken nearly seriously enough."

"No, I mean it. What could be more difficult? Do you still write?"

"Not since I've been teaching. Ironic, isn't it? As demanding as the advertising business was, I still had the energy after a twelve-hour day to write in the evening. Teaching leaves me too drained to write."

"What about vacations?" Scanlon remembered that Lillian had told him that one of the few virtues of teaching was the long vacation, which she could devote to her writing.

"I seem to have gotten out of the habit. Mother used to illustrate my books." Lillian reached over and placed her hand on her mother's arm. Mrs. Bloemer's illustrating days were long over.

"Were they a commercial success, your books?" Scanlon asked before she drifted off to nostalgia.

"Hardly," she laughed. "My last royalty check was for a dollar-fifteen." The price of a six-pack of low-grade beer, Scanlon thought. But he was also interested in this business of writing children's books.

"How do you go about it? I mean, how can you, as an adult, know what appeals to their little minds?" Lillian started to reply, but Scanlon interrupted. "How do you decide on language? You know what I mean?"

"Yes, I do indeed." Lillian dragged deeply on her fresh cigarette, leaned her head back delicately, and blew a cloud of smoke toward the low ceiling. Her neck was so thick, as thick as Johnny's grandmother's had been with goiter. "You have to guard against condescension. Children are not miniature adults."

"Once upon a time still in vogue?"

"It still has the power to enchant me."

"Me, too. What age did you write for? Is that a stupid question?"

"Preschoolers. It's only after they get to school that they begin to distrust their imagination."

Scanlon remembered vividly the day he learned how to tell time, and the sense of power and relief he'd felt, having despaired up to that point of ever learning the skill. It was the year before he started school.

"Yeah. They learn to read and write and figure and tell time. Terrible things to have happen to creative little minds." Scanlon hadn't meant the sarcasm, but sometimes he was powerless to help himself.

"But they have to sacrifice so much." Lillian sighed and removed her half-smoked cigarette from the silver holder, replacing it with a fresh one. "They have such a wonderful logical system before the schools get hold of them. What goes up doesn't have to come down, necessarily."

"We can't remain children forever." Now, in his mind's eye, he was looking down upon the bare bottom of Johnny Labalm having his diaper changed on the bed in the front room, the bed on which his grandfather later died. "Is there a technique to getting into their psyches?"

"You must try to project yourself. Go back to your own childhood. Once the physical reality is summoned, the emotional associations come easily enough."

"How do you know if you had a normal childhood?"

"It's not difficult to know if you've had a particularly happy or a particularly unhappy childhood. Do you know, really? I suspect yours was unhappy."

Scanlon reached in his pocket for his own cigarettes. Lillian offered him a big table lighter with a cut-glass base. Sweat streamed down his face. Despite her excess weight, Lillian showed no sign of being bothered by the heat. "Do you mind if I take off my jacket?"

"Of course not. Are you too warm? Mother is so sensitive to draft. I try to keep it warm for her." Scanlon struggled out of his jacket, wondering where on earth Lillian Bloemer got the notion he had an unhappy childhood.

"You're wrong about my childhood," he said, folding his jacket and laying it across his lap, inside out.

"I suppose next you'll tell me you're not a Gemini," Lillian said, rising from the love seat. "Don't go away. I'll be right back." Their drinks didn't need replenishing. She's either off to the bathroom or to fetch the tarot cards, Scanlon thought, disarmed by her casual identification of his "sign." It would have been easy enough for her to look up his birth date in Winship's office. Why would she bother? Lillian returned with a wooden breadboard bearing a small loaf of freshly baked bread and a wheel of soft cheese.

"Hope you like Camembert," she said, laying the board and some large cloth napkins on the coffee table. "Would you mind slicing the bread?"

"Are you an astrologer, or what?" Scanlon cut into the soft, hot, aromatic bread.

"I used to give readings for friends in New York for fun. I got pretty good at it, too." Lillian tore off a corner of one of Scanlon's thick slices of bread, spread a small amount of cheese on it and handed it on a napkin to Mrs. Bloemer. Not accustomed to eating in this fashion, Scanlon watched carefully so that he could follow Lillian's example instead of wolfing his down the way he would have liked to do, he was so hungry. Mrs. Bloemer nibbled delicately.

"This is sensational," Scanlon said.

"Tell me about your happy childhood, then." For all her physical grossness, Lillian ate as gracefully as her mother. Everything, in fact, about Lillian

Bloemer and her mother—their home, their possessions, their hospitality—spoke of grace and gentility. Scanlon felt like a peasant in their company. He drained his Scotch like one, and Lillian was immediately up to make him another. The late afternoon light was quitting, and he wondered if he should turn on the lamp beside Mrs. Bloemer. Before he could offer, she reached out and switched it on herself without taking her eyes off her work.

"You do beautiful work, Mrs. Bloemer," Scanlon said, all of a sudden feeling the alcohol coursing through his brain. Mrs. Bloemer didn't answer. She had that half smile on her lips; Scanlon was mesmerized by the speed of her crochet hook. "My aunt crochets a little. Nothing like you, though." Perhaps she was recollecting a pleasant girlhood memory. Maybe that's the way it was with senility, coming back full circle to childhood. Lillian was back with another drink for him.

"Where were we? You were going to tell me about your childhood."

"My memories of childhood are poor, I'm afraid. I'll never make it as a children's writer." He had no desire to probe into his childhood for Lillian Bloemer's amusement or curiosity.

"Don't get the idea that it's a passive exercise, Jack. It's hard, demanding work."

"I've never had a creative impulse in my life."

"If you say your childhood was happy who am I to dispute it?"

"What about your astrological instincts?"

"It's really none of my business."

"It wasn't entirely happy. There were good times and bad."

"Are you more comfortable with your jacket off?"

"Yes, thank you." Had he insulted her? Did she actually expect that he'd be willing to reveal facts about his childhood? Perhaps he had misjudged her, and she was nothing more than a tiresome, nosy old maid. Once again there was a breach in the conversation; there was the loud rhythm of the grandfather clock, the crackling of dry birch in the fireplace. "Looks like it's starting to come down hard. Maybe I'd better get on the road," Scanlon said.

"Should I trust you behind the wheel with three drinks? You're welcome to stay for dinner."

"Thanks, but my aunt's expecting me. I'm all right to drive. Really." He felt the effects of the drinks but more in his limbs than in his head at the moment. In this room he could have easily sweat out as much alcohol as he'd imbibed. Besides, he'd driven his car with more drinks than this in him.

"Let me fix you a cup of strong coffee before you go. You can spare that much time." Lillian got up.

"It'll only keep me awake." Lillian had to look at him a moment before laughing.

"Humor me, Mr. Scanlon. It's instant. Won't take a minute." Lillian left to make him coffee. He felt trapped in the room with its heat, the excess of furniture, Mrs. Bloemer's proximity.

"I'd like to have a look at your work sometime," Scanlon said when Lillian returned with his coffee.

"Aren't you sweet. I'll bring my books to school tomorrow. How's that for calling your bluff?"

"Come on, Lillian." Scanlon raised the cup to his lips. It was too hot to drink. Everything about the Bloemer household was too hot. He could let it come to room temperature and it would still be too hot to drink.

"Drink it, Mr. Scanlon. I won't allow you to drive in your condition."

"What condition?"

"You've had three drinks. No one has ever been allowed behind the wheel of an automobile after three of my drinks. Would you like to phone your aunt and tell her that you'll be a little late?"

"That won't be necessary." Scanlon sipped loudly. "Jesus."

"Let it cool, Mr. Scanlon." Lillian, back beside her mother on the love seat, studied him, and though he wasn't looking directly at her, Scanlon was aware of her scrutiny.

"How about if I walk you a straight line? What'll it take to convince you I'm all right to drive?"

"Finish your coffee and we'll see."

"It's snowing like crazy. If I stay much longer, it won't make any difference how sober I am." Scanlon put his jacket on, felt for his car keys in the right pocket. He'd left them in his overcoat.

"If necessary you can stay the night. We have a fairly comfortable spare room."

"I've got papers at home to correct."

"There are always papers to correct."

"Tell me about it." Scanlon tested the coffee again, and risked scalding himself just to get some down. "The paperwork is the big reason I'm getting out of teaching."

"You think you're the only one behind in his paperwork, Mr. Scanlon?" Lillian was beginning to get to him addressing him as Mr. Scanlon all the time. In fact, Lillian Bloemer was giving him the creeps.

"I really should be on my way now, Lillian. Thanks for the drinks, the great bread and cheese, the conversation, the coffee ..."

"Not until you've finished your coffee, Mr. Scanlon," she said, as if she meant to do something about it if he didn't finish his coffee.

"It's too hot and I have to be going. I'm really sober enough to drive. If I'm killed on the road, you can tell everybody you warned me. All right?" Scanlon moved toward the vestibule. "It was nice to see you again, Mrs. Bloemer," he said over his shoulder to the old lady. He left the steaming cup of coffee on the table beside his chair. Lillian made no move to escort him to the door. He couldn't go rummaging in her closet for his overcoat. "All right, I'll finish my coffee," Scanlon said, returning to his chair. Her reputation for willfulness was richly deserved. Lillian Bloemer watched him sip and blow his way through the coffee, and when he'd finished she tried to talk him into another cup. This time he was able to convince her that he was indeed sober enough to drive his car. She got his overcoat out of the closet.

"Thank you for coming, Jack. It was a pleasant afternoon, for Mother and me at least. I'm sorry if you think I'm unreasonable, but I'd rather be thought eccentric than have to carry around the guilt for someone's untimely death. I hope you understand."

"Of course. I'm sorry I gave you a hard time. Thanks for everything, and don't forget to bring those books to school tomorrow. I really wasn't bluffing."

"Please drive carefully."

Chapter Sixteen

Children's stories, Scanlon thought as he slid down under the covers, happily drunk, ready to be overtaken by sleep. What could be so hard about writing a story for kids? Everyone has been a kid; everyone has gone through the same experience, more or less. The trick would be to reclaim that experience in ways that were meaningful to the ones who were going through it now, he imagined. He wouldn't know where to begin. Maybe it couldn't be that hard to do, but Scanlon didn't know where he'd begin if he had a mind to do it himself.

Once upon a time, in the Northeast Kingdom of Vermont, there lived a happy little eight-year-old boy named Johnny Labalm.

Johnny lived in a big brick house on a quiet street with his grandparents, who doted over him so much that certain people were worried that he'd soon be spoiled rotten.

Among his friends were twelve-year-old Eddie Leclerc, who taught him to masturbate, and Alvin Farr, a ten-year-old who planned the Mary Alice McGinnis fiasco, which may have influenced Johnny's whole life.

One day, Johnny was in the woods behind his house with Eddie, Alvin, and a drip by the name of Milton Nash. Eddie, who had already reached puberty, was leading the others in a circle jerk. There they were, the four of them, their little peckers (all except for Eddie who had a man-sized whang) held with a strangler's grip in their sweaty fists, stroking for all they were worth to achieve the effect Eddie compared to Fourth of July fireworks. Eddie was the only one capable of such pyrotechnics, the rest of them having to settle for a mere tickling sensation and to admire Eddie's prodigious output of gism with awe and envy.

Alvin Farr, who claimed to have fucked several girls since he turned ten in April, likened his dry orgasm to the ringing of bells in his stomach. If Alvin's boast of sexual encounters was dubious, it was common knowledge that Eddie Leclerc had screwed so many girls he'd lost count.

"It's time we got Labalm fucked," Eddie Leclerc announced calmly, shaking out his thing and tucking it back in the fly of his dungarees. "High time this boy had his first piece of ass. What about that girl lives next door's always hanging around? Wanna fuck her, Labalm?"

"Yeah!" exclaimed Alvin Farr, putting away his own pecker. "Mary Alice McGinnis. I'd fuck her myself if she weren't so young. We'll get her for Labalm." Mary Alice McGinnis was six years old and was always trying to get Johnny to play house with her and her damned dolls. At six, she was already very motherly. Johnny had never been keen on the idea of playing house with her, but he wouldn't mind fucking her, whatever that amounted to. Eddie and Alvin were always going on about it being the greatest feeling in the world, and that to have fucked was as important to the attainment of true manhood as going to war. Why they referred to it as a "piece of ass" was a question Johnny Labalm was afraid to ask for fear of being thought a baby.

"I got an idea," Alvin Farr said, all excited. Stupid Milton Nash, who looked like Jughead in the funny books, was still playing with himself after everyone else had finished. Eddie was disgusted with him and predicted that he'd grow up foolish.

Alvin's ingenious plan involved wooden kitchen matches and a brand of magic that would play on Mary Alice's astonishing gullibility. It would be Johnny's mission to steal a box of the matches from his house; Alvin himself would take responsibility for the ruse to lure Mary Alice into the woods behind the big brick house. Those woods were where Johnny had acted out his fantasies. He had been Daniel Boone tracking and evading scalp-hunting redskins; the noble Robin Hood lying in ambush of the rich; the U.S. Marine slithering on his belly in the jungles of Okinawa (where his Uncle Ira had been for real) flushing out Jap snipers in the trees. Now, it was Alvin Farr's scheme to use these same woods as the site of the seduction of the unsuspecting Mary Alice McGinnis.

Mary Alice came willingly, as Alvin knew she would when he promised her that there was magic to be found in the enchanted forest. She was never without her Raggedy Ann, and her mother made sure she was impeccable in a different dress each day, colorful and crisp, tying her long honey-colored banana curls in bright ribbons. As they walked toward the woods,

Johnny carrying his ill-gotten box of matches in a brown paper bag, he felt excitement such as he had never felt before welling up from his groin to his chest. But there was also a heaviness in the pit of his stomach, and he looked over his shoulder once before they entered the woods.

Alvin led them to the place where the boys went to smoke cigarettes and jerk off, a little clearing, a plateau on a sloping hill protected at every approach by dense undergrowth. They weren't long into the woods before Mary Alice began asking when she could expect magic. Alvin kept her moving along the narrow trail, where low branches and brambles stung her cheeks and bare legs, threatened to tear her pretty yellow dress, with the promise that very soon there would be magic. And when they finally arrived at their destination, Alvin Farr wheeled around to face Johnny and Mary Alice, his eyes narrowed to slits like a cat's. Johnny had never seen such a face on the boy before, and it made him a little afraid. Mary Alice, tired and cranky from the difficult walk through the woods, demanded a show of magic now. Alvin told her she'd get her magic as soon as she lifted up her dress and showed them what she had under there. To Johnny's surprise, Mary Alice happily obliged. She sat on the ground on damp leaves and pine needles in her immaculate yellow dress and pulled down her underpants, Raggedy Ann clutched firmly at her side. Johnny was stunned at the nakedness of her crotch. He'd never seen anyone without a pecker before. He was at once thrilled and repelled. Mary Alice, having done what was asked of her, demanded again to see evidence of magic. Alvin went into his routine, declaring that he could make the Spirit of the Enchanted Forest reveal himself only by making him angry. For her part, Mary Alice would have to stand with her face against the bark of an evergreen tree in order to interpret the Spirit's message. Mary Alice wasn't so sure she wanted to deal with an angry Spirit, but Alvin assured her that she had merely to pull down her pants to appease the Spirit. Alvin nudged Johnny as he spoke this nonsense, which Mary Alice found plausible enough to press her pretty little forehead against the rough bark of a pine tree. While Alvin Farr chanted gibberish to the Spirit of the Enchanted Forest, Johnny made ready a bunch of wooden matches, the heads of which Alvin would smash between two rocks to produce a report as loud as a gunshot. Mary Alice's little shoulders recoiled at the noise, and she was convinced that the Spirit was indeed angry, and that she must therefore again lift her dress and drop her pants. The acrid smell of sulfur in their nostrils, Alvin explained to her, was the Spirit's bad breath.

They performed the ritual in the woods on two more occasions before Alvin decided that Mary Alice McGinnis was "ripe for picking." Now that she was a true believer in their magic, the next step would be a cinch. In his heart, Johnny would have been content to let things stand as they were, but that would be inviting the scorn of Alvin, and worse, Eddie Leclerc, who had received progress reports on Mary Alice's seduction.

"My uncle's the janitor at the trade school," Alvin told Johnny one day. "Once in a while I bring him his lunch pail. Now that school's over, he's washing and waxing all the floors. Tomorrow he'll be finished in the basement, so we can go down there and nobody'll bother us. The door'll be open, and he's the only one around. He should be up on the second floor by ten."

Alvin planned to get Mary Alice in the basement and convince her that the doors had somehow locked behind them; the only way out would be to summon a new kind of magic. This time the magic required a lock, which she would provide, and a key, courtesy of Johnny Labalm. Johnny had merely to insert his key in her lock and the doors would open. Mary Alice had no problem whatsoever with this concept.

But as little Mary Alice McGinnis lay there on the polished tile of the basement classroom—the desks and chairs all stacked neatly against a wall for the summer, Alvin Farr standing with his hand on the knob of the heavy gray door that led to the corridor, an awful twisted smile on his face—with Johnny Labalm staring down at the by now familiar hairless labia, he was paralyzed with fear. His throat was suddenly so parched he could barely swallow, and his hands had gone clammy.

"Hurry up, for Christ sakes," Alvin whispered. "We ain't got all day. What're you waiting for?" Johnny could do nothing, not even speak. Mary Alice smiled and Johnny was enraged at her stupidity, her willingness to go along with Alvin Farr's absurd magic. He stood there, mute and motionless. "You gonna fuck her or what?"

Johnny shook his head.

"You're fucking hopeless, Labalm," Alvin said, jerking open the door and walking out of the classroom leaving Johnny alone with Mary Alice on her back on the floor, starched white dress hiked up around her chest, underpants around her ankles, waiting for lock and key magic to open doors for her. When Alvin opened the door without benefit of Johnny's magic, Mary Alice's brown eyes opened wide. Johnny ran out of the room before she could question him.

It had to have been with the exuberance of pure innocence that Mary Alice McGinnis related the story of Alvin Farr's and Johnny Labalm's magical powers to her mother. More likely, Mrs. McGinnis had become suspicious at the sudden appearance of her ordinarily immaculate little girl's soiled dresses, and had pressed her for an explanation. In any case, when she called Johnny from her front door as he was playing with his parachute on the big lawn in front of his house, he knew instantly what it was she wanted.

"Johnny, I would like you to tell your grandmother what you and your friends have made Mary Alice do," she said in an even voice, with such an absence of anger in her manner that Johnny went cold all over the way he had that first day in the woods when he looked upon Alvin Farr's slitty-eyed leer. He muttered something and ran off in the direction of his backyard. He sat down on the back steps, trembling, unable, out of a fear that made him dizzy and short of breath, to go inside and do as Mrs. McGinnis had asked him.

Next thing he knew, he was running along the short path through the woods that led to the dirt road to Eddie Leclerc's house, his head hot, his eyes filled with tears, his breathing rapid and shallow.

The Leclercs lived in a square, white house with a slanting, corrugated tin roof and a screened-in front porch. Johnny had spent many a warm summer night sleeping on the musty smelling, creaky porch glider. He was a frequent visitor to the Leclerc household and was treated like one of the family, which was to say, ignored for the most part. The house was down off the road, in a valley with vegetable gardens in the back, front, and on one side. Mr. Leclerc worked in the foundry where Johnny's grandfather had put in fifty hard years. During the short growing season he worked the gardens for relaxation, though what he did looked a lot like backbreaking work to Johnny. The Leclercs looked older than normal parents, closer in age to Johnny's grandparents. Eddie was their only child, and like Johnny, had things pretty much his own way.

Eddie was down in the tomato garden beside the house, helping his father weed when Johnny arrived. Johnny stood around for a long time watching Eddie and his father on their hands and knees pulling at weeds around the young tomato plants, neither of them acknowledging his presence he was such a fixture around the place.

Eddie's father wore a broad-brimmed hat and a long denim smock that looked like it would be hot to wear in this weather. Eddie had on dungarees and a T-shirt. When they finished weeding, Mr. Leclerc said "Hello Johnee," in his French accent, and then moved on to other chores leaving Eddie and Johnny standing alone in the early summer garden, Johnny trying to find the courage to tell Eddie what had happened to him.

"You hard-on," Eddie said when Johnny was finally able to blurt his story out. "Come on. Give me a hand with the two-by-fours." Johnny helped Eddie haul lumber up the hill beside the house to their secret campsite. They were building a shack, which would be their "clubhouse." For now, they were the only members. Knowing Johnny's penchant for blabbing, Eddie had made him promise, upon pain of having the bird shit pounded out of him, not to breathe a word to anyone about the camp until it was finished. Johnny shuddered at the thought of being pummeled with Eddie's big-knuckled fists. "So what are you gonna do now, you dumb fuck?" Eddie said, dropping his armload of boards on the ground in front of the shack's doorframe. He grabbed a handful of chokecherries from one of the many bushes around the campsite and stuffed them in his mouth. Johnny was worn out from lugging heavy boards up the steep hill through the underbrush. He sat down to catch his breath before telling Eddie that he hoped that he could hide out at his place for a few days until he could figure out what to do next. What he didn't say was that he also hoped that Eddie would be the one to figure out what he should do next.

"If we moved our asses we could have the camp built in a couple days, and you could hide out here. I could sneak food up to you. Shit, they'd never find you." There was still a lot of work to do before the shack would be functional, work Eddie would do himself for the most part, Johnny's contribution involving no more than handing Eddie nails and boards, running errands. Eddie's lips were red from chokecherry juice. Johnny didn't eat them because he didn't like the way they made his mouth pucker. "And you never even fucked her. So all this shit is for nothing." Eddie shook his head in contempt and disbelief. Johnny felt himself start to cry. "For crimus sake, don't start bawling," Eddie said. "Let me think."

They could hear the faraway sound of yells and shrieks coming from the Lion's Club swimming pool, less than a quarter mile from where they were, but separated from their secret place by what Eddie assured him were unexplored woods. It had the effect, however, of reminding Johnny that he hadn't escaped the real world of retribution.

It couldn't be said that Johnny Labalm's story ended happily, but neither did it end in the awful confrontation with his grandmother that he imagined it would. It just ended. Johnny stayed with the Leclercs for three days; Eddie acted as liaison between Johnny and his grandmother, reassuring her that Johnny was indeed at his house, but more importantly reconnoitering for signs of trouble.

Johnny returned home after Eddie's scouting reports suggested that there was no immediate danger, and surely and inexplicably everything was as it had been before he ever got involved with the whole Mary Alice McGinnis episode. It was as if her mother's summons and ultimatum had been a dream. Nevertheless, Johnny kept his distance from the McGinnis house in general, Mary Alice McGinnis in particular. For weeks he was on edge in fear that the whole matter would resurface as soon as he put down his guard, and he would be made to pay in the manner in which he himself believed he should. No such thing happened. In the fall of that year, after his grandfather's death, his grandmother was forced to give up the big house. She and Johnny had no choice but to move in with Aunt Lilly and her new husband, Howard, in New Hampshire. For a long time, Johnny believed that this was the way he was being punished for his wickedness. It was severe punishment indeed to be cut off from the only home he had ever known, taken away from all his friends, though no worse than he deserved.

S: Bob, want to read a little story about something that happened to me when I was eight years old?

Kennedy poured them each a stiff one in the trusty Styrofoam. His hemorrhoids must have been flaring up because he grimaced as he poured. Scanlon tossed his notebook on Kennedy's desk.

S: There's this woman at school used to write children's books. She almost had me convinced I could do it, too, if I put my mind to it. Tell me if you think this would be suitable for a children's story.

Kennedy must have been a speed-reader. He finished reading in less time than it would have taken Scanlon to tell it out loud.

K: I doubt that anyone would mistake this for a children's story, though I'll have to concede to you, children are involved. Why do you suppose Mrs. McGinnis never went to your grandmother with her story?

S: I don't know, Bob. Honest. It's a big mystery to me and probably always will be now that my grandmother's been dead for ten years.

K: Can't you speculate? Do you think it really changed your whole life?

Kennedy had his shoes off, his feet up on his paper-strewn desk. Today, he had on white athletic socks, dirt-rimmed around his shoe tops.

K: You don't have to speculate if you don't want to, of course.

S: I haven't thought about this for a long time, and you know my memory.

A long time. He doubted that he'd ever thought about it before. Some how, the talk with Lillian of his unhappy childhood, and the business about children's stories had triggered the memory. He could have imagined the whole thing, made it all up, for all he knew.

K: Did this all happen to you, or is this all made up?

Scanlon laughed at Kennedy the mind reader.

S: You are truly amazing, Bob. I toast you.

Scanlon raised his cup and drank to his shrink's clairvoyance.

S: This took place quite a long time ago. Yeah, I suppose I could have made all of it up. What do you think about that, Karnak? OK, suppose Mrs. McGinnis really did go to my grandmother.

Scanlon paused to consider the implications of this idea, which had rolled out of his mouth rather than his brain. Kennedy wiggled his toes making Scanlon wonder why some people had smelly feet and others didn't.

K: Yeah.

S: It could have happened, I suppose. It's pretty unlikely anything would have come of it, though.

K: Why?

S: My grandmother was so blind to my faults, Mrs. McGinnis would have had as much chance of being believed as she would if she'd accused me of molesting her. But she could have spoken to my grandmother. That can't be ruled out. We'll never know the truth. I'm not about to track down the McGinnis family for their version.

K: Wouldn't your grandmother have given some indication that Mrs. McGinnis had said something to her? Couldn't she have said some thing like "I want you to stay away from that McGinnis family. All they do is spread lies," or something along those lines?

S: Good point, Bob. I can't remember a conversation like that. She may have said something, she may not have. The fact is, I was never made to face up to what I'd done to that kid. I'm sure of that at least.

K: You're absolutely sure?

S: Absolutely.

Kennedy reached over to pour Scanlon more whiskey, bending from the waist without taking his feet down from his desk. The effort got him red in the face. Scanlon held out his cup.

S: Take it easy, there, big fellow. We don't want to tempt a stroke when my therapy's coming along so smashingly, do we?

K: I'll outlive you, Scanlon.

Kennedy poured himself a dollop and leaned back, his finger going to his temple as if under its own volition.

S: You act like you don't believe me.

Scanlon looked up at the patchwork ceiling with its stalactic paint chips poised overhead.

S: It would help if you fixed this rat hole up a little. Your budget can't afford curtains for the fucking windows? A little fresh paint? This is more like an interrogation room than a shrink's office.

Scanlon made an arm sweep to encompass the room.

S: You can't hang a picture on the wall, have Janet bring in a potted plant?

K: I'll get my decorator on it first thing Monday morning.

S: You think I've got serious hang-ups, don't you?

K: I wouldn't go that far. Tell me why you were so anxious for me to read this story.

S: I don't know. I thought you might be pleased. It's got so much psychological stuff in it. I thought you might get off on it.

K: You made this up for my benefit?

S: Hell, no, Bob! This isn't made up, not all of it.

K: You're saying the essence is there, right?

S: Yeah. The essence. I don't know what the truth is now any more than I did two months ago. Two years ago. Ever. It's too hard for me, Bob.

As usual, Scanlon was drinking too fast; he'd finished his second cup before Kennedy had started on his refill. Kennedy had his fingers together on his big chest now, church-steeple fashion. He seemed deep in thought.

K: What if we just take all this as if it were the literal truth and see where that leads us. What do you say?

S: Sure. Whatever you say.

K: Don't just acquiesce, for Christ's sake.

S: What do you want from me?

K: A little cooperation would be good.

S: All right.

Scanlon raised his hands in surrender.

K: Why don't you tell me how you feel about the subject matter?

S: I don't know how the fuck I feel about the subject matter. Why do I bother telling you this shit if you have to ask me all these questions?

K: That's not a very smart thing to say, Jack.

S: I don't feel like dealing with smart things if that's all right with you. What, are you pissed at me for criticizing your dungeon office?

K: What I'm pissed at is all the time we're wasting with your evasiveness. You want help or not? If you don't, there are plenty of people I could be talking to who do. Make up your mind, Jack.

S: Are you serious or just wearing the rag today?

K: I'm serious. I don't have time to hold your hand anymore.

S: In that case, why don't you try fucking yourself.
Scanlon stood up. Kennedy told him to sit down.

S: Why should I? I don't need anybody to hold my fucking hand, you fat fuck. Scanlon was trembling, his face hot with anger and whiskey.

K: Sit down, Jack. I'm sorry. I was trying to shake you up, get you off your ass. Looks like I succeeded.
Kennedy chuckled. Scanlon sat down.

S: I'm glad you think it's so funny, asshole. Scanlon waved his cup at Kennedy. For that I'll need another drink.

Kennedy poured him a small portion. When Scanlon calmed down, Kennedy asked him again how he felt about that episode in his life.

K: Don't think about it. Just say whatever comes into your pretty head.

S: This one of them word association tests?
Scanlon spoke with a hick inflection.

K: Sex is what we're talking about here. Am I right? Now that you're divorced, what are you doing about sex, if you don't mind my asking?
Scanlon laughed.

S: Jesus, do we have to talk about that?
Kennedy sighed.

S: What, are you going to dump on me now because I don't feel like talking about my nonexistent sex life?

K: Why did you tell me about this particular incident? I don't think I've ever heard you go on at such length about a subject.

S: Just came out. I don't know why.

K: How old's your daughter?

S: Six. What's Lucy got to do with anything here?

K: About the same age as this Mary Alice kid.

S: My guess is that Mary Alice is a little older by now.

K: All right, wise guy.

S: What are you after, Bob, in your twisted mind?

K: Remember why you came here in the first place?

S: Yeah.

K: You claimed you dreamed you murdered your child. Later you said that was a lie. Now I assume that you were lying about the content. Am I right? I mean, you did dream something, right?

S: I forget. Scanlon tossed back the rest of his whiskey.

K: Now, this six-year-old from your childhood turns up out of the blue. If you were in my place, Jack, what would you think? You said yourself that the story was lousy with 'psychological' stuff. You're right about that. Don't you think I might naturally make the connection between your daughter and this Mary Alice McGinnis? Wouldn't you, in my place?

Scanlon was in a panic. He couldn't remember whether or not he'd revealed to Kennedy the true content of his dream. He couldn't have; if he couldn't do it now he couldn't have before.

S: I don't remember what I dreamed, Bob, and no, I don't see that there's an obvious connection between Lucy and Mary Alice. Could it be that you're trying too hard?

K: Tell me if I'm wrong. You had an incestuous dream.

S: No.

K: Don't worry about it, Jack. It's no big deal. I've had dreams like that myself. It's not uncommon. It doesn't make you a freak or anything. Is this what's got you all up tight?

S: That's the trouble with modern life, Bob. Everything's so out in the open. There's no mystery, nothing that can't be explained away by some half-assed theory about human personality. Life's become so ho-hum. I could confess to mass murder, and you'd tell me that doesn't make me a bad person. Is there anything that has the power to shock you, Bob?

K: Yes, as a matter of fact. I'm still put off by indifference, if you really want to know. I can understand mass murder easier than unconcern.

Scanlon was exhausted, enervated, as if he'd lost a lot of blood.

S: So, what now?

K: Why don't you let me ask you some questions. Try not to second-guess me. All right? You trust me enough to play it this way?

Kennedy's voice had softened, returned to the soothing, conciliatory, forgiving one that could have had something to do with why Scanlon really did trust the man in the first place.

S: Fire away.

K: Your dream was incestuous wasn't it?

S: Yes.

K: To have dreamed about murdering your own child is less alarming to you than having dreamed about having sex with her. Is that fair to say?

S: Yes.

K: There are certain types of women you can't even imagine having sex with. Am I right?

S: Yeah. So what?

K: So-called nice girls?

S: Depends on the nice girl.

K: On what does it depend?

S: What she looks like. How she acts. The usual things. I know all about this idea, Bob. I took intro psych in college.

K: Are you aware that you used the word "immaculate" twice when you were telling the story?

S: You kept count? I'm impressed. What of it?

K: What does the word suggest to you?

S: Purity. Spiritual purity. Like the Immaculate Conception, sex without the stink and stain.

K: Exactly.

Kennedy looked self-satisfied, a look that didn't please Scanlon.

S: You're telling me that I've got these sexual hang-ups, and they're what's at the root of my problem? You been hiding in the bathroom with the Kinsey Report or something?

K: That's not all of it. I'm just trying to find out where it fits in the total picture.

S: What's next? Toilet training? I've been told that I learned to use the flush toilet by the time I was a year old. I always thought that was pretty advanced. What are you going to tell me, it set me back ten years?

K: And what about Johnny's paralysis and anger at Mary Alice in the class room? This was at the threshold, as it were, of sexual passage. That seemed fairly pointed, Jack. What do you make of it?

S: You'd like to know if this was Jack Scanlon's or Johnny Labalm's perception, right?

K: Well, what about it?

S: I can't be sure. My recollection of specific emotions is unreliable. Maybe I was angry and paralyzed with fear, or maybe just paralyzed with fear. What do you think?

K: It doesn't matter what I think. Right now I get the impression you're steering an evasive course.

S: What can I say?

K: How old were you when you lost your virginity?

S: That's a queer way to put it, Bob. I associate the phrase with girls, not guys.

K: Really? Well, you're right in the literal sense. What if I asked you when you got your first piece? Would that be more agreeable?

S: Much better, thank you.

Scanlon lowered his eyes and stared at his hands resting in his lap. He didn't like the turn of the conversation.

K: What's the matter? You uncomfortable with the subject?

S: Yes, as a matter of fact. I'll probably need another cup of the mash if we're going to talk dirty.

K: I don't know. I'm feeling mine a little. Maybe we'd better cork it.

S: It's your hooch. What are you looking at?

K: You. Who else?

S: You think maybe the booze has knocked out some of my memory cells?

K: We could both stand to lay off the sauce a little.

S: Fuck that.

K: Right.

Kennedy poured them each another small one.

S: I was eighteen. I tell everybody who asks, sixteen.

K: How come?

S: Sounds more stud-like.

K: What were the circumstances?

S: Professional relationship. Back room of a Tijuana bar.

K: How did you feel about that?

S: Like a fraud.

K: Why?

S: The manly art of fucking involves conquest. When you deal with professionals, they're the ones in charge.

K: So you've got sex, and war, and conquest on the same conceptual level?

S: In my gut, if not in my head.

K: And in your gut you think of sex as dirty and evil, don't you?

Kennedy's voice was getting phlegmy from the whiskey.

S: I wouldn't go that far, Bob. A little naughty, maybe, but evil? I wouldn't go that far.

Kennedy's stockinged feet were back up on his desk. He had his whiskey cup resting on his big belly, and his thick eyebrows were a continuous line across his frowning forehead. His big, veiny nose was aflame from whiskey drinking, and the broken blood vessels in his jowly face were in bloom as well. John L. Lewis. That was who Kennedy reminded him of. All he needed was a big overcoat, a felt hat and a stogie and he could double for the old labor boss. Kennedy had all his intellectual powers mustered to fathom Scanlon's pathetic psyche. Scanlon felt self-indulgent, even silly, talking about himself, showing all his warts. What did it matter in the end? Who cared? Did he even care himself? Kennedy looked like he cared. Was he this way with all his patients?

S: You thinking about something really profound, Bob, or just nodding off?

Kennedy looked up and smiled. He had a warm smile, and when he used it he didn't look at all like John L. Lewis, who probably never smiled.

K: Just trying to figure you out, Scanlon. You're not always a lot of help.

S: Don't you like a challenge every now and then?

K: Yes, but not right now, I'm afraid. We've gone a bit overtime. I've got a lot of paperwork to do. That's the bad part about Friday.

S: Tell me about it. You think we're getting anywhere?

K: I think we're doing better than we have been. We'll go wherever you feel comfortable, but not too comfortable.

Kennedy struggled out of his chair and started his paper-scooping ritual.

S: I guess you won't be receiving next week.

K: I'll be going to my wife's family for Thanksgiving. See you in two weeks. You got anything special planned for the holiday?

S: No. Catch up on sleep, have dinner with my aunt and uncle. That's about it.

K: Well, have a good one, then.

S: You, too.

Chapter Seventeen

Scanlon was lying in bed Thanksgiving morning listening to voices that, in his semi-conscious state, could have been dream voices. Then Willie Goodwin's braying laugh and Althea's cigarette cough brought him fully awake.

Alice had invited the entire Groveton branch of her extended family for Thanksgiving dinner: Willie and Althea and their kids except for Billy, who was spending the day with his girlfriend's family; her older sister Jeanette and her husband Rudy, and Mrs. Royer, the family matriarch. Scanlon rolled over and closed his eyes but couldn't get back to sleep with all the sound coming from downstairs. Sighing, he threw back the covers, got out of bed and struggled into his clothes in the too hot room. He'd tried unsuccessfully to remember what he'd dreamed. It couldn't have been any good; he felt heavy-limbed and his stomach was upset and his mouth sour from last night's heavy drinking. Somewhere in a shadowy part of his mind lurked something formless that caused him to shiver from more than early morning stupor. He would have liked a couple more hours sleep. Instead, he went downstairs without bothering to shave. Maybe this weekend he'd start a beard, give Winship something else to stew about.

"Good morning, Johnny. Did we wake you?" Alice said to him in the kitchen where everyone was gathered except the kids, who were watching TV.

"No. My internal alarm doesn't know this is a holiday."

Mrs. Royer sat at one corner of the kitchen table like a dowager queen, though there was nothing remotely imperious about her. She always looked stone-faced, however, belying her shy, gentle nature. As usual she was impeccably "groomed," a word he'd often heard her daughters use to describe their mother, as if she were a show horse. At seventy-four years old, and after giving birth to and rearing eight children practically by herself (her husband died when she was in her twenties), she still made her own dresses, invariably of dark, homespun cloth befitting her modest way of life. Hair neatly coiffed, makeup applied discreetly, a neat pearl choker at her neck, Mrs. Royer's only visible imperfection was a wart the size of an eraser head on her chin from which grew a single black hair. She spoke very little English and was so unobtrusive that in a few minutes one hardly knew she was in the room.

"It's about time you dragged your dead ass out of bed," Willie Goodwin said from his chair at the head of the table near the refrigerator where the beer was, and handy to the open cellar door where he tossed his empties. "Sleep your life away you ain't careful." Willie leaned back in his chair and got Scanlon a beer out of the well-stocked refrigerator. "Get rid of some of this goddamn food, Alice," he said, tossing a bottle at Scanlon, taking him by surprise. He caught the bottle clumsily, with both hands. "Catch like a goddamn girl," Willie observed. Scanlon's attention was unwillingly drawn to his uncle, whose lap was full of Althea. Althea had her arm around Ira's neck. She had on a tight-fitting, pink, mohair sweater, which made her breasts appear larger than Scanlon remembered them, one of which Ira pretended to tweak, falling just short of the mark and eliciting a squeal from Althea.

"You son-of-a-bitch," she said to Ira, not sounding angry. Ira winked at Willie Goodwin, whose look was something like a sneering smile or a smiling sneer. He grunted and took a long swallow of beer, his big Adam's apple working like a piston in his lean neck. Alice was busy at the sink scrubbing carrots with a brush, her back to Ira and her sister. Mrs. Royer, her hands in her lap, was a study in impassivity. Jeanette and her husband, Rudy, sat at opposite ends of the table; neither of them seemed interested in Ira and Althea. Scanlon felt like yanking the slutty Althea out of his uncle's lap.

"She been tryin' to get his pecker up all morning," Willie said to Scanlon, and yawned showing a maw full of bad teeth. "Ira ain't got no interest in pussy at his age."

Rudy Thibeault, whom everybody in the family except his wife and Mrs. Royer treated like a fool, laughed like one at Willie's remark. Rudy was thin, and his thinning red hair was matted to his fragile looking skull as if it had been painted there. Scanlon doubted that his IQ could match the temperature Alice kept the house. Rudy boasted of his military exploits even though he knew everybody was aware that the closest he ever got to combat was maybe in the bars of Phenix City, Alabama, where he was stationed for the duration of his enlistment. If he weren't such a fool, he would have been unbearable. He had an Adam's apple that rivaled Willie Goodwin's for size and independent motion, and he wore his wristwatch on the shirt cuff of his right arm. He and Jeanette deserved each other, she not operating on very high wattage herself. She lacked her sisters' energy and personality. Scanlon had been surprised to learn that she was a Royer woman, in fact. In contrast to the hyperthyroidal Alice and Althea, Jeanette was stocky in build and phlegmatic in nature. Her placidity she no doubt inherited, undiluted, from her mother.

"How are you, Joh-, Joh-, Johnny?"

"Good, Rudy. Yourself?" Scanlon said. Willie shook his head at Rudy's stammering. Ira and Willie constantly made fun of Rudy and put him down. Jeanette either didn't notice, chose not to notice, or simply didn't care. Then nobody seemed to notice or care that Ira was practically fondling his wife's sister at seven-thirty of a Thanksgiving morning. Mrs. Royer was unperturbed; Willie, if anything, was offering encouragement, and Alice was more interested in her carrots than what her sister was doing with her husband. Or so it seemed to Scanlon. Rudy, of course, was a fool.

"Want some bacon and eggs, Johnny? Ira's making breakfast," Alice said.

"You know me and breakfast."

Willie had eaten hours ago, but if Ira was doing the cooking, he'd force some more down. Ira was the celebrated skillet wizard at hunting camp, a legend in his own time, Rudy haltingly reminded everyone.

"You sure? Dinner won't be ready till after one," Alice said, scrubbing dirt from her carrots into the sink. Ira demanded to know how many would be wanting breakfast. Alice and Althea declined, everyone else, except Scanlon, put in their orders.

Ira tickled Althea's ribs to get her off his lap so he could get busy with the bacon and eggs. Scanlon offered to help, even though he was never allowed to help in the kitchen.

"How the hell you expect me to find anything in here with all this goddamned beer?" Ira said, crouched in front of the refrigerator.

"Nothing worse than a reformed drunk," Alice said.

Ira found a carton of eggs and a package of bacon, and squeezed between Althea's chair and the hutch, lingering at Althea's shoulder longer than Scanlon thought he should have. And Althea was in no hurry to pull her chair in to let him pass.

"I'll give you exactly one hour to get your elbow out of my crotch," Ira said, shooting a wink in Willie Goodwin's direction, then rolling his eyes in mock ecstasy. Althea pretended to be interested in Jeanette's conversation with her mother. Scanlon looked away. Willie tossed his empty beer bottle over his shoulder through the open cellar door, cupping a hand to his ear to listen for the sound of breaking glass. The bottle struck the stone wall with a hollow thunk and dropped unbroken into the cardboard box on the landing.

"Shit," said Willie. Scanlon was too inhibited to send his empties down the stairs this way. Ira finally made it to the stove, and soon the smell of frying bacon filled the room, making Scanlon's mouth and eyes water. Ira was happy to oblige him when he asked if he could change his mind about breakfast.

"I-, I-, Ira's going to make someone a f-, f-, f-, fine wife someday," Rudy said, honking out a laugh. Willie shook his head again, his lips moving slightly.

"Might as well baste the bird while you're at the stove," Alice said to Ira.

"Can't you see I'm busy, Mother?" Ira snapped. Scanlon said he would baste the turkey, and got up quickly to do it before anyone could object.

"How many eggs can you eat, Johnny?" his uncle asked as Scanlon pulled the roasting pan out of the oven.

"Two will be good," Scanlon said, really wanting three or four. Basting the turkey nauseated him. He remembered only now how much he disliked turkey. Once, when he was in high school, he'd gotten drunk on cheap whiskey the night before Thanksgiving and became throwing-up ill at dinner the next day at the first taste of turkey skin. He hadn't been able to eat turkey since that time without feeling ill. He imagined he could force down some white meat just to be polite.

"Sunny side or over easy?" Ira wanted to know, cracking open an egg one-handed into the bacon grease.

"Over easy." Scanlon was sweating from the oven heat. Tears were in his eyes. He chugged beer to settle down his queasy turkey stomach.

What would Stambaugh make of this scene? Scanlon pictured his family down on the island gathered on the sprawling front lawn of their mansion to have their photograph taken; they'd be the kind of family that would have it printed up for Christmas cards.

Stambaugh, a sweater tied at his neck, would be tossing a football to one of his younger brothers. There were bound to be younger brothers, and a sister in prep school.

He hadn't spoken to Stambaugh since the day he and his college roommate ganged up on him in Stambaugh's apartment. Even if Stambaugh had repeated his invitation for the weekend, Scanlon was almost sure he would have told him what he could do with his precious island.

In the other room, he could hear the Goodwin boys arguing over a TV program. Althea had warned him that Donny would be asking to be taken bowling after dinner. Althea had the mistaken idea that Scanlon didn't want to take the kid bowling, when in fact he actually looked forward to it. Procrastination rather than aversion was the reason he hadn't followed through on his promise to take Donny again after the first time back in September. She didn't want Donny to be a nuisance to anybody. Althea may have had her sluttish ways, but she wasn't completely insensitive. Willie, on the other hand, Scanlon wasn't so sure about. Willie seemed always to be watching, filing information away in secret places in his mind for future reference. There was no doubt more to Willie Goodwin than met the eye. The nature of it was out of Scanlon's and, apparently, Althea's reach.

This morning, Willie and Althea's reconciliation seemed anything but on firm ground. Sitting there at the kitchen table, swilling beer after beer, on his face an expression Scanlon couldn't decide was bitterness or amusement, Willie Goodwin's wheels were turning. He knew something. What?

"Give us a poon tang report, Johnny," Willie said. "Them Fairfield girls treatin' you right?" Scanlon winked for lack of a comeback and lifted his beer bottle to his lips, marveling at Willie's knack for smelling prurience in the air.

Eggs sizzled in Ira's fry pan. Jeanette changed chairs with her husband so she could be next to her mother, to jabber at her in French. Mrs. Royer, trance-like, nodded from time to time, but had little to say herself. Rudy pestered Ira at the stove, trying to interest him in what he faced at Peck's Hardware store where he clerked. Alice finished with the carrots and was now on the attack against the butternut squash, using a potato masher to pulverize it into submission. Althea, now that Ira was busy, turned her attention to Scanlon.

"How's school, Johnny?" Her eyes were booze watery and full of sadness. She had on more makeup than Scanlon was used to seeing on her and the fact that it was early in the morning made him wonder what was up. The truce she had with Willie, it was obvious to see, was uneasy. Was the garish makeup job a disguise for her wounded pride?

"It's nice to have a few days off. Teaching's harder work than most people think." Althea blinked sympathetically. He glanced at Willie to see his reaction to this lament of the hard-working schoolteacher. Willie's grin remained enigmatic. Althea was good and drunk. Scanlon was beginning to wish he was, too. "How're the kids?" he asked.

"Donny's gonna want you to take him bowling," she repeated. "You don't have to."

"I want to, Althea."

"I hear that you-, you-, you," Rudy started to say to Scanlon.

"Spit it out before you choke on it," Willie said, winking at Scanlon.

"Eggs over easy," Ira announced. "English muffins'll be up in a jiffy. Let's have your plate."

Scanlon went to the hutch for a plate and accepted Ira's eggs and bacon. His uncle didn't look him in the eye. Scanlon sat down and didn't look up until he had cleaned his plate. Another beer was waiting for him, courtesy of Willie. Althea had slipped into the chair next to her husband.

What had Rudy heard? There were too many people in the kitchen today to suit Scanlon. It wasn't uncommon to have such a gathering. On Sunday mornings there would often be this many people, sometimes more, gathered in the tiny kitchen to gossip and drink beer. Today, Scanlon felt smothered. Mrs. Royer, sphinx-like, listened and nodded as the tireless Jeanette delivered her litany in that abrasive French-Canadian accent. His head began to ache; the room pulsed in and out of focus. He thought he was going to be sick. He belched and swigged some beer to kill the nausea and the aftertaste of eggs.

Ira stood at the stove, spatula in hand, and asked if anyone wanted seconds. Scanlon caught him winking at Althea, but so did Willie. Ira wasn't trying to hide anything. What bothered Scanlon was Ira's remoteness from him. He would have expected that his uncle would close ranks with his own nephew against the Royer "clan." He complained often enough how overwhelmed he felt by them. And Ira's outrageous flirting with Althea bothered him in a way he couldn't explain. If there was really anything going on between them, they probably wouldn't be so blatant about it. Unless all this openness was a smoke screen to lull everybody into believing that it was all good-natured fun, when in fact they were screwing each other blind in private. If this was Althea's idea of revenge, she was wasting her time because Willie Goodwin couldn't have cared less what his wife did, and with whom, in private or public. And Scanlon doubted that Althea would do anything herself that might hurt her sister. For his part, if Ira strayed from his marriage vows from time to time, he had enough sense not to do it under Alice's nose, and certainly not with her sister. It was all too bizarre, too improbable. Despite the common sense of it, Scanlon had doubts. Today he felt like a stranger among these people, including his uncle.

"When we gonna eat?" Donny wanted to know as he came into the kitchen tugging at his crotch. "Smells purty good in here," he added in his imitation of cowboy talk. Althea had gotten the kids to agree to haircuts for Thanksgiving and the barber had gone amuck with his clippers on poor Donny's head, leaving divots on both sides and one beauty in the back. All the Goodwin boys, except for Billy, who was involved with a girl, were made to wear the crew cut. Scanlon remembered with chagrin the crew cut he'd had to endure in boot camp that made his ears look so enormous and out of proportion to the rest of his head. He lived in fear the whole ten weeks that his hair wouldn't grow back by the time he'd have to go home on leave.

Donny made a face when Alice told him that turnips were among the vegetables cooking for dinner. She promised him in a whisper that he wouldn't have to eat them, even if his mother put up a fuss, as they both knew she would.

"What else we havin', Alice?" Donny loved to eat, but not as much as he loved to bowl.

"Well, there's mashed potatoes and gravy. And there's cranberry sauce, and two kinds of squash, and carrots, and sweet potatoes because your father likes them, and peas and onions and dessert." Alice said dessert with special emphasis. "Plenty to stuff that face with." She had a soft place in her heart for the slow-on-the-draw Donny, as did Ira, though Ira showed favoritism to Davey because the kid shared his passion for fishing.

"What's for dessert, Alice? Mince pie, I hope. That's my favorite." Donny glanced over at Scanlon and shot him a sly, conspiratorial grin. "We still goin' bowlin' after dinner, Johnny?"

"Sure thing, pal," Scanlon said.

"Will you for Christ sakes stop pestering Johnny," Althea said.

Donny helped Scanlon put in extra leaves for the dining room table, and even managed to get himself seated next to Scanlon. Ira, the only adult besides Mrs. Royer who'd had nothing alcoholic to drink, carved the turkey and served everyone who wanted it a little white meat. The kids argued over drumsticks, and to Donny's credit, he deferred to his younger brother, Eddie. The promise of an afternoon of bowling had got him more agreeable than usual. For his part, Scanlon worried how he was going to pay for all this bowling.

With Mrs. Royer, a strict Catholic, present, Scanlon was surprised that Ira didn't go through the pretense of saying grace. Alice had to practically drag Ira, a convert as Scanlon had once been, out of the house to mass on Christmas Eve and Easter. Mrs. Royer attended six o'clock mass faithfully every Sunday, and was reputed never to have missed a service on important holidays. Althea hadn't attended services since she'd been married to Willie Goodwin, but Jeanette and Rudy were regulars. Since the Church of Our Lady of Fatima burned down two years ago, they had to attend mass at St. Patrick's and put up with Father McMahon and all his Irishness. Scanlon found himself, to his surprise, disappointed that grace had not been said. Mrs. Royer, flanked by Althea and Jeanette, seemed not to notice the omission. She listened patiently to Jeanette's incessant chatter, without much change in expression, and she proved to have a robust appetite, unlike her daughters who picked at the food on their plates. If it was to the Lord she was thankful for her bounty, she would apparently see to the proper expression of thanks in private. Willie was a self-proclaimed "Home Baptist," and since Althea had abandoned the practice of attending mass, the children had been raised with no particular religious inclination. They were Catholics in name only, and this condition couldn't have pleased Mrs. Royer. It was hard to know if her manner toward Althea was deliberately cool, Mrs. Royer was so undemonstrative.

"Yes sir," Donny said, loudly enough for everyone at the table to hear him, "I could bowl six strings, no problem." Scanlon wondered how much six strings of bowling would cost him. He had about nine dollars to his name.

"Would you just stop it, Donny, with the goddamn bowling," his mother said, giving him a bleary-eyed look of reproach.

"When I get done here," Scanlon said, surveying the table laden with bowls heaped high with steaming food, "I may not be good for two strings." Donny's jaw fell.

"Might as well not even go if we're only gonna bowl two strings." Althea cocked her head and gave him one of her if-you-don't-stop-right-now-you're-going-to-get-it looks. But Donny only pouted, and his lower lip began to quiver.

"And if you don't eat them goddamn turnips there won't be no bowling at all for you, mister," Althea threatened.

"Will you the Christ get off his back," Willie said. "He don't like turnips no better'n I do."

"Can we not have any arguing on Thanksgiving?" Alice said quietly. "I told Donny already, he don't have to eat the turnips if he don't want to."

"What about me?" little Eddie demanded in the name of justice and fair play.

"Yeah, and me," Davey piped in.

"No," Alice said in mock exasperation, "nobody has to eat turnips if they don't want to, but you don't know what you're missing." Mrs. Royer said something in French to Alice to which Alice replied no. Scanlon had given up trying to pick up French words spoken by members of the Royer clan.

"Don't worry, pal," Scanlon said, scrubbing Donny's hair stubble with his knuckles, "we'll get in six strings if you have to bowl mine, too." Maybe he could get away with letting the kid bowl by himself.

"Hurray!" Donny shouted, and in his exuberance sent a forkful of gravy sodden mashed potatoes toward the ceiling. Donny's brothers cheered and everybody laughed except Althea who glowered at him. But Donny was too pleased with himself to have his spirits dampened by any dirty look his mother could serve up. Everyone was laughing and happy because of what he had done.

Scanlon declined at first, then gave in to Alice's offer of pumpkin pie with whipped cream. He was already so full he was afraid everyone could hear his belly gurgling. He was even too stuffed to drink the beer Willie brought him from the kitchen.

"We goin' bowlin' now?" Donny wanted to know.

"In't that cute," Althea said to Alice without sarcasm, "Donny and Johnny goin' bowling."

"If I can fit my gut behind the wheel," Scanlon said.

"Take mine, you want to," Willie offered. Willie drove a big '60 Chrysler.

"Thanks just the same, but I wouldn't trust myself in the snow with your big rear end."

"Talkin' of big rear ends," Willie said, goosing Althea as she cleared away dishes. Althea didn't even jump.

"Keep your hands to home, you bastard," she said, wearily.

"Not room enough on your big ass for Ira's and mine, too?"

"Go and fuck yourself." Althea, Jeanette, and Alice saw to clearing the table. Mrs. Royer sat on the sofa in the living room and looked at TV. Ira took Wednesday's newspaper with him into the bathroom; Rudy joined Mrs. Royer in the living room. Scanlon was grateful and relieved that Eddie and Davey hadn't asked to be taken bowling, too. And he was gloomy again about what might be going on between Althea and Ira. He went upstairs to get his coat and to check on his money. He had eight, not nine dollars, as he thought he had. Donny might have to bowl by himself after all. He could beg off, claim he was too stuffed from dinner.

In the kitchen, as Scanlon struggled into his overcoat, Willie Goodwin pushed a ten dollar bill in his pocket.

"No need for you to pay for the kid's bowling." Scanlon protested feebly.
"Take it. Jesus Christ," Willie said.

"I really don't mind taking him, Willie."

"Good. Then you shouldn't mind me paying for it."

"Jesus, Willie."

"Don't argue, goddamn it," Willie said with a wink, as if he knew how strapped Scanlon was for money. He should have forced Willie's ten dollars back at him but he did no such thing.

As Scanlon and the hyperactive Donny Goodwin went out into the gray, late afternoon, colder than any Thanksgiving day in his memory, he fingered the smooth ten-spot in his coat pocket feeling the way he did as a kid after he'd swiped junk off the counters of the five-and-dime. He sighed, wondering if he'd ever grow up.

Chapter Eighteen

"I was disappointed that you didn't make it down for the weekend," Stambaugh said, blowing into his coffee cup. Scanlon was surprised to find him in the teachers' lounge where he had never seen Stambaugh before.

"What are you talking about?" Scanlon drew hot water from the aluminum urn for his own coffee.

"I half expected to see you down at the Vineyard last weekend. You do remember that I invited you?"

"I couldn't have made it if I'd wanted to. What was the other half expecting?"

"I don't understand. You've gone out of your way to avoid me ever since that day with Stewart. Would you mind telling me what's wrong?"

"You're supposed to be a bright guy, Douglas. You figure it out. And don't get the idea I've gone out of my way to avoid you. I'd spend that kind of energy on your account?"

Cynthia Sinclair burst into the room, characteristically upbeat, ready to seize the day though it was not yet 8:00 A.M.

"Good morning, gentlemen. How are we this fine morning?"

"Good morning, Cynthia," Stambaugh said. Scanlon grunted, turning his back on her.

"What are we so grumpy about this morning, Mr. Scanlon? Too much turkey, I'll wager. If I had a single morsel more I swear I'd start to gobble." Cynthia released one of her high-pitched laughs. Scanlon closed his eyes, working hard not to say something rude. "Did you have a nice time down on that marvelous island, Doug?" Cynthia asked. "I haven't been to the Vineyard since college. I won't tell you how long ago that was. Did you go down to visit Doug, Jack?"

"No," Scanlon said, turning to look at Stambaugh who was staring at the floor.

"Oh, dear. Why on earth not? I certainly wouldn't have passed up an offer like that."

"I had other things to do," Scanlon said, his eye on Stambaugh. Cynthia blathered on about her own Thanksgiving spent with her widowed mother in Burlington. Who else had Stambaugh told about inviting him to the island for the weekend? Why hadn't he offered again after the way he and his friend had treated him in Stambaugh's apartment? He couldn't be so obtuse as to miss the fact that Scanlon's feelings had been bruised.

The bell rang for homeroom. Stambaugh hurried out the door before Scanlon could say anything to him. Cynthia, blithely ignorant of the tension between the two men, asked Scanlon if he would help her organize the Christmas Pageant. She'd been doing it all by herself for the past twelve years and it was time she had some help.

"I can't think of anything I'd rather do less," Scanlon said, and left Cynthia standing in the teachers' lounge with her bright red lipsticked mouth agape. He got no farther than the stairs before he regretted it, but when he went back to apologize she was gone.

Later that morning, he stopped by Cynthia's classroom and waited for her to finish erasing the blackboard.

"I don't know what got into me this morning, Cynthia. Can you ever forgive me? It had to have been the devil's work." Scanlon tried for his sheepish grin.

"You're forgiven only if you'll agree to help with the pageant."

"All right, but I can't imagine how I could be any help."

"Trust me, Mr. Scanlon. I'll find a way." Cynthia had on the white blouse with ruffled front, and plaid skirt cinched at the waist by the wide, black patent leather belt that she'd worn to Winship's party in September. To picture Cynthia in a sexual act was beyond his imagination.

"How did you hear about Doug inviting me down to Martha's Vineyard?"

"Oh, heavens, I can't remember exactly. Just came up in conversation I would imagine. Douglas is such a nice boy, don't you think? A little too serious sometimes, but such a gentleman."

"Yeah."

"I should have the both of you over for drinks before things get so busy I don't have time to think. We don't socialize nearly enough. It's really a shame."

"That would be nice. Well, got to brace myself for bio class. Thanks for understanding about this morning."

"Oh, good grief, think nothing of it," Cynthia said, waving him off. "Go dissect your frogs."

Stambaugh waited for him outside Scanlon's classroom at the end of school. He clutched books against his chest and had on his earnest face. Scanlon fussed with his keys longer than he needed to. Ever since Winship had spoken to him about locking up after himself, Scanlon had been vigilant.

"What can I do for you, Douglas?" Scanlon said, face to the door.

"You could stop being childish for starters."

Scanlon wheeled around to face Stambaugh. "Where do you get off talking to me like that?"

"I was under the impression we were friends."

"Yeah? What gave you that impression?" Scanlon brushed by Stambaugh, and walked toward the south stairs. By the time he reached the first landing Stambaugh was beside him.

"I don't know what I did to offend you, Jack, and I won't know unless you tell me. Why don't you come over for a beer? If you're determined to end our friendship, I think I at least deserve an explanation."

"An explanation," Scanlon sputtered, at a loss for anything further to say. All he could do was stare fiercely at Stambaugh who held his stare, pain and determination in his eyes. Scanlon felt himself yielding, the way he always yielded whenever he confronted obstinacy that matched his own. "You and your asshole friend, Stewart what's-his-name. You were about as ... I don't know." Scanlon dropped his eyes and sighed heavily.

"I'm really sorry, Jack. It's funny, Stewart thought you were the one being aggressive. I can understand why you two didn't hit it off, but you left so abruptly I thought there may have been something else." Stambaugh stopped and shook his head.

"Didn't hit it off," Scanlon laughed, "that's the understatement of the day."

"It's because of what I said about your inferiority complex, isn't it?" Stambaugh said, nodding his head as if to say, of course, what else could it be? "Still, I'm surprised you didn't take to Stewart. He was very popular at school."

"The guy's a dink. He treated you like his valet. What, did you clean his room in college?" Stambaugh's mouth opened, as though he'd had the wind knocked out of him.

"We were best friends. We're still good friends."

"Hah! With friends like that ... I felt like you guys had some kind of inside joke going and you had me up to be the butt of it, if you're interested in how I felt. How's that?"

"I don't know what to say, Jack. You don't think I could have done anything like that, do you?" Nobody could look injured in quite the way Stambaugh could. He couldn't have displayed more visible pain or incredulity if his mother told him she didn't love him and never had.

"Jesus, mercy, Doug. It's not that big a deal. I was out of sorts from a run-in with Winship. It was all my fault. Forget it." Stambaugh stared at the floor, shaking his head. "Come on. Snap out of it." Scanlon punched Stambaugh's shoulder lightly. "Let's go get that beer."

"I had no idea you felt this way, Jack. Honestly." Stambaugh's suffering brown eyes seemed on the verge of tears.

Scanlon looked over his host's record albums while Stambaugh opened two bottles of German beer for them.

"The Mamas and the Papas?" Scanlon said. "Are you serious? Jesus." Stambaugh's taste ran from psychedelic ("Ultimate Spinach" and "Strawberry Alarm Clock" were the actual names of musical groups, groups Scanlon had never heard of) to baroque (many Telemann, Vivaldi, and Bach).

"You like the fucking Mamas and Papas?" Scanlon said as he was handed a foil-necked bottle of beer. He thought German beer was overrated, but he'd never admit this to Stambaugh who brought out his Austrian stein for the occasion.

"They're honest."

"You need counseling, Doug." Scanlon sat down on the big sofa and allowed himself to sink into the hydraulic cushion. Stambaugh flipped through his albums.

"What would you like to hear, Jack? How about some nice Mamas and the Papas? What classical do you like?"

"You got Bartok?"

"No. Reminds me too much of modern jazz." Stambaugh smiled. "How about Berlioz?"

"Why don't you put on some string quartet stuff. Something quiet." Scanlon wasn't in the mood for cultural game playing.

"Brahms all right, since I'm in the B's?"

"Sure." Leave it to Stambaugh to have his albums alphabetized. That was another essential difference between them—aside from the obvious inherited ones—Stambaugh led an orderly life; Scanlon's was chaotic.

"Were you able to get away at all during break?" Stambaugh asked, sitting in his upholstered rocking chair.

"Not unless you count sleeping fourteen hours a day getting away. I used the waking hours to get caught up on paperwork. I feel like a new man."

"Until the next surf comes in. You ought to try reading a hundred history term papers sometime. I won't miss that part of teaching."

"So what's it going to be? The army or Canada?"

"I think Canada." Stambaugh lowered his eyes; his face looked troubled. Scanlon wished he hadn't been so flippant.

"So you've made a decision. When will you go?"

"I'll finish the school year. I expect I'll have to make my move as soon as school ends, though." Stambaugh smiled bravely.

"You really intend to go through with this?" Scanlon asked, as if it were only now that he understood that Stambaugh meant business.

"You doubted me?"

"Have you thought this all the way through? Do you understand what this means?"

"Yes, Jack. I've thought about little else this year."

"Christ," Scanlon said, peeling a strip of label off his bottle.

"You think I've made the wrong decision. I know."

"I don't know. As I told you before, I'm ambivalent. I don't know what's scarier, facing dying in combat or living life in exile. Anyway, Canada's too freaking cold for my blood." Scanlon chugged half the bottle and wiped his mouth with the back of his hand. Stambaugh looked abstractedly at his shoe. Brahms added to the solemnity.

"Change to some of that psychedelic shit if you want to, Douglas. I'd like to hear what a band that calls itself "Ultimate Spinach" sounds like. We could both use cheering up."

Stambaugh put on a record that was pure gibberish to Scanlon's ear but which he claimed to like just to be polite.

"What about your C.O. petition?" Scanlon asked.

"I don't remember telling you I applied. How did you know?"

"You told me, remember? That night in the Groveton House." Scanlon remembered too late that he'd heard about it from Winship. He didn't think this was the time to bring it up, given Stambaugh's state of mind.

"I couldn't have. I hadn't filed yet. Winship must have told you. He's the only one who knew, except for Stewart."

"So maybe it was Winship. What difference does it make?"

"It just seems odd, given your relationship with him, that he'd be sharing confidential information with you."

"All right, all right. Let me explain." Scanlon recounted his conversation with the principal.

"Well, that would explain your frame of mind the day you met Stewart," Stambaugh said, his eyes narrowing.

"I came over here intending to tell you all about it but ... well, you know how it turned out. I owe you for clueing me on that turd, Sorenson, though. You were right. Nothing came of it. And I don't think anything's going to come of this other deal, either. You know Winship, all fucking talk and no action."

Stambaugh laughed. "If he thinks I'm using my classroom as a forum for radical politics wait until he finds out that I've invited some SDS kids from Clifton to speak to my classes," Stambaugh said with as much irony as Scanlon had ever heard from him. Clifton was the little college nearby, a haven for the radical left, hippies and other assorted freaks of nature.

"When is all this supposed to happen?"

"Soon. Very soon." Stambaugh's lip curled in a sardonic smile.

"Can't wait." Scanlon drained his beer, hoping Stambaugh wouldn't be so characteristically slow in offering a refill.

"Even if Daryl doesn't raise a stink, the kids will probably stone them." Stambaugh produced another mirthless laugh. "If only he knew how resistant to new ideas these kids really are, he wouldn't lose a wink over me, or SDS, or the international Communist Party. Nothing can budge these kids. If Joe McCarthy were running for president he'd win Fairfield by a landslide."

"Aren't you exaggerating a little there? What about Scott Pettingill? Samantha Burnham? They strike you as right-wingers?"

"There are maybe a handful in the whole school. It's frightening when you stop to think about it. The youth of America is mobilizing to bring down the established order and here I am stuck in the nineteenth century. These kids would have been right at home with the Republicans in Miami last summer. It's enough to make you vomit."

"I don't think they're as bad as all that. They don't know what they believe in yet. What do you expect? They're isolated up here; they spout their parents' beliefs. They'll change when they hit college." Scanlon felt hypocritical commenting on the ill-formed beliefs of Fairfield High kids when he wasn't sure himself what he believed in. Doug Stambaugh had no such doubts.

"Sure. How many do you think will end up in college? Ten percent? What about the rest of them?"

"Don't despair, my friend, don't despair. You got another brew in your Lilliputian refrigerator?" Scanlon got up from the sofa.

"No. This is the last of it. Take the rest of mine. I don't care for beer anyway."

"Has Stewart decided to flee, too?"

"He's going to Stockholm over Christmas break to visit friends. I wouldn't be surprised if he didn't return."

"It's one thing to run out on your country but to break a teaching contract. That's what I'd call moral turpitude." Scanlon sat back down with the rest of Stambaugh's beer.

"You're not serious." Stambaugh said, looking uncertain.

"What do you think?"

"Sometimes with you I can't be sure." Stambaugh got up to change the record. "What would you like now?"

"How about some Dylan? You must have everything he recorded, right? I wonder if he was ever drafted. You think he'd go fight in the jungle, Doug?"

"I don't know. I can't imagine him being asked to go into combat in the first place. He'd be too valuable to them as an entertainer."

"You're probably right, though I can't imagine the rednecks fighting in Nam would have much interest in a guy who writes songs like "Masters of War." Tell me the truth. Isn't there a part of you that's dying—forgive the phrase—to know what it's like?"

"Not even a small part of me."

"When I was a kid, my best friend's brother was killed on Pork Chop hill. That's in Korea, Doug. He was seventeen; went into the Army when he was sixteen. His old man swore to the recruiters he was seventeen. Another friend of mine lost his kid in Vietnam. I don't know where, exactly. Someplace out in the jungle. His kid was seventeen, too. Seventeen must be a bad age for soldiers."

"The government would love to have a whole army of seventeen-year-olds. They have no fear of death." Stambaugh was dead earnest, as usual.

"I feared the hell out of death when I was seventeen, and I wasn't close to any threat of it. I went into the peacetime Navy when I turned eighteen. Sometimes I feel guilty as hell because I sleazed by between wars. Not that guilty." Scanlon laughed. "I wonder how many Fairfield kids will buy it in Nam?"

"I've heard plenty of them claim that they can't wait to go."

"Is that why you've been bad-mouthing the war in your classes?"

"Is there anything wrong with expressing an opinion?"

"I guess not, as long as you make the distinction between opinion and whatever to your students. Of course, history, beyond so-called objective facts, is just somebody's opinion anyway, right?"

"Some opinions are better than others, Jack."

"You think Winship would give a fuck if you were gung-ho for the war in your classes?"

"I doubt that his passion for objectivity would be so ardent," Stambaugh said, indulging in a rare expression of sarcasm.

"We'll see how deep his passions run when your SDS buddies appear." Stambaugh was slipping into a funk by the looks of him. "How are you going to join the overthrow of the establishment if you're freezing your ass off in Canada?"

"I wouldn't have any more of an opportunity in Vietnam."

Scanlon had little sympathy or understanding for Stambaugh's eagerness to become part of the subculture dedicated to social revolution. Then, maybe he'd been relegated to a subculture all his life without knowing it. Stambaugh's subculture, unlike Scanlon's, had a political identity and political ambitions.

"There's no other way? You can't join an anti-war movement or something? Go to jail if you have to?"

"How long do you think draft evaders last in jail?"

Scanlon had no answer. "I don't suppose your family has any influence in Washington." Stambaugh frowned, as if the implied question were absurd. "What? Some people do have influential families in Washington," Scanlon added. "The question's not that off-the-wall, is it?"

"I come from a middle-class family. We have no influence in Washington or anywhere else."

"I wasn't aware that your average, middle-class family owned property on Martha's Vineyard," Scanlon said. Stambaugh just looked puzzled again. "But what the fuck do I know?"

"You're doing it again, Jack."

"Doing what?"

"Your inferiority routine."

"I'm trying to help. Fuck you, if you don't want my help."

Stambaugh sighed. "I know you're trying to help. I appreciate it, even if I don't sound as though I do." Stambaugh's voice had taken on a flatness, a resignation. Scanlon felt like a jerk for acting hypersensitive, like one of the girls he taught instead of the man of the world he liked to fancy himself at times.

"I tell you, Doug, and I'm not just blowing smoke. I don't honestly think I'd have the guts to run. I mean it."

"Thank you for saying that. I've had my share of doubts about my motives. Maybe you've been right all along; maybe I am coward. When you said it that time, I couldn't think about anything else for days."

"I was trying to jerk you off. I didn't really mean it. Trust me. I don't think you're a coward and never thought so for a minute. Maybe just for one minute." Scanlon meant to inject levity into what was becoming a serious interchange between them; he was in no mood for serious conversation.

"Tell me about Vietnam," Stambaugh said.

"What can I tell you? I was four days in Saigon in 1960. Who'd ever heard of the place in 1960? This war we hear about on the news is taking place somewhere I've never heard of. I've been there in time and space only. You know as much as I do."

"Tell me anyway," Stambaugh said in that flat voice. "Humor me."

"It's been eight years. I don't remember anything worth telling."

"Try."

"I'd need more to drink, and you're all out." Scanlon put a point on his argument by draining the rest of his beer.

"I've got something else, I think. Some sherry. Can you drink that?" Stambaugh went to the kitchen and came back with an almost full bottle of Duff and Gordon dry sherry and a small water glass. "Here," he said, pouring sherry to the brim.

"All right," Scanlon took the glass from Stambaugh, careful not to spill. He sipped the top off the sherry, leaned back and sighed. "You're not going to find anything I tell you useful."

"I'll decide that for myself. Now tell me all about your four days in Saigon." Stambaugh leaned back in his rocker, both arms out straight on the wooden arms, and closed his eyes.

"I wonder what Saigon looks like now, after the Tet show?" Scanlon said after he'd described to Stambaugh his four-day sojourn in the city.

"Don't expect me to send you postcards from Saigon, Jack," Stambaugh said, smiling without showing his teeth, his eyes still closed.

"My little tale hasn't persuaded you to turn over and take up arms against the little yellow people?"

"Not really."

"You're not impressed with the domino theory of Communist expansion in the Far East?"

"Not impressed in the least."

"What will you do in Canada, Doug?"

"I haven't any idea."

"You'll send me a postcard from Canada, won't you?"

"Of course."

Chapter Nineteen

"I almost collided with Bambi and her family," Scanlon said to Rachel Patterson who had greeted him at the kitchen door. Inside, the kitchen was fragrant with something bubbling in a red casserole pan on the old-fashioned black stove.

"Deer cross the road at night all the time," Rachel said, helping him off with his coat, "and Bambi's a him, not a her. You have to be careful after dark."

"I was practically on top of them. You must have heard my brakes."

"Come on in the other room. Doug's in there."

"I didn't see his car."

"He came over with Josh after school. Maybe you'll be a dear and take him home." Rachel had on a denim mini-skirt and white ski sweater; her hair was shorter than he remembered it. Rachel found a way to speak to him without meeting his eyes, but he wasn't sure if she were doing this on purpose.

"Be glad to." Scanlon wondered if Rachel was punning "dear" with him.

Stambaugh and Josh Patterson were in the study, where an inferno raged in the fireplace, sending out a wall of breath-sucking heat, and making shadows on the walls of the darkened room. Stambaugh had on a blue blazer over a tattersal shirt; Patterson wore a heavy ski sweater that looked handknit. Wearing his synthetic, marked down V-neck sweater, Scanlon felt already at a disadvantage. Patterson's big rolltop desk—the one he claimed to have pulled out of the dump—lay open, cluttered with school papers folded lengthwise. Scanlon's heart lurched at the sight of them. Neither Stambaugh nor Patterson appeared to be drinking.

"Josh, why don't you see what people want to drink. I'll get cheese and crackers," Rachel said, and left the men alone.

"Good to see you, Jack," Patterson said, extending his hand, as if he hadn't seen Scanlon in a long time instead of maybe three hours.

"Nice to be seen," Scanlon replied. Patterson chuckled politely. Scanlon wondered if Stambaugh had unburdened himself to Patterson in the hours they'd spent together.

"You're a bourbon man if I remember correctly," Patterson said. His scalp was pink in the part of his thin blond hair, his nose and cheeks red, as if sunburned.

"Right. I'm impressed."

Patterson left to make drinks, and Scanlon was alone in the room with Stambaugh, the stifling fireplace heat, and the eerie flickering shadows. Stambaugh hadn't spoken a word since Scanlon's arrival.

"That's some fire," Scanlon said, sitting on a Victorian sofa with burgundy velvet upholstery that looked like it could have been at home in a New Orleans brothel. He didn't remember it from the last time he visited. It was at least out of the path of the direct heat. Stambaugh remained close to the fireplace, blue blazer and all. "Be careful, Douglas, you could spontaneously combust." Stambaugh flashed an enigmatic smile. Scanlon studied the wide painted floorboards between his feet, waiting for something else to occur to him to say.

Patterson returned with drinks. There was nothing for Stambaugh who was in the habit of being abstemious. He continued in his prolonged silence as well. Rachel followed closely behind her husband with a plate of cheddar cheese and crackers. Patterson and his wife drank white wine, Scanlon bourbon on the rocks.

"Oh, Josh," Rachel said, hugging herself, "that's a delicious fire." Scanlon felt sweat trickle down his sides.

"Can't beat elm for heat output," Patterson said, looking at his conflagration with pride. Scanlon got to his feet when he saw that it was plain nobody intended to sit down. Rachel offered him the plate of cheese and crackers.

"Never cut good bourbon," he said, taking a line from Joe E. Lewis. He tried without success to engage her eyes, but she had turned to offer snacks to Stambaugh and her husband. While Stambaugh and Patterson chewed on cheese and crackers, Scanlon sipped iced bourbon. Too soon he emptied his glass; Rachel hadn't touched her wine and Josh had taken perhaps one or two little sips. Here we go again, Scanlon thought.

"Heard the new Stones album?" Patterson asked Scanlon.

“I doubt it.” What he knew of the Rolling Stones, or any other rock and roll group, came from what he heard inadvertently on the radio, and since he'd been in Vermont, not even that.

“Let's wait until after dinner for that,” Rachel said, giving her husband a private look.

“OK,” said the amiable Josh Patterson. Still not a peep from Stambaugh.

“We'll be sitting down to dinner soon,” Rachel announced to the room with somewhat less exuberance than Scanlon was used to hearing from her. Scanlon excused himself to use the bathroom but really to escape the dry, oppressive heat of the fire and to pour himself a quick swallow of whiskey from the bottle Patterson had graciously left on the counter by the kitchen sink. Rachel had the tavern table set for dinner: pewter dinner plates with matching wine goblets, heavy silverware with long-tined forks, cloth napkins and heavy-looking pewter candle holders.

Everyone fell silent when Scanlon returned to the study, or so it seemed to him. Patterson scolded him for not helping himself to another drink. Scanlon claimed not to have seen the bottle and to not be the type who snooped around in his host's cupboards.

“It's over by the sink. Go on, help yourself. We have a little time before we eat, don't we, Rache?” Patterson said.

“Twist my arm,” Scanlon said and went back to the kitchen for a refill.

Then they were sitting down to Rachel's pungent Coq Au Vin, and Stambaugh had still not uttered more than a few words in Scanlon's presence. Patterson carried dinner conversation practically by himself, acting as if nothing were out of the ordinary, content to let Stambaugh eat in silence. After his third goblet of burgundy, Scanlon had had enough of Stambaugh's melancholy. “What's bothering you tonight, Doug?” he asked, catching the Pattersons in an exchange of meaningful glances. If he'd committed a breach of decorum, he didn't care. They knew what they could do with their decorum.

Stambaugh sighed. “Bad news from my draft board. They've refused to reclassify me. I have ten days to request a hearing.” Stambaugh stared woefully at the food on his plate. That was it? Couldn't he have said this earlier? Scanlon was baffled.

“Jack had a close call with some deer on the road tonight, didn't you, Jack,” Rachel interjected, this time making sure to make eye contact with him. Scanlon had drunk enough not to be intimidated by mere good manners. Stambaugh was *in extremis*. What harm was there in having it out in the open? He held Rachel's gaze. Patterson was at his shoulder with more burgundy.

"I'm aware of Doug's situation with his draft board, if you're worried about that," Scanlon said, hearing the slur in his words, his tongue sliding over them like slippery rocks. The Pattersons looked at each other again, worry in their eyes.

"It's true," Stambaugh said, "Jack knows the whole story." Scanlon was momentarily jealous of the fact that Stambaugh had confided in the Pattersons without informing him. Then neither had he said anything to the Pattersons about Scanlon's part in the drama.

"Well," Rachel said, idly stirring the contents of the casserole dish with the serving spoon, "I think we shouldn't talk about anything unpleasant this evening." She had one eyebrow raised, and it had the effect of destroying the symmetry on which, at least in Scanlon's eye, her beauty was founded.

"You're right," Scanlon said, "let's not jeopardize this polite evening with talk about real life."

"Jack," Patterson said in a low voice, eyes on his plate. Rachel let the serving spoon drop and smack against the side of the casserole. She gave Scanlon her profile; he could see her jaw working. Stambaugh moved his lips and shook his head slightly.

"Please. This is all my fault," Stambaugh said in his quiet voice.

"Bullshit, Doug," Scanlon said, throwing his napkin on his plate, not caring if the Pattersons wrote him off as a vulgarian.

"Jack," Patterson repeated, a little louder. Rachel squared her shoulders, put on her haughty expression, as she assessed Scanlon.

"So I'm a little smashed," Scanlon said before Rachel could comment on how much he'd had to drink. "It wouldn't hurt you people to loosen up a little yourselves."

"I think we're about ready for dessert," Rachel said, getting up. She busied herself removing dinner plates from the table while the men sat in awkward, eyes-averted silence.

"What's the problem here, Rachel?" Scanlon said as Rachel brought a bowl of white grapes, sour cream and brown sugar to the table.

"I just think it's important to keep a social evening pleasant," Rachel said, having got control of her pique. "There's a time and place for discussions about real life, as you call it." Scanlon couldn't help himself now.

"Yeah. Doug looks in the mood for an evening of social pleasantries."

"Please, Jack. It's all right. I'm really sorry," Stambaugh said.

Rachel began to serve dessert. Without thinking, Scanlon lit a cigarette, earning a look of distaste from Rachel. What did he ever see in her? He looked for a place to butt his cigarette. He got up and extinguished it under the water faucet. Rachel had removed the burgundy from the table and Scanlon knew that there would be no more to drink this evening and that he'd end up in the Groveton House as soon as he found an opening to excuse himself, to escape.

After dessert there was coffee but no brandy, and certainly no cigars. Stambaugh worked hard to act cheerful. Scanlon, however, made no effort to hide the way he felt. He sulked over coffee and back in Patterson's study where Josh prepared to put on the new Rolling Stones album, Scanlon brooded on the Victorian sofa. The Pattersons paid him no attention; Stambaugh was getting the hang of being cheerful, exchanging light conversation with the Pattersons while the music played at low volume on the hi-fi. Scanlon wondered what all the fuss over this new album was about if they didn't want to pay attention to it.

"So what's your draft status, Josh?" Scanlon asked, interrupting Rachel in mid-sentence. For a moment there was only the incongruous sound of Mick Jagger of the Rolling Stones invoking sympathy for the devil. Patterson, poker in hand, stood in front of the fireplace, coaxing more flame out of a dying elm log. Rachel sat cross-legged on the floor; Stambaugh faced Patterson, elbow on the mantle, one hand thrust in his jacket pocket. Scanlon found this tableau funny and began to laugh. "Shit, Josh, you look like I asked you how often you had sex with your wife, or something."

Patterson gave him his what-a-tasteless-thing-to-say look. Rachel, when she'd recovered from the remark, explained in her chilliest voice that Josh had been classified 4-F because of flat feet.

"Maybe if we put our minds to it we can get Doug's arches to fall," Scanlon said. Josh and Rachel turned away from him, as did Stambaugh who now had both hands in his pockets as he stared wretchedly into the fireplace. "So this is what you guys learned in the Ivy League? To be politely rude?"

Rachel snapped around to face him. "Well, it's obvious that wherever you went to school ..."

"You're absolutely right," Scanlon interrupted, having lost his stomach for insulting his host and hostess, "I've got the social graces of a mollusk. I'm very sorry." Scanlon felt more weary than contrite, but he convinced the Pattersons, Rachel at least. She graciously forgave him and refused any talk from him about having to leave.

"We had a long talk with Doug before you arrived," Rachel said, getting up to stand beside Stambaugh. "We care about what happens to him. It's not the way you think." Why this couldn't have been revealed two hours ago puzzled Scanlon.

Scanlon said, "I just thought we'd have a chance for a creative solution if we put our heads together. What about this hearing you have ten days to ask for?" he asked Stambaugh. Stambaugh looked at Rachel as if asking for permission to answer.

"He has ten days to submit his request in writing for a personal hearing," Rachel offered.

"What good will that do? If they turned down your written petition, what makes you think they'll have a change of heart? Doug?" Scanlon wanted to hear it out of Stambaugh's mouth.

"I'm counting on a procedural error or, better yet, improper procedure by my draft board. They have to grant me a hearing if I request it within the stipulated time period. I can take witnesses to the hearing if I want. How would you like to come and testify for me, Jack?" Stambaugh asked with an ironic laugh.

"What, you think I wouldn't want to? Or is it you think I'd be a lousy witness?"

"It's just that I know how you feel about the whole thing. I may disagree, but I respect your position."

"Rache and I will go with him," Patterson said, as if he intended to make Scanlon feel like odd man out. Rachel squeezed Stambaugh's hand.

"So you guys are pacifists, too?" Scanlon asked.

"Of course," Patterson said.

"What will you say? Won't the review board, or whatever they're called, just think of you as a couple more flakes if you come off pacifistic?"

"Jack, for crying out loud," Patterson said, exasperated.

"You could have a point, Jack," Stambaugh said, rubbing his elbow as if it were sore.

"What kinds of questions do you think they'd ask a witness?" Scanlon asked Stambaugh pointedly, meaning to exclude the Pattersons.

"Oh, I imagine they'd be pretty routine. How long have you known the objector? In what capacity? What can you offer in the way of evidence of the objector's sincerity? Have you influenced him in his position in any way? They'd probably ask about his own views on the issue. Things like that. That's why I think your point is so interesting. If someone were to appear as a witness for an objector who was not himself a pacifist, well, this could be salutary."

"I doubt having a warmonger for an advocate would be salutary, Doug," Patterson said.

"I never suggested Jack was any such thing," Stambaugh hastened to say.

"I didn't mean Jack, necessarily," Patterson said with a sly smile.

"He meant Rachel," Scanlon said.

Patterson pretended interest in the dying fire. Rachel had sat back down on the floor, put her arm around her husband's leg, and leaned against him. Scanlon had to restrain himself from saying something disparaging about marriage.

"What about you?" Scanlon asked Stambaugh. "What kinds of questions will they ask you?"

"They'll try to bait me. I'm sure of it. Try to provoke me into contradictory statements. I got a pamphlet, last time I was in Cambridge, to help me prepare for this."

"I could imagine the kinds of questions they'd ask. I know the ones I'd ask," Scanlon said.

"Why don't we role-play, then," Rachel said, excited all of a sudden. "You be the inquisitor, Jack. Josh and I will be witnesses. This could even be fun."

"I ought to be going," said Scanlon, getting up, his head beginning to ache from the hot room and all the liquor he'd drunk. "You need a lift to Fairfield, right, Doug?"

"I'll take him home, Jack," Patterson said.

"No. It's on my way." Scanlon paused and looked at Patterson. "Oh, I get it. You think I'm *non compos*. But you don't mind if I drive home by myself."

"I don't mind riding with Jack," Stambaugh said. Scanlon stood in front of Patterson, a good head shorter than his host.

"Why is it all right if I drive home in my condition but not all right to take Doug with me? Can you answer me that?"

"You're being belligerent, Jack. That wasn't my reason for offering to drive Doug back to Fairfield ..."

"Please!" Rachel said, winding her arms around her husband's waist. "Stop this silly arguing." She nestled her head in his chest and glowered at Scanlon like a petulant little girl.

"Thanks for dinner, Mrs. Patterson," Scanlon said, bowing.

"Yes, it was a wonderful dinner," Stambaugh added, moving to Rachel to give her a peck on the cheek. Scanlon hung back, apart from the three of them, in this moment so close together they could have been dancing. He was angry, and jealous.

"We'll have to do this again soon," Patterson said. Scanlon almost laughed out loud just to be rude.

Chapter Twenty

Scanlon decided to drive through Crawford Notch south, because it was a more direct route (but also more treacherous) to Garrison than through Franconia Notch. In any case, it was the farthest he would have driven his car since coming to live in Vermont, and he was so nervous about getting caught in a mountain snowstorm, he stopped to buy a six-pack of beer to keep him company and give him moral support on the trip.

No snowstorms. The roads were clear through the Notch; the sun even shined briefly. Driving his little car, six friendly beers on the seat beside him, Scanlon felt free for a change. In the canyons of the White Mountains flanking the road through Crawford Notch, he stopped several times to get out of the car and admire these great slabs of rock that rose sharply to the overcast sky. Scrubby alpine vegetation, deep snow, high altitude. He was giddy with the height, the air, the beer. He stopped at the entrance to the Notch, at a big four-story summer resort hotel, perhaps the very place his mother had worked many years ago, before the war. Perhaps the very hotel where she had met his unknown father. Conceivably the place where he was conceived. He stopped behind a snowbank to piss away the two beers he'd drunk since leaving Groveton. The air was so cold, so thin, he had to work to breathe comfortably, surrounded by those presidential range mountains. Railroad tracks wound around the base of one of these mountains; a few hundred feet above the tracks he could see a large house with weathered shingles. It had a private dwelling look about it rather than a weather or observation station. Home of a wealthy recluse? From where Scanlon stood, the house looked inaccessible.

By the time he reached North Conway, he had drunk all but one of the beers. In New Hampshire, there was more litter along the road than in Vermont. Did this mean that Vermonters were more sensitive to natural beauty than the good citizens of New Hampshire? He had been careful not to toss his empties out the window the way he used to do when he drank beer in cars back in high school. He was also alert to the way he was driving, having consumed so much beer; careful not to speed, mindful of his vision; the minute he began to see double, he resolved to pull over.

Traffic was heavy coming north, practically nonexistent southbound. A steady stream of cars bearing loaded ski racks passed him on Route 16. He'd never been tempted to take up skiing. This herding behavior he couldn't understand either. In winter they herded to the slopes, in summer to the beaches. He'd take solitude any day. He checked his rearview mirror for cops before taking a swig. He didn't mind having no radio in his car, not that radio signals could be received in these hills. Today he was at peace with his thoughts. At the base of Mt. Chocorua, outside West Ossipee, he thought of Lucy for the first time today. By the time he hit Ossipee, he was depressed.

In Milton, in a little store with a gas pump outside, overlooking Three Rivers Pond where he often came to swim as a teenager, Scanlon stopped to pick up another six-pack, his chest heavy with nostalgia and sorrow.

He pulled into the Stacys' driveway thoroughly drunk, almost rear-ending their Karman Ghia.

"Jesus. I don't believe this," George Stacy said, picking at the crotch of his dirty chinos.

"Who do you have to fuck to get invited to the party?" Scanlon said, brushing by George Stacy into the living room, carrying what was left of the six-pack he'd bought in Milton. The party Scanlon referred to was going on at full volume in the apartment across the hall.

"Fucking college girls. Moved in when school started," George said, eyeing his old friend. "What brings you back among the living?"

"You call this living?" George and Elaine Stacy lived in a big, white gingerbread, four-family apartment house on the north side of Garrison. The Stacys' apartment was in the back, added on as an afterthought, it seemed. The apartment was cozy enough, with a step-down kitchen and a nice attic that Elaine used as a workroom. There was no guest bedroom, so Scanlon would be put up on the living room sofa if the Stacys were inclined to allow him to stay the night. That was no longer a certainty.

"Hey, you're shitfaced already. What's with the hair lip?"

"Where's Elaine? She'll be tickled to see me. Here, help yourself." Scanlon handed George the carton of beer before sitting down heavily on the sofa bed with the paisley throw. He didn't take off his coat. "I'm bushed from the drive. What is it with VWs?"

"Where'd you come from?" George swung the carton at his side. He had on a sleeveless sweatshirt that showed his hairy-ape upper arms. Scanlon thought he'd lost some more hair on top, though. His friend did not look overjoyed to see him. Elaine would probably throw him out.

"Vermont. That's where I live now. You'll never guess what I'm doing."

"Time for manslaughter is what you'll be doing if you drive a car in your condition. When did you get a driver's license?"

"So, where's your old lady?"

"In bed."

"It's after one."

"We went out last night. Stayed up late. Take off your coat. I'll open us a couple beers." George started for the kitchen. Scanlon tossed him the church key he had in his coat pocket.

"Save yourself some steps," Scanlon said, shrugging out of his coat, letting it stay behind him on the sofa. "How come you're not watching college hoop on the tube?"

"I just got up, thanks to you." George snapped open two beers. He handed one to Scanlon and flopped into a wing chair torn to shreds by Rose, the black cat Elaine doted on like a baby. "So what is it I'll never guess you're doing?"

"Teaching school. I'm a high school science teacher. How do like that?" George Stacy studied the label on his bottle, not registering any surprise at Scanlon's news.

"I'm back in school myself. Graduate school of business. Elaine's bringing home the bacon now. Makes for a very pleasant relationship. Wait'll she wakes up and finds you here." George drank long and belched. His lips were red and moist. He looked like he hadn't shaved for a week, but Scanlon knew it was only a day's growth.

"I'll be leaving after this beer. Don't worry. What do you see of my mother? Big bad Bill Scanlon still on the scene? What about Keith and Billy? They still around?"

"You don't have to leave. You know Elaine. She'll be pissed at first, but that'll be that. You know how she is."

"I don't want to be any trouble."

"Oh, no. You wouldn't want to be any trouble. Let me have your coat." George Stacy took Scanlon's coat and hung it up in the closet off the living room. Rose, the cat, appeared and jumped up on Scanlon's lap. Scanlon stroked its sleek pelt; the cat began to purr and rub against his chest. "Kick her off if she bothers you."

"You know I like cats."

"Yeah."

"You hungover?"

"Big time."

"Beer'll fix you up. Yeah, I love cats. Good thing, too, where I'm living. Aren't you curious about my life?"

George got up and switched on the television, which sat upon the top shelf of a brick-and-board bookcase displaying his love of literature and high culture. "Let's see if the UCLA-Nevada game's on." Scanlon sighed and drank beer.

"Who're you talking to, George?" Elaine's voice came from the bedroom, which in this odd apartment had doors off the kitchen and living room.

"Jack's here," George replied. There was a long silence. Scanlon listened. George sat on the edge of his chair, his eyes on the TV screen, his cheek twitching from time to time.

Elaine appeared in the doorway dressed in a terry cloth bathrobe. An unlighted cigarette hung from her mouth, and her hair was in a tangle. Elaine, with the dangling cigarette in her mouth, reminded Scanlon of his mother for an instant.

Elaine Stacy stared at Scanlon. Scanlon stared back. Her face was puffy and sleep creased. "It is you. God help us," she said, finally. She produced a book of matches from her bathrobe pocket and struck three duds before she got one to ignite. She tilted her head when she lit her cigarette. In Scanlon's blunted state of consciousness, the whole scene was ritualistic: George Stacy sitting on the edge of his chair, half his attention on the TV screen, the other half on his wife who stood above them like a high explosive lighting her own fuse.

"In person," Scanlon said. "I've got a lot of nerve coming here, haven't I?"

Elaine looked him over like shabby merchandise. "Looks like you've had several bottles of nerve. How long have you been up?" she asked George.

"Not long," George said, eyes still on the TV.

"I got him up. Sorry," Scanlon said.

"And you're already drinking?" Elaine said.

"I gave him the beer," Scanlon said. "He's just being a good host."

“Sure.” Elaine shook her head. “I’m going to put on some coffee water. I don’t suppose either of you wants coffee.” Elaine left the room without waiting for an answer.

Scanlon drained his beer and rose to his feet, the sofa springs creaking loudly.

“Where are you going?” George asked.

“I’m leaving.”

“Sit down.”

“Look, I know where I’m not wanted.”

“Spare me.” George looked at the ceiling. “Just sit down. I told you how she’d be. Let her wake up, have her coffee.”

Scanlon did as he was told. On TV, a couple of sportscasters with headphones were talking about the UCLA-Nevada match-ups. Could anyone in the world match up with Lew Alcindor? No one known to either of these announcers.

“So, what are the Celts’ chances this year?” Scanlon asked George who was a rabid basketball fan, pro and college, even high school. Scanlon used to follow the Celtics but had little interest in college ball.

“Not a prayer. This is Philly’s year in the east, and they’ll fall to Lakers in the finals.” George’s eyes were fixed on the TV. Scanlon knew that he wasn’t really welcome, that he was making George uncomfortable and Elaine angry. Maybe that was why he had come. To pay them back for last New Year’s Eve. But he’d already paid them one memorable visit since that evening, a visit he didn’t imagine the Stacys would forget for a long time. So why didn’t he feel the account was settled?

The living room walls had been repainted since his last visit. A mustardy yellow, a color a torturer might choose for a room in which he wanted to break his victim psychologically. Elaine had a touch for decorating that made the screaming yellow walls hard for Scanlon to figure. There was the paisley throw on the sofa, her “antiqued” red milk can, a linseed-oiled blanket chest that served as coffee table. She framed her own prints: Vermeer’s *Woman With a Water Jug*, Caravaggio’s *Bacchus* (who reminded Scanlon of Romeo Boudreau), Dega’s *Absinthe Drinkers*, Van Gogh’s *Self Portrait*, all hanging today. Nothing Cubist, George’s taste in painting, was visible, and Elaine said she had outgrown the French Impressionists a long time ago, so that took care of Scanlon’s interest in art. No, the wall color didn’t figure.

The music from the apartment across the hall, which had subsided since Scanlon’s arrival, suddenly increased in volume. The closet off the living room was all that separated the Stacys' apartment from the one next door. Elaine came in the room carrying a mug of coffee.

"I'm not putting up with that," she said to George. George didn't look at her. Scanlon could tell he was boiling inside. The music was so loud he could scarcely hear Elaine. "Are you going to do something about those people?"

"They're high on pot," George said, scratching at his belly. "It won't do any good to talk to them. I've tried before when they were straight. You know it does no good to talk to them."

"Young girls twist George around their little finger," Elaine said to Scanlon. "Well, I'm not so easy to twist." Elaine stalked out of the room, presumably to put on some clothes and go have it out with the pot-smoking neighbors.

"You want me to go over there?" Scanlon asked George. "Maybe they'll invite me to their party. Then I'll invite you guys and everything'll be cool."

"Right." George was still intent on watching the TV.

"How young?"

"What?"

"How young are these girls next door?"

"College girls. I told you. Three of them. Must be majoring in public relations. They party every night, all day and night on weekends. You wouldn't believe the traffic up and down those stairs. Sometimes you can even hear them fucking in the next room. They fuck in groups sometimes."

"Can't say I share their taste in music." On TV, Lew Alcindor got the ball in the low post and hooked it in off the glass. George shook his head in admiration. The music next door stopped abruptly, and Scanlon realized that his stomach muscles had been contracted. When the music stopped his muscles relaxed. Then it started up again, the same tune as before, louder this time. George clenched his fist, his eyelids fluttered.

"No shit, George. I'll be happy to go over there and have a word with them. This is bullshit."

Elaine came back, dressed in stretch slacks and sweater, a wild look in her eyes. He wouldn't have been surprised to see smoke coming out of her ears. George had always been a live and let live guy, but this was more than even he should be expected to tolerate. Yet he left it to Elaine to play the heavy. She flung open the door and let it swing full force against the wall. She pounded on the door across the hall so hard with her fist Scanlon expected to hear it splinter. In a moment there was another surge of volume as the door opened. Scanlon listened for Elaine's voice. All he could hear was the din of rock music. Then Elaine was back, and shortly the music stopped. Scanlon's muscles relaxed once more.

"Ah, that's better," Scanlon said. "Good going, Elaine." She stopped to glower at her husband before she marched out of the room. She didn't even look in Scanlon's direction. "I think that may be my cue," Scanlon said, getting off the sofa again. Elaine was suddenly back.

"You don't have to leave, Jack. Maybe George will even stray from his lower class habits and turn off the TV when he has a guest." George looked at her, and then at Scanlon to roll his eyes before getting up to punch off the TV.

"I should go. I've got to pay my mother a visit, find out what the kids are up to."

"We don't see you for months. Sit down. Have another beer. One more can't do you any more harm than you've done to yourself already." Elaine pulled the last bottle out of the six-pack on the floor and handed it to him.

"What did you say to your neighbors? George, toss me my church key."

"I reminded them of the laws concerning marijuana and suggested that if they didn't want the police visiting their party, they damned well had better not play their hi-fi loud enough for me to hear it." Elaine sat down in the shredded wing chair vacated by George and lit up a cigarette. "You want one, Jack? You still smoke, don't you?" Scanlon accepted her cigarette and even allowed her to light it for him with her delicate little Ronson, which seemed too small for her large hand. "George is trying to quit, aren't you George?"

"Third time this month," George said.

"So what have you guys been up to?" Scanlon sat back down on the by now rumpled paisley throw. Without thinking, he put his feet up on the blanket chest earning him a look from Elaine. He removed them immediately.

"Never mind about us. What about you?" Elaine said.

"Jack's a schoolmaster. There's a sobering thought." George brought his empty bottle to his lips and sucked out the last of the foam.

"That doesn't surprise me, really," Elaine said. "No, I'm not surprised at all. I'm pleased to hear it, Jack."

"Thanks. I'm lousy at it, I'm afraid."

"I don't believe that." Elaine crossed her legs. She was barefoot. Her feet were big but graceful with long, shapely toes, well-groomed nails, no polish.

"Hope you're not modeling your style on some of our high school teachers," George said.

"You could do worse than teach like Swenson," Elaine said, determined to punish her husband for not dealing with the neighbors. Jon Swenson had been Garrison High's flamboyant math teacher, unorthodox, creative. He'd come into class with a wastebasket over his head, teach the whole period without removing it. He'd ensconce himself on the lecture desk like Scheherazade and make quadratic equations come to life. He'd snap the girls' bras, make fun of the jocks, and give a kid a B even if he hadn't earned it if he thought the kid had what it took. Yes, he could do worse than model himself after Swenson. Except he didn't have Swenson's natural aptitude and talent for the work.

"George tells me you're back to supporting him again." This remark brought color to George's face, a snort from Elaine.

"Thanks, friend," George said.

"Do you hear from Katie? How's Lucy? Have you seen them?" Elaine wanted to know.

"Since late August, since I've been in Vermont, I've received exactly one letter, if you could call it a letter, from Katie reminding me of my financial obligations and that if I missed another payment she'd have the law all over my ass. I talked to Lucy once on the phone. She was very distant with me, very distant." Scanlon's voice started to break.

"I'm so sorry, Jack," Elaine said.

"You got plans to go out there?" George asked.

"I can't afford it." The Stacys looked at each other. "I literally cannot goddamn afford it. How much do you think I make teaching school? I got rent to pay, expenses. How much do you think I have to cough up a month for support? I can't fucking afford it!"

"All right, Jack," Elaine said, trying to sound reassuring, "we understand."

"What if I run out for some more beer?" Scanlon pushed himself off the sofa.

"Great," Elaine said, exhaling smoke from her nostrils, "just what we need."

"I've got a microeconomics exam on Monday," George said, "and I don't understand squat about microeconomics."

"And you're not going to understand any more about the dismal science by studying one more lousy day, either. Why don't we go around to the Social Club." Elaine could only laugh.

"I'm telling you, Jack, I can't do this shit anymore." George looked ill at ease, as well he should. On Scanlon's last visit, he and George went off on a two-day drinking spree. Scanlon left the Stacy household in physical and emotional shambles.

"How long before you spoke to him again after the last time I was here?" Scanlon asked Elaine.

"Not for a very long time. What do you want from us?"

"I just want to have a little fun."

"I thought you were broke. You have enough to piss away on booze, but you can't afford to visit your child. You're a terrific father, you know that, Jack?"

"Fuck you, Elaine," Scanlon said, bringing George to his feet.

"Maybe this time you really ought to leave. In fact, why don't you just get your coat and get the fuck out of our lives."

"That's fine with me." Scanlon got his coat from the closet. "That suits me just fine." He was shaking inside and out. There were many things he should say to these people. He couldn't think of any of them. Elaine got up and put her hand on his sleeve, her arm around his shoulders.

"Jack, don't go like this. Sit down and talk." She stroked the back of his head. He wanted to stay, to talk, to have his friends back.

"It's too late. It's been too late for a long time." And he left in this overly dramatic fashion, regretting it as soon as he was on the first landing but too full of pride and sorrow and stupidity—and beer—to go back inside where perhaps his only friends in the world were.

Stupefied, he drove the loop around the Garrison shoe factories where his mother had toiled for years. He drove for maybe a full half hour, round and round. The sky was low and gray with the threat of snow. Snow left on the ground from the last storm was dirty from car exhaust and factory smoke. Garrison never looked dirtier to him, this old mill town.

Finally, he drove uptown and parked across the street from the apartment house, a two-decker, where his mother lived with Bill Scanlon. He sat in the car, smoked cigarettes and watched the house. It was on Garrison's main drag, and the traffic was heavy on this Saturday afternoon. He watched the house until he grew numb from the cold. No one went in while he watched, no one came out. There was a light on in the living room, the room that faced the street. Was Bill Scanlon on the couch, drinking whiskey with beer chasers, watching the UCLA-Nevada game until he passed out? What would his mother be doing? Crossword puzzles? Where were Keith and Billy now that they were both out of the service? Scanlon was conscious of his own foul breath in the VW's confined space.

Shivering from the cold, sick to his stomach from too much beer and not enough food; sick with grief and heartache and confusion. He started up his little car and drove north.

Chapter Twenty-one

"Johnny? Johnny, you up there? There's a lady down here to see you." Befuddled, Scanlon wasn't sure Alice's voice came from his dream or from downstairs. "Johnny?" He opened an eye to look at the alarm clock on his nightstand. Eight-thirty. His head jerked off the pillow involuntarily.

"Jack? If you're not well, you should have called in. Daryl's covering your classes for the time being but he can't do it all day. Jack?"

Scanlon recognized Madelaine Winship's voice. He got out of bed. The room went momentarily out of focus. He stumbled backward to a sitting position on the edge of the bed.

"Oh, my God." Scanlon held onto his throbbing head with both hands.

"Jack?" Madelaine's voice seemed right in the room with him. He felt incapable of speaking in a normal voice. Was he still in a dream? What was Madelaine Winship doing in Groveton, in his aunt's house?

"I'm here," he finally managed to croak. "My alarm didn't go off. Tell Daryl I'm on my way."

"Well, I think you should be the one to call him," Madelaine replied. "I have things of my own to do."

"All right." Scanlon hurried to the bathroom, dropped to his knees and flipped up the toilet seat and got sick in the bowl. His eyes watered; his nostrils stung; his head pulsated.

Alice called up to him again, "You all right, Johnny?"

He couldn't answer, only nod his head, as if this would tell Alice anything. Then she was knocking on the bathroom door.

"You want me to call a doctor, Johnny?"

"No, Alice. I'm all right now. There's someone you can call for me if you don't mind." Scanlon gave her the school number and asked her to tell Winship's secretary that he'd be there in half an hour. He wrapped his arms around the base of the toilet bowl, rested his cheek on the rim and drooled. His insides erupted again, but nothing came up. "My God. Oh, my God."

Scanlon's classroom was darkened. Winship was showing his biology class a filmstrip on the circulatory system of the perch. Scanlon slipped in the door quietly and sat on a three-legged stool in the back of the room. Winship lectured on the perch's two-chambered heart, its low-pressure shunt to the gills in contrast to the hearts of amphibians, birds, and mammals. Kids were quiet, attentive. Even Romeo Boudreau seemed to be awake, his chin, in profile, propped in his dirty hand. Scanlon had never used any of the A-V equipment—the filmstrip machine, the movie projector—and he was too embarrassed to admit to Winship that he didn't know how to operate it, he a former industrial engineer.

Since Winship had come down on him about the condition of the lab, Scanlon hadn't set up any new experiments. It seemed that all he did these days was lecture and give quizzes and tests. It was only a matter of time before the kids revolted. For a moment, sitting on the low stool, Scanlon thought he would be sick again. He swallowed a big wad of saliva and the nausea passed. Winship changed frames and looked over his shoulder at Scanlon.

"That's all for today," Winship said just as the bell rang. The kids left the room quietly. Scanlon approached Winship so he wouldn't have to deal with looks from his students.

"I'm sorry about this, Daryl. I forgot to set my stupid alarm."

Winship gave him the once over then turned his attention to the filmstrip machine. "I wanted to cover the marine fish's adaptation to a saline environment, but time ran out. I think it's important that they know this," Winship said, replacing the spool of film in its canister. "You'll be sure to bring this up when you meet with them tomorrow."

"Yeah, sure." Scanlon had no idea how marine fishes were adapted to a saline environment.

"I covered relative humidity in your first period general science class. I had my old sling psychrometer in my file cabinet. Gave them a demonstration. They like demos."

"Thanks." The last demonstration Scanlon had done in general science was the collapsing can trick, to show the effect of atmospheric pressure. It hadn't worked because the stopper he'd used in an empty duplicating fluid can was too small. Instead of the can collapsing under the weight of the atmosphere, the rubber stopper was sucked, or rather pushed, into the can. The effect was maybe more dramatic, if not the one he'd expected. The result was that his confidence had been shaken, and he hadn't found the courage to try another demonstration since.

"I wouldn't worry about oversleeping." Winship looked him up and down. "By the looks of you, you ought to be back in bed. Go on home, if you want. I can cover the rest of your classes."

"Thanks. I'll be all right. Sorry Madelaine had to be inconvenienced."

"No inconvenience. She was in Groveton anyway. It wasn't out of her way." Winship unplugged the filmstrip machine and wound the cord around its base. "Would you mind bringing this back to the A-V closet?"

"Not at all." Scanlon's chemistry students were arriving for class.

"We gonna see a movie?" Roy Hardwick asked, his eyes lighting up at the sight of the filmstrip machine.

"There aren't any dirty movies about chemistry on the market, Roy," Scanlon said, tucking the machine under his arm. Before he could get out of the room, three more kids asked Scanlon if there was going to be a movie. He hurried to the A-V closet with the confounded machine.

Stambaugh had invited him to bring his eighth period study hall kids to the open discussion with the hippies from Clifton. They were meeting with his history class and any others who had a free period and were interested. What Scanlon would like to have done was dump his kids on Stambaugh and go home early. He'd made several trips to the men's room with the dry heaves during the day. Aspirin couldn't begin to compete with his headache; several times he thought he would faint. He gave spot quizzes in all his classes, and divided his time between the toilet and the malodorous teachers' room sofa.

There was standing room only in Stambaugh's classroom. Two long-haired boys in denim jackets sat on Stambaugh's desk in the front of the room. Scanlon recognized them immediately as the boys who'd accompanied Samantha Burnham to the dance the night Winship had confronted her.

Scanlon came in the room as one of them uttered the words "shit work." He seemed to be directing his remarks at Donald Dubois.

"There's got to be some kind of incentive," Dubois replied, "or else people won't produce." Dubois' statement was met with loud applause. The hippies looked at each other and smiled. The one who'd said shit work had thick eyebrows that grew in a near uninterrupted line over his long, thin nose. On his left cheek bloomed a large, pigmented mole, and his dark, shoulder-length hair was tangled and unwashed. Scanlon's insides recoiled at the thought of Samantha Burnham in this boy's dirty embrace. The other boy's hair was lighter, if not cleaner. It also grew to his shoulders. On his small chin was a wisp of goatee.

Goatee held up his hand for order, an insolent smile on his face. When the room quieted, he slid off the desk and stood up, both hands thrust in the pockets of his filthy jeans.

"That's a typical capitalist argument," he said of Donald Dubois' incentive position. "It's how the powermongers keep the people slaves to the profit motive."

"Why don't you move to Russia, then, if you're so much against free enterprise?" Dubois countered. More applause, loud whistles and foot stomping.

"Yeah," added Romeo Boudreau, "and take the niggers with you." Scanlon was surprised to see Romeo there. He wasn't one of Stambaugh's students.

"That's another familiar attitude we have capitalism to thank for," Mole Cheek said, and was greeted with boos and more foot stomping. Stambaugh was being proved correct in his assessment of the right-wing leanings of Fairfield High students. Scanlon never dreamed it was as passionate as this.

The discussion, as Stambaugh had advertised it, was in danger of getting out of control. In Scanlon's opinion, it was Stambaugh's responsibility to step in and restore order. Josh Patterson was hemmed in by students in the back of the room. He was the only other teacher present besides Scanlon and Stambaugh. Should he do something himself? Would Stambaugh think his authority was being usurped if he stepped in and took charge? If Winship should decide to make an appearance, he'd have the whole room dispersed in no time. Stambaugh held his seat in the first row, appearing outwardly calm in the face of what looked like total chaos to Scanlon. The hippies sat on Stambaugh's desk looking extremely smug.

It was Scott Pettingill, finally, who took matters in his own hands, standing on a chair, both arms raised above his head, and whistling for order. Almost at once, the room fell quiet.

"We live in a free country, in case you guys have forgotten," Pettingill said, voice quavering, "and in a free country everyone has the right to express himself, no matter how unpopular his opinions may be. I don't agree with these people any more than you do, but I think they deserve a right to say what they got to say." With that, Scott Pettingill stepped down.

Goatee asked if anyone had a question. For a long moment there was only silence as Scott's chastening lingered. Then someone, Scanlon couldn't see who from where he stood, asked Mole Cheek how long he thought socialism would last in the United States if it were to become the system tomorrow. Before Mole Cheek had a chance to respond, Junior Darling started to go on about how no country in the world, not even Russia, was a hundred percent socialistic. He said that in Russia, and even China, capitalism was practiced under the table, and that anyone who argued for pure socialism was politically naive.

Mole Cheek reached in his jacket pocket and came back with a reefer between his fingers. He proceeded to light up and before even thinking, Scanlon heard himself say, "Put that out."

Goatee looked at Stambaugh. "I thought you said this was going to be a free discussion. No interference from teachers."

"Discuss all you want," Scanlon said, before Stambaugh had a chance to say anything, "but you don't get to smoke dope in this room, pal."

Mole Cheek shrugged his shoulders and snuffed out the reefer with his thumb and forefinger.

"Another thing you guys got to learn," Goatee said, "is to say fuck you to authority." Scanlon wasn't used to hearing the word fuck uttered in public, and in the presence of young females.

"That's right," Mole Cheek said. "Authority figures keep the worker down and in his place. That's where the authorities want them to stay, too. That's how they maintain power and the status quo. You've got to give authority the finger. You got to rise up and take over. Start by taking over this school. Throw out the pigs in authority."

"Fucking A," Goatee assented. "Right on."

How long would Stambaugh allow this? Patterson, standing a head above every kid around him in the back of the room, was laughing silently but with such gusto his face had turned crimson. Kids were getting restless. The hippies' revolutionary message was not winning over any converts at Fairfield High. They began to talk among themselves, to ignore the two zealots from Clifton College. Their mere association with that school had probably lost them any credibility with these kids in the first place.

"You all been fucking brainwashed by the system," Goatee said. "Come on, Max, let's split. Hey, thanks a lot for having us to your fascist school, there, mister," he said to Stambaugh. Samantha Burnham appeared in front of the room to stand between the hippies, looking defiantly out at her "fascist" classmates. Scanlon held his breath.

"Go on back to your faggot school," someone shouted, "Fucking commie. Take her with you." Scanlon couldn't see who had spoken. The voice was not familiar. Samantha whispered something in Mole Cheek's ear. He nodded his head and smiled. Scanlon felt a spasm of dizziness again. He pushed his way out of the classroom, out of the building into the fresh air.

Outside, Scanlon gulped cold air. Three yellow buses were idling behind the building near the gym. Exhaust smoke billowed from their tail pipes in great clouds suspended in the cold, still air. He stood beside his car, shivering and keeping an eye on the front door to see if Samantha came out with the hippies. He scanned the parking lot for a VW bus or one of those vans their kind seemed to favor. He saw no unfamiliar vehicles. Kids were beginning to come out of the building, to board buses, get into their cars, or wander off on foot to their homes.

When it was clear that Samantha and her companions would not be coming out through the front door, Scanlon got in his car and started the engine. He waited a few moments longer, watching the front door. No one else came out of the building. Besides his own car, only Winship's and Higgins' remained in the lot. Scanlon slipped the gearshift into first and drove away.

Chapter Twenty-two

Maybe out of deference to Kennedy, Scanlon felt obliged to recount in his journal the strange dream he'd had the day Madelaine Winship came to his aunt's house.

"All rise," I hear Winship say. "The Honorable Robert C. Kennedy presiding in the case of the People versus John Scanlon." Winship is a uniformed court bailiff. Bob, you come shuffling out of chambers brushing the front of your judge's gown. You've spilled coffee or whiskey on it. I can see the sleeves of your seersucker jacket under the gown. You need a shave, as usual. You motion everyone to sit down. I'm at the defense table and I remain standing.

"Why aren't you seated, like everyone else?" you ask me.

"I want to make a motion to dismiss," I say, lawyer-like, wondering what the C in your middle name stands for.

"On what grounds?" you ask me, studying your gavel as if it were an artifact.

"On the grounds that the People have no, uh, probable cause," I say.

You ask the prosecutor, who happens to be Daryl Winship and has changed out of the bailiff's outfit into a natty, three-piece pinstriped suit, what is meant by the term, probable cause.

Winship replies with some gibberish like "A man who has himself for a lawyer has a fool for a client," consults his notes and suggests that we get on with the "show."

You pound your gavel and say, "Let us proceed. Do you have any opening remarks, learned counsel? Do you wish to call a witness, take a recess, badger the defendant?" Then you pull a Styrofoam cup from under the bench and slurp from it.

"Your honor," I start to say.

"I object," Winship shouts. "That is hearsay. Inadmissible. The jury will ignore the defendant's last remark."

You sustain the objection and direct Winship to call his first witness. Then you lean back and close your eyes. Winship gets back into his bailiff's outfit and swears in my ex-wife with a back issue of *Seventeen* magazine. Katie's wearing a bouffant wig, a tight mini-dress and spiked, blue suede heels with sequins. I wonder if she has brought Lucy. I crane my neck to scan the gallery behind me. All I see are my students in the audience, life sciences on the right, physical sciences on the left.

They raise their fists when they catch my eye. Someone shouts, "Right on, Prince!"

Winship, in his role as prosecutor, asks my wife how long she has known the defendant. He leers at me and traces his finger along Katie's bare arm. Then I spot my stepfather in the back row of the jury box. He's thumbing through a 1950 edition of *Police Gazette*.

"A lifetime," Katie answers.

"What have you done with Lucy, you cunt?" I shout, and pound the table with both fists.

"Mr. Scanlon," you say, Bob, waking up from your nap and reaching for your gavel, "one more outburst like that and I'll have to ask the bailiff to remove you. Will Mr. Scanlon's counsel please counsel him to refrain from any further such outbursts?"

I clench my teeth and promise no more such behavior from my client.

"Just how long is a lifetime, Mrs. Scanlon?" Winship asks Katie, replacing his bailiff's uniform back in its box.

"I prefer to be addressed as Mrs. Durand. That's my maiden name, you know? That son-of-a-bitch," she says, pointing a long-nailed finger in my direction, "that selfish bastard sitting there who got me pregnant and made me quit high school just when I was starting to get asked out a lot, ought to have his dick cut off and stuffed in his mouth the way the A-rabs do it. He always put me down, made fun of me every chance he got, especially In front of his friends with their college diplomas. He was a filthy pig. He always left his scuzzy shorts and smelly socks strewn around the bedroom for me to pick up after him, cook his meals, work eight hours a day and take care of the baby. He never took me out anywhere, but he didn't mind staying out all night himself, drinking and screwing around with other women..."

"What about you?" I shout. "Tell the court how you were playing hide the meatloaf with Murray Klein, our saintly landlord."

"I'd just as soon not talk about that person anymore," says Katie, meaning me, "unless you don't mind me barfing right here in the courtroom."

"Did the defendant beat you? I mean did he strike you in any way as to bring physical harm upon you?" Winship asks. I notice Winship's fly is open. The jurors seem embarrassed but instead of putting their hands over their eyes, they have them over their ears. I'm surprised to see Samantha Burnham in the jury box. She's not listening to Winship's questions, however, because she's absorbed in another Hermann Hesse novel. Looks like *Steppenwolf* from where I'm sitting.

"I must object to this line of questioning," I say, "unless counsel can show relevance."

Winship requests permission to approach the bench. I want to approach, too, but Winship pouts and says he asked first. Winship whispers something to you, Bob, I can't hear. It sounds something like tamper or Tampax.

I wonder if now I'm being accused of tampering with the jury, or tampering with their Tampax. I won't be maligned by this fool. I ask again to approach the bench.

You deny my motion, Bob. You gavel the bench and tell us to proceed. I'm beginning to sense a conspiracy, a fix. I realize that Katie has been staring at me. I can't bring myself to look at her.

Winship says, "Your witness," and winks at the jury.

I don't have any questions for my ex-wife.

You excuse Katie from the witness box, and pour yourself a splash of whiskey. You don't offer me any, and I'm miffed at you for being so selfish with your booze.

"I want to know exactly what it is I'm being charged with," I ask you, trying not to sound as testy as I feel.

"I'd caution defense counsel against undue familiarity," you snap at me, scowling from beneath your big eyebrows. Peripherally, I see Winship snatch *Steppenwolf* out of Samantha Burnham's hands. He gives her a severe tongue-lashing and a week of detention. I notice my mother for the first time. She's in the women's section of the jury box working a crossword puzzle so she won't have to look at me. It dawns on me that Winship has stacked the jury and probably has you in his pocket as well.

I say that I'd like to declare a mistrial.

You tell me that this is not done nowadays. You ask Winship for corroboration.

"Absolutely," Winship says. "That hasn't been done for a long time, a very long time. Any man who defends himself in a court of law has a fool for a lawyer. That's it!" Winship applauds himself. My students boo Winship and stamp their feet. Someone yells, "Shit head!" You belch and gavel for order in the court. Winship reaches for his bailiff's togs in case he has to clear the courtroom. I turn to my students and hold up my hands for quiet. They fall silent immediately.

You order Winship to call his next witness.

"I call Mary Alice Farr, nee McGinnis to the stand." Winship swears in a frumpy Mary Alice Farr, nee McGinnis with a copy of *Family Circle*. Alvin Farr, balding and big-bellied in a T-shirt that has "USA Drinking Team" written across the front, gives me the hairy eyeball from the jury box. I feel like I'm at the gates of hell where you have to relinquish all hope. Mary Alice has forgotten to remove her apron before coming to court, and I can see, even from where she sits, that her hands are red and chafed from years of house slavery. She's also a lot fatter than I remember her at six years old.

"Please tell the court, in your own words, about your relationship with the defendant, John Scanlon, alias Johnny Labalm." Winship looks over at me and narrows his eyes.

"He made me take down my panties, and he promised me magic."

"And did the defendant deliver the magic he promised?" Winship realizes that his fly is open. He turns his back to the jury and zips up.

"No, he didn't. I had to take down my panties lots of times, and I didn't get magic once."

I can't take it anymore. I jump to my feet shouting, "That's a damned lie, your honor. You got plenty of magic, young lady. All the magic you wanted. And I'd remind you that you're under oath and you could go to jail for a long time for lying. So just stop your lying. Let the record show that defense counsel has warned this witness." I make sure that Cynthia Sinclair, today's volunteer court stenographer, gets the message about my caution of the witness. Cynthia, who is decked out in a plaid skirt and a high-necked, ruffled-front blouse, pecks rapidly at her steno machine.

Just then, Raymond Burr, broad-shouldered and dead-panned, comes into the courtroom and takes a seat next to me. He apologizes to you for being late, blaming the damned LA traffic. At the mention of LA, I request a change of venue.

"I'll make the motions around here from now on, Mr. Scanlon, if that is your real name," Perry says to me, putting me in my place.

Then you tell me that the court has assigned Perry to my case, and you give me this insider's wink. I immediately tell Perry to ask Mary Alice if she understands the consequences of perjury. He just looks at me as though I'm mold.

"The defense has no questions," Perry says, opening his briefcase. I ask him if maybe he's got a drink in there. All he has is mouthwash.

Winship is too lazy to get back into his bailiff's outfit so he lets the next witness take the stand without swearing her in. Rachel Patterson wouldn't take the oath on anything except maybe *Town and Country*, I think. Winship wouldn't have that in his stack of swearing-in magazines anyway.

I ask my attorney if he had noticed that the witness had not been sworn in. "If that's not grounds for dismissal, I don't know what is. She'll lie through her teeth, and there's nothing the State can do to her because ..."

"I know the law, Mr. Scanlon," Perry says.

I wonder what F. Lee Bailey is doing, or Pearl Bailey. Was she still married to Louis Bellson? Rachel wears no makeup. She's the picture of Protestant-Virgin-White America, though I don't imagine she can still be an actual virgin after almost three years of marriage to Josh.

Winship fawns all over her, asks where she was educated, how long she's been living in Burton.

"Rosemary Hall and Bryn Mawr. I came out in 1962, in New York. My father is also a successful attorney like yourself, Mr. Winship. That man," she says, pointing accusingly at me, "the one with the hideous mustache, sitting next to Perry Mason, tried to seduce me in my own kitchen while my husband was not five feet away in the bathroom, correcting social studies tests." Rachel lowers her head. A tear wanders down her wholesome cheek. My ex-wife, who has taken her place in the jury box, wags her finger at me.

I ask my counsel if there isn't some sort of upper limit on the number of people who are allowed to serve on a jury.

"The more the merrier has always been my motto," says my lawyer.

"Tried to seduce you? A Bryn Mawr alumni?" Winship acts incredulous.

"Isn't it alumna?" I ask Perry who shushes me.

"It's simply beyond comprehension." Winship shakes his head at the enormity of my depravity and pats Rachel's smallish hand. "Your witness, Mr. Mason."

"I have no questions for the witness at this time. I reserve the right to redirect at a later time, however."

"How come you never do any cross-examining until the show's almost over?" I ask Perry. "It's maddening."

The jury now consists entirely of women: Laraine McFarland, looking whorish in a tight sweater; Rachel Patterson, still in agony from her ordeal of having to dredge up the memory of that sordid evening with me in her kitchen that smelled of home-baked bread; Mary Alice Farr, nee McGinnis, who has Raggedy Ann in her lap; and my mom, bent over her crossword puzzle, eyes squinting through cigarette smoke. Alice, Althea, and Mrs. Royer are playing honeymoon whist, and Cynthia Sinclair has taken her place in the box, steno machine and all. Lillian Bloemer is dressed like Shirley Temple in *The Good Ship Lollipop*, and I have to admit, it makes her look younger. Mrs. Bloemer has Clytemnestra, a champagne angora, and a dead chipmunk in her lap.

Winship calls my mother to the stand, and there is a collective gasp from the jury and spectators. Mom is sworn in amidst whispers that sound like escaping steam, her right hand raised, her left placed on the confiscated copy of *Steppenwolf.* "Can he swear people in like that, out of uniform?" I ask Perry.

"Clothes don't necessarily make the man. Let me handle this, Mr. Scanlon. I've been to law school. Yale."

"What can you tell the court about the defendant, Mrs. Scanlon? What kind of baby was he? When did he start to display the kind of attitude that ... well, shall we say the kind of attitude that brings him before the court today?" Winship has his thumbs hooked in his vest and drums his chest with his fingers. He looks very sure of himself.

"He was a good baby. Always slept through the night, never complained. Learned to use the flush toilet by the time he was, let's see, eight months old. That's advanced, don't you think? What's a seven letter word for illegitimate?" Mom asks you, the judge.

You call Winship to the bench to consult over the answer to twenty-nine down. You guys break up, shaking your heads.

"I've got the last four letters, T-A-R-D," Mom says.

"Retard?" Winship offers, looking up at the bench for your approval. But your attention is inside your whiskey cup.

"That's only six letters," Mom replies, chewing the eraser of her pencil.

"Why don't you ask her where she was during those years I was really flushing toilets?" I can't help myself from shouting. Perry tries to restrain me.

Mom has a cigarette in her mouth. She asks Winship for a light. You beat him to Mom's cigarette with a kitchen match. You scratch it and light Mom up.

"You got an ashtray in this place?" Mom wants to know.

"Just use the floor," you say with an ingratiating smile.

"When did he go bad, Mrs. Scanlon?" Winship continues, thumbs back in his vest. "When did he start to break your heart?"

"I think it was when he started smoking leaves wrapped in notebook paper and traveling with a bad crowd. He was eleven, too young to be smoking leaves. Leotard?" Mom says, writing, then erasing. "No. Doesn't sound right."

Winship has been shaking his head at Mom's testimony as if he can't believe a boy could be so cruel to his mom. He asks her if she feels well enough to continue. Mom is a little vexed by twenty-nine down but agrees to remain on the stand a while longer.

"What else can you tell the court about the defendant, Mrs. Scanlon?"

"Who?" Mom's attention is on her crossword puzzle.

"The defendant," Winship reminds Mom. "John Scanlon, alias Johnny Labalm and God knows how many other aliases and deceptive identities."

"He never liked being called Johnny and as soon as we left Groveton—God, was I ever glad to get out of that place—he told all his new friends that his name was Jack. Naturally, we couldn't send him to school with a last name like Labalm so we registered him as Scanlon, John Scanlon. The Jack was his idea."

"So the defendant was in the habit of lying at a very early age. Very interesting."

I elbow Perry and ask him if he's going to object.

"I'll be the judge of that," he says, and looks over his shoulder for someone. Paul Drake, maybe, with the crucial evidence that will clear me of these trumped up charges. I look, too. No sign of Paul Drake. And all my students are gone. They should be so quiet when they leave my classroom.

"Oh, Jack became an accomplished liar as he got older," says Mom, cheerfully. "It got so you could never tell when he was lying or telling the truth. Especially if he wanted his way. He was a thief, too, of course. His father and I were heartbroken when we found out about this habit of his of stealing things."

"Make her stop referring to that asshole as my father," I say to Perry. You must overhear me because you get self-righteous and tell Perry to keep me under control or you'll have me removed from the courtroom. You're really into this role, Bob.

"Mrs. Scanlon." Winship pauses for dramatic effect, lowers his head as if it bears the weight of heavy responsibility and grasps the rail of the witness box, which I notice is ornate, curly maple, not at all what I'd expect in an LA courtroom. "Mrs. Scanlon, I'm going to ask you a question which will no doubt cause you some pain. The court will understand if you don't choose to answer, won't it, Judge Kennedy?" Bob, you've got your shoes off, your feet up on the bench. There is a hole in the big toe of your right sock. You nod in the affirmative.

"If I can only get twenty-nine down I could crack this baby. Come on, counselor. Judge. Put on your thinking caps. I won't ask Jack for help. He was never any good at crosswords. Sometimes I thought he even resented me for doing them. Could never understand that boy. Never talked to his mother like a normal son. Not like Billy, and not like my Keith, my favorite. Jack was sullen, always brooding and unhappy, always lying and stealing and traveling with a bad crowd. Once I had to go down the street and take him away from those hoodlums he hung around with at the pool hall. Took him right by the ear and dragged him down the street right in front of his friends. Don't think they didn't laugh. Made him promise me he'd never go near that poolroom and those hoodlums again. He promised, but I could tell he had no intention of keeping it.

"He'd skip school for weeks on end, spend all his time in that poolroom when he wasn't working at the delicatessen—that place didn't have such a good influence on him either—drinking liquor and stealing and being a hoodlum and a liar."

"I object, your honor," Perry finally says. "The witness is leading the prosecution."

"Sustained. Stop leading the prosecution around by the nose, Mrs. Scanlon."

"But your honor," Winship says, "I haven't even asked my potentially very painful question of the witness."

"All right, all right," you say, "Never mind. Only stop your whining." You smile at me and wiggle your toes.

"Mrs. Scanlon, I don't think you're leading me around by the nose. You're only trying to find out the truth about the defendant without subjecting yourself to any more pain than you've no doubt had to endure already by being the mother of this, this ..." Winship uses his hand to make a circle, to search for the word that will properly describe the nature of my despicable existence.

"Let's be careful, learned counsel," you say. "We don't want a slander suit on our hands."

Winship agrees to withdraw the question. You want to know what question. I notice that your face is flushed and you're busy at your temple. Winship tells Mom to continue. He's got his hands together like he's praying. I look over my shoulder. My students are back in the audience and I'm relieved.

"He turned his back on us when he got married. He was never the same after that. I tried to tell him she was no good, but when did he ever listen to his mother? She was nasty neat, that girl, and the way she spoiled the baby. It was disgusting. I tried to be nice to her, to give her advice about Jack and the baby, and how to cook meals, but she'd have nothing to do with me and my husband. She turned Jack against us, too."

"Mrs. Scanlon, I'd like to follow up on this idea of neatness, if you don't mind. You say that his wife, his former wife," Winship says, glancing at Katie Durand in the jury box who is sitting on my stepfather's lap. They are clearly French kissing and not listening to anything Mom has to say. Winship blushes and turns back to Mom. "If the defendant's former wife was, as you say, neat to a fault, how would you describe the defendant's personal habits? Would it be fair to describe him as a slob?"

"True, he was never very neat, but I'll take that over what she was any day. You couldn't put out a cigarette and she'd be taking the ashtray away to clean it. I always had to remind Jack to pick up his clothes, to wash the dishes, to take a bath. It wasn't till he was in high school, when people started to tell him he stank, that he took more than one bath a month."

"Thanks, Mom," I say.

"Could you trust him to lock the door after he left a room?" Winship asks, excited with this line of questioning.

"He wasn't very good at that, either." Winship scribbles notes on his yellow legal pad. "In fact, we were relieved when he decided to join the Navy, not that he had much choice in the matter. It was either the Navy or the jail."

"This is a travesty," I protest. "Make her tell the truth, Bob. You know my side of the story. You can't tell me you believe the things she's saying under oath."

"The court will recess for five minutes. I would like to see counsel in chambers." You literally stagger to chambers, Bob. Perry and Winship hurry after you. Mom is left on the witness stand with only her crossword for company. I glance over at the jury box to see if Katie and my stepfather are still at it. A paper airplane floats over my shoulder and lands on the judge's bench. I swivel around to see if I can spot the culprit. Everyone in the audience looks ceilingward, trying to appear innocent. It wouldn't be professional for me to talk with any of them, or to say something to Katie and my stepfather about their lack of good manners in the jury box. I would have thought Rachel Patterson would step in and give them a lecture on decorum in the courtroom. I wonder where Josh could be? And Doug Stambaugh? I could use a couple of defense witnesses, character witnesses as it were. Where were George and Elaine? Ira, where was Ira? There's one person who would stand up for me, no question about it. Never trust a shrink is my motto from now on. Who would have suspected that you moonlighted as an LA circuit judge, Bob?

Is that Lyle Higgins dry-humping Cynthia Sinclair in the jury box? I can't believe my eyes! They're fully clothed, but she has her legs wrapped around his waist, he has his hands on her buttocks. I have to look away.

Madelaine Winship appears with a brown-bag lunch for her husband, the prosecutor. She has on a slinky, pink chiffon dress, black-net stockings and her sequined sunglasses. The dark roots are gaining on the rest of her brassy hair.

"You seen Daryl?" she asks me. "I brought him some tuna sandwiches and chips. You want a brownie, Jack?"

"No thanks, Madelaine. How's it going? How do you like LA?"

"Beats Fairfield, but I'm getting really tired of the commute every day. It's like leading a double life. I don't have to tell you about how that feels, do I, Jack?" Madelaine gives me a wink.

"No, I guess not." I'm starting to feel really miserable. "Maybe you wouldn't mind going over there and tell my stepfather to stop fondling my ex-wife. There is such a thing as appearances."

"It's not my job to tamper with the jury. That's Daryl's business. I should be going. Good luck with the trial, Jack. Don't forget the Christmas party Friday night."

"If I'm not in prison."

"Oh, right." Madelaine giggles and waddles out of the courtroom, swinging her big can for the benefit of the senior boys who pretend to throw up.

Winship comes out of chambers alone and looks worried. He's got on his bailiff's jacket, and lawyer trousers. If I weren't so polite by nature, I'd have laughed out loud. The judge appears moments later. But wait! You're no longer the judge, Bob. It's Bill Scanlon! My stepfather! I look quickly toward the jury box and sure enough, Katie is sitting alone and looking very pleased with herself. She's replaced her bouffant wig with an Afro, and at first glance could pass for Angela Davis except for the blue eye shadow. Mom has vanished from the witness stand. I look for her in the jury box, feeling panicked. She has disappeared.

"All rise," Winship says, solemnly. "The Honorable Bill Scanlon presiding in the case of the People versus John Scanlon, alias ...?"

"Yeah, yeah," I say. "Where's my lawyer? Where's Perry?"

"Button your lip, kiddo," my stepfather snarls, removing his judge's robes. He's more comfortable on the bench in his short-order cook's whites. I admire his jacket with the front buttons on the diagonal. "If I want shit out of you, I'll squeeze your head." Bill Scanlon laughs himself into a coughing jag at his own wit. His face is all red; the blood vessels in his neck bulge out and his eyes are popped.

It wouldn't bother me to see the bastard choke to death.

"Why aren't you in school today?" the judge wants to know. "How many days have you skipped this marking period? You think I don't know what you're up to, wise guy? I've seen all your excuse notes. I paid the principal a visit yesterday. He showed me all of them. You know how long I could put you away for forgery? You been hanging around that fucking poolroom again, after you promised your mother you wouldn't. You make me sick. Bring exhibit A to the bench, counselor." Winship produces a stack of my forged absence excuses and carries it to the bench.

"I'm entitled to counsel." I try to say it calmly while in a rage inside. My stepfather, the judge! "Where's my lawyer?"

"The court has appointed a new one. Perry's got a pressing engagement with Della Street. Hah, hah, hah." Judge Scanlon's laugh is as obscene as it ever was. As if on cue, Doug Stambaugh appears beside me, lugging an army duffel. He's out of breath and wearing a bulky ski sweater with a diamond motif on the front, despite the one hundred-degree LA temperature.

"Got here as soon as I could, Jack. You wouldn't believe the traffic on the Hollywood Freeway." Stambaugh opens his duffel and pulls out the *Handbook for Conscientious Objectors*. "This will be like the Bible from now on, Jack. We can't miss." Stambaugh waves the handbook at Judge Scanlon as if to taunt him.

"Who's the fruitcake?" Bill Scanlon asks.

"This is Doug Stambaugh, my defense attorney and friend."

"He's a Communist sympathizer, your honor," Winship says in his shrill voice.

"Well, call the FBI if he's a commie," the judge says impatiently. "We've got important business to conduct here without wasting time on pinko fags."

"I think the FBI's on lunch break right now, your honor." Winship consults his watch.

"What's going on here, Jack?" Stambaugh wants to know. He scratches his silky-haired head. "I thought I was the one on trial. I thought you were defending me. What is this?"

I sink deeper into despair. I lay my head down on the table and try to sleep. I feel a hand on my shoulder. I think it belongs to Doug, and I push it away.

"If you don't want me to defend you, you miserable bastard, I got other things I could be doing," says Abe Cohen, my first boss, existential philosopher, delicatessen proprietor, divorced and abandoned like me. And now Abe Cohen is counsel for the defense of his young employee of seven years to whom he was father, brother, Dutch uncle, and drinking buddy. A right-footed bowler and chainsmoker, Abe never sat down to a regular meal after his wife left with his two daughters. He would nibble at Genoa salami, drink cold coffee with curdled cream, and smoke four and a half packs of Chesterfields a day. He drank sweet wine laced with vodka and listened sixteen hours a day to Mantovani records in the deli. "Have you done your algebra homework, schmuck?"

"I don't get quadratic equations." I wonder where Stambaugh could have gone. "I'm glad you're going to be my lawyer, Abe. You, more than anybody, know what I went through with those people."

"So what are you charged with, you miserable little bastard?" Abe asks, jabbing my arm playfully.

"Who knows?"

"What's the kid charged with?" Abe has put on a few pounds and there is black hair growing on his Semitic nose, and out of his big ears. His chest hair curls over the front of his shirt, and if he didn't shave he could pass for a werewolf. I'm so glad to see my old boss I could kiss him. I can feel my fortunes beginning to turn for the better.

"Crimes against humanity," Winship says, picking up his legal pad. "Shall I read you the list?"

"Of course you should read me the list, you fool. How do you expect me to defend this miserable little bastard if I don't know what he's charged with?" Abe rolls up the cuffs of his plaid shirt to reveal his thick, hairy wrists.

"That's it!" Mom yells from the spectator's gallery. "Thanks, Abe." She fills in twenty-nine down and slumps in her chair with relief.

"Indifference," Winship begins, "neglect—let's see, one, two, three—I get nine counts; sarcasm, too many counts to count, self-deception, emotional sloth. You really want me to go on?"

"Yes, I want you to go on."

"Insincerity, selfishness, self-pity, self-indulgence of the kind we can simply list under gluttony; lust for inappropriate objects of lust; failure to clean up or lock up after himself; failure to send cards on Mother's Day; failure ..."

"That'll do," Abe says, stroking his hairy nose with his forefinger. "I'd like to call my first witness for the defense." There's whispering and foot shuffling in the courtroom. Judge Scanlon sends Mom to the Ginnies for spaghetti take-out. "The defense calls Mrs. Fanny Labalm."

Uncle Mitch escorts Grammy to the witness stand. She has on a nice, gray dress, wire-rimmed glasses, black, high-top shoes with laces, and lisle hose. She's four feet eight inches tall and bowlegged. I hope she remembered to bring her false teeth. Mitch helps her onto the witness stand. Grammy shakes her fist at Judge Scanlon whom she has always despised.

"How's it going, sister?" the judge says out of the corner of his mouth, city slicker style. Grammy sputters and almost loses her teeth. Winship rummages around on the prosecutor's table for something appropriate with which to swear in Grammy.

"Your honor," Winship says, the whine back in his voice, "this is most distressing. The People were not informed about the existence of this witness, and I haven't got a thing on hand I can use to swear her in." As luck would have it, Abe has an extra National Bohemian salami in his briefcase he can offer Winship to use to swear in Grammy.

"And what is your relationship to the defendant, Mrs. Labalm?" Winship asks Grammy in his condescending way.

"I'm his grammy, you eediot," says Grammy. My chest fills with emotion.

"I'm sorry I didn't come to your funeral, Grammy." I start to sob. "I couldn't. That's the truth, Grammy. I had to report back to duty. There was no way I could get out of it."

Winship raises an eyebrow. "Is this true, Mrs. Labalm? Did the defendant, your allegedly loving grandson, in fact fail to attend your funeral?"

"He had good reason," Grammy says. "Johnny had his Navy duties to attend to. Johnny was my little boy, and they took him away from me. His mother was no good, and she went and married that good-for-nothing jailbird and took my Johnny away from me." Grammy starts to weep. Mom returns with a carton of spaghetti for the judge, and a portable TV.

"Did you remember to ask for extra sauce? Hot sausages?" the judge asks Mom with threat in his voice. Mom tells her husband to go shit in his hat and plugs in the TV so Grammy can watch cop shows while she's testifying.

"It is alleged," Winship continues, "that the defendant slept with you in the same bed until the age of eight. Is there any truth to these allegations, Mrs. Labalm? Let me remind you that you are under oath."

"Objection," Abe says. "Question is irrelevant and immaterial."

"How to go, Abe," I say. "Where'd you learn that lawyer talk?"

"Overruled. Witness will answer the question," Judge Scanlon says, sucking spaghetti through his brown teeth.

"Watch out, you eediot!" Grammy screams at the TV as Eliott Ness and a couple of his Untouchables are about to walk into a warehouse ambush.

"I'd like a psychiatric examination of the witness, your honor, to determine competence," Winship says, not even worried about Eliott Ness's fate.

The judge's mouth is full of spaghetti and hot sausage. He waves his fork in assent, and you, Bob, appear from chambers to cross-examine Grammy psychologically.

"Grammy." You take Grammy's tiny hand in your giant paw. "Why didn't you punish Johnny for things he did to Mary Alice McGinnis?" But you're blocking her view of the TV and she gets angry and whacks you out of the way.

I say, "Leave her alone, you two-faced shit."

You riposte in a really grown up way by saying "Look who's calling the kettle black. You couldn't even be bothered to attend your poor grandmother's funeral, and after she raised you practically from scratch. What's the real reason you didn't attend the funeral, Jack? I don't want to hear about any military obligation either. I want the truth."

Abe tells me that I don't have to answer your questions. He tells me to take the Fifth Amendment.

Grammy is looking straight at me and crying. She knows. She knows I lied. I get up out of my chair and move toward Grammy. Winship intercepts me and Mitch leads Grammy out of the courtroom before I can explain.

"I couldn't face it, Grammy," I yell after her. "I couldn't face the pain of losing you."

"That's a lie, ladies of the jury," you say. "He didn't attend his grandmother's funeral because he was having too good a time. He had other things to do. Isn't that right, Jack?"

"How would you know that? I never talked to you about that. Where do you get off making statements about which you know not a thing?"

"Sloth is one of the charges against you, is it not?"

"What's that got to do with my missing Grammy's funeral?"

"You're out of line, Kennedy," Abe says, brandishing his salami at you.

George Stacy appears from behind the judge's bench where he's been yukking it up with my stepfather. There are spaghetti stains down the front of his shirt. "He may be out of line, but the fat guy speaks the truth," George Stacy says, sitting on the edge of the defense table, shoving a toothpick into the corner of his mouth.

"All right, smart guy," Abe says, "let's hear what you got to say about it."

"Swear in the witness," Judge Scanlon says to Winship, who is struggling into his bailiff's trousers, being careful this time to zip up. He shows George Stacy several magazines, asks him to pick the one with which he'd like to be sworn in. To my surprise he chooses *Playboy*. Elaine would hit the ceiling if she were here. I look toward the jury box, half expecting to see her there with the rest of the hostile women in my life. If she's there, I can't see her.

"Where were you on the day of Grammy's funeral?" you ask George. Winship tugs at your jacket and whispers in your ear. "Oh," you say. "Sorry." You sit down at the prosecutor's table; Winship clears his throat.

"Where were you on the day of Mrs. Labalm's funeral, Mr. Tracy?"

"Stacy, asswipe. I was with the defendant. It was a Saturday. Jack was home on leave before heading for his new duty station on the West Coast."

"And when was the defendant scheduled to report for duty?"

"Not for another week."

"I see," says Winship, stroking his chin, a supercilious smile on his tanned face. "Not for a week. So, in your opinion, he would have had time to attend his grandmother's funeral if he chose to do so. Is that correct?"

"Yeah. He could have gone," George continues, rubbing the spaghetti stains deeper into the fabric of his shirt. Elaine will crucify him for doing that to a stain. "What is it, two and a half, three hours tops, to Groveton from Garrison? His mother, and the judge here, offered to take him up with them."

"Yet despite Judge Scanlon's and his mother's generous offer of free transportation to his allegedly beloved grandmother's funeral, the defendant refused to attend. Is that correct, Mr. Daley?"

"That's about it. Sorry, pal," George says to me. "I'm under oath."

I'm numb. George Stacy speaks the truth, as far as the facts go anyway. The court has no interest in my motives, the ambivalence that was in my heart at the time.

If Winship decides to pursue the circumstances further with this witness it will be all over for Jack Scanlon, alias Johnny Labalm.

"Your honor," Winship says, "the People could rest its case right now with confidence that the jury would return with the proper verdict. Your honor?"

His honor is sound asleep, snoring mightily with his mouth open, his cook's jacket splattered down the front with spaghetti sauce, like blood.

"Give it a rest, counselor," Abe says, moving toward the witness stand. "Let me have a crack at this wise guy."

"I'm not through with my questioning. You'll have to wait your turn."

"You miserable prick," Abe says to Winship before returning to the table. "How'd that moron get to be DA?"

"He apprenticed as a high school principal." I'm still wondering why Ira isn't here. How did Alice and Althea and Mrs. Royer get here if Ira or Willie didn't drive them? None of them would set foot on an airplane. Ira is my only hope. I ask Abe what he's going to ask George on cross.

"I knew all about how you were clipping me for beer and cigarettes and small change, you miserable little bastard," Abe says, drinking cold coffee. "You think I didn't know?" I begin to shake. I feel on the edge of an emotional collapse. Involuntary sobs erupt in my chest. "Your only chance now, you little prick, is to throw yourself on the mercy of the court. Beg forgiveness. You don't deserve forgiveness, but you can't lose anything by trying. Myself, I wash my hands of you." Abe picks up his Chesterfields and splits. I'm alone at the defense table, sobbing out of control. I realize that I am naked. Have I been this way through the whole trial? Where is Ira?

"Ira, Ira," I sob. The jury and spectators begin to leave the courtroom, single file. Mom stops by the defense table to ask me if I know a five-letter word beginning with G, meaning deceitful, cunning. She wanders off without waiting to see if I know it. I'm still bareassed and crying at the table after everyone is gone.

I hear the sound of something knocking against furniture. I look up from my crying to discover Ira, the janitor, sweeping the room. Crazy Nick Costa, still suffering from the effects of shock treatments, is Ira's helper.

"Ira," I say, "where the hell have you been? What are you doing here, Nick?" They don't hear me. They act like they don't even see me. Silently they move furniture, push their brooms, no expression at all on their faces.

Chapter Twenty-three

S: This will be my first drink since Tuesday. I haven't missed it, if you can believe that.

Kennedy poured their whiskey.

K: Good for you. But you must know that it's bad luck not to drink on Friday the thirteenth.

Kennedy had given up wearing neckties. Jackets, too. The collar and cuffs of his pinstriped shirt were frayed. Scanlon was relieved to find that Kennedy hadn't stepped completely out of character. As if he read Scanlon's mind, Kennedy's finger found its way to his temple. He leaned back in his chair and slurped whiskey the way Judge Kennedy had done in Scanlon's weird dream.

S: You superstitious? Really?

K: Not really, Jack.

S: Neither am I.

Scanlon was playing a game with himself, deliberately postponing his first taste of whiskey. He turned the cup in his hands, let the fumes rise to his nostrils.

K: What's going on with you?

S: Not much.

K: Why the abstinence?

Kennedy sucked in a lot of air, put his feet up on his desk. He had on loafers, the heels worn down on the outsides, his white sock visible where the sole parted company with the vamp on the right shoe.

S: You still off cigarettes?

K: You were right. I fell.

Kennedy got his cigarettes out of his middle drawer, offered one to Scanlon and lit up.

S: Smokin' and drinkin', drinkin' and smokin'. Ain't we a pair, Bob?

Scanlon took his first sip. It tasted like more. He took a good swallow this time and dragged deeply on his cigarette.

K: Health is wealth. I'll stop tomorrow. But today. Today is my day.

Kennedy drained his cup; Scanlon did the same and Kennedy refilled them.

S: You know a woman named Madelaine Winship?

K: Name's got a familiar sound. Like someone you're associated with.

S: My principal's old lady. Works for the welfare department, I've been told.

K: Oh, yeah. Bleach blonde? Yeah, I've met her once or twice. You're worried she knows about you? Don't be. She doesn't.

S: How can you be sure? She could have spotted me coming or going. You can't know for sure.

K: People around here talk. I would have heard.

S: Oooo, that's reassuring.

K: Have you heard anything at school that would tell you she knows?

S: Couldn't say for sure. So much weird shit goes on there, who could tell?

K: What kind of things?

Scanlon told Kennedy about oversleeping and having Madelaine in his aunt's house, about the Clifton hippies and his weekend in Garrison, his "lost weekend."

S: Ray Milland had nothing on me, except for the DTs. Wait till you read about the dream I had Sunday night. I wrote it all out so I wouldn't forget anything. It was that kind of dream. You won't believe it.

K: Let's have a look.

Scanlon handed Kennedy his notebook. Kennedy swiveled toward the window, opened up Scanlon's notebook, and began to read and massage his temple.

When he'd finished, Kennedy closed Scanlon's notebook, chuckled up a wad of phlegm, and disposed of it in his filthy handkerchief.

S: How're your piles these days, Bob?

K: Don't ask. You don't expect me to believe you remembered this dream in this kind of detail, do you? You're getting to be a regular fucking raconteur.

S: Maybe I embellished a little. Nick's a kid I hung around with in high school; Abe is just like I described him, my boss in the deli from the time I was a sixth-grader. He was like a father to me. Abe, that is. Nick flipped out in California. Brother had him committed to the funny farm.

They fucked his brain over with electric shock therapy. He's never been the same. The other people you've heard me talk about, right? What's your view on shock treatments?

K: They scare the shit out of me, if you want to know. There are a few more in here I'm not familiar with. Tell me more about this Abe.

S: As I said, he was like a father to me, whatever that's like. Maybe more like an uncle. Nobody's father would let them get away with the shit Abe let me get away with.

K: So why did you steal from him?

S: I don't know.

Scanlon drank some whiskey and leaned his head back against the chair. Kennedy's bald use of the word steal made his insides twitch, triggered his sweat glands.

K: What's the matter? Too hot in here for you? I forget, you got a thing for hot rooms.

Kennedy got up and opened the window. Scanlon took off his jacket and laid it across his lap. He loosened his tie, drank some more whiskey.

S: What hit me?

K: Disturbing associations would be my guess.

Kennedy turned back to the window, hugging himself against the draft.

S: You don't have to have it open that much if it bothers you.

K: It's all right.

S: I'm thinking of maybe driving out to California, Christmas break, to see my kid.

K: That's a lot of driving.

S: You don't think I should go?

K: Why don't you fly?

S: I won't go.

Scanlon got up and closed the window. He looked out over the gully at the backs of the tenements. The snow in the gully had gotten dirty. The sky was gray. The gray sky, dirty snow, the squat tenements with the ever-present laundry hanging on the porches conspired to put him in a low mood.

S: I'd never make it across this continent. I'd get lost for sure. I'm always getting fucking lost in my car.

K: All the more reason to fly.

S: I'm definitely not going. For one thing, I can't afford to fly.

K: What's another thing?

Scanlon turned to look at Kennedy. Kennedy studied his whiskey, rubbed his temple. The room was too hot again. Scanlon reopened the window a crack and sat back down.

S: What do you think it means, my dreaming about you that way?

K: First thing comes to mind is that you see me as your judge. As I keep telling you, I'm no dream man. What do you think it means?

S: You're always turning it back on me. It's getting old. What do you take me for, a moron? I thought we were friends.

K: Sorry. Force of habit. Friendship is important to you, isn't it, Jack.

Scanlon looked up from his whiskey.

S: You make it sound like a revelation. Wouldn't you guess that it's important to everybody?

K: Not to the same degree with everybody. No, I wouldn't say so.

Kennedy had on his thoughtful face.

S: My inventory of friends is shrinking fast, Bob.

He reminded Kennedy of his falling out with the Stacys.

K: What about this Stambaugh?

S: There's a barrier between us. We're too different. I can't think of a single thing we have in common except for being schoolteachers. He doesn't like to drink, he doesn't share my taste in music. He comes from a different world.

K: If a shared interest in boozing is one of your criteria for friendship, I guess that would make us blood brothers.

Kennedy laughed. Scanlon thought it had a sardonic ring.

S: I don't think that's the only thing we have in common, Bob.

K: Right. We're both hooked on cigarettes.

Kennedy laughed again, laughed himself into one of his coughing fits.

S: Someday you're going to choke to death.

Scanlon put his elbow up on the back of his chair and looked out the window. Kennedy had his dirty handkerchief out again. Out of the corner of his eye, Scanlon saw him inspect it as if he were looking for a clue to the corruption in his lungs. The thing was probably crawling with tubercle bacilli.

S: You should be hospitalized.

Kennedy folded up his hanky as if it contained diamonds and stuffed it in his back pocket.

K: You can count me as your friend, Jack. But you've got to understand that we've also got a professional relationship. I got an obligation to try and help you. You got an obligation to cooperate. After this is over, maybe we can concentrate on just being friends.

S: After this is over? Is this shit ever over?

K: There'll come a point when you and I won't be able to go any further.

S: Assuming we've gone somewhere at all. I don't feel much different now than I did the day I walked through your door.

K: You may not *feel* different, but I think you are different.

S: How?

K: I'd rather you figured that out for yourself.

S: You asshole, Bob.

K: You going to California, or not?

S; No, I told you.

K: Why?

S: I think it would be too dangerous.

K: It doesn't have to be that way, Jack. You've got a little time. Don't make up your mind yet. Give it some more of your attention. Next week we'll talk more about it.

Chapter Twenty-four

Al Noyes' tenor sax man was legally blind, which wasn't such a startling condition for a gentleman in his late eighties. Al himself looked like he might never see eighty again. Al played drums. On the base drum, in script, was written "Al Noyes and His Rhythm Boys." Al hadn't been able to keep a reliable piano man since Charlie "Duke" Dube passed away after thirty-five years with the band. The guy who sat in tonight was young, maybe fifty-five, with thin, veiny arms and thin, gray hair combed straight back. He looked bored.

Percy Mackay played "Melody of Love" with enough vibrato to make Freddy Gardiner envious. Al tried to keep the tempo with his brushes, but he wasn't clicking with the young piano man who kept squinting out at the room as if he were looking for someone.

Scanlon held his breath on Percy's high notes as if he expected the old gent to blow his last. Ira and Alice were the only couple on the floor, gliding to their own inner music over the black and white tiles like Arthur and Kathryn Murray. There were only a dozen or so people in the lounge on this Friday the thirteenth; one other woman besides Alice, a woman swaying in her chair as if she were being buffeted by wind. She was too drunk to stand, let alone dance.

"That was smooth. Real smooth," Scanlon said to Alice and Ira, applauding their return to the table. "You don't see that kind of dancing anymore." Ira rolled his eyes and pretended to be tuckered out. Tonight he had his gray suit on, his hand-painted palm tree and hula girl tie. Alice wore a black dress with big shoulders, a dress she might have worn in the forties when she and Ira were courting. She drank Black Velvet with beer chasers; Ira, ginger ale. Alice drank whiskey only on special occasions, like Friday the thirteenths.

"Well, I tell you," Alice said, sliding into the metal chair with vinyl seat and back, "we used to dance every Friday night, years ago. Before your uncle quit drinking. Like pulling teeth to get him out of the house now."

"I'm a working man, Mother," Ira said, winking at Scanlon. "I can't be staying up all hours of the night, dancing." Ira normally worked Saturday mornings, but tomorrow he had off because of inventory. Scanlon had agreed to come along with them after Kennedy had got him a head start on bourbon that afternoon. Like Alice, Scanlon drank whiskey and beer.

"Used to be able to drink all night and work all day. That was before he started acting like an old man." Alice lit up a cigarette, searched her purse.

Scanlon hadn't been in the American Legion lounge in a while. Nothing had changed since the days he'd spent here as the Swish Kids team mascot. Upstairs, Johnny Labalm had learned to shoot a fair stick on the pool table with leather-thonged pockets. This was where the legionnaires met, wearing their silly piss-cutters, to discuss their right-wing political philosophy.

The lounge smelled powerfully of booze, as if the bartender washed down the tables with gin. "Melody of Love" had taxed the Rhythm Boys enough for them to take their second break of the evening. Al Noyes, an arm at old Percy's elbow, assisted him down from the bandstand and led him to his table. The piano man stayed on his stool and drank from a glass that had been sitting on top of his instrument. He smoked and drank and squinted out at the dark room, running a hand nervously through his thin hair. Percy and Al Noyes drank shots and beers at their table, oblivious of the piano man. It wasn't nine o'clock yet. Scanlon would have taken bets that they wouldn't last till eleven.

"How long have they been playing here Friday nights?" Scanlon asked.

"Long as I can remember," Ira said, looking at Alice. "Since before the war, right, Mother?"

"Since before World War I, if you ask me." Alice smoked one of those recessed filter-tip cigarettes, leaving a scarlet smudge of lipstick on it. This was the first time he'd seen her gussied up since he'd been back in Groveton. Her skin condition seemed under control, thanks to her regular trips to Hanover and all the expensive medication and lotion. She was alarmingly skinny, though. She couldn't have weighed ninety pounds. And Alice was on her way to being very drunk tonight. Her snippy remark about the Rhythm Boys gave Scanlon the feeling that she was about to pick a fight with Ira.

"Old Percy worked with your grandfather for years at the foundry," Ira said.

"And he's got his gold watch to prove it," Alice said. She sipped her Black Velvet and started to sway herself, slightly. Scanlon finished his drink and asked Alice if she'd like another. At the American Legion, you got your own drinks at the bar. Scanlon stood at the bar several minutes before he was acknowledged by the old man in the red, bow tie who was serving drinks. "Remember the Pueblo" on a three-by-five card was tacked on the wall, and "What You Hear Here Stays Here." And a cartoon depicting a hapless little man run through the middle with a giant screw, captioned, "Work hard, do your duty, and you will receive your reward." Just to be a wise guy, Scanlon ordered a martini. The bartender shook his head without saying a word. Scanlon left the bar with two shots of Black Velvet and a bottle of beer.

Back at the table, Ira and Alice were turned away from each other in silence.

"Here you go, Alice." Scanlon placed his aunt's drink in front of her.

"Thanks, Johnny."

"You remember George Denault, Johnny?" Ira asked Scanlon.

"Yeah. One of the Swish Kids, right?"

"That's right. And he's sitting over there in the corner." Ira nodded toward the far corner of the room where two men faced each other across the table over a cribbage board. Scanlon recognized George Denault at once, although the man had packed on a few pounds since his Swish Kids days.

"I'll be dipped," Scanlon said. "He hasn't changed much. He'd never recognize me, I'll bet." Denault had been his Uncle Mitch's best friend. They drank and caroused together until Mitch met the woman he eventually married. All the fun stopped for Johnny Labalm when Mitch got engaged to Joyce. When Johnny was introduced to his uncle's fiancee, Johnny knew that things were never going to be the same again. Later, when Mitch asked him what he thought of Joyce, Johnny told him she reminded him of an alligator. It became a standing joke. He hadn't seen either of them since he was in high school. Ira said Mitch and Joyce still lived in Maine and were childless, like Ira and Alice.

"Want me to call him over?" Ira asked.

"I guess the Rhythm Boys have conked out," Alice said, shaking her head. The piano man was gone from his stool. Percy Mackay and Al Noyes sat quietly at their table, looking old and conked out. Percy's tarnished saxophone rested, center platform, in front of his chair. Scanlon had a sudden urge to go up on stage and try a few licks on the horn. How good would he have been if he'd stuck with it? No worse than Percy Mackay. He didn't want to talk to George Denault.

"I don't think so, Ira. I don't want to have to ..."

Before he could finish, Ira was up and moving across the room to Denault's table. Ira stood and chatted with Denault and his companion, then pointed over to where Scanlon and Alice sat. Denault looked their way and shook his head. Then he pushed back his chair and rose, hitching up his trousers. He had an enormous belly, but his face was youthful, much the way Scanlon remembered it. He had a full head of brown hair with a big pompadour fashionable in the forties, cleft chin, boyish good looks. The belly looked incongruous on him.

"I recognize you up close," George Denault said, shaking Scanlon's hand. "The eyes. How you doing, half-pint?"

"Good, George. You haven't changed a hell of a lot. Still playing hoop?"

"Got a basket rigged over the garage door for the kids. Shoot a round of horse once in awhile. My days up and down the court are over." Denault grabbed two handfuls of belly. "What are you up to these days, Johnny?"

"Johnny's a schoolteacher," Alice said. "Can you imagine?"

"Whereabouts?" Denault asked.

Scanlon had no choice but to tell him. He was frankly surprised that he hadn't bumped up against more characters from his past after encountering Laraine McFarland.

"They call him the Prince, at school. The kids do," Alice said. Scanlon cringed.

"No shit," Denault said, starting to grin.

"Can you imagine?" Alice said.

The Rhythm Boys were back on stage. Scanlon hoped Alice would drag Ira to the dance floor. The four of them, Scanlon, Denault, Ira, and Alice, watched attentively as the trio prepared for the next set. Scanlon held his breath again as the old men tottered onto the platform stage; the piano man waited, bored, for Percy to hook up his tenor, for Al to climb behind his snare drum.

George Denault said, "There's talk that Percy's been dead for ten years, and Al controls him with wires."

Percy Mackay licked his mouthpiece, consulted the sheet music that he couldn't possibly see, being legally blind, and without waiting for the downbeat, began to play a reedy interpretation of "Harbor Lights." Al and the piano man caught up, more or less, a half bar later. Scanlon had to work to keep from laughing out loud. Ira and Alice got up to dance.

"Them two know how to fox trot," said an admiring George Denault.

"Yeah. You don't see dancing like that anymore," Scanlon said, feeling as though he'd used that phrase before. They watched Ira and Alice float around the booze-sticky tiles, not in synch with the Rhythm Boys but with a rhythm of their own invention, it seemed.

Scanlon remembered how his Uncle Mitch always complained back in the Swish Kids days about how lazy George Denault was on defense. Depended on his flashy head feints and quick moves to the basket, then dogged it in transition. All the natural talent in the world and lazy as a fat dog in the sun. Now, George looked relaxed, languid, slouched in his chair, his legs extended all the way to the edge of the dance floor. He had on penny loafers and white socks. Maybe what Mitch had seen as lazy was only relaxed.

"See anything of Mitch these days?" Scanlon asked him.

Denault pulled in his legs, sat up straighter in his chair. "Comes down once or twice a year to play golf with Butch White. Remember Butch? Owns the Cadillac-Olds franchise in town. I was sure your uncle would go into business with him. Bet he's kicking himself in the ass now he didn't. Anyways, Mitch comes down here for old times' sake and that's about all I ever see of him. He's way the hell up in Maine, anyway."

"I haven't seen him in years myself."

"You never much liked Joyce, did you?"

"That was an official joke. I was jealous as hell at the time. What did I know? I got over it. I got nothing against Joyce."

"Yeah," George said, drinking beer from the bottle, "Joyce was good people. Ain't seen her in years. Mitch never brings her down on his golf trips."

Scanlon wasn't sure how Alice felt about Mitch's wife or Joyce about her and Ira. If Mitch never brought her with him on his Groveton visits what did that say?

On the dance floor, Ira dipped Alice as "Harbor Lights" came finally to an end. They returned to the table in discord, however. Ira was tired and wanted to go home; Alice was drunk and in no mood to do anything but stay and drink and dance some more. How many chances did she get to dance these days? They had all come in Ira's car, and unless someone wanted to walk the three miles home, they would have to leave together.

"I don't know about you, Ira," Alice said. "You don't have to get up tomorrow. Anyone would think you were Percy Mackay's age the way you act." Alice picked up her empty glass and set it down hard on the table.

"I got to have my beauty sleep, Mother." Ira winked at George. Denault grinned and sucked on his beer bottle.

"It's not even ten o'clock. You just hate for me to have any fun." Alice's words came out mushy. She rapped her glass on the table and ordered Ira to go up and get her another drink. Her beer was gone, too.

"Goddamn, Mother," Ira said, getting up slowly, hand on his lower back like an old man, "I'm tired." He grinned and winked at Scanlon and Denault when he said it, but Scanlon could see the fatigue in his eyes.

"Why don't we take Ira home," Scanlon offered, "then I'll bring you back in my car if you want."

"There you go, Mother," Ira said, pleased with this solution.

Alice looked steadily and hard at Ira.

"Let me buy you a round before you go," George said. "I might not be here when you get back." Ira's shoulders sagged.

"We won't be that long, George," Scanlon said. "What do you say, Alice?"

Alice angrily snatched her purse from beside her chair and got up. She started walking a crooked line to the stairs. Ira shrugged his shoulders and followed.

"In case we don't get back before you go," Scanlon said, standing and extending a hand to George Denault, flashy forward for the Groveton Swish Kids of 1946, "it was good to see you after all these years."

"Me, too, Johnny," Denault said, wiping his hand off on his trousers before shaking with Scanlon. "Those were the days, huh?"

"You bet." Scanlon finished his drink and followed his aunt and uncle up the stairs.

When they got home, Alice went straight to bed. Scanlon drank a beer and chatted with Ira for a few minutes about his Swish Kids days, then Ira went to bed.

Chapter Twenty-five

"How they hangin', Mr. Scanlon?" Danny Picard got out of his chopped and channeled '57 two-tone blue Chevy. Every sudden movement sent a jolt of pain through Scanlon's tender skull, including the effort to get out of his VW. "Uh oh," Danny said when he got a look at Scanlon.

"Don't say another word," Scanlon said, reaching carefully in the back seat for his books. On the floor was a paper bag with two bottles of emergency get-well beer, in case it got Monday-morning rough.

"Tied it on good last night, huh?"

"Don't be a wise guy, Danny. Have some sympathy." Danny walked with Scanlon to the gym entrance.

"I'll bring you some of my old man's home brew some time. Stuff'll put hair on your balls." Danny held the door open for Scanlon. They surprised Grace Ouemette and John Pike smooching under the stairwell. Pike was the center on Coach Sorenson's team and had been pursuing the voluptuous Grace Ouemette since September.

"Carry on," Scanlon said. Grace smiled and nuzzled her hair-sprayed head under Pike's chin. Pike, six foot two, blushed. Danny rubbed his forefingers together, naughty-naughty fashion.

"Pike's blushing 'cause we caught him with a boner," Danny said on the way up the stairs. "Grace is just a cock teaser. Pike'd have better luck with his fist."

"Thanks for that information, Danny."

"Don't mention it. See you in study hall."

Scanlon went out to his car during lunch period with the intention of having at least one of his medicinal beers. He found both bottles turned to slush in the cold VW. He sat shivering in the little car, his forehead resting on the steering wheel, his innards all twisted around from Sunday night's drinking. He'd so far not taken a drink while school was in session, unless that time he chaperoned the dance counted. He was profoundly disappointed in himself for being out in his car for this purpose, and now that he wouldn't be able to have his get-well beers, even more disappointed.

Danny Picard startled him, tapping on the passenger side window.

"You all right in there, Mr. Scanlon?" Danny had on a smile, but it was a worried smile.

"Yeah, Danny, I'm all right. A little tired is all." Scanlon was embarrassed to be caught in such a vulnerable position; not half as embarrassed as he would have been if Danny had caught him swilling beer.

"Ain't you cold out here with no coat?"

Scanlon opened the door and got out of the car. He was cold, to be sure, cold and sick in body and soul. "I didn't plan to be out here long. It's gotten colder instead of warmer since this morning. Jesus," Scanlon said, hugging himself, "what a place to live."

"Careful how you talk about God's country."

"What are you doing out here, anyway? Come on, let's get inside before we both freeze to death." Scanlon jogged to the front door, Danny trotting easily beside him.

"Days like this I come out and start the car a few times to keep her warm. You don't have to worry with your VW. Starts every time all the time. Right?"

"Most of the time. It's a good car." Scanlon leaned against the wall in the vestibule, short of breath.

"You're in great shape, Mr. Scanlon. Sucking air after a twenty-yard jog. How many packs a day you doing?"

"Down to three. Don't you have anywhere to go? Like a class?"

"I don't have nothing till eighth period study. Thought I'd go down to the cafeteria and hump boxes." Danny walked up two steps and vaulted over the banister back down to the floor.

"You're a regular gymnast, Picard."

"You like that? Watch this." Danny Picard executed three perfect cartwheels down the corridor and disappeared out the south door.

"Mr. Scanlon!" Cynthia Sinclair exclaimed on the gym stage after school, "you look like death warmed over." It was one of his grandmother's favorite expressions.

“What y’all want me to do for you today, ma’am?” Scanlon asked in his southern accent. “How ‘bout I take the girls’ chest measurements.”

Cynthia put on her flustered act and whacked Scanlon across the arm to show her appreciation of his devilishness. He was on the mend from his hangover, thanks to a half-hour catnap on the teachers’ lounge sofa. His recovery was short-lived as Cynthia soon had him on his hands and knees laying down masking tape on the stage floor for the placement of backdrop flats for the pageant. His head was athrob again in no time, his insides back in turmoil.

“Jack, I mean it,” she said after a while, “you look a fright. I think you should take yourself home to bed. You’re coming down with something. And be sure to drink plenty of liquids.”

“You can be sure of that,” Scanlon said, not putting up any argument. “I’ll be good as new tomorrow.”

“See that you are. There’s more work to be done, and time is running out.”

Cynthia had never followed up on her intention of having Scanlon and Stambaugh over to her place for drinks. What did an over-forty old maid do at night in the winter? Scanlon collected four stacks of tests from his desk and was half way down the stairs before he remembered that he’d forgotten to lock the door. He climbed back up the stairs swearing at himself. His door was wide open. Winship was in his room, opening drawers at lab stations.

“Something I can help you with, Daryl?”

Winship stood up quickly, looking startled. “Oh, I thought you’d gone.”

“As you can see, I haven’t. What are you looking for?”

“Nothing. A pair of scissors.” Winship fished a pair of rusty dissecting scissors from the drawer he had open and hurried out of the room. Scanlon watched him all the way to his office.

Scanlon opened all the drawers himself. He found only dirty beakers, flasks, and filthy test tubes, half of them broken; Incomplete dissection kits; rusty scalpels, needles, scissors and probes with flesh sticking to them. There were gum and candy wrappers, paper towels with obscenities written and drawn on them, burnt matches—general chaos. Winship had been conducting a secret inspection. Why hadn’t he said his piece then and there? Because he’d been caught sneaking around, that was why. Scanlon slammed the drawers shut, one after the other.

"What were you really after in my room yesterday?" Scanlon asked Winship in the teachers' room as the principal opened an envelope of cream substitute for his coffee. They were alone in the room and Scanlon heard himself blurting the question out before thinking. Winship didn't answer right away, and Scanlon, who was sprawled on the sofa, waited, his hands shaking from nervousness and the effects of last night's drinking. The humming electric clock above the coffee urn filled his brain. Winship turned to face him. He put his coffee cup down on the scarred table, his foot up on a chair. He rested his forearms on his knee.

"I'd heard complaints that the condition of the lab stations represented a safety hazard. I went to see for myself." Winship turned his hands over as if inspecting them for cleanliness. "I'm sorry to have to say the complaints were legitimate."

"Who complained?"

"I don't think that's important, Jack. What is important is that this isn't the first time you've had this problem."

"I got the lab cleaned up, didn't I?"

"Good God, Jack!" Winship shouted, "are you serious?" Winship lifted the chair off the floor and brought it down forcefully. Scanlon recoiled at the noise.

"You don't want a teacher. What you want is a domestic, someone to tidy up. I never pretended to be a neat freak."

"Listen to me, Jack. I know what a good job you're doing with the kids. I know how much time you give them, and I want you to know I appreciate it. You think it's easy for me to have to say these things to you? Well, it's not, believe me. But doggone it, part of your job is seeing to it that these little things get done. No matter how mundane you think they are. You've got to think about safety. About cleanliness. They're as much a part of the educational process as the subject you teach. These kids need to learn good housekeeping habits."

Scanlon looked up at Winship in disbelief. He was about to argue against this point of view but Winship interrupted.

"I know you think this is nonsense, but I'm serious, Jack. Education at this level doesn't involve intellectual matters. Habits of action as well as thought are important, in my view. Most of these kids' formal education ends when they leave Fairfield High."

"Isn't that all the more reason to pay attention to developing their critical faculties and let cleanliness be damned?" Scanlon asked, cringing from within at his own hypocrisy.

"Jack, Jack," Winship said, shaking his head at Scanlon's *naiveté*, "most of these kids will end up mucking out cow stalls the rest of their lives. Or raising babies. Or working low-skill, low-paying jobs where their survival depends on how well they manage their budget and their household, not how astute they are at reading between the lines of some *New York Times* editorial, or how adept they are at recognizing the politician's lie."

Before Scanlon could get in his licks about Winship's low opinion of Fairfield High kids, the bell rang for homeroom. His talk with the principal had him on edge all day.

"I've got to talk to you, Doug."

Stambaugh was slowly erasing the blackboard, two large hardcover books held against his chest with his free hand.

"Did you hear me? I said I've got to talk to you."

"I heard you, Jack," Stambaugh turned around and snapped chalk dust off his fingers. He looked remote, abstracted; he avoided Scanlon's eyes.

"Well?"

"I'm pretty busy."

"You're pretty busy? You can't spare me two minutes?" Scanlon felt himself start to shake. "To hell with you anyway. Who needs you?" Scanlon slammed the door on the way out of Stambaugh's classroom.

Stambaugh caught up with him in the parking lot as he was getting into his car.

"I'm sorry. I've got a lot on my mind." Stambaugh invited him up to his apartment and as they were climbing the stairs he stopped to warn Scanlon that he had nothing to drink in the house.

"You make it sound like I can't come to your place unless I get a drink. What do you think I am?"

Stambaugh turned to him and frowned before he unlocked the door. Scanlon found it odd he should find it necessary to lock his door in Fairfield.

Inside, several cardboard boxes were stacked against the wall, and Stambaugh's bookcase, the one Mrs. McKenzie had her man make especially for him, was empty.

"You getting ready to split? What's the story, Doug?"

"My C.O. hearing is coming up next week. I want to be ready for the worst."

"Oh." Scanlon sat down on the sofa. Seeing the empty bookcase, the boxes of books, filled him with the kind of dread he associated with moving. He'd moved too many times in his life to count. And Stambaugh's dilemma, which up to now occupied only an abstract part of his consciousness, seemed all too real.

"What was it you wanted to talk to me about?" Stambaugh sat in his favorite rocker and fingered his keys.

"You'd just up and leave? Right in the middle of school?"

"If I have to. I wouldn't if I had any other choices."

"They'd allow you to finish the year, wouldn't they?"

"They would."

"Then ..."

"I'd have to act fast," Stambaugh interrupted. "If I waited until June, I'd lose the element of surprise. They'd expect me to stay out the year. This buys me more time."

"As soon as Winship realizes you've fled, he'll report it. How much time do you think you'll gain?"

Stambaugh didn't answer. He slapped his keys against his thigh, his forehead creased in thought. Had he lost weight? He looked gaunt, dark around the eye sockets as if from lack of sleep. Scanlon had forgotten what he wanted to talk to him about. He asked Stambaugh if the Pattersons would accompany him to the hearing.

"No."

"I got the impression they were going to be in your corner. When we had dinner over there that night."

"I haven't said anything to either of them about the hearing."

"I see. You want me to go with you? I mean," Scanlon added quickly, pointing his forefingers at himself, "you *are* telling me about your hearing so I don't consider it too presumptuous to ask."

Stambaugh produced one of his enigmatic smiles. "That's very kind of you, Jack. I've given it a lot of thought and decided I should stand alone on this. If I can't argue my own case persuasively, why should I depend on someone else?"

"I'm not sure I follow that logic, my friend, but I guess you know what you want. If you change your mind, the offer stands. I mean it." People who tagged "I mean it" on their earnest promises always annoyed Scanlon. Now, here he was using the phrase himself.

"I thought you had something you wanted to discuss. We've talked about my problems *ad nauseam*. It wouldn't have anything to do with our beloved principal, would it?"

"I'd forgotten, to be truthful." Scanlon cocked his head, as if to listen to what he'd just said.

"What is it?"

"What I just said. You know, 'I'd forgotten, to be truthful,' the sound of it. You could interpret it as 'I'd forgotten to be truthful,' you know what I mean? A little pause, a tiny comma, and the whole meaning of things changes. As if one could forget to tell the truth." Scanlon laughed. "I guess you could forget *how* to tell the truth altogether, but there's not much chance of forgetting to tell a particular truth. You know what I'm saying?"

"I would be very surprised if there were." Stambaugh raised an eyebrow at Scanlon as if he were looking at someone deranged.

"Yeah. Winship's all over me again." Scanlon told him about his latest conversation with the principal. He would have preferred not to, now that he had learned of Stambaugh's crisis, but there really wasn't any way to avoid it after his little display of indignation in Stambaugh's classroom.

"There aren't many issues on which I agree with Winship. I'm on his side with this one, Jack. You are what might be described as a consummate slob. I personally have no quarrel with slobs, but Winship is obviously of a different mind. Frankly, I think he has the right to insist that you do as he wishes."

"Yeah, of course. I wasn't trying to suggest that he's overstepping his authority or anything. What gets me is that he's not man enough to say 'Look, Scanlon, clean up this pit or find some other line of work.' No, he's got to bring on this crap about its educational value. You see what I mean? I accept his authority. What I can't stomach is his sanctimony."

Scanlon was surprised to discover that Stambaugh looked bored and wasn't going out of his way to hide it. He studied his fingernails, looked over his shoulder, inspected his watch, wiggled his foot. Scanlon got up to leave. Stambaugh made no move to stop him.

"I appreciate your offer to go with me to the hearing, Jack. It means a lot to me."

"Sure. I'll be seeing you." Scanlon left with his feelings and his pride injured again.

Alice had overcooked the franks causing them to split. Ira was not pleased to be served split franks. Scanlon didn't see the big difference between split franks and unsplit, apart from the obvious one. Franks were franks.

"You know I don't like my dogs split like that, Mother," Ira complained. Scanlon rarely heard his uncle criticize Alice's cooking.

"Well, pardon me, your highness."

Alice and Ira hadn't exchanged a civil word since the night at the Legion. Lucky had taken to moping by the hassock in front of Ira's chair, his muzzle resting between his front paws. He'd look up at Ira with those sad, watery eyes that asked, "what's wrong, Dad?" And no sooner would Alice get comfortable on the sofa than Nanette would be in her lap.

"You cut your own tree?" Scanlon asked, "or buy it off the lot?" He referred to Christmas trees. He remembered from his Johnny Labalm days how Alice always over decorated her trees; always too many icicles, and smothered in angel hair.

"I take her down with one blast of the twelve gauge. There's a good crop over in East Groveton. Got to snow shoe in this year, though," Ira said. "Want to come along?"

"I've never tried snow shoes."

"Nothin' to it. Pass me the brown bread, Mother."

"When are you planning to go after it?" Scanlon slathered soft butter on his brown bread. The idea of snowshoeing in the deep woods appealed to him.

"Saturday."

"I don't know why you're so late this year," Alice said. "We always have our tree two weeks before Christmas. We won't even have it a week before, this year." Alice shook her head, displeased with Ira's Christmas tree procrastination.

"Yes, Mother," Ira said, with his familiar eye rolling.

"I saw that look," Alice said. "You're not fooling anybody."

"Huh?" Ira cupped his hard-of-hearing left ear.

"You heard me." To Scanlon Alice said, "He hears good enough when he wants to."

Ira grinned at Scanlon.

"You know where I could get my hands, or maybe my feet, on a pair of snowshoes, Ira?"

"Oh, I think maybe we could rustle you up a pair." Ira put away four split franks without any problem. He pushed his chair back from the table and patted his belly. "I'm full, Mother. Be fartin' all night, too."

"Well, aren't we refined," Alice said.

Scanlon had eaten three franks himself, along with two helpings of yellow-eyed beans, and three slabs of brown bread, two beers. It was the kind of meal that would put him to sleep the minute he started grading test papers. Just as well. Asleep he wouldn't be tempted to keep on drinking.

Chapter Twenty-six

Winship called it the "recreation room." He could have as easily referred to it as the "blue room." The wall-to-wall carpet, pills and all, were bright blue; barnboard walls, stained blue.

Extraneous furniture had been removed to make room for dancing; the lights were turned low. Scanlon arrived feeling no pain. Madelaine greeted him at the door and ushered him into the blue room. Cynthia Sinclair was there, and the Sorensons, and to Scanlon's surprise, Lillian Bloemer. No sign of her mother tonight. Madelaine had on a red velvet dress that accentuated her thick middle.

"How nice you came early, Jack. You can help Cynthia with *hors d'oeuvres*, since you work so well together. The pageant was splendid. Congratulations." Madelaine squeezed his hand.

"Early? What time is it?"

"Cynthia," Madelaine called to Cynthia Sinclair who was chatting with Daryl Winship near the white-clothed card table, which bore several bottles of liquor and mixes, a bucket of ice cubes. The bar acted on Scanlon like a force field. "I've got you an assistant." Cynthia held a highball glass to her small bosom. Scanlon moved toward the bar, Madelaine at his side. Rob and Jackie Sorenson ignored him, seeming to be engaged in intense conversation with Lillian Bloemer, which of course Scanlon knew to be a big fake. Would he be asked to "rescue" Lillian again tonight?

Winship had put out only inexpensive liquor. Even a brand of Scotch Scanlon had never heard of. But it was Scotch, inexpensive or not, and he had Lillian to thank for giving him a taste for it.

"M.Y.O.D.?" Scanlon asked Winship. Winship gave him a blank look. "Make your own drinks?"

"Oh," Winship said. "Sure, help yourself. Tall glasses or short, take your pick. When the ice gets low, you can get refills in the kitchen. Every man for himself."

Scanlon turned his back to the others so they wouldn't see him pour three fingers of Scotch over ice. An open bottle of club soda had gone flat, so he added a splash of water from the pitcher.

"Merry Christmas," Scanlon said, raising his glass.

"Same to you." Winship clinked glasses with Scanlon. Cynthia didn't let them drink until they'd clinked hers. Scanlon sipped his drink and discovered that it was stronger than he expected. Madelaine poured from the water pitcher into a long-stemmed martini glass and dropped a lemon twist into it.

"Water with a twist of lemon. That won't get you very far, Madelaine," Scanlon said, as she joined them.

"What are you talking about? This is my famous martini with a twist. I made a pitcher. Keep your eye on it and let me know when it gets low so Daryl can make a fresh batch."

"Jesus," Scanlon said, looking into his glass.

"What?" Madelaine asked.

"Nothing. Merry Christmas." Scanlon drank more cautiously this time and noted mentally that martinis complemented Scotch nicely. And he was already feeling warm and magnanimous. He'd worn his blue blazer and a white turtleneck sweater. The blazer would have to go because Tommy Winship was preparing the fireplace, and the room was too hot already for Scanlon's liking. Winship had on the same Irish fishing sweater he'd worn at the September party, which caused Scanlon to wonder if he ever conferred with his wife on the subject of appropriate dress for social occasions. Sorenson was relaxed and casual in white shirt and slacks; his wife had gotten dumpy after giving birth and wore a miniskirt that made her look dumpier. Cynthia could always be counted on to dress in bad taste. Tonight she held to form in her pink chiffon party dress and black patent leather shoes that tied with white ribbons. What would Dennis Kitchell bring to this sartorial hodgepodge? Lyle Higgins?

In the course of the next hour, all the Fairfield High faculty had arrived. Stambaugh came in close enough behind the Pattersons to make Scanlon wonder if they hadn't come together. And if they had, did this mean that Stambaugh had changed his mind about having them to his hearing? Scanlon experienced a tug of jealousy. He went to the bar to prepare himself another Scotch and martini. This time he was more generous with the martini mix.

Everyone except for Stambaugh seemed prepared to throw caution to the wind tonight. It had been a long fall, made to seem longer because of the early arrival of snow and winter-like weather. For Scanlon, it had been a grueling emotional stint. What the teachers needed to do now was relax, let their hair down. Scanlon kept an eye open for the chance to talk to Rachel. With all he'd had to drink, he was prepared to give her another chance. It was only the Christian thing to do. True, he had never been sure of himself where women were concerned, but hadn't she kissed him? He hadn't imagined that. There had to have been something behind that act. It seemed not unreasonable to assume so in his present state of mild inebriation.

It was Rachel who intercepted him on his way to the bathroom. She had been in the kitchen, chatting with Madelaine Winship, and was on her way to join the party in the recreation room when their paths crossed.

"You were about to snub me, weren't you," she said.

"I didn't see you, actually. If I had, I probably would have snubbed you, yes."

"You don't like me anymore." Rachel put on her pouty face. Tonight, he found it alluring again.

"What makes you think I ever liked you?"

"Woman's intuition." She leaned her shoulder against the door jamb and peeked up at Scanlon from beneath her long eyelashes. She had on a white turtleneck ski sweater and black slacks. Her perfume was strong in his nostrils.

"What're you drinking?"

"Nothing." She showed him her empty hands.

"We can't have that. Come on, I'll get you some wine." Scanlon made a move toward the recreation room. Rachel grabbed his arm.

"Bring it to me outside. I need fresh air."

"It's freezing out there."

Madelaine appeared, carrying a jug of white wine. "What are you two plotting?"

"Jack's going to take me outside and seduce me in the snow."

"I'll need to ply her with wine first," Scanlon said, relieving Madelaine of the jug. To Rachel he said, "I'll get you a glass."

"Jack, you can't have all of that," Madelaine said.

In the kitchen, Scanlon found a glass in the cupboard and poured a generous portion for Rachel, the temptress. His heart raced; his hands shook so much he spilled wine on the counter.

He returned to find Rachel and Madelaine sitting next to each other on a cushioned window seat in the dining room. Their heads were very close together, as if they were sharing a secret. Rachel, he recalled, had always defended Winship against criticism, but he wasn't aware that she was tight with the principal's wife as well. Scanlon handed Rachel her wine, gave the jug back to Madelaine. He'd left his own drink in the kitchen. The women accepted their wine and bottle without looking at him. He hurried back to the kitchen to fetch his drink and returned to find Rachel and Madelaine gone.

"I thought I was supposed to be outside seducing you," Scanlon whispered in Rachel's ear in the recreation room where she had joined her husband and Doug Stambaugh. How would Patterson react if he took Rachel in his arms, buried his face in her hair? What would Rachel do? Right now, she acted as though he weren't in the room. She didn't acknowledge his tender whisper.

"I think Jack has something he wants to tell you, Rache," Patterson said, looking arch and amused enough for Scanlon to notice.

Scanlon offered Patterson his hand. "If I can't bang your wife, Josh, at least let me shake your hand." Patterson's hand was big and damp; he looked confused, not sure he should be amused or insulted. Stambaugh looked down at the floor.

"Bet I can tell what Douglas is thinking," Scanlon said. "Here we go again, he's thinking. Scanlon drunk again and boorish, waving his inferiority complex around like a flag. Right, Douglas? Well, screw you if I embarrass you."

Patterson put an arm around Scanlon's shoulders and tried to steer him away from his wife and Stambaugh. Scanlon resisted.

"Don't condescend to me, you fuck." Scanlon flung Patterson's arm away and in doing so sloshed his drink on Rachel's sweater. Madelaine hurried across the room toward them. Conversation, which had been lively and high-pitched, suddenly ceased. Rachel dabbed at her wet front with a cocktail napkin, her face flushed. The room went out of focus for Scanlon for a moment. Then it was Winship and Higgins who moved in his direction from across the room. Scanlon saw double. Soon, Higgins had a tight grip on his arm. Madelaine led the way; Winship got hold of his other arm and assisted Higgins in whisking Scanlon to the kitchen.

"I'll put some coffee water on," Madelaine announced.

"Just have a chair, there, young fella," Higgins said. Winship pulled a chair out from the kitchen table. "Easy does it." They sat him down and stood over him.

"I don't want any coffee," Scanlon said.

"You'll feel better," said Madelaine.

"That's right, Jack," Winship added. "A nice cup of coffee, you'll feel right as rain."

"You people make me sick." Scanlon started to get up, but Higgins had a firm hand on his arm.

"Why don't you just sit quiet, Mr. Scanlon, and let Mrs. Winship make you a cup of strong coffee." The room was in motion, wheeling like a carnival Tilt-A-Whirl.

"He looks like he's going to be sick," Winship said. Higgins jerked Scanlon out of the chair and pushed him toward the bathroom. Scanlon went limp, allowed himself to be literally dragged out of the room.

Higgins left him alone in the bathroom. He dropped the toilet cover and sat down, face in his hands, elbows on his knees. The spins stopped. There was no nausea. The Winship's bathroom was also blue. Blue wallpaper with a pink floral print, blue sink, blue bathtub, blue toilet seat. The toilet paper was blue. There was a bowl of blue, scented soap balls in a painted china bowl on the toilet tank. The room smelled blue. It would be nice to take a shower. There was a window next to the blue sink large enough for a man to crawl through. What about his coat? To hell with it.

Scanlon got up and flushed the toilet. He ran water in the sink, surprised that it didn't flow blue. He opened the window next to the sink, but it was no good because of a storm window behind it. He'd have to escape by some other route.

"Feel better?" Madelaine said to him in the kitchen as if he were her little boy. Higgins sat at the kitchen table looking hard at him over his bifocals. Scanlon's arm was sore where Higgins had gripped him.

"Yes. And very embarrassed. I'd like to go, If you'd be kind enough to tell me where I can find my coat."

Higgins laughed. "You're not going anywhere in your condition, buster." Winship had left the room. Madelaine poured hot water in a coffee mug. Music drifted into the kitchen from the recreation room, the sound of laughter and loud talk.

"Why don't you go and cut a rug with your lovely wife," Scanlon said.

"And why don't you just sit down and drink your coffee instead of being such a wise acre," Higgins replied.

“Now just stop it,” Madelaine said, bringing Scanlon’s coffee to the table.

“I don’t want this, Madelaine,” Scanlon said, pushing the steaming mug away from him.

“Are we going to have to go through this again?” Madelaine referred to the last time Scanlon had been a guest in her house and she’d had to persuade him to drink black coffee before he was allowed to drive his car.

“I don’t need coffee.”

Higgins snorted. “You’re drunk as a lord. Now do as you’re told. Drink your coffee.”

Scanlon pushed away from the table and knocked over his chair getting up. He walked toward the dining room. Higgins was quick to intercept him.

“Take your hands off me,” Scanlon said, turning around, off balance, to face Higgins whose jaw was set and determined.

“What is going on in here?” Lillian Bloemer wanted to know. “Jack, are you all right?”

“Ask the commandant, here,” Scanlon said. “Ask my keeper.”

“Our friend’s three sheets to the wind, and he won’t mind his hostess and drink his coffee like a good boy. I may have to get out the switch.” Higgins was smiling now, in his unpleasant way.

“He looks all right to me,” said Lillian.

“Well, he’s not all right,” Madelaine said, emphatically. “Didn’t you witness his little scene in the other room?”

“No.” Lillian looked puzzled. “What scene?”

“I spill a little booze on Snow White’s sweater and everybody gets bent out of shape,” Scanlon said, moving closer to Lillian. “I am not drunk, and I do not want, nor do I need, your coffee, Madelaine.” Why was it that everybody always wanted to force black coffee down his throat?

“Where do you keep the switch, Maddie?” Higgins asked, looking around the room. Tommy Winship came into the room bearing a tray of dirty glasses. He had that wait-till-the-kids-hear-how-their-bio-teacher-behaves-when-he’s-trashed look.

“I am not drinking your coffee. Get used to it. And if it isn’t asking too much, I’d like to have my coat so I can be on my way. Is that asking so much?” Scanlon saw two of Madelaine Winship.

“You’re not fit to drive,” Madelaine said, stalking out of the room. Momentarily she returned with his overcoat, then turned and left again before he could say anything more. Higgins shook his head and followed Madelaine, leaving Scanlon, the hopeless case, alone with Lillian Bloemer.

"Why don't you stay a while longer, Jack? You're not going to abandon me to these bores."

"Afraid so, Lillian." Scanlon lost his balance putting on his overcoat and bumped hard into the kitchen table.

"You are a little tipsy, you know. Perhaps you should listen to Madelaine."

"I'll be fine."

"The roads aren't in the best shape."

"I'll be all right." Scanlon started for the kitchen door so he would not have to encounter any more of his colleagues.

"Jack! Stop acting like a child!"

Instead of walking out the door, as he should have done, Scanlon paused, and faced Lillian, one hand on the doorknob. Lillian sat at the kitchen table, one fat leg crossed over the other. She scrutinized him through those awful thick lenses, one elbow on the table. She held her empty silver cigarette holder between her fingers. Scanlon felt himself swaying in his tracks. There was nothing he could do about it. He was drunk and he knew it. Now, he saw two of Lillian Bloemer.

"I really think you might sit for a few minutes, Jack. You could do that at least if you're determined not to drink any coffee."

"I'll sit down if you get me my drink from the other room." Scanlon lurched toward a chair across from Lillian. "Hey, I think you may be right. I could very well be too drunk to drive. I'm obviously too drunk to walk."

"And you want me to get you more to drink?" Lillian inserted a cigarette in her holder and asked Scanlon for a light. He fumbled around in his coat and jacket pockets, all thumbs, and came out with a limp book of matches with the cover torn off. He offered them to Lillian.

"A gentleman would light it for me," she said.

Like a man with arthritic fingers, Scanlon tried in vain to strike a match. Lillian took the matches from him gently and lit her own cigarette. Stambaugh came in the room followed by Josh Patterson.

"Is he all right?" Patterson asked Lillian Bloemer, as if Scanlon were unconscious or not present.

"He's peachy keen," Scanlon said. And to Lillian, "Tell Mr. Patterson that I'm quite all right and thank him for his concern."

"You're all broken out in hives," Stambaugh said, with his worried expression.

Scanlon touched his face with his fingertips. "I don't feel hivey." His face *did* feel hot.

"Good grief," said Rachel when she came in to see Scanlon, "what's happening to you, Jack?"

"He's having a hive reaction," Lillian said. "Nothing to worry about. I've seen him this way before."

"What?" Scanlon asked. The only possible opportunity Lillian would have had to see him in this condition was the day he'd visited her and her mother. Why hadn't she said anything then?

"Alcohol is known to bring on that reaction. You broke out the time you were at my house, whether or not you were aware of it."

"Should we call a doctor?" Rachel asked. She looked at Scanlon as if he were covered with running sores, her fist full of her husband's jacket sleeve.

"Why don't you all just leave me alone," Scanlon said, rising and immediately sitting back down. The room tilted again when he stood.

"He should have coffee, shouldn't he?" Rachel asked Patterson.

"Don't mention that word in Mr. Scanlon's presence," Lillian said, laughing, cigarette smoke spewing from her mouth and thick nostrils.

"I think he needs fresh air," Stambaugh said. "What do you say, Jack? Why don't we go out for a little walk."

In the meantime, Winship and Madelaine had come back to the kitchen, followed by Lyle Higgins and Cynthia Sinclair. They all had advice to give on the help and maintenance of Jack Scanlon, Fairfield High faculty's problem drunk. Scanlon rested his forearms on the kitchen table, put his head on them and closed his eyes. Inside his head, the world spun round and round.

Chapter Twenty-seven

K: It's coming up on the anniversary of your wife leaving you. How're you handling it, Jack? How're you feeling?

Scanlon drank a little bourbon before he answered Kennedy. It had been poured and waiting for him when he entered Kennedy's office.

S: Haven't given it a thought. I got enough to worry about without dredging up old business.

K: Heard from your daughter?

S: Just a card. Stupid fucking Christmas card Katie no doubt picked out. Had her pedestrian taste all over it like fingerprints.

K: She tell you she loves you?

Scanlon looked at Kennedy, but Kennedy's attention was out the window.

S: Who?

K: Your daughter. Who else?

S: Yes, but ...

K: You don't trust it.

S: Why should I? After all these months, why should I trust anything? All it said was Merry Christmas, Daddy, Love, etc.

K: Nothing from your ex? No word as to how things were going?

Kennedy had his shoes off again. His white socks were dirty, but his feet didn't stink.

S: No. Nothing.

K: I thought you might go ahead and make the trip out. I really did.

S: You disappointed? Sorry.

K: How're you going to deal with this if you don't go out there?

Kennedy dropped his feet off the desk abruptly and sprang upright in his chair.

S: Let it fade away like an old soldier.

Scanlon finished off his whiskey and tapped his cup on the corner of Kennedy's desk.

K: That's a mature attitude.

Kennedy poured more bourbon in Scanlon's Styrofoam, more for himself. His nose was redder than usual today. Scanlon suspected his counselor of getting a head start on him. He was in a holiday mood again.

S: I suppose getting shitfaced with me every Friday afternoon is mature. Not to mention professional.

K: Nothing in the book says we have to have refreshments. It's fine with me if we dispense with the practice.

S: Sure, Bob.

K: You sound dubious.

S: Are you telling me you provide this only for my benefit? You're hooked as much as I am, maybe more.

K: So you think you're hooked?

S: Yes, I do.

K: How's that?

S: I said, yes I do. I think I'm hooked. All right? I can admit it, at least. Say it out loud. Can you claim as much?

K: I think so, Jack. I've been going to AA for years, saying it out loud for a long time. I don't have any illusions.

Scanlon laughed.

S: AA's done you a lot of good. My stepfather used to attend the occasional meeting. He used to say only losers went regularly. He'd only go so he could feel superior to the losers. You can't be serious, Bob.

K: I'm very serious.

S: The folks down at AA know about you? If they do, they can't look too favorably on your habits.

K: They're aware of my habits. Maybe you'd consider coming to a meeting.

S: So I can booze with a clear conscience?

K: Not quite. In fact, the opposite. The conscience works overtime after you've attended a few meetings and then fall.

Scanlon balked at the idea of AA meetings. It was one thing to admit to yourself that you were not completely in control of your drinking, another to go whining about it in public in front of a lot of drunks and losers.

S: I think I'll have to respectfully decline your kind offer.

K: You afraid?

S: I don't think that's it. They sound like a waste of time, is all. You're a walking example.

K: A lot of people would disagree.

S: Thanks anyway, Bob. But no thanks. Why don't we make a deal, Bob. Let's say no more booze at these sessions. That way I won't have to feel guilty for your drinking and mine, too. What do you say?

K: Deal.

Kennedy picked up the bottle and tore away the wrapper. There was maybe an inch left. He measured out the last of it carefully, and held the bottle suspended for a moment over the wastebasket before dropping it. He made a bombs away whistling sound.

K: Here's to the last drink we'll ever have together.

Kennedy toasted and threw back his drink. Scanlon did the same.

S: How long do you think this'll last?

K: If you don't bring anything in, I promise I won't.

Kennedy squashed his cup in one hand before depositing it on his desk. Scanlon tossed his empty cup in the wastebasket.

S: What a lousy pact. I feel rotten.

K: Me, too.

They sat in reflective silence for several minutes. The events of the evening at Winship's Christmas party intruded painfully into Scanlon's thoughts. He had been reluctant to share the details of the evening with Kennedy, up to now. There was still something that told him to show Kennedy only selected parts of himself. He wanted Kennedy's approval as a man more than as a professional. Kennedy was prepared to reveal his own weaknesses. It didn't seem right, on balance, that Scanlon should withhold his own embarrassments. He was toasted enough by now to let down his guard.

S: How would you like to hear about what an ass I made of myself the other night?

Kennedy listened without interrupting as Scanlon reconstructed the evening. Telling it was more difficult than he thought, as his memory proved fuzzy in several places. For example, he wasn't clear on the details of how he got home. Somebody drove his car back to Groveton. Whether he was driven in his own car, or rode with somebody else, he couldn't be sure. And he was vague about the details of being sick in Winship's kitchen. It was horrific enough to remember that he'd gotten sick at Winship's kitchen table. And the look of surprise and disgust on Rachel Patterson's face the instant before his insides spilled out on the kitchen table was burned in his memory. But after that, he had no memory.

S: I'll never be able to face them. How can I after what happened?

K: You have a choice? When classes resume you're going to have to face them.

S: I have the choice of not returning. I can just split and be done with them.

K: You'd never do that. You're too much of a Yankee to pull a disappearing act like that.

S: I don't know about that, Bob. All I know is I'd rather do anything than have to face those people again. It's as simple as that.

Scanlon was sweating and shaking, wishing there was more to drink.

K: You really think it will be as bad as all that? Think about it. Did you do anything so terrible? Anything any one of us isn't capable of doing?

S: You don't know these folks. You don't know what I've had to put up with from them already, before this happened.

K: Somebody drove you home, you say?

S: I guess so. Who can remember? I can't really remember.

K: Somebody must have driven you home. You didn't drive yourself, right?

S: Right.

K: And somebody cleaned you up?

S: I guess so.

Kennedy paused to rub his temple. In the silence, Scanlon was conscious of Kennedy's adenoidal breathing, a kind of wheeze that reminded him of the way his stepfather breathed, everything through the nose, through some air passage obstruction.

K: Starting to snow.

S: Yeah. That's all it ever seems to do around here. No wonder everyone in Vermont owns a Ski-Doo. Kids are after me all the time to ride with them.

K: So why don't you?

S: I don't know. Maybe I will one of these days. Frankly, they scare me. I nearly ran one over crossing the road the other day. It's a weird pastime, if you ask me.

K: Yeah.

S: Where do you go for these AA meetings?

K: Masonic Temple. Monday nights.

S: No shit? The Masonic Temple? That's where my stepfather used to go. Can't be easy to keep your anonymity in a town the size of Groveton.

K: I don't suppose it is. I don't live here.

Scanlon had been seeing Kennedy for three months, and he had no idea where the man lived. He knew nothing of Kennedy's personal life apart from the fact that he'd lost his thirteen-year-old daughter to leukemia.

S: So where do you live, Bob? If that's not too personal a question.

K: Lancaster.

S: That's kind of a haul, isn't it?

K: I don't mind. I find the drive relaxing.

S: I never was able to relax behind the wheel. The time I start to relax is the time I have my fatal accident. I don't think that's the way I want to check out. You?

Kennedy shrugged his shoulders.

K: As long as it was quick.

S: You're right. Quickness is everything.

There was another awkward pause, an uneasy silence between them; the only sound in the room, Kennedy's labored breathing.

S: Bob.

K: Yeah?

S: You think we were a little hasty with, you know, the abstinence thing?

Kennedy looked at Scanlon over the tops of his glasses and grinned.

K: Maybe a tad hasty. You know the saying, a foolish consistency is the hobgoblin of small minds, or words to that effect?

S: Yeah. I catch your meaning.

K: What're your plans for New Year's Eve?

Scanlon had a moment of intense anticipation, for it sounded to him as though Kennedy might be on the verge of inviting him to share the evening with him.

S: I don't have any plans.

K: Me neither. Never make a big deal out of New Year's Eve. Stay home, go to bed early, make no resolutions. That's my motto.

S: Yeah. Good motto. I think my aunt's throwing some kind of small party. I don't know. I might visit my mother, my brothers. I haven't any idea, really.

Scanlon was disappointed that Kennedy hadn't invited him to his home for New Year's Eve.

K: So, next time I see you it'll be nineteen sixty-nine.

Kennedy shook his head at the rapid passage of time.

S: Yeah. The year I turn thirty. How much worse can it be than nineteen sixty-eight? Answer me that.

K: Hard to imagine a worse year than this one.

S: I'm not making any fucking resolutions either, if you're interested.

K: Don't blame you. Why make resolutions you know you're not going to be able to keep? It's self-deceit.

S: I'm glad we share this pessimism, Bob. I'd hate to think that my shrink was some wishy-washy Pollyanna.

Kennedy laughed.

K: It takes more than empty promises to change your way of life, Jack. You know that.

S: Yeah.

In fact, Scanlon wasn't sure he knew that at all. Kennedy seemed to be losing interest in him. For his part, Scanlon felt he was treading water. He was impatient for change. He wanted to wake up one morning to find that his whole life had changed. He yearned for optimism, sobriety, hope for the future, for his personal future and for mankind's. He was tired of being pessimistic, hungover, depressed, fearful, bored, always physically exhausted. It was no way to live. He wanted to be in love. But he was scared of that more than anything else.

K: At the risk of sounding trite, let me wish you a happy New Year, Jack. Think of the New Year as an occasion for hope. You've got youth on your side, despite what the flower children say. Don't lose heart. See you in a couple weeks.

Chapter Twenty-eight

"You've gained weight."

"Can I come in?"

Scanlon's mother left the door open and walked away from him into the apartment. There was no light in the cold hall that smelled of stale cooking, exactly the way it had the last time he was here. He went in and closed the door behind him.

"You're the last person I expected to see at the door. You want coffee?"

"No." He noticed a folded-up afghan on the sofa instead of his stepfather. The living room was too tidy. Bill Scanlon was on a bender.

"There's nothing else if you don't want coffee."

"I don't want anything." This was a lie. What he wanted was a very strong drink. If Bill Scanlon was indeed on a bender, there would be nothing of that sort in the house. Scanlon followed his mother into the narrow kitchen. There was a pile of needlework on the table; she sat down and picked it up. Her hair was grayer, and she'd put on a little weight herself. Her face had more color than the last time he'd seen her.

"What brings you here out of the blue?"

"I had some free time. Keith and Billy around?" He made a point of not asking for his stepfather. His mother expressed her displeasure by not looking at him. He supposed it was no more than he deserved, having been silent and out of touch for over a year. But when had she ever looked at him, really looked at him as if he were her son, someone worthy of her attention? Scanlon sat down; already sorry he'd come.

His mother laughed harshly and stabbed at her needlework. "Those two idiots." She pronounced idiots "eediots" just like her mother, Johnny's Grammy. "Act like common criminals, dope peddlers. You'd think Keith would've learned his lesson. Thinks he knows it all. 'Oh, Ma,' he says, 'you worry too much. I know what I'm doing.'"

"Great."

"This might not have happened if you'd been around."

"Are they living here with you?"

"I won't have no dope peddlers under my roof."

"So where are they?"

"They got their own place. Corner of Walnut and Main. Spend all their money on clothes, dope, and hi-fi records. Billy spent eight hundred dollars on a hi-fi. Eight hundred dollars. Lot of good his hi-fi's going to do him in jail."

"You still at the shop?"

"I haven't worked there since I kicked the old man out. I'm at the university now, cleaning. I've got my driver's license and a used car. I like being independent. I like living alone, too."

"You really kicked him out?" Scanlon was surprised. Surprised and resentful. Why couldn't she have done it years ago when it would have counted for something? Maybe all she really ever wanted was to be left alone, to live by herself, to be "independent." "Where is he now?"

"Taken up housekeeping with a woman with three young kids. Lives up by Gilman Park when he's not in some beer joint or the Social Club." Dorothy Scanlon laid her needlework on the kitchen table and sipped coffee. In the needlework frame was a beach scene with blue sky, sandpipers, and beige sand.

"When did you take up needlework?"

"Couple months ago. I like working with my hands."

"What about your crosswords?" Scanlon got his cigarettes out of his pocket and offered one to his mother.

"Gave those up two years ago. You don't remember? Haven't done a crossword in ages. Where have you been all this time? What is it, over a year?"

"You heard about Katie and me?"

"She's got your daughter, hasn't she? Where are they, California? How could you let her take Lucy? What about me? I'm her grandmother."

"I've got no rights in this thing." Scanlon lit his cigarette, looked around for an ashtray.

"Use this." His mother pushed her saucer in front of him. "So are they in California or not?"

"Yes."

"California. Is that where you've been?"

"No." Scanlon brought his mother up to date on his life since last New Year's Eve; he saved telling her that he was living with Ira and Alice for last.

"Couldn't you have called, at least?"

"It's been a very confusing year. I thought it best if I stayed away from certain people and certain places for a while."

"You couldn't let 'certain people' know that you were alive?"

"I'm sorry. I told you, I wasn't feeling that great. I'm still not feeling that great, to tell the truth."

"You should see a doctor if you're not feeling good," his mother said, back at her needlework, letting the sarcasm in her voice be heard. Scanlon hadn't mentioned that he was seeing Kennedy. She'd flip out if she knew he was going to a shrink. "How can you stand to live in the same house with Alice? I'll never understand how Ira puts up with her. Her and that family of hers. I'm surprised you still got your ears."

"I don't mind Alice. She's been great to me. I don't mind her at all."

"Talks too much to suit me."

His mother had always gone out of her way to find fault; always looking for the flaw in someone's character, the skeleton in the closet. No wonder he'd grown up cynical.

"I kind of like teaching school."

"I hope you like teaching it better than you liked going to it. God help your pupils if you don't."

"People can change."

"Yes. For the worse, from what I've seen of people."

"You still got the cat? What was his name?"

"Got hit by a car. I don't want no more cats."

"You don't have to let it go out. Cats are happy in the house, if you start them out that way." How many pets had died because of her neglect he'd hate to count. They were forever getting run over, poisoned, lost. She'd never spend a dime to take them to the vet. In his mother's view, animals were happier shifting for themselves. It was nature's way.

"I don't want no smell of cat box in the house. You must know what that's like, living with Alice."

"I don't even notice anymore." Scanlon got up to turn off the dripping faucet. It continued to drip. The kitchen was narrow, and there was no window. He liked big kitchens with plenty of windows, like the Pattersons' kitchen. Every place he'd ever lived with his mother and stepfather had been small and dark. When they first moved to Garrison from Vermont, they lived in a rundown four-room shack with unfinished wood floors. The only source of heat was an oil-burning kitchen stove. One week that first winter it got so cold the pipes froze. They moved the bed his mother and stepfather slept in into the kitchen, and that was where the whole family slept—his mother, stepfather, Keith and Billy and himself—together, just to keep warm. The cat they had at the time ran away, and Scanlon envied him.

"You just stood by and let her take Lucy?"

"She had the law on her side. What could I do?"

"You should have taken her here to me, before that damned fool got a hold of her."

"You mean I should have kidnapped her? You can go to prison for that sort of thing." The last place he'd have brought his daughter was here, even if he had been inclined to kidnap her.

"Couldn't you find a lawyer who could prove she was an unfit mother?"

Scanlon laughed. His mother wanted to know what was so funny.

"What's funny is that she wasn't an unfit mother. She was a good mother."

"She was so good a mother she wouldn't let her daughter have nothing to do with her own grandmother. If that's what you call a good mother, I'd like to see your bad one."

Scanlon ran a hand through his hair. "What good does it do to talk about it now? Where did you say Billy and Keith were living? I thought I'd swing by, see what they're up to."

"They don't keep normal hours. You never know when they're going to be home or out on the streets selling dope. Only time they come see me is when they want me to chauffeur them someplace in my car. Neither one of them got a license."

"Maybe I'll drop around their place, then."

"What'll it be, another year before I see you again?"

"It's not that easy for me to get away. I don't have a lot of money."

"How rich do you think I am, cleaning rooms?"

"I don't see what your poverty has to do with mine. I don't have money to do a lot of traveling."

His mother's mouth was set in a familiar grim line, the one he'd come to associate with Bill Scanlon's absence. Now, since Bill Scanlon was absent involuntarily, was the mouth for her oldest son? What did she expect from him? He hadn't intended to return after seeing Billy and Keith, but then he heard himself asking his mother if it would be all right if he came back for supper.

"Of course you can stay for supper. Stay as long as you want. What, are you on vacation?"

"Yeah, but I got a lot of work to do back in Groveton. It's really not all vacation. People don't understand what teachers are required to do."

"Looks like a pretty easy life to me."

"It's not the way you think. Listen, I'll be back around five. That all right?"

"I usually eat earlier than that."

"Well, why don't you tell me what time you want me to be here."

"Five's all right."

"Well, I'll be seeing you."

Scanlon searched the mailboxes in the vestibule and found his half-brothers' box with their names handwritten on adhesive tape. They lived on the second floor. He climbed the stairs, tentative and nervous. How long had it been since he'd seen either of them? Five years? Five years ago they were teenagers.

Their door was open a crack. He knocked. There was no answer. He knocked again and stuck his head inside.

"Keith? Billy?" he called. No answer. Could he have the wrong apartment? He opened the door all the way. The room was bare except for a sofa bed on castors. There were worn places along the walls where furniture would have been. It looked like Keith and Billy had moved out. There were doors off the bare room to the right and left. Scanlon decided to have a look.

The door on the right led into a kitchenette. The countertop was littered with dirty dishes, beer bottles, ashtrays full of dead butts. Scanlon opened the refrigerator and found an open package of cold meat, some American cheese, a small jar of mayonnaise, pickles—four bottles of beer. He closed the refrigerator and investigated the room off the left door of the empty living room.

Two mattresses with wrinkled sheets and tangled blankets; a dresser with all the drawers open, underwear and socks spilling out of them; more ashtrays on the dresser and on the floor beside the mattresses. Against one wall, a sophisticated looking hi-fi set, record albums strewn around the floor; on the wall, a life-sized poster of some rock musician with long hair and a red bandanna around his head. A closet door was wide open, revealing lots of colorful shirts, several pair of fancy shoes on the floor. Anybody could have lived here. The hi-fi was the only evidence that maybe Billy was one of the occupants. Nothing else he could see triggered any associations of these two boys with whom he had shared nearly ten years of his life.

He heard muffled voices from the hall, heavy footsteps on the stairs, and though it was probably Keith and Billy, Scanlon was apprehensive, as if he were in the apartment illicitly. He had been out of touch with these kids for so long.

Billy came in first, Keith right behind him. Scanlon planted himself in the middle of the living room to greet them, feeling exposed and anxious.

"Holy shit!" Billy exclaimed. Keith blinked several times as if the light was too bright, and his mouth opened a little.

"You were expecting Jimi Hendrix?" It was the only psychedelic rock personality Scanlon could think of.

"Cool stache," Keith said of Scanlon's mustache. Both Keith and Billy had shoulder-length hair; Keith wore his in a ponytail, Billy's hung free, impossibly tangled, but clean. They were both sticklers for personal cleanliness, even if their fastidiousness did not run to keeping an orderly or clean house. Billy sported a droopy Fu Manchu himself, almost too pale to notice.

"Ain't seen you in a coon's age," Billy finally said to Scanlon. Did he hear rebuke in his half-brother's voice?

They sat around on the mattresses in the bedroom, listened to records and talked. Scanlon drank beer, Keith and Billy smoked reefer. Scanlon told them about his visit with their mother. His brothers nodded their heads like hipsters, squinting through the sweet smelling marijuana smoke, so thick it had Scanlon giddy just breathing it. He'd refused their offer of "hits."

"Ma's been weird since she dumped the old man," Keith said.

"She was cool for a while there, just before the shit hit the fan," Billy said. "Shit, she even used to smoke a little with us, dig Hendrix. As soon as he was gone, she changed. Got a set of wheels, started doing that needlework shit, whatever you call it. Started handing out shit about how we were living. She changed like overnight. Weird."

"Yeah," Keith assented. "Real weird."

"I noticed she's stopped smoking cigarettes, too. And no more crosswords," Scanlon said. Keith and Billy looked at each other. Scanlon realized that this was old news. "She says you guys are dealing."

"Man," Keith said, drawing out the word like the hipsters, screwing his face all up, "she makes a big deal out of such small shit. We sell a lid here and there, a few bags two, three times a week to friends. She's got us hanging on street corners peddling to high school kids. I wouldn't sell drugs to no high school kid. She's so off the wall these days you wouldn't believe it. Anyways, we only sell enough to pay for our own. Right, Billy?"

Billy nodded, his eyes shining. Scanlon wondered how they paid for the clothes, and the hi-fi, if they sold only enough to satisfy their own dope needs. There was no mention of their jobs. Keith bragged about how he'd logged exactly fifty-seven acid trips since getting out of Portsmouth brig. Billy lagged a few trips behind but was gaining.

"You're not concerned about what that stuff does to your brain? I mean, you're swallowing powerful chemicals. Nobody knows for sure the long-term effects."

"They know," Keith said. "Timothy Leary studied all that shit at Harvard. LSD's harmless as aspirin."

Hearing their tales of acid trips, stories of the strange and wonderful psychic effects of mescaline and peyote, struggles with reds and blues and whatever primary colors of pills, had Scanlon feeling anxious. His own little bout with diet pills seemed harmless, so "establishment" by comparison.

They thought it was extremely cool that he was teaching high school.

"You made it with any of the high school chicks?" Billy wanted to know.

"Not yet, but I'm hopeful." Scanlon gave them no more encouragement. By now they were stoned enough not to be able to hold onto too many concepts at once anyway. The conversation veered off in one direction, then the other, and there was a lot of laughing over things that weren't that funny.

Scanlon finished off the four beers that were in the refrigerator, and Billy offered to go out for more. The store was only next door. Billy didn't even bother to put on a jacket. Scanlon was alone with Keith. He had always had an easier time talking to Keith than to Billy. He expressed his concern again about their drug use, the way they were living their lives.

"We're cool, Jack. Don't start in. You sound like Ma."

"I don't care how small time you say you are. Selling dope, even to your buddies, can get you in jail for a long time. And I'll bet civilian jails are no more pleasant than military ones."

"I'm not going to jail, for Christ sakes."

"What about him?" Scanlon jerked his thumb toward the door, after Billy had left. "He's not famous for his good judgment, you know."

"You don't know what's shakin', Jack." Keith had his hand up to halt, his head shaking slowly from side to side. "You don't understand the scene, all right. So just be cool, Jack. We know what we're doin', so just be cool."

Scanlon sighed and fell back on the mattress, empty beer bottle on his chest. He closed his eyes. He heard Keith get up to change the record. His half-brothers were now into the psychedelic music scene with all its synthetic sound production. What did they hear? What Scanlon heard was noise and cacophony—chaos.

Billy returned with two six-packs of "stubbies." Scanlon gave it one last try. "Look at yourselves," he said. "You really think the cops haven't noticed you? The way you dress, the way you got your hair? You're probably under surveillance right now." Billy yanked a beer out of the paper bag and, grinning like a lunatic, tossed it to Scanlon. "Well, I've said my piece."

"All right," Keith said. "Now let's get fucked up."

"Yeah," Billy said, opening a beer for himself.

Resigned, Scanlon lay back against the wall. "So where do you conduct your business?"

"We don't run no scores from the apartment, if you're worried," Keith said.

"Tell Jack about last week with the acid," Billy said, falling down on the mattress beside his blood brother, holding his middle, jackknifed in a laughing fit.

Keith had been downtown, on the corner by the savings bank, waiting for an out-of-town buyer when a police cruiser came screeching up to the curb. Keith knew right away that they were looking to shake him down. He reached in his pocket and downed about five tabs before the cops got to him and spread him out. Stayed high for eighteen hours. Crash-landed in the pad of some chick he'd never met before.

"These crashes sound like a lot of fun," Scanlon said.

"You don't do five tabs, normally," Keith said in all earnestness. "What do you want?"

"What a fucking way to live," Scanlon muttered. "What time is it?"

There was no clock in the apartment and neither Keith nor Billy owned a wristwatch. Scanlon had the sense that it was later than five o'clock, which was the time he said he'd be back to his mother's for supper.

"Who gives a fuck?" Billy said and found the question enormously funny. He rolled around on the mattress seized by another laughing jag. Scanlon struggled to his feet. He hadn't told them he was expected back at their mother's. He didn't tell them now. It was dark outside.

"I've got to be going. Got an appointment at five." Scanlon swayed a little on his feet.

"Well," Billy said, between snorts of laughing, "plan on being tardy." Billy lapsed into hysteria this time, apparently finding the word tardy apt and hilarious in light of Scanlon's newfound vocation. When he'd played out his latest fit he told Scanlon that it was five-thirty when he'd gone down for beer, at least that was what the wall clock in the store said. Even by Billy's sense of time, truncated by marijuana, that put it at well after five. Their mother had little patience with lateness. Scanlon dropped back down on the mattress.

"So where's the old man hang out now that he's banished? You guys see any of him?" Scanlon asked.

"I seen him a couple weeks ago," Billy said, "comin' out of the Social Club, drunk on his ass."

"You talk to him?"

"Fuck no. I got nothin' to say to that motherfucker." On the subject of his father, Billy found nothing amusing.

"He's still a horse's ass," Keith offered. "Still runnin' off at the mouth in bars about what a fucking star he was in high school. Makes everybody around him feel like puking. Someday somebody's gonna shut out his lights."

Billy said that the old man had tried to hit him up for a couple of bucks that day outside the Social Club. Billy just turned his back and walked away. He told it as though he were proud of what he'd done, but Scanlon had the feeling his half-brother didn't feel pride so much as shame. Whenever Billy felt bad about anything at all he blustered and strutted around like a rooster to cover up. Protested too much, as Shakespeare would have put it.

"The prick's incorrigible," Scanlon said, in a low voice, as if to himself.

"What the fuck does that mean?" Billy demanded. "I can guess. He's a total fuck-up, right?"

"Right," Scanlon said.

"You still got that wicked vocabulary, huh, Jack," Keith said, smiling. He was goofy from marijuana, his pupils as big as dimes.

"Haven't you guys got any other kind of music? Those guitars are wearing me down," Scanlon said.

"Remember the time you were in high school, you came home drunk and puked in our bedroom?" Billy asked Scanlon.

"Not likely I'll forget that any time soon. You saved my ass on that one. That was decent. I owe you one." Billy had taken the blame for being sick, letting Scanlon off the hook with his mother.

"He'd have squealed on me," Keith said, changing the record.

After a certain number of drinks, Scanlon became susceptible to sentimentality. That was what was happening to him now as he reminisced with his half-brothers after being so long out of touch. And Keith and Billy were no less inclined to be taken with nostalgia, even when it touched on their common, unpleasant experiences with the tyrannical Bill Scanlon senior. How many times had any one of them been awakened out of a sound sleep to get dressed to go to one restaurant or another for take-out for Bill Scanlon, just arrived home from an evening of heavy drinking with a powerful appetite? Or to be sent after his paycheck at some restaurant job he'd quit without giving notice to attend to his frequent benders?

"Listen," Scanlon said, "I was pulling that duty before you guys were allowed up past eight o'clock."

He couldn't compete with either of them for the beatings, though. Bill Scanlon had struck him only once in their years together, for stealing from the Garrison Country Club pro shop. With Billy and Keith, especially Billy, hitting was an everyday possibility.

"He was a mean motherfucker," Billy said through his teeth. "I couldn't count the times I could have killed him."

"Me, too," Keith said. "Even Ma."

Even Scanlon had fantasized about murdering his stepfather. But Keith offered the fact that their mother had contemplated the act herself as if this were privileged information. Keith was his mother's boy. They all knew and understood this. He had a way of talking to her that neither of the other two could fathom. To Scanlon, especially, she was an enigma, and he to her, he imagined. She and Keith were soulmates; with Keith she shared everything, and it would have been a mistake for Scanlon to say what was on his mind at the moment concerning their mother's culpability in their rearing. He had a sense that Billy might understand, perhaps even be sympathetic, but not Keith. No way.

"So how come neither of you jokers has a driver's license? Ma told me how you're always mooching rides."

"Keith can't get one for another year because of his BCD," Billy said.

"And shit for brains got nailed for DWI two months ago. He's grounded for another four months. What are we supposed to do? Walk?"

Scanlon said, "Ma must be something to see behind the wheel of a moving vehicle."

The boys laughed hard and tried to describe to Scanlon how their mother looked, both hands on the steering wheel holding on for dear life, her head all that could be seen through the driver's side window, like a kid.

"She drives about fifteen miles an hour, and on the highway she stays in the breakdown lane. She won't let neither one of us drive, even with her in the car."

"Why should she?" Scanlon asked. "Why should she let unlicensed drivers behind the wheel of her car?"

Billy answered with a loud fart. Farting was Billy's claim to talent; if Keith was a natural athlete, Billy could outfart him and just about anybody else he'd ever met.

"Chew on that for awhile," Billy said with a stoned grin. "Put that in your pipe, light up, enjoy a good smoke."

Keith tried to counter with a fart of his own, feeble compared to Billy's cannon shot.

Bill Scanlon was an unconscionable farter. That was where the boys had picked up the habit. Bill Scanlon's flatulence knew no bounds. He was no more constrained at mealtime than in mixed company. There, he seemed to say, take that. It's my right as a man to fart if and whenever I feel like it. You want to make something of it? You want to step outside? There was defiance in Bill Scanlon's farts; not so much in his son's. Billy, now that he was on the fringe of the hippie culture, laid claim to the fart as a form of natural expression. Scanlon remembered that he'd started doing it to get attention, the poor, love-starved kid. He thought big Bill Scanlon would love him more if he could match him in flatus.

"If it weren't the car, she'd find something else to bitch about," Keith said.

"That's a fact," Billy concurred, squeezing off another liquidy fart, face all contorted in exaggerated effort. "The woman gets off on bitching. Don't bother me. That's the way she is."

"So let her chauffeur you, but don't hound her to let you drive. You get caught behind the wheel without a license you'll be a long time becoming eligible again," said big brother, big half-brother. The boys ignored him, tolerated him.

"Where you stayin'?" Keith asked him. "Wanna crash here?"

"I got to get back. There's shit to do."

"Maybe our suite ain't good enough for his highness the schoolteacher," Billy said, just joking.

"For Christ's sake, Billy," Scanlon said, overreacting.

"I didn't mean it," Billy said. Soon, he fell asleep sitting upright, back against the wall. Scanlon talked for a while with Keith, and drank beer, then Keith succumbed to sleep, and Scanlon found himself drinking alone. He was too awake to drop off the way they had done, too sleepy to want to drive anywhere in his car on a night like this. His mother would be angry with him for not showing for supper. The question was, should he stop by to see her before he left in the morning? Leave a note? Go on his way without another word, as if he'd never been here in the first place? Billy and Keith snored contrapuntally. They were so different from him; no one ever believed they were even related, let alone shared the same mother.

Scanlon awoke in the first light, his body aching at every joint, his mouth rancid from beer and cigarettes. He tried to sit upright and pain shot through the top of his skull. His trousers were all twisted around his waist and crotch. He lay back on the hard mattress and looked up at the whitewashed, molded tin ceiling. He had to squint from head pain and from the pale light that filled the room and hurt his eyes. Then he realized that Billy and Keith were not in the room, a room stinking of marijuana and dirty socks. And it was cold, very cold. Scanlon shivered so hard his teeth began to clatter. He went into a fetal position, hands tucked between his thighs for warmth, but it was no good. He rolled over and pushed himself up on his hands and knees, his head pulsating, a little wave of nausea rolling up into his throat. He hadn't gone to the bathroom once last night for all the beer he'd drunk. He didn't remember seeing the bathroom yesterday, now that he needed it urgently. Scanlon lurched to his feet and hit the wall with his shoulder. Where were his brothers? What the hell time was it?

There was no aspirin in the medicine cabinet. There was nothing, in fact, in the cabinet. If the boys kept toothbrushes or toothpaste, they kept them hidden. The sink was black from dirt. Their mother would have apoplexy in such a bathroom. Where were they? Out peddling dope so early in the morning? Or was it early in the afternoon?

Scanlon looked out the bedroom window at the empty street. Everything looked frozen, still. No traffic. Only parked cars. He panicked when he couldn't see his VW across the street until he remembered he'd parked it around the corner by the grocery store. He wouldn't have put it past his brothers to take off with his car.

The little VW creaked and groaned when Scanlon got in. The gearshift was so frozen in neutral he feared it would snap off in his hand. He pumped the gas pedal twice; the ignition sounded dead on the first turn, then the engine turned over, sputtered two or three times and hummed to life. He let the engine idle, waited for the windshield to clear, still not knowing what he would do about his mother, not even knowing what time of day it was.

Scanlon left the car to idle and went to the grocery store on the corner for cigarettes. The door was locked, the inside dark. He peered through the glass door looking for the clock that Billy talked about last night. He saw no clock, only shelves of canned goods, a meat case, scale, and beer cooler. Seeing a beer cooler made him want a cold one. They had drunk all of Billy's two six-packs last night, Scanlon most of them. All this need.

VWs took forever to heat up. He sat shivering, his breath freezing on the inside of the windshield, all the windows rolled up inviting carbon monoxide poisoning. He got the dry heaves and opened the door to retch on the curb. His sound echoed off the frozen street. After he was finished, Scanlon listened. Nothing. It was as if sound itself had frozen solid. Not one car had passed since he'd been out here.

Scanlon drove past his mother's two-decker, twice. The market next to her apartment house was closed, too. His craving for beer and cigarettes heightened. He drove slowly down the deserted main drag looking for signs of life. The west face of the City Hall clock said eight-ten. Where was everybody? Where had Keith and Billy gone? Had they left the night before, while he was asleep?

Fandy Guyer's little store next door to City Hall was open. Scanlon parked and went inside, shaking from hangover and anticipation. Fandy was standing behind the counter of the narrow store, crowded with display stands and grocery shelves, reading a magazine. A skin magazine no doubt, knowing Fandy's reputation. Randy Fandy he used to be called, and if his hair had thinned some since Scanlon had last seen him there was no mistaking his dour puss. The legend in Scanlon's youth was that Fandy fancied young boys. Liked to have them come to the back room to show them fishing tackle and live bait. Then he'd spring his dick on them, reputed to be no less than a foot long, soft.

This morning, Fandy looked pale, in no mood for pederasty. He lived upstairs over the store, and had not been averse, Scanlon remembered, to being awakened at any hour of the night to sell illicit beer. He wasn't fussy about ID, either.

"How's it going, Fandy?" Scanlon acted cheerful, not expecting and not getting any sign that Fandy Guyer remembered him from his high school days, of his late night, or early Sunday morning beer business. Garrison was small but not so small that, like Groveton, everyone knew everyone else. Fandy nodded, glancing briefly at Scanlon, wetting his finger with his tongue before turning a page. "Place is like a ghost town this morning. What's the deal?"

Fandy looked up from his magazine, puzzled. "What do you expect on New Year's Day?"

"Right. Happy New Year."

"Umm." Fandy was back in his magazine. If it were true that he liked little boys, Scanlon couldn't imagine little boys liking Fandy, unless his fishing tackle was extraordinary, or Fandy himself, in the seduction of youth, became somehow transformed. Ordinary eyeglasses, ordinary nose, ears, mouth; ordinary thinning hair. The kind of guy who could stick up a bank in front of a dozen witnesses who'd give a dozen different descriptions he was so nondescript. Scanlon was disarmed to learn that it was New Year's Day, 1969. No one had mentioned anything about last night being New Year's Eve. How could he have forgotten such a day?

"Let me have a pack of Winstons," Scanlon said, looking around the store as if there was something else on his shopping list. "And you better make it a couple six-packs of beer. It's OK to buy beer before noon on New Year's Day, right?"

Fandy didn't answer. He bagged two six-packs of low-priced beer, as if he could tell by looking at Scanlon that he wanted low-priced beer, and pulled down a pack of cigarettes off the rack behind his head. He laid them on the counter. Scanlon felt like a derelict.

"This cover it?" Scanlon laid down three singles. Fandy swept them off the counter and rang up two-dollars and thirty-five cents on his ancient cash register. He slapped Scanlon's change on the counter and got back to his magazine. Scanlon tried to sneak a look at the magazine, but he saw only color, no detail. Buggerer's monthly, he was expecting?

Back in the car, Scanlon's hands trembled as he fumbled around in the glove compartment for his church key. He had trouble getting his cigarettes open for all his shaking. When he finally got one to his lips he discovered that he was out of matches and the car lighter didn't work.

"Shit!" he said out loud. His head started to pound again. He managed to get a can of beer open, to drink long and deep before dealing with his lack of matches. All he had to do was walk back inside Fandy's store and ask for some. He chugged a whole can and belched, savoring the malty kick-back. He had to force himself out of the car and back inside the store. Fandy charged him a penny for two books of matches.

Scanlon sat in front of Fandy Guyer's store on this New Year's Day, 1969, drank down two more quick beers, smoked a couple of cigarettes. He was shivering so violently the little car shook. He popped a fourth beer and got into first gear, not knowing at all what he wanted to do, where he wanted to go. All alone in this young New Year with no inkling about how to begin. There were places he could go, but none of them was quite right. He couldn't go back to the Stacys, and now it was clear to him that he would not return to his mother's. Who knew where Keith and Billy were? What did Fandy do in his wretched apartment above his squalid little store? Besides bugger little boys?

He started south, changed his mind at the first traffic light and reversed direction. He drove down steep Irving Street toward the house he lived in for a year when he was in sixth grade; a tiny, five-room cracker box, all but hidden behind a duplex in a small neighborhood of derelicts and displaced shanty-towners. He remembered the family that lived in the house, if it could be called that, on the corner. He remembered the mother, a stoop-shouldered, leather-faced hag who smoked constantly and had a mouth that would have made Althea blush. He'd never been sure exactly how many kids were in the family, only that they were all retarded in varying degrees, one or two severely. The eldest boy the neighborhood kids called "Shittum" because he always walked around with a load in his pants and a retarded grin on his face that seemed to say, "I've shit myself again, but there are worse things that could happen." The oldest girl had been in Scanlon's sixth-grade class, and because she was so hopelessly and irrevocably ugly, had been called "Pretty Alice." Hereditary myopia due to inbreeding deficiency, he imagined, forced her to wear big thick-lensed goggles. Her snarled hair, the color and texture of broom straw, had never known shampoo. To school she wore poor, ill-fitting dresses, the kind you'd see worn by old ladies, gotten from welfare grab bags. And try as hard as she might, Pretty Alice couldn't learn. She was promoted along because teachers didn't know what else to do with her. They marked time until she turned sixteen and could be legally cut loose from the system. This age, Pretty Alice reached by eighth grade. She just sort of vanished. Scanlon imagined her being sexually exploited, of giving birth to defective babies whose fate would be like her own; her own father could likely be the father of her children. What went on behind the curtainless windows in that crooked, malodorous house on the corner occupied the imaginations of Scanlon and his neighborhood pals on end.

Kids, in various stages of undress, were forever spilling out of the doorless entryway, even in dead of winter. The father was an itinerant laborer, like Bill Scanlon, employed between benders when he could find menial work. He was rough-hewn, prone to violence when he was drinking, home only sporadically, but when he was home, the neighborhood knew it. His wife's braying, hectoring voice reverberated through the street, the wailing of beaten children increased in frequency and intensity, and the arrival of the police cruiser could be anticipated with precision. Then Mr. Shantytown would be escorted out of his castle, a uniformed cop on each arm, while his Gorgon stood out on the sidewalk in her dirty bathrobe (several filthy undressed kids wrapped around her legs), shaking a crazy fist at him. Once her bathrobe fell open. The neighborhood had been treated to a glimpse of her great sagging dugs, her swollen belly, her hairy pudendum, and Scanlon had been shocked, confused, repulsed.

There had been one daughter, however, Rose he thought her name might have been (like the Stacys' cat), who seemed to have survived the genetic struggle for survival, who got through school, who found some decency and a life for herself as a practical nurse. All of this he'd heard secondhand, years later. Got herself married to a hard-working stiff from a normal background. And Rose had been decent enough herself not to turn her back completely on her despicable family, even if in the opinion of everyone who had one she would have been perfectly justified not to look back.

Now the house was gone without a trace. What was left was an empty space, piled high with dirty snow. The house he'd lived in was still standing, looking like a normal home with fresh, white paint (it had been brown and anything but fresh when he lived in it), black shutters, a wrought-iron fence out front, and a black door knocker. He drove on.

Main drag traffic was picking up. It occurred to Scanlon that he was expected at his job tomorrow. He was unprepared, unwilling, unable to decide whether or not to return. He missed Bob, missed swapping shots out of Styrofoam, of playing cat and mouse mind games with the big slob. He found himself parked in front of his mother's house again. The lights were out in the front windows. Would she be working on New Year's Day? Cleaning up after college kids? So, he cleaned up, in a manner of speaking, after high school kids. One job was as menial as the other. No, she wouldn't be working on a holiday—the college would be on break. He popped open another beer, his fifth, and sat for awhile, drinking and shivering in the tiny, cold car. He watched his mother's windows, the front door. For maybe ten minutes he sat like this. He finished number five, opened number six. Then a light went on in the front window. He slipped into gear and drove away from the curb very slowly.

In Alton, he realized he was on the wrong road and sleet started to fall. Scanlon headed west, not feeling equal to the challenge of Crawford Notch in what would more than likely be a snow squall there. His reason, muddied by six beers, did not inform him that he would eventually have to negotiate Franconia Notch, every bit as treacherous as Crawford. Like choosing between the dope that Keith and Billy used to wreck their health and the alcohol that ruled his life.

He was in Belmont, having made no progress north, and down to five beers. Snow mixed with the sleet. He stopped to pick up more beer. The storekeeper told him he couldn't sell him beer in his condition. What condition? He was in fine condition; who was this jerk in this hick town telling him about his condition?

By Plymouth, traffic was at a crawl on I-93. Scanlon grew sleepy; his ninth beer had gone warm, untouched between his thighs. The windshield was beginning to ice up. He got off the highway. Route 3 was no better. He got sleepier, his eyelids dreadfully heavy. He knew he should stop. He lost consciousness south of Lincoln-Woodstock just long enough to leave the road; he jerked awake in time to see the looming evergreen. He wrenched the steering wheel to avoid colliding with the tree and sent the VW skidding across the road into the oncoming traffic lane. Then he was tipping over, and everything went into slow motion. Old, uncorrected test papers, festering on the floor in the back of the car, rained down around his head. He rolled once, twice, the sensation of wetness in his crotch, the sense of calm, of relief. Lights out.

Chapter Twenty-nine

K: You're goddamned lucky to be here. You know that, don't you?
S: Yeah. I know.
K: You got a bruised right shoulder? That's it?
S: Luck of the Irish.
K: I'll drink to that.
Kennedy did just that, and Scanlon matched him.
K: What are you going to do about transportation?

Scanlon laughed and told Kennedy that he'd have to depend on Lyle Higgins, who lived in East Groveton and had to pass his place every morning on his way to school.

S: I'm at his mercy, in a way. I now have to get up before dawn with my uncle because Lyle Higgins has never arrived at school later than six-thirty in the twenty odd years he's been teaching there. And I have to hang around after school until he decides he's ready to go home.
Scanlon smiled. Kennedy chuckled.
K: Still, you've got your health, such as it is, if not your independence or your dignity. How did your principal take it?
S: He was a sweetheart. Told me to take all the time off I needed. Prick would no doubt be scouting for my replacement if I took time off.
K: You trying to say you don't trust him?
S: About as much as I trust my insurance company.
K: You should be behind bars, Scanlon.
S: You're having a good time with this. I'm inches from oblivion and you're giving me the needle.

Kennedy was of the opinion that whenever you could put one over on the Angel of Death it was cause for rejoicing, wisecracking, drinking. He'd made a special trip to the liquor store when Scanlon had called to tell him about his accident. For occasions like these the moratorium was lifted.

S: It was mighty irregular, Bob. The trooper asked me how much I'd had to drink. I'm stinko, and the car reeks of beer. I can't remember what I said, but it wasn't the truth. He writes something in his little notebook—I'm sitting in the cruiser with him—and I don't think he even looks at me. He probably wanted to get the hell out of there and home to his family before he turned his cruiser over the way I did my VW, I don't know. There was no walk-the-straight-line talk from this dude, nothing. He had to know I was blitzed. I should write an angry letter to the head of the State Police. Complain about how they're soft on drunk drivers.

K: Your uncle came all the way down there in that weather to get you?

S: Yeah.

Scanlon wondered for a moment if Kennedy was hurt that he hadn't called him instead of his uncle.

S: I'd have called you, if I'd had your number.

K: I don't drive on icy roads.

Kennedy said this too matter-of-factly to suit Scanlon.

S: Not even for your patients? Your clients?

K: Clients? Especially not for my clients.

S: You're an unfeeling prick.

Kennedy grinned and raised his cup. Scanlon raised his own cup in toast.

S: In fact, you're such a first-class asshole, it makes me wonder why I keep coming back.

K: Maybe this is where you feel you can be yourself.

S: Spare me.

Scanlon appraised his counselor. Kennedy was digging in his ear with a fat forefinger.

S: You're pretty sure of yourself today, doctor. Wouldn't be the whiskey?

K: Let's enjoy it while we can. After today the cork's back in the bottle. Our next drink will be the farewell one.

They clicked Styrofoam and drank to the time they'd say good-bye to each other for good. It had a quieting effect. Scanlon inspected his fingernails, while Kennedy massaged his temple and looked out the window at the snow-filled gully.

S: You know what, Bob?

Kennedy turned toward Scanlon, finger at his temple, and raised one thick eyebrow.

S: The idea of a farewell drink doesn't appeal to me that much. In fact, it kind of scares the shit out of me.

Kennedy frowned and peered into his cup as if maybe he'd discovered an insect swimming in his bourbon.

S: You trying to tell me something, Bob?

K: I suppose I am.

Kennedy swiveled back to the window. He'd lost the right elbow patch on his winter jacket, the hound's tooth, too-tight-to-button jacket that looked like it had been under siege by moths.

S: Well, are you going to sit there like a hard-on or are you going to say something to reassure me?

K: I'm not so hot at saying things like this.

Kennedy's voice was phlegmy. He picked up the pace of his finger massage.

S: You're leaving, aren't you, you prick.

K: Not until June.

S: June?

K: Yes. I'm going to have to do some residential clinical work for a year, year and a half, to finish my doctorate.

Kennedy turned to Scanlon and smiled.

K: That's what you always wanted from me, wasn't it? Credentials?

S: Fuck you. Where are you doing this residential clinic?

Scanlon couldn't look at him.

K: Cambridge. I've done my work at Harvard.

S: Excuse me. I've been dealing with another fucking Ivy Leaguer all this time? What a laugh.

Scanlon could tell that Kennedy was looking at him hard.

K: A lot can be accomplished between now and June.

S: Forgive me, but I don't see any point in trying.

Scanlon was aware that he was sounding sorry for himself with his wee, I'm-so-unhappy-I-could-cry voice.

K: Come on, don't be that way.

Scanlon remembered the Benny Goodman tune "Don't Be That Way." Heard it for the first time on Nick Costa's hand-cranked Victrola.

S: Yeah, look at all the progress we've made so far.

K: I don't agree. You know how I feel about that.

S: Yeah, I know how you feel. But I don't feel any better now than I did in September. In fact, I think I feel worse. Totally out of control instead of only partially. Look at me. Look what I almost did to myself. What I could have done to someone else. Look, for Christ's sake.

Scanlon pointed his forefingers at himself.

S: Maybe you feel all right. Maybe you're the one who's been making all the progress around here. I know it hasn't been me.

Kennedy chuckled, his big belly rippling under his shirt.

S: Now what's so fucking funny?

K: Any fallout from your Christmas party performance?

S: Not to my face. Who knows what they're whispering about behind my back?

Kennedy chuckled again, and Scanlon was getting annoyed with him.

K: And what about your pal the draft dodger? He come back?

S: Yeah, Doug's back. I'm wondering now if he'll really go through with it if his draft board sticks it up his ass, as we both know they will. With the guys we got in power now there are no acceptable arguments for C.O.

Scanlon saw, in his mind's eye, all those boxes stacked against the wall in Stambaugh's apartment, the empty bookcase, the desolation. He'd been surprised to find Stambaugh back after Christmas break. He hadn't said anything to him, but he was so sure that Stambaugh had been seriously preparing to flee that seeing him in the corridor that first morning back took him by surprise. Lyle Higgins, ever the chatty one on their early morning commute, had tried, in his heavy-handed way, to probe him on Stambaugh's intentions. It hadn't taken long for the word to get out about his C.O. petition. By now, thanks no doubt to Winship, the entire Northeast Kingdom was aware of it.

K: And the teaching? Feeling any better about that?

S: I'm still crummy.

K: Maybe you should try a different approach. Could it be you're fixed in your mind about what makes for good pedagogy?

S: I'm sure you're right about that. What do I know from pedagogy? All I have for my examples are my high school teachers and college professors. I wouldn't know where to begin to try something new. If I could talk to my colleagues I might be more inclined to give it a try, but I get the feeling they're not much better off than I am. Teachers at Fairfield High don't seem all that hot to share their incompetence. Is that the way it is with your crowd, Bob?

K: You have to find a way to feel competent yourself. Then you can take the initiative with your colleagues on professional interaction.

Scanlon had to smile at the important sounding phrase "professional interaction" when he thought about it in the context of Winship, Dennis Kitchell, and the rest of the Fairfield High teacher corps.

K: When I taught in grad school, we put a high premium on sharing ideas. I think it makes for a healthy climate.

S: All right, Bob, I'm convinced. Prescribe me some competence tablets, then I'll start interacting meaningfully with my colleagues. Fuck them, anyway. I don't owe them professional anything.

Kennedy shook his big head and smiled, putting his lips to his whiskey cup as if it were hot coffee he was drinking. He held the Styrofoam with both huge paws, like a little boy. How will I ever get along without this walrus? Scanlon asked himself. Kennedy read his mind.

K: You feel like I'm deserting you, don't you.

S: Yes, I do.

K: You know, I can't prescribe competence tablets for you but I could get you on some medication that might settle you down some. In your gut.

S: No thanks, Bob. No drugs. And you got a right to your own life. Best thing you could do is get off this dead-end street. I'll be all right. You said yourself I've made progress. So don't worry about me.

Scanlon looked up at the ceiling, and reflected on all the phrases used in conversation that had been turned into songs. "Don't Worry 'Bout Me," for example.

K: I'm a natural worrier. But you're right. I think you have made progress, even if I know you're being a wise guy by saying so.

S: You're probably just saying that to make it easy on yourself for leaving me in the lurch.

K: You talk about yourself differently than when you first started coming.

Kennedy shifted in his squeaky chair and screwed up his face in pain from his ever-present hemorrhoids.

S: I talk a good game, Bob. You must have figured that out by now. But I don't have clue one about what to do with or about my life. I'm still on a treadmill, and I'm hitting the juice more than ever.

K: And now you're saying it out loud. Could you have made that statement five weeks ago?

S: It doesn't change a thing.

K: The change will come in time.

S: One hopes before I spread myself or some other poor fucker out over the interstate.

K: So don't drive your car when you're toasted. What's so hard about that?

S: What drunk have you ever met had any sense when he's torched? Besides, I enjoy a couple of brews when I'm driving. Takes my mind off the road.

K: Fucking wiseass.

Kennedy wasn't joking.

S: I'll try to do better. When did you say you were leaving? June? Think you can break me of my lethal habits in five months?

K: I can't cure you of anything, Jack. I can't cure myself.

S: You should see a shrink.

K: What were you doing way down in New Hampshire?

S: I was down in Garrison paying a visit to me old mum and kid brothers.

Kennedy's eyebrows rose. Scanlon watched his face for more reaction, but all Kennedy had for him were the eyebrows.

K: Well?

Kennedy reclined in his chair, whiskey cup balanced on his belly the way he liked to do.

S: My mother? Well, Bob, she finally got around to tossing my stepfather out on his ear. A little late to do me or my brothers any good but she seems better off herself. She says she likes the independence. Got herself a driver's license, her own car. Gave up smoking and doing crossword puzzles. That's what I call turning your life around. Think I could do all that, Bob?

K: Tell me about your visit.

Scanlon pleated the rim of his cup. Kennedy wasn't offering refills.

S: I had no business going down there. I don't even know why I went.

K: So why do you think you went?

S: Because I'm ruled by impulse. I just do shit without thinking sometimes, without considering the consequences. You must know that about me. If you don't you should.

K: What were you up to just before you took off for Garrison? You remember how you were feeling?

S: I don't know. Antsy. I'm always antsy, restless, on edge. Only time I don't feel like I don't want to be somewhere else is when I'm in here or in a good bar. And there aren't any good bars around here. So that leaves this place. God help me.

Scanlon folded his hands in prayer to the flaking ceiling.

S: Sister Marie, where are you in my hour of need?

K: What did you do New Year's Eve?

S: Hung out with my half brothers.

Scanlon couldn't bring himself to admit to Kennedy that he'd lost track of New Year's Eve. Kennedy would only try to make it connect in some deep, psychological way with the events of New Year's Eve 1967. That wasn't fair to Kennedy. He wasn't that kind of shrink. Nevertheless, he didn't bring the matter up. He asked Kennedy how he'd spent his New Year's Eve. Kennedy shrugged and said he'd gone to bed early. There was still the pretense of abstinence in his household. It was only here in the office, and only with Scanlon, that he strayed from the pledge.

K: You should maybe see more of your brothers, talk to them about what it was like for all of you as kids.

S: I've got seven and eight years on them. We come from totally different points of view.

K: That doesn't invalidate what you had together. They must have been toddlers when you went to live with your mother and stepfather, right?

S: The first thing comes to mind is all the times I had to baby-sit the little bastards. I had to do it every day for one whole summer, the summer my mother decided that if the family was going to survive she'd better find a job. I spent my summer vacation baby-sitting two holy terrors every working day of the week. They were around five and six years old and we lived in this cramped, two-room apartment on the third floor. The apartment house was on one of the busiest street corners in town. The two of them, Keith and Billy, learned to panhandle strangers for small change and spend it on candy at the corner store. My mother had to hang signs around their necks, it got so bad. Don't give this boy money or candy, the sign said. People thought this was adorable. They gave them more money, more candy. And they fought with each other from the time they woke up till the time they went to sleep. I was a morose thirteen-year-old, resentful for having to waste my precious summer looking after two street urchins when I should have been playing ball with my friends, swimming, or doing just about anything except what I was doing.

Furthermore, I was in love with the fourteen-year-old girl who lived with her aunt downstairs. She was fourteen, but she acted twenty. Treated me like a kid, a younger brother. I put up with her condescension because I would have put up with anything from her. She was beautiful, though I can't remember any details about how she looked. I remember large breasts. Maybe that was what I was really in love with, those knockers. No, she was nice, and kind, and didn't seem to mind talking to me. I was skinny, and sullen, and hated bathing, so with girls

I was no star. Can't even remember her name. She used to tell me all about high school, and dating, and how you were supposed to go about courtship in high school. She was very experienced in the area of court ship. She had boys pulling up to the curb in their cars practically every night that summer.

K: You must have been jealous.

S: That would be putting it mildly. It only made my condition worse. I used to lie around on the bed and listen to the radio and feel extremely sorry for myself. I'm not making light of it now, don't get me wrong. I remember real, palpable suffering that summer. Those were days when popular music was even worse than it is now. This was pre-rock and roll. You'd hear crap like "How Much Is That Doggy in the Window," or "Harbor Lights," and shit like that. I used to listen in total agony, waiting to hear a song I liked. I fantasized like crazy in those days. My imagination was limited on sexual stuff with the chick downstairs, so I used to daydream a lot about being a sports star. Football, baseball, hoop, whatever was in season.

S: I was just thinking, Bob. All the candy and soda my kid brothers consumed from their panhandle money, and I was a bit of a soda pop junky myself.

K: What about it?

S: You think kids learn addictive habits, or do you think we're born that way? What do you think? Were you a candy man as a kid?

K: Yeah. Weren't we all? I'm still hooked on Hershey's Kisses.

S: So you think we learn how to become junkies?

K: I don't think the news is all in on that story.

S: I guess that makes me your moral superior, Bob. I can live nicely without Hershey's Kisses. I feel better already.

K: Here, have some more.

Kennedy poured Scanlon more whiskey. None for himself.

S: Now you want me to drink alone?

Scanlon put his cup on the edge of Kennedy's desk.

S: I'm not so bad off I want to drink here by myself.

Another lie welled up from his groin.

K: You don't have to pretend with me. Drink up.

Scanlon meekly retrieved his whiskey. He took a delicate sip. Kennedy waited; he checked out his fingernails, then poured himself a little whiskey. Could he be drinking just to make Scanlon feel at ease, so he wouldn't feel like the only lost soul in the world? What if Kennedy wasn't an alcoholic after all? What if the drinking was just some therapeutic technique? He looked to Scanlon like a hard-core drinker, though, with his incandescent nose.

K: You said once that your mother was never affectionate.
Kennedy said this as if to himself.

S: Did I? Well it's true. At least not with me. Actually, not with the kids either. Not really. Not even Keith. Nothing physical where she was concerned. Bill Scanlon was the affectionate one, but only when he was drinking. Then the affection could turn to violence just like that.
Scanlon snapped his fingers.

S: I take after my mother.

K: You weren't affectionate with your wife?

S: You're shitting me. We despised each other. The whole marriage was a total sham.

K: What about with your kid?

S: Yeah. I used to make over Lucy quite a bit, for me. I don't think she liked to have me handle her; I think Katie influenced her in ways I'll never know about. Let's not talk about this.

Kennedy's huge fist was around his cup, his fingers completely encircling it. It looked to Scanlon as if he were about to crush it, whiskey and all, make it disintegrate. Kennedy struck him as enormously powerful physically.

S: I know what you're thinking, Bob.

K: What am I thinking?

S: You're thinking I ought to get this business with my father over with once and for all. You think I'm making more of it than I need to. I should ask the question, put all the *angst* to rest. Am I close?

K: It's not what I was thinking about at this precise moment. But since you've brought up the subject, who's in the best position to give you the scoop on your old man?

S: My old mother. Not so old as mothers go. She was eighteen when I was born. A child mother, really. But I suppose that's all relative. I see kids at school eighteen who I couldn't imagine giving birth, let alone caring for a child.

K: How old was your wife when she had your daughter?

S: Not quite eighteen. Look at her. Maybe there ought to be a law, like the drinking age—no childbearing before the age of twenty-one. I.D. required at the door. Except, whatever else Katie is, she's not a bad mother, not completely bad anyway. I guess she can't really be blamed for poisoning Lucy's mind against me.

Scanlon barked a laugh.

K: What?

S: You're really leaving, you asshole? Abandoning me like my child bride, like my child mother? I think maybe I'll call it quits now, while I'm feeling loose. I think this'll be it for me. You don't mind, do you?

K: If that's what you want.

S: When have I ever known what I want? You're putting me out like the fucking cat, going off to make a better life for yourself.

Scanlon tore pieces off the rim of his cup and put them on Kennedy's desk.

K: You think I'm trying to better myself on your time, Jack?

S: That's crazy, if you'll pardon the expression under these circumstances. You got a right to do whatever you want. Go where you want. I just don't see any point in continuing, knowing that it's going to end so soon. Where do you think we'll be in June? Honestly. I'll ask you again, where do you think we are now? I mean compared with September? And please don't ask me where I think we are.

Kennedy sighed, massaged his big nose and inspected his fingers.

K: You're more willing to peek inside than you were in September. Who knows where you can be by June? Personally, I think you should keep coming but as I said, that's your decision.

Kennedy signaled the end of their time together with his usual paper rearranging. He looked remote, almost professional.

S: I'll try it one more week.

Chapter Thirty

Alice sat in the backseat next to the beer cooler, nursing her third bottle. Scanlon sat up front with Ira. He was on his third as well, wondering if Alice had stashed the Black Velvet in the picnic basket in case of an emergency. There was a whole case of beer in the cooler, however. Alice maintained a steady stream of non-sequitur chatter and navigational advice. Ira's eyes rolled whenever she gave directions or her discourse got really off-the-wall, or when she chastised him for not listening to her, which he wasn't.

Ira wanted to head for Franconia Notch, Alice wanted Crawford Notch just to be contrary, Scanlon thought. Ira called it Snawford's Crotch. As Ira had predicted, the snow was too deep in the Notch for picnicking. The plows had left snow piled halfway up the utility poles. It might as well have been January for all the snow. Franconia wouldn't have been any different. Ira conceded that much to Alice after first gloating a little.

"What'd I tell you, Mother? When you going to listen?"

"Drive through," Alice ordered. Ira groaned and protested but did as he was told.

Scanlon was happy to be riding and drinking, not caring one way or the other whether they stopped for a picnic or not. In fact, if pressed, he'd opt for not stopping. He liked being a passenger, was getting used to it after all these weeks without his own car, thanks to the bureaucratic incompetence of his insurance company. He was lulled into a sweet torpor by the motion of Ira's big Ford and the beer he'd drunk. Not a care in the world, as Grammy used to say.

They were heading south on Route 16 and Scanlon felt a twitch of something in his heart (sadness?) that might have had something to do with the time he'd driven down to Garrison to visit the Stacys.

"Look at it, Mother." Ira pointed out the high snowbanks that flanked Route16 by way of reminding Alice of his earlier warnings. "Like driving through a tunnel. Never seen nothing like it. No different here than it was in the Notch. I'm for turning around. What about you, Johnny?"

Scanlon could tell that Ira was eager to get back home. The only time he enjoyed leaving the house was in the fall during deer hunting season. The trips to Alice's relatives in Massachusetts and Connecticut he made with utmost reluctance. He hated driving in what he termed "city traffic," which was any traffic beyond the Vermont border, especially those confounded traffic circles and interstates.

"Pull in there," Alice said, stabbing her bony finger over Ira's shoulder. She pointed to the entrance to a State Park with a closed-for-the-season sign hung prominently over the padlocked wooden gate.

"Can't you read, Mother? We can't go in there. We could be arrested for trespassing."

"Who's gonna see anybody trespassing on a Sunday?" Alice replied.

"There is the small matter of the gate," Scanlon offered, sublimely indifferent.

Alice suggested that Ira drive around the gate, and it was clear to both Ira and Scanlon that this was her wish and therefore Ira had better find a way around that gate. There were snowbanks on either side with a narrow passage on the left made by Ski-Dooers, that to Scanlon didn't look wide enough to accommodate a VW let alone Ira's beast of a Ford Fairlane.

Ira managed to squeeze through the slot between the snowbank and gatepost, the car listing dangerously to starboard. He got through with inches to spare and Scanlon was even a little excited by this innocent trespass.

Inside the grounds the road was clear of snow, but the picnic tables, which Scanlon was surprised to see out at all, were buried up to the seats. Ira drove along the winding road while Alice turned to the right window, then the left, then back to the right, like a hyperactive child, looking for a spot where they might unpack and enjoy a picnic lunch to celebrate the arrival of warm weather. Even Alice, the optimist, had to know that in Vermont winter was never over until at least May.

They came to a sand pit and a lot of construction equipment left around as if abandoned: dump trucks with the State of New Hampshire Department of Parks seal on the doors; backhoes and earthmovers with their huge, deep-treaded tires that Scanlon had once seen listed in a catalog for eight-thousand dollars. Alice spotted a pile of sawhorses and then a stack of lumber. She ordered Ira to stop and sent Scanlon and her husband out to fetch a pair of sawhorses and a broad piece of plywood. It was cold, even in the bright, high-noon, early-April sun. Scanlon and his uncle hauled the sawhorses and plywood over to a muddy patch of ground near the car and set up the serving table while Alice got busy unpacking the picnic basket. The first thing she did was remove the beers from the cooler and plant them in a snowbank like brown, guided missiles.

"Want a beer, Johnny?" Alice chirped, happy to be out on a picnic. Sure, Johnny wanted a beer. Johnny could always drink a beer. Ira and Scanlon stood by as Alice prepared the table. She decided against using her good tablecloth on the rough plywood and hoped the men could live without that little amenity.

"We'll try to manage, Mother," Ira said, seeming to finally relax and enjoy himself, to get into the spirit of Alice's adventure.

Alice stood back from the crude table hands clasped at her breast, a frown on her over-made-up face, to appraise her work.

"Something wrong?" Scanlon asked.

"Forgot candles," Alice said, laughing.

"Candles? Jesus H. Christ." Ira laughed so loud it echoed around the empty park and bounced off the heavy equipment right back at them.

"Oh, shut up," Alice said, and Scanlon worried that she'd taken Ira wrong.

"Well, seeing we're here, might as well eat." Ira took a plate off the stack at the edge of the table and started to serve himself ham, potato salad, rolls and margarine. Alice sat in the backseat of the car with her beer; she would have nothing to do with food beyond its preparation. Scanlon wasn't hungry either, but he got behind Ira with a plate and loaded up out of habit and not wanting to risk hurting Alice's feelings. By the time he finished serving himself, he was shivering from the cold. He plucked a beer out of the snow and crawled in the front seat of the car his hands so numb he could barely move his fingers.

"Did you need another beer, Alice?" Scanlon asked his aunt, turning to look at her in the back seat. "Shit."

"What's the matter?" Alice asked him.

"My neck. Something snapped. How stupid can you get?" Scanlon referred to himself and he hoped, hearing how it sounded, that Alice didn't think he meant her.

"Have Ira give it a twist. It'll be all right."

"Sure," Scanlon said, "and have Ira unscrew my head. I'll be all right." Scanlon tried turning his head to one side then the other. He felt pain, a sharp, stabbing pain to the left, nothing when he looked right. "Shit."

"Here," Ira said, "get out of the car and let me get you in a headlock."

"Really. I'll be OK. It'll work itself out. I'm always doing this. It's no big thing." As far back as he could remember, Scanlon had never done this to himself before. He could picture himself reporting for school tomorrow wearing one of those stupid foam collars. A shooting pain rose from the base of his neck to the top of his head and spread like a wave to his left shoulder. I'm going to be paralyzed for life, he thought, raising his bottle to his lips. This gesture brought on another spasm of pain.

"Shit."

"I'd get me to a chiropractor if I was you," Higgins said to Scanlon Monday morning on the drive to school. Scanlon could now only look in the straight-ahead direction. If he wanted to see what was going on to his left or right (he'd lost the right side overnight somehow), he had to turn his whole body, like a robot.

"Chiropractor? You're kidding. Some states don't even allow those clowns to practice."

"Wouldn't know about that. Suffered back pains myself some years ago. Woke up every morning for two years having to spend fifteen minutes getting my clothes on. Went to three different doctors. They were consistent in one thing. Writing out prescriptions for expensive pills that didn't help. Brother-in-law put me on to this chiropractor up in Irasburgh. One whack from that gent and haven't had lower back trouble since."

"How long do you think a thing like this could last?"

"Had mine for two years, like I said."

"Jesus."

"Any word yet on your insurance?"

"Car insurance? No. And if I don't hear from those jokers pretty soon I'm really going to raise a stink. How long has it been? Over three months? It's outrageous." Scanlon waxed indignant for Higgins' benefit, in case he had the idea that Scanlon was just mooching rides from him. He had offered to help with the gas. Higgins had refused him. Had to make the trip anyway, he said, with or without Scanlon.

"I'd change companies, I was you, after this is settled."

Scanlon would have been more aggressive with his company if he didn't believe that part of the delay in settling had something to do with the way in which he'd wrecked his car. They hadn't said anything to him straight out, but with bureaucracies you never knew.

"I'm beginning to wonder if I'll ever get a settlement. Without it I can't get another car. I appreciate your hauling me back and forth like this. It must be getting old for you."

"No trouble 'tall. You're right on the way. Maybe you ought to hit'em with a whiplash claim." Higgins chuckled but Scanlon had actually weighed the merits of the idea. Not that he had the inclination or the nerve to submit a fraudulent claim, no matter how shabbily he felt he'd been treated.

"What's this guy's name in Irasburgh?" Scanlon asked. His uncle wouldn't mind driving him to Irasburgh. Scanlon thought about what it would be like to be able to look only straight ahead for two years.

"Can't remember, offhand. Have to talk to the wife's brother. Keep your eye out for that nigger preacher up there, especially if you bring along a white woman."

Scanlon should have reminded Higgins of what a stupid, bigoted remark that was. Instead, he kept quiet, staring straight ahead out the window at Route 2, needing no excuse, in his condition, to not turn and give the math teacher a reproachful look. He'd all but forgotten about the Irasburgh incident anyway. It had its day in the press and now it was over. Not in Higgins' mind, apparently. Kids throwing rocks through the preacher's windows because he'd been accused of sexual intimacy with the white wife of one of his parishioners. Signs with racial slurs on his front lawn, his kids harassed in school. It never occurred to Scanlon to wonder if the charges were true. What if they were? Did that justify rocks through his windows? The signs? Folks in Irasburgh barely tolerated a Negro clergyman. A Negro clergyman who stepped out of line, especially when it involved sex with white women in general, married white women in particular, was asking for the lynch mob, a burning cross, retribution. For a day or two, the matter had the attention of the national press. Scanlon thought it had all blown over. Now Higgins was stirring it up. Maybe it was Higgins who gave Romeo Boudreau all his ideas on race.

"Don't fancy nigger talk, do you, Mr. Scanlon." Scanlon could see, peripherally, Higgins looking at him. "You liberals got no stomach for straight talk."

"Hasn't that dead horse taken enough of a beating?"

Higgins laughed. They hit the final hill before descending into Fairfield. The sun held the Methodist Church steeple just right, and it took their attention off the subject of race.

"Ain't that a pretty sight," Higgins observed. Scanlon wondered if this rustic fracturing of the language he tended to lapse into was affectation.

"Yeah, that's nice. Nature imitating art." This remark earned a guttural laugh from Higgins.

"How you going to manage teaching class with a neck like that?"

"Good question. I'll teach from the back of the room. Call it progressive education."

"Hmm."

"We ever going to see the last of this snow?" Scanlon asked in all earnestness as they turned into the parking lot rimmed with mountains of filthy snow.

"No tellin'."

"What's wrong with your neck?" Samantha Burnham asked Scanlon in eighth period study hall where her attendance was rare enough. To be spoken to directly by her was rarer yet, an occasion to take notice. The few words that he'd exchanged with her this year had been at his instigation and had always centered around her attendance, or lack of it, in study hall, the exception being the time she'd laid him low with that withering remark after the Danny Picard incident. Now, here she was asking after his neck. His palms were all clammy, and he was conscious suddenly of his heartbeat. She leaned toward him, elbows on the lecture desk, her lovely chin cupped in both delicate white hands. Her eyes, oh those eyes! Those lashes and that mole on her chin. Then he was reminded of Mole Cheek and his mood darkened.

"Old combat wound. Acts up now and then during a thaw."

"Sure." Samantha smiled, and all thoughts of her hippie boyfriend vanished for Scanlon.

When he told her the real story of his neck, she laughed. Such a mirthful sound, he had to laugh, too, at himself. Kids were coming into the room, scraping chairs, making conversation, but Scanlon was aware only of Samantha. She took her seat, her eyes never leaving his, so unabashed it was he who finally had to look away. The whole period he stole looks in her direction, his brain over stimulated with possibilities. She had shifted her attention to a paperback book.

Once, he caught Danny Picard staring at him with a fat grin spread across his pockmarked face. Scanlon looked back at him cross-eyed. The period ended, and Samantha left the room without so much as a glance in his direction. Danny got his attention with a lascivious insider's wink.

Scanlon waited for Higgins in the parking lot, his neck stiffer than when he woke up, his spirits low. Then Samantha was beside him, her head tilted, a small frown creasing her smooth forehead that had just a hint of blond down above the brow.

"What you need is a massage, a neck rub," she said to him. His heart thudded, and blood rose to his head like hot mercury.

"Oh? Know where I could get that kind of treatment?"

"I'd do it for you, but my father's supposed to be picking me up." She swung her shoulders and arms back and forth, her body torquing as if she were getting ready to go into a spin, like a figure skater or a ballet dancer. She got up on point. "Of course there's always the chance that he won't show up. With Daddy you can never be sure. In which case, I would take care of you."

Take care of me, Scanlon thought, growing slightly faint.

"Well?" Samantha said, with a beautiful frown.

"I'm waiting for Mr. Higgins. And with Mr. Higgins you can always be sure. How about a rain check?" It was all he could think of to say to inform this girl that he could think of nothing that would give him more pleasure than to have her hands on his stiff neck. It had come out sounding faintly prurient, and he regretted having said it. Samantha merely shrugged, as if her offer of a neck rub was completely impersonal, a service she'd perform for anyone if she was in the mood.

Lyle Higgins did appear before Samantha's father, and as they drove out of the parking lot Scanlon would have given anything to be able to turn his neck for a last glimpse of this creature standing alone like the patron saint of high school parking lots. Then Mole Cheek and Goatee were back in his thoughts, characters who would no doubt intrude in his fantasies, day or night.

When Scanlon awoke the next morning from active and confusing dreams, his neck was back to normal. Was he to take this as a sign? Samantha, of course, had attended his dreams but not in any tangible or satisfying way. She was a presence, a filmy, elusive, insubstantial presence. He remembered none of the specific details, not the way he remembered his courtroom dream. Nothing he could bring to Kennedy even if he were inclined to discuss dreams of Samantha with him. Some things were simply not meant to be shared. His relationship with Samantha had taken on a sudden, new direction. And knowing that this was bordering on adolescent fantasy, his thoughts were nevertheless crowded with Samantha as he waited on the front lawn for Higgins to collect him. The air was softer this morning, the sun up, promising more snow melting. The snow had already receded from the front steps to the edge of the road revealing the small patch of lawn. Another week of temperatures in the fifties or low sixties would take care of the rest of it; the snowplow-created mountains on the roadsides could take longer.

An insect flew by Scanlon's nose, and he felt a little spasm of joy. He wished it were Friday. He would like to talk to Kennedy today: let the poor bastard see him in a good mood for a change.

Higgins' Ford appeared around the corner, his right blinker flashing. He'd have to think of something appropriate to pay Higgins back for his generosity.

"How's the neck this morning?"

"Gone. I mean it's like there was never a problem with it. What do you make of that?"

"Probably faking it all along. Good way to get sympathy. I saw that Burnham girl offering her sympathy yesterday." Higgins turned, and to Scanlon's astonishment, winked.

"What are you talking about?" Scanlon forced out a laugh that made him sound like a man with something to hide.

"You don't have to play innocent, Mr. Scanlon. We got eyes in our head."

"That's ridiculous, if I understand what you're suggesting. That's really crazy."

"What is?"

"What you're suggesting. It's, it's ... I don't know ... crazy."

"And what is it you imagine I'm suggesting?"

Scanlon, now capable of turning his head, saw that Higgins was either toying with him, or on a fishing expedition.

"I wouldn't presume to imagine such a thing."

Higgins laughed. Patches of green were beginning to show up on the rolling meadows along Route 2. Higgins observed that by this time next week you'd never know we'd just been through the worst snow winter in seventy-eight years.

"It'll all be forgotten except for when you're telling your grandchildren about the winter of '68-'69," Higgins said.

Grandchildren. Scanlon couldn't imagine Lucy as a bride, as pregnant, as a mother herself, suckling a child, his grandchild. It was beyond his comprehension. What he saw, in his mind's eye, was an unhappy little girl with damp, blond curls plastered against her skull, propped up in bed with pillows, sucking her thumb, tugging at her ear, with that stinking security rag in her tiny fist. Then he thought of his grandmother and grandfather who had reared him the way his mother should have reared him, who'd spoiled him rotten and given him the happiest moments of his life.

"Here we are," Higgins announced.

"Ah, yes," Scanlon said, cranking his door handle. He got out of the car and stretched, still tentative where his neck was concerned, but happy to have the use of it back so soon. He glanced surreptitiously around the lot, but it would be too early for Samantha. How did she get here? Bus? Was her father reliable enough to depend on for rides to school? The answer was assuredly no, given her frequent absences. He hoped today would not be one of her absent days.

"Into the breach," Scanlon said with uncommon enthusiasm, rubbing his hands together the way Higgins liked to do. Higgins noticed.

"Full of piss and vinegar this morning."

"It's spring, and I'm in love," Scanlon replied without thinking.

Higgins' eyebrows rose causing his bifocals to slip down his nose.

"Today," Scanlon announced in first period biology, "you begin taking responsibility for shaping your own curriculum." He looked out upon the collective blankness he'd grown accustomed to seeing and which would no doubt account heavily for his leaving the teaching business. Only today, it being spring-like, and he being in love, Scanlon was undaunted. "That's right. As of today you're in charge of your own fate." He had not the slightest idea where he was going with this nonsense. For once, he seemed not to be concerned with consequences. He was full of something, he didn't know what. Shit is what Romeo Boudreau would tell him he was full of, if he continued this euphoria into fourth period.

"No more lectures," Scanlon continued "No more objective tests, no more spoon-feeding and regurgitation. I'm licked. From now on we're giving over to affective education." Scanlon looked out at the faces. Nothing. "Relevance is what they want, relevance is what they'll get," he said, more to himself this time than to the class.

"How'll we get graded?" Donald Dubois, always the practical young man, wanted to know.

"I don't know. Grade yourself. Give yourself whatever you think you're worth."

Donald Dubois shrank down into his seat, not at all satisfied with his teacher's abrupt pedagogical change in direction. In fact, no one received

Scanlon's new, "progressive" approach with enthusiasm. They just looked up at him from their tablet armchairs as if he were demented, which in a way he was, except this time it felt good. Had he achieved that elusive spontaneity he'd always felt was out of his reach? Fourth period and Romeo Boudreau would be the acid test. With his chemistry students, he'd get a more enthusiastic reception. They were juniors and seniors, always ready for anarchy. With his freshmen, Scanlon wasn't so sure. He would see how he felt third period.

"Aren't any of you curious? No questions?" The answer was frozen on their glum faces. Not only were they not curious enough to ask what he was up to, they were seconds away from marching to the principal's office and have him come down here with his gaff hook and butterfly net to take their teacher away to Waterbury.

"I'll bet you're not comfortable with the idea of grading yourself. Is that it? You think you'll give in to selfishness and give yourself a better grade than you deserve. Am I right?"

Was he imagining this or were they frowning? "Sure, some of you might overcompensate, be too hard on yourself, not wanting to appear dishonest, or overly conscious of grades." Scanlon paced the floor in front of the lecture desk, careful not to step on the first row kids' feet, gesticulating like a Baptist preacher. "You're worried about what your parents will think. Wouldn't they be pleased to see an "A" next to biology on your report card? Would they have to know how it was gotten? Of course they wouldn't. So what are you afraid of? Mr. Winship?" Some kids began to squirm, others smiled, maybe thinking this was just another one of Mr. Scanlon's lame jokes.

"You can't expect us to be fair if we grade ourselves. We're just kids." It was Denise Marcotte who finally brought him down. The little redhead, the snake lady, who had given up on monogamy and who never said boo in biology class. Fairness. A concept he'd never considered. When you're acting spontaneously, there's little room for this plodding kind of logic. Fairness. Now their faces were pleading, having been given a voice by Denise Marcotte, who Scanlon had trouble sometimes thinking of as just a "kid."

"So does this mean you don't want to dictate your own curriculum? Write your own grades? Take responsibility for your own learning? You want to just keep doing what we've been doing? What about relevance?"

Junior Darling asked Scanlon if there was going to be a unit on sexual reproduction, since he seemed to think relevance was so important.

"Don't you get enough of that at home?" Scanlon joked to deadpan stares.

"All right. We'll get into sex. It's almost spring anyway, what the hell." Another joke floated heavily and crash-landed. Scanlon retreated behind the lecture desk and opened the biology text, thumbing pages without looking at them. "Where were we last time?"

Eighth period study hall. The bell had rung five minutes ago and there was no sign of Samantha Burnham. Scanlon was disconsolate and it showed, at least to Danny Picard who sat in his chair, arms folded across his chest, smirking at Scanlon. He knew everything, and he would use this knowledge to make Scanlon's life miserable, not out of malice but playfulness.

Scanlon motioned him up to the lecture desk. Danny obliged, slowly extracting himself from his narrow seat, not once taking his eyes off Scanlon.

"You look like a possum eating shit," Scanlon said, getting a whiff of Danny's powerful body odor. Since the warm spell, Danny was back to wearing T-shirts to school, T-shirts he wore to shop and to class.

"Don't know what you're talking about." Danny slouched against the lecture desk, poking through Scanlon's papers with his index finger because he knew this annoyed him.

"Don't be cute. How would you like me to throw your ass in detention for chewing gum?"

"What gum?" Danny bit the wad of gum between his teeth and bared them. "You mean this gum? Dentist said I should chew gum all day. Keeps the shit out from between the teeth." Danny's teeth were beyond ever getting clean. In ten years, he wouldn't have a natural tooth left in his head.

"I want to know why the smirk. You got a secret?"

"I ain't got no secrets."

"You going to graduate?"

"I better."

"What about your English? You talked to Miss Sinclair about last marking period?"

"Cynthia and me got an understanding." Danny hadn't yielded the smirk.

"Cynthia, is it?" Scanlon nodded. "Such familiarity. How long have you and Miss Sinclair been on a first name basis?"

Danny smiled and made a show of chewing his gum. He couldn't know anything about Scanlon's feelings for Samantha. How could he? And if he was operating on a hunch, nothing had happened between Scanlon and the girl so far that could reinforce it, and Scanlon wasn't about to say or do anything that would fuel this smart-assed kid's speculation.

"You know, don't you, that if you don't pass English you don't graduate."

"You don't have to worry. I'm gonna pass English." Danny looked too sure of himself to be bluffing.

"You getting help with your compositions?" As far as Scanlon knew, Danny had no friends among the competent writers. It wasn't likely that his fiancee, Norma Woodruff, high-school dropout and cosmetologist in training, was writing his papers for him. He seemed very sure of "Cynthia." If he'd struck a deal with her he wouldn't be bold enough, or foolish enough, to let it get out. Even if he did think of Scanlon as an ally, Danny didn't strike him as the kind to take chances. It could be that he didn't care one way or the other about passing English. There was the question of why he'd stuck it out at Fairfield High this long, so obviously out of his element, only to throw it away a few weeks before graduation. He had to want the diploma.

"What worries me," Scanlon said, "is you don't look worried enough."

"Don't lose no sleep over me." It was as if Danny were telling Scanlon that he should attend to his own problems, and furthermore, that Danny had inside information on the nature of Scanlon's troubles.

"Still planning to tie the knot after graduation?"

"Yup. Me and Norma been making final plans all this week. You coming to the wedding?"

"If I'm invited. I suppose you'll want a gift."

"Damn straight."

"You sure you're all right in English, Danny?"

Danny Picard flashed the thumbs up sign and went back to his seat.

Chapter Thirty-one

Lying in bed that night on the edge of sleep, Scanlon tried to conjure up images of Samantha and himself on platonic assignations in green spring fields, sitting amidst spring flowers, speaking obliquely of love. His efforts failed, and he was overtaken by sleep and another dream involving his daughter.

He awoke next morning with the sour memory, the same hollowed out feeling in his stomach as the last time he'd had such a dream.

Bob Kennedy had on his spring wardrobe for Scanlon's Friday visit. The seersucker suit for most seasons was back. Kennedy hadn't bothered to have it cleaned, and for some screwed up reason he couldn't figure, Scanlon was glad he hadn't.

Scanlon went immediately into the dream, and Kennedy went immediately for his temple, his attention, as usual, out the window at the gully with its dregs of spring melt.

S: Please don't ask me to recount the events of the day, Bob.

Kennedy ignored his sarcasm.

K: You involved with this woman again, your colleague's wife?

S: Not a chance.

He couldn't possibly get into it with Kennedy about Samantha. He was having enough trouble with the dream.

K: Well, as I told you before, these things are fairly common. I wouldn't make too much of it.

S: Exactly how much of it do you think there is?

K: Hard to say.

There was no whiskey. Kennedy would have to pick now to show resolve.

S: I can see how you could pass it off as an aberration if it was a one-shot deal. Now I'm not so sure. It's like a recurring thing, you know? Just when I think maybe things are starting to look up, wham.

Scanlon smacked his fist into his open palm. Kennedy jumped a little.

K: Don't let it throw you. For Christ's sake it's spring. Look for yourself.

Was he supposed to look out the window to confirm that the season had changed? He felt worse for bringing up the dream. Should he offer to dash out for a jug? If he was in a crisis wouldn't bourbon serve him well, as it had in crises past?

S: How you doing with the sauce, Bob?

K: Nothing for six weeks. Yourself?

S: Hah! Nothing for twelve hours.

K: What's the story with your car?

S: Don't get me started on that subject.

K: So you're still without transportation?

S: I got transportation. I just don't have my own car. I ride with Higgins every morning, every afternoon. On weekends I'm grounded. I hate to ask my uncle to use his car.

K: How are things looking up? You mentioned it a while back. Just when things were starting to look up, I think you said.

S: I said that?

Scanlon laughed.

S: You must be hearing things. Looking up? No, things are still looking down. I don't even write in the diary anymore.

K: You sound disappointed.

S: Do I? Maybe I am. Maybe I enjoyed it, even if it was starting to get a little sickening.

K: How come you stopped?

S: It wasn't hard. If I could stop drinking as easily as I stopped writing I'd have it knocked. It was probably going to Garrison, racking up the car. Got me out of my rhythm. It took a little discipline to do the writing, you know? It wasn't just something that came naturally to me.

K: I realize that. It might do you some good to try and get back in that routine.

S: I don't know, Bob. Nothing seems worth the bother. I'm exhausted, you know? Really fucking beat. In here.

Scanlon pointed a finger at his head, cocked his thumb and shot himself through the skull.

K: I get the feeling that something is coming to a head, you'll pardon the expression. I want you back in the diary. Carry the goddamn thing around with you if you have to.

S: I don't think I can. I can't very well walk around all day with my note book. Be realistic.

Kennedy's eyes were bright; he looked younger all of a sudden, probably the direct effect of being off the booze for six weeks. If he thought he could postpone turning thirty for a few years, Scanlon would quit himself. In a minute.

K: Do it. Indulge me for a change.

S: Indulge you? What the fuck have I been doing for six, seven months?

K: Indulge me some more.

S: So you can skip out after you've had your way with me?

K: Just this last once.

Scanlon panicked again at the prospect of not having Kennedy there for him on these Friday afternoons. To start seeing someone else would be pointless, and Kennedy had suggested no such thing, which wasn't to say that he might not suggest it in the future. Scanlon hoped he wouldn't. He wanted always to think of their association as something special, one of a kind.

S: So you want me to keep a running chronicle of my fun-filled days.

Scanlon shook his head, half-smiling.

S: I can see this thing throwing me into an even deeper funk.

K: What's to hurt by trying?

S: OK, Bob. For you.

K: Thanks, Jack, but it's for you.

S: We'll see.

Danny Picard kicked open the door, and Scanlon quickly closed his notebook. He tried to tuck it under his legs, like a kid trying to hide something from his parents.

"How do, Mr. S," Danny said, grabbing a fistful of keys off his belt. He shouldered a box of evaporated milk.

"What's up, Danny?"

"Not my dick. How come you're sitting on that notebook? Trying to hatch it?"

"None of your business," Scanlon said with a playful smile.

"Writing your memoirs?"

"Get bent."

Danny laughed and unlocked the storeroom door. "I got about twenty more of these just like it out in the hall, you feel like breaking a sweat." Danny faced Scanlon, feet spread, one hand on his hip, the case of milk on his shoulder. He had on his mischief face. Scanlon itched to write something about him in his notebook.

"I don't perform stoop labor, thank you just the same."

"Why're you hiding that notebook?"

"I'm not hiding anything, you nosy shit."

"Yes you are," Danny sang.

"You'll go to any length to avoid honest work, won't you, Picard?"

"What would you know about honest work?"

"You're on the threshold of impertinence, young man."

"Only threshold I'm on's this scuzzy teachers' room. I wouldn't be caught dead hanging out in here."

"You don't like this room?" Scanlon asked. "What's not to like about it? Is it the khaki walls that offend you? The cement floor? The asbestos pipes grate on your sensibilities? What?"

"I got work to do. See you eighth." Danny went about hauling boxes of evaporated milk.

Cynthia Sinclair bustled through the door, exuding energy and purposefulness. This time Scanlon didn't make the mistake of trying to hide his notebook.

"We missed you at lunch, Mr. Scanlon."

"I couldn't face the brown bag offering."

"There was nice chopped ham salad sandwiches and chocolate chip cookies. And a nice, red apple. It was excellent." Cynthia had acquired her own Snoopy coffee cup. No more Styrofoam for her. She held her nickel poised over the slot in the coffee fund box before letting it drop, as if Scanlon would challenge her for copping free coffee. She mixed herself a cup with two envelopes of fake cream and three lumps of sugar.

How would she react if he pulled her down onto the mildewy sofa and reached up under her dress? Scanlon smiled. Cynthia noticed and demanded to know what was on his wicked mind.

"Nothing too wicked, I assure you."

"I don't believe you."

Lyle Higgins came in talking in Daryl Winship's ear. Scanlon fingered the metal rings of his notebook. Neither Winship nor Higgins so much as glanced in his direction. They were deep in discussion about the bond issue snag, miffed over the foot-dragging antics of some members of the school committee. Too important an issue to be bothered with a peon like Scanlon. He didn't care one iota about either of them, but here he was sitting on this musty sofa feeling hurt and rejected. He caught Cynthia watching him. He averted his eyes. If she wore less makeup, less of that lipstick in particular, and if she let her hair down, got contact lenses, somehow acquired a better figure and an acceptable personality, she might be considered attractive. Such mean thoughts.

Danny Picard came into the room grinning like an inside dopester. Scanlon quickly closed his notebook and slipped it into the top drawer where he kept his evaporating dish ashtray hidden.

"You don't look glad to see me, Mr. Scanlon. What're you trying to hide in the drawer?"

"Sit down, you baboon."

Danny laughed and slung one long leg over the back of the tablet armchair. He sort of fell into his seat, sending the chair scraping across the floor. Julie Moreau made a face at Danny's antics, wrinkling her nose as if his behavior gave off a disagreeable smell, a smell equal to his rank body odor after an hour of humping dry goods down in the cafeteria. But Danny was his own man, oblivious of the judgments of his peers. And now Scanlon was a little jealous of him, too.

He was tempted to take out his notebook during study hall. Danny would be at the lecture desk in a flash, putting his nose where it didn't belong. Samantha Burnham arrived ten minutes late. The fact that she had arrived at all had Scanlon's heart accelerating, blood pounding through his temples. She walked straight to her usual chair without a look in his direction, without so much as a feeble explanation for her tardiness, indifferent to his signals of love. He meant nothing to her and he was suddenly angry.

"I suppose you have a good reason for being late, Samantha," he heard himself saying. Everyone looked up at him. Had the remark been so outrageous?

"I'm sorry," Samantha said, reaching into her handbag. "I was seeing Mrs. Gallagher." Samantha produced a white slip of paper and held it up for him to see. Presumably a note from Connie Gallagher, the district nurse, but it could have been any scrap of paper, a bluff from the cool Miss Burnham. What could she be seeing the district nurse about? VD? Birth control advice?

"May I see that?" Scanlon asked her.

Samantha came to the lecture desk, an impertinent little smile forming on her mouth. She handed him the note with the district nurse's letterhead.

"Why didn't you give me this when you came in?" Scanlon pretended to scrutinize the note as if he doubted its authenticity, but he was really only trying to cover up his embarrassment.

"I must have had something else on my mind. Sorry."

She sounded almost genuine. Scanlon softened, daring to look up from the note into her face.

"Nothing serious I hope," Scanlon said, dying to know what it was that took her to the nurse.

"No. Just trouble with my period."

Scanlon dropped his eyes, fingered the textbook on the lecture desk.

"Surely, you don't have to look that up in your biology book." There were her elbows on the lecture desk again; her exquisite chin found its way into her cupped white hands.

"I'm glad it's nothing serious then," he said with a little voice. He took a chance and raised his eyes.

"Am I making you uncomfortable?" she asked in almost a whisper. Behind her Danny Picard snorted, and there was much shuffling of feet in the room.

"Well, thanks for the note. Maybe you should go back to your seat," Scanlon said, thinking what a stupid, idiotic thing that was to say. Samantha backed away, eyes fixed on Scanlon who held her stare long enough to elicit a smile from her, one that was anything but impertinent.

Alice was tuned into Merv Griffin, flanked by Lucky and Nanette on the sofa. Cats on the back of the sofa, on the arms, on the braided rug, on the coffee table. Alice looked shrunken, lost in the menagerie. She had the afghan over her lap. The temperature in the room was eighty-five if it was a degree. She was so absorbed in the show that she didn't notice Scanlon's presence. He stood in the middle of the room, watching the screen until Alice became aware of him. She looked up, startled.

"Sorry, Alice. Didn't mean to surprise you. I thought I'd have a beer, if you don't mind. Yourself?"

"Can't dance." Alice laughed and raised her bottle to the light to inspect the dregs before drinking them off.

“I still got a pile of work to do before supper,” Scanlon said on his way to the kitchen.

“Didn’t I tell you? We’re going to Althea’s for supper tonight. I thought I told you. Guess not. Getting forgetful in my old age. Soon as Ira gets home and washes up, we’re going over.”

“I should probably skip Althea’s,” Scanlon said before realizing how presumptuous it was of him to assume he was also invited to the Goodwins for supper. “Think she’ll mind?”

“Donny might mind. Probably waiting to hound you to take him bowling after supper. I’ll just tell them you’re busy.”

Scanlon climbed upstairs feeling like a fraud, but spending an evening with the Goodwins was the last thing he needed.

Chapter Thirty-two

"I've ordered white mice," Scanlon announced in biology class fourth period. "What do you think of that?"

"Can we dissect them?" Denise, the snake lady, asked.

"They're not for dissecting. They're alive. I thought you might be interested in using them for an experiment on behavior, you know, mazes and that sort of thing. This is a chance for you to make up your own simple experiments, carry them out and report your results like grown-up scientists."

"Then can we dissect them?"

"Denise." Scanlon almost wisecracked at Denise's expense until he remembered that she might be fragile.

"Yeah," Junior Darling said, "that would be neat. Better'n them rubber pigs."

"Those rubber pigs," Scanlon said. "Anyway, they're on order, and when they arrive it's going to be your responsibility to see to it that they're cared for. They've got to be fed and especially watered properly, and their cages have to be cleaned regularly." Scanlon hadn't thought about what he'd use for cages, and now that he'd brought up the subject, anxiety began to mount.

"I ain't feedin' no rat, 'less it's to my cat." Romeo Boudreau, Scanlon might have known, would have his say.

"Mice," Scanlon said, wanting to add something caustic to put Romeo in his place, but held back. "Not rats, Romeo. Mice. Little white ones that not even you would be mean enough to feed to the cat." He couldn't hold back completely; he was no saint. Romeo merely smiled, but Scanlon thought he detected a flicker of pain, a bit of a wince behind it. As usual, Scanlon felt terrible for his mouth.

“What about the containers they come in? Can’t you keep them in there?” Winship asked.

“There’ll only be a couple of containers. I need to separate them into several groups, you know, experimental, control, and all that.”

“You should have thought about that before you went and ordered them,” Winship said, stroking his chin. Even as Winship treated him like a child, he seemed to be thinking, searching for an answer to Scanlon’s white mice dilemma. “Why don’t you have a talk with Dennis. Maybe he can fix you up with something down at the shop. Better yet, why don’t you have your kids do the cages? Dennis won’t mind if they use his wood scraps. How much could it take? Yeah, try Dennis.” Winship seemed pleased. Scanlon had to admit to a certain excitement of his own, along with relief, for Winship’s idea was perfect. Why hadn’t he thought of it himself?

The shop teacher, dressed in his greasy mechanic’s smock, directed the hoisting onto blocks of a Ford engine. The engine was poised over the hood of a 1965 Mustang, suspended by chains from a pulley rigged on the high ceiling, and Kitchell was waving one hand like a traffic cop to get the kids working the pulley to center the thing over the blocks. Kitchell and his auto mechanics students were so absorbed in their task that they didn’t notice Scanlon. Or they noticed him and chose to ignore him. Either way he felt stupid and out of place, as if he were a witness to a primitive ceremony, some kind of pagan ritual.

He was surprised not to see Danny Picard there, for Danny was hard-core when it came to shop. Even Danny couldn’t be expected to spend all his time with his passion; he did take other courses.

“Now swing her around,” Kitchell yelled, “let her down on the dolly. We’ll put her up by hand.” Ross Chance and Bucky Cailiff, their faces as intent and earnest as brain surgeons, guided the engine out of its cradle and eased it down onto the dolly. Kids should be so purposeful in his classes. He was envious. And Kitchell was a popular fellow, maybe even as popular as Scanlon.

Kitchell glanced at Scanlon, his eyes flickering as he processed this interloper with whom he had not spoken five words all year. What are you doing here? What do you want? These were the questions, Scanlon imagined, that were on Dennis Kitchell’s mind. He walked away from Scanlon toward a large desk against the wall next to the ramp that led outside. For a moment, Scanlon forgot why he had come down here. Kitchell stood by his desk, pretending to study something attached to a clipboard. He was deliberately ignoring Scanlon, forcing him to make the first move.

"Dennis, I've got kind of a weird favor to ask of you," Scanlon said from where he stood, clear across the vast, high-ceilinged shop, his voice echoing. It got Kitchell's attention. He looked over at Scanlon, put his clipboard down on his desk and produced a rag from his back pocket. He began to wipe his hands. Scanlon approached.

"What can I do for you?" Kitchell asked.

You could look at me for openers Scanlon said to himself, wanting to grab the man by the shoulders and turn him around. Kitchell was wiry, lean, and probably one mean s.o.b. Tough and Vermont taciturn, stubbornness coded into his genes. Scanlon explained his problem while Kitchell finished wiping grease from his hands, not once looking at Scanlon. Scanlon wondered what he did out here when it got really cold outside in the dead of winter.

"Well, I can't have kids in here working on them. They'd get in the way of classes. How many you say you need?" Kitchell stirred papers around his desktop the way Winship always seemed to do.

"Four would be ideal. I could get along with two, but four would be ideal. If that's not too much of a problem, I mean."

Kitchell did some pencil calculations on a note pad. Scanlon, beholden to this man, waited in an anxious state, like a teenager asking for the family car.

"Take a few days."

"That's all right. There's no hurry, really. You sure you don't mind?" When you're too ingratiating, Scanlon had learned, you get people's attention. Kitchell finally deigned to look at him as if he were too stupid for words. Well, Scanlon thought, fuck you, I'm getting my cages. He must remember to thank Winship for his bright idea.

"Thanks, Dennis. I really appreciate this. A few days, you say? That's great."

"Three or four days. Week at the most."

"Thanks." Scanlon retreated before Kitchell changed his mind. He hurried to his notebook.

Chapter Thirty-three

"You got a letter today, Johnny," Alice announced, as if he'd won the Irish Sweepstakes. Scanlon thought it might be from Lucy. He hadn't received anything from her since the pathetic Christmas card.

"Where is it?"

"Put it on your dresser."

Scanlon took the stairs two at a time. The letter, which Scanlon held in his trembling hands, was postmarked Garrison, New Hampshire, and the neat script he recognized right away as his mother's, handwriting he hadn't seen since he'd been in the Navy. What did she want? Money? How could so many people expect money from a resource as poor as Jack Scanlon, annual income five thousand and change? He tossed the letter on the bureau without opening it. He got undressed and lay down on the bed, intending to stay down for only a few minutes. He fell asleep, and when he woke up it was dark. He'd missed supper. They didn't bother to call him down for supper anymore. He was hungry, and what was more he wasn't particularly interested in a drink. He turned the lamp on beside his bed and glanced at the bureau, at the unopened letter. He half expected not to see a letter, to realize that the letter had been part of a dream. It wouldn't be the first time his dreams merged with reality in a way that made it difficult for him to distinguish one from the other. He listened. It was quiet in the house, not even the sound of the TV downstairs. It was only eight-thirty, too early for even Ira to be in bed. Scanlon got up and slipped into shirt and trousers. He went downstairs barefoot, walking softly in case Alice and Ira had gone to bed after all.

Ira was asleep in his chair, Lucky curled up on the floor at his feet; Alice was on the sofa, on her side, her hair up in curlers; one eye flickered when

Scanlon came in the room. The TV was on; the volume turned so low as to be inaudible.

Scanlon felt stranded. He'd seen Alice's eye open, then close. She knew he was there and she obviously did not want to talk to him. Alice not wanting to talk was cause enough for distress, but to find his aunt and uncle dozing off in the living room during the shank of the television evening was panic making.

"Alice," he whispered, and Alice's eye flickered again. "Alice," he repeated, "you awake?" Lucky stirred, let out a sigh and went back to sleep. Ira's glasses had slipped down to the tip of his nose. His mouth was open. Scanlon was surprised his uncle wasn't snoring. His breathing was regular and quiet, yet Scanlon felt as though he had stumbled upon a pair of corpses. He had a sudden urge to drink a beer. He tiptoed into the dark kitchen and opened the refrigerator, holding his breath. To his relief there were plenty of brown beer bottles stuck in among the casseroles, packages of foil-wrapped leftovers, bottles of this and that. A family of eight could have lived for weeks off the contents of that refrigerator. He was no longer hungry, only thirsty for beer. He pulled out a bottle wondering what life would be like free of dependence on appetite. Any appetite—food, drink, sex, power—all of it.

When he returned to the living room, intending to continue back upstairs, Alice was sitting upright.

"I woke you up," Scanlon said, glancing at his uncle who was still dead to the world.

"Must've dozed off," Alice said, rubbing her eyes with her fists like a kid, like his Lucy used to do. Scanlon wondered why Alice had put her hair up. Was she due for another trip to Hanover tomorrow?

"Ira's really conked out," Scanlon said, sitting on the edge of the rocker not intending to linger.

"Wake up and go to bed," Alice said, as if talking to herself. "Lucky, wake your father up. Take him to bed." Lucky snorted. A ripple of muscle moved along his backbone, but he held his position. He took orders only from his "father." With Lucky and Nanette, it was difficult not to anthropomorphize.

"Sorry I missed supper. Dozed off myself."

"Knocked on your door. Some boiled potatoes and ham in the fridge. Peas. Help yourself. That beer looks pretty good."

Scanlon got up quickly to fetch Alice a beer. Ira was awake when he returned.

"How's it going?" Scanlon asked his uncle, setting Alice's beer down on the coffee table.

"Fell asleep during the news. Probably won't sleep the rest of the night now. Wake up feeling like a warmed-over turd."

"That's a laugh," Alice said. "He can sleep anytime except Sunday mornings and during deer hunting season. He'll be sawing wood in half an hour."

Ira grinned and winked. One of the blessings Ira had received in this life was the ability to sleep straight through the night and wake up refreshed in the morning. He had this gift even when he was drinking, Alice had said. Scanlon wondered if he snored himself. Katie had never complained. About everything else concerning his existence she complained. Never about snoring.

"Now that the snow's almost gone, we should plan another picnic," Scanlon said.

"Oh, I thought having it in the snow was fun. Huh, Ira?"

"Eh?" Ira cupped an ear toward his wife.

"Jesus, he's deaf," Alice said. Scanlon had heard this conversation, or conversations enough like it not to be able to tell the difference, many, many times since he'd been staying with his aunt and uncle. Each time he was saddened a little more, though on the surface it was harmless enough, almost playful.

"Yeah, we could go up to Beaver Falls," Scanlon said with false enthusiasm. "You remember Beaver Falls, Ira? Over in North Fairfield?"

"Oh, sure. Swam there all the time, we was kids. You know where it is, Mother? Couple miles from Letourneau's on the North Fairfield road. Next left takes you out to Father Jerry's."

"Beaver Falls. I know where it is. I'm not stupid." Alice sounded insulted, as if intelligence had anything to do with knowing where Beaver Falls was.

"Excuse me," Ira said.

"We used to swim there, too," Scanlon said to avert any more unpleasantness between them. "Eddie Leclerc always said there were bloodsuckers in the water below the dam. You ever see any bloodsuckers, Ira?" Scanlon made a point of speaking loudly and directly at his uncle, more for Alice's benefit than Ira's because they all knew that Ira's deafness was selective.

"Heard that, too. Never saw one myself, and we swum there nearly every day. Been years." Was that a shadow of nostalgia crossing his uncle's face? Ira used to tell wonderful stories about his childhood on the "Hill" during the Depression. Scanlon's mother turned up in most of his uncle's stories because as kids they were very close, as close as any of the eight kids in the family were to each other. His mother was something of a tomboy when she was a young girl. Unlike today's youngsters, Ira would be quick to say, kids in his day had to invent their own amusement. They never had a problem finding things to do. This was before radio was commonplace in the homes of the poor, let alone television. Relievo. Kick the can. Red Rover. Games kids seldom played nowadays.

Scanlon had lived on the "Hill" briefly himself, shortly after coming to live with his mother and Bill Scanlon. Hill kids were different from village kids he'd discovered, more resourceful in ways that Ira described the kids of his youth. So it was with the boys on the Hill. In retrospect, he couldn't remember any Hill girls, but there must have been girls. He was ten years old at the time, and girls mattered not at all. He remembered the summer in particular, those long, warm days spent playing baseball in the upper pastures, using dried cow flaps for bases. Evenings, when there was a good movie playing in town, the Hill boys would walk as a group the four miles to the Palace. They did everything together, which included playing some of those Depression games Ira liked to reminisce about. Scanlon had been sad to move away from the Hill, almost as sad as when he had to move away from Groveton altogether.

"Bloodsuckers." Alice shuddered just saying the word.

"They're good for you, Mother. Suck all that shit out of your blood." Ira used to say that about people he considered weak, morally if not physically—that they had shit in their blood.

"Better'n having shit for brains," Alice riposted.

"Now, Mother." Ira's eyes were bright with mischief.

"Aren't you hungry, Johnny?" Alice asked.

"Not really. Anyhow I've got to lose some weight." His trousers were way too tight in the waist and rear end; his gut hung over his belt like Kennedy's. He'd probably look like Kennedy when he got to be his age. How did Ira stay so thin, the way he packed away the food? By not drinking like a fish every day of the week was how he stayed thin.

"Clothes cost money these days," Ira said, reading Scanlon's mind.

"Yeah. Everything costs." Scanlon shook his head solemnly, as if he were privy to some great economic wisdom.

"Well, it's a good thing beer's cheap," Alice said, holding her bottle up to the light, then taking a swallow from it.

"Amen." Scanlon swilled his beer, too. At a buck a six-pack, it was hard to complain about the price of beer, to be sure. Even the so-called premium beers could be had for only thirty or forty cents more. Whiskey was another story. It was still cheaper in Vermont, with the State exercising price control, than it was in Massachusetts. Scanlon drank more whiskey when he lived in Boston. He was also making twice as much money and wasn't being bled dry with support payments to an ex-wife.

"So what did Dot have to say?" Alice asked. For a moment Scanlon wasn't sure whom she was talking about. "Your mother," she added.

"Oh, not much." Scanlon picked at his beer label. "She got rid of her old man, you know. I told you that already, didn't I?"

"Bill was quite a character, huh, Ira. Liked his drink."

"Well, I guess," Ira said. "We tied on some good ones, him and me."

Scanlon remembered the time, right after Ira's discharge, when he was home for good, and he and Bill Scanlon got drunk together one night and took it in their heads to start training for local smokers. Ira was in pretty good shape, having done some boxing when he was in the carrier division. But he hadn't actually stepped into the ring for a few years. And who knew about Bill Scanlon? Who could separate truth from fiction where he was concerned? That was the year before his mother and Bill Scanlon took Johnny Labalm away from Groveton.

Ira would work out with Bill Scanlon on the heavy bag for a half hour, skip a little rope, and for their road work they'd jog downtown to Proyer's beer parlor and get tanked. Ira couldn't pass the physical because of his bum kidney. His troubles really began that year. Now he was operating with high blood pressure on top of the single kidney.

It wouldn't do anybody any good to try and explain to them why he hadn't opened his mother's letter. Could he explain it to himself?

"How're the kids, your brothers?" Alice asked. Scanlon was hard put to remember the last time Alice had been so curious about his family. Had she steamed open the letter and read it herself? Scanlon was irked at himself for thinking such a thing of Alice.

"They're all right. My mother's not thrilled with the way they lead their lives, but then she's not crazy about how I'm living mine either." He wished he hadn't said that. Alice's interest was stirred, and Ira seemed more attentive, leaning forward slightly in his chair as though expecting more to come. Even Lucky had rolled over on his back and had one eye open to stare at him. "She thinks I should have stayed in industry where the money is," Scanlon added. To their credit, and to Scanlon's relief, Alice and Ira had never in all the time he'd been with them asked any hard questions about his real reasons for coming back to Groveton. They knew, of course, that he'd split with his wife and that he had a daughter, and that he was looking for a fresh start. But that was all. They knew nothing of the circumstances around which he'd lost his job at Consolidated. They could have guessed it involved his drinking. How hard could that be? He couldn't remember now what story he'd given them last April. Was it already a year? Another year was rapidly slipping away. Soon he would be thirty. And then what?

Dear Jack,

Well I got another cat after I swore up and down I'd never have another cat in the house. He's so cute. All black except for two white front paws and a little white mustache (like yours). I named him Mittens because of the front paws. He's full of the devil, and I taught him to fetch like a dog. I never seen the beat of it. He looks a lot like Sneakers, the cat we had on the Hill. You remember Sneakers? He was your favorite. Remember when Keith dropped him off the second story porch and he landed on his feet? Poor thing. Were you home the time he got on top of the refrigerator and got the turkey down on the floor? Was that Thanksgiving or Christmas? The years go by. I must be getting old. I can't remember what happened yesterday, but things years ago I remember clear as a bell.

The old man was around yesterday begging me to take him back. He was on a toot, and he's broke and looks like hell. I almost gave in again. Don't worry. I didn't. I got no more use for him and his drinking. Should have got rid of him years ago.

Mittens is trying to chew my pencil while I'm writing. How many cats does Alice have these days? How does Ira put up with it? Whenever I think of their house, I think of cat box. Ira was never crazy about cats, even as a kid. He loved dogs. Alice likes those French poodles. I can't stand them. They're so nervous. Keith and Billy told me you came to visit them. I thought you said you were coming back for supper. I guess you're pretty busy with your new career. Keith is going for his license Monday. He's got a chance to drive truck for Dewey Linen. It pays good. Maybe a paycheck coming in regular will keep him from peddling dope. Billy met a girl and is talking about applying down at the Navy Yard. If they don't get arrested and thrown in jail first. Keith had a run in with Duchek the other day and had to go down to the station. Remember when Duchek brought you home that time? How Keith hates that man. I told him he was only doing his job, but Keith thinks Duchek is out to get him. Well son, I got to get to bed. Five o'clock comes early. Hope everything is going good for you up there. Glad I don't have to live in Groveton anymore. Write when you get the chance.

Love,
Ma

Dear Ma,

Thanks for your letter. Sorry I took so long to answer. You're right about my being busy. I used to think schoolteachers had it knocked. Four or five hours a day, long vacations, the whole bit. Not true. Teachers work harder in nine months than most people do in a year and a half. I'm not exaggerating.

Alice and Ira are fine, and they have five or six cats. I know they have two dogs, Lucky and Nanette. Lucky is Ira's dog, and Nanette (one of those toy poodles you say you can't stand) is definitely Alice's. They've been like saints. Not Lucky and Nanette. Ira and Alice. Putting up with me all these months, who else but saints would do that? They've been a damned sight better to me than you and your husband ever were. And frankly, I resent the way you look down your nose at Alice. Who are you to pass judgment? So you finally got rid of your cancer. I suppose I should be happy for you. I'm afraid all I can report feeling is resentment, deep resentment for the years you inflicted your husband on Keith and Billy and me. And I haven't forgotten all the allotment checks I sent home while I was in the Navy so you could finance that pig's drinking sprees. Now you want a dutiful son who comes home for supper at five, who writes when he has the chance, who'll be around to look after his younger brothers so they'll refrain from selling dope, to keep them out of jail where they probably belong. You want a lot. My question to you is what's in it for me?

Finally, I think you owe me the courtesy of informing me of the identity of my father. If that's not asking too much. Is it so selfish of me to expect this information from you? I'm glad you've finally found peace of mind, that you're independent, drive your own car and do needlework instead of those crossword puzzles. You deserved all of that years ago. So did I. So did Keith and so did Billy. Don't you think you could get outside yourself just long enough to grant me this one small favor? I won't ask another thing of you, I promise. And my mustache isn't white. Yet.

Your son,
Jack

Scanlon stuffed the letter in an envelope, addressed it, even stamped it. He left it on the bureau beside his mother's letter to him, not really intending to mail it. Two days later he came into his room to find the letter gone. Alice had noticed it while she was cleaning his room and had decided to mail it for him.

Chapter Thirty-four

"Where you want the cages?"

"Cages?"

"Them cages for the rats."

"Oh, those cages," Scanlon said to Dennis Kitchell after the light came on regarding the cages he'd forgotten about completely. Not only had he forgotten about them, but now that they were a reality he had no idea where he would keep them. There was no room in his lab, and he doubted Josh Patterson would agree to keep them in his classroom. "Why don't you have them brought in here."

"Here? In the teachers' room?"

"Yeah."

"I don't know about that. They're gonna stink. People don't want to drink their coffee and eat their lunch around the stink of rats. I don't think Daryl will want you keeping them down here."

"You're probably right. I'll ask him, though. Can you hang on to the cages until I get this straightened out?"

"I guess so." Kitchell didn't seem pleased as he peered at his jagged, dirt-packed fingernails with something like a pout on his pointy face.

"I'll get back to you by lunch time. OK?"

"I guess so." Kitchell left the teachers' lounge without saying any more to Scanlon. It was to Kitchell's credit that he'd finished building the cages on the very day the beasts were due to arrive. Now, where could they be kept? If not in the teachers' room, where?

"Daryl," Scanlon said to Winship in his office before homeroom period began, "I have a favor to ask."

"A favor?" Winship glanced up from the perpetual stack of papers that he was busy sorting into piles.

"Yes. Remember those white mice?"

"I seem to remember white rats. Due today, aren't they?"

"I thought it was mice." Then he remembered that Kitchell had said rats, too. Rats were not what he wanted. Had he really ordered rats, not mice?

"No. We definitely ordered rats. I've got the purchase order here somewhere." Winship pawed through the various stacks of papers.

"Rats, mice, whatever. I was hoping you could help me out." Scanlon presented his case. Winship was not keen on the idea of keeping rats in the teachers' room for reasons Dennis Kitchell had already expressed. With newfound tact, Scanlon asked Winship if he had any ideas on where they might be stored. Winship went down the list, which he discovered was short, before coming to the realization that the teachers' room was perhaps the only logical place they could be kept, unless he wanted them in his office which he most assuredly did not. It would be only for a few weeks; teachers could adjust. Scanlon couldn't wait to tell Kitchell and treat himself to the shop teacher's reaction. He hurried downstairs to the shop before the bell rang. Kitchell wasn't there. He trotted downstairs to the teachers' lounge to find only the lingering smell of Cynthia Sinclair's fruity perfume. The bell rang. He would have to wait until lunch to needle Kitchell.

Winship announced the arrival of the rats over the public address speaker in Scanlon's classroom during biology class. The kids cheered. Scanlon went to Winship's office on the run.

On the floor in front of Winship's desk were two large boxes with red lettering and ventilation holes in the sides through which the whiskered snouts of Scanlon's cargo were probing. Trudy Lester sat uncomfortably at her typewriter, glancing frequently at the boxes.

"Feel like poking your finger in there, Trudy?" Scanlon asked her, picking up a box carefully and offering it in her direction. She recoiled.

"Get those nasty things away from me. They stink." They stank indeed. He would hear from his colleagues about how they stank. Feeling like a little boy on Christmas morning, Scanlon stacked one box on the other and hurried back to his biology class carrying his load of rodents like a gift-bearing magus.

Denise Marcotte wanted to hold one, let it crawl up her arm; Romeo Boudreau wanted to poke a couple of them with a dissecting needle to see what it would take to get them angry enough to bite. Most of the kids were content to let them stay in their boxes, to watch their pink noses at the air holes.

"What are we going to do with them?" one kid asked.

"We gonna dissect them, or what?" Tommy Winship wanted to know. His eyes were bright and wicked at the prospect of cutting into a live creature.

Scanlon wasn't sure himself what was in store for them. He had a vague hope that the kids might come up with some simple maze-training experiments on their own. Now that the rats were a smelly reality, the question of materials for the construction of mazes occurred to him. And food. What would he feed the things? He searched the outside of the boxes for paperwork, for instructions on the care and feeding of white rats. He found nothing. How had he ever survived as an industrial engineer? What had become of his advanced planning skills?

"Be right back. Don't fool around with the boxes. Romeo, I don't want you tormenting those things. You hear me?" Scanlon jogged back to Winship's office to see if Trudy had the paperwork. There was only a bill of lading, no instructions of any kind.

"What am I going to feed them?" he said out loud to himself.

"You can feed them to my cat," Trudy said.

"Where's Mr. Winship?" Scanlon didn't wait for her reply. He hurried back to his classroom.

"Denise! What are you doing?" Plump little Denise Marcotte had rats on both arms, one crawling around to the back of her neck; she was reaching in the box for another one with which to festoon herself when Scanlon came in. The one on her left arm was a large male with huge swinging testicles like hazelnuts. The others were smaller, females, probably juveniles. They sniffed Denise up and down her freckled arms as if she were a giant hunk of walking cheese. The one at her neck was nuzzling in her hair. Their fur looked dry and brittle, and their tails were naked. Scanlon got a look at their awful yellow teeth and felt a chill. The other kids stood their distance from Denise, laughing and pointing. Denise was oblivious of them, the rats her only concern.

"Denise, I think you should put them back. You can play with them later if you want."

"They should have something to eat," she said, placing them tenderly with both hands back in their boxes. Scanlon doubted seriously that he'd ever be able to reach into those boxes full of rats with their hairless tails and yellow slanted teeth. What have I done now? he asked himself.

"Would you stay a moment after class, Denise?" he asked as the bell rang. "You like the rats, Denise?"

"Sure."

"How would you like to take care of them?"

"Sure."

"You'll have to see to it that they're fed and watered and their cages are kept clean. Every day. Think you'd want to do that? I'm only asking because you have a certain way with animals. And I'll bet anything that these guys don't have any hang-ups about monogamy."

Denise smiled. "I'd love to take care of them. Thank you, Mr. Scanlon."

"Not at all. Mr. Kitchell has cages all ready for them. They'll be living in the teachers' room. Just think, Denise, you might even get to listen in on the interesting conversations of teachers."

Denise smiled again, gathered up her books to her plump bosom and went off to her next class, toeing out.

Kitchell's boys had done a first-rate job on the cages. Sheet metal sides and backs with a slide out bottom also of sheet metal. Wire mesh for the fronts. He'd even thought to design slots in the sides for water bottles.

"These are sensational," Scanlon said with genuine admiration. "I had no idea. I mean I was expecting something banged together out of plywood. I'm impressed."

Kitchell grunted without looking at Scanlon, his sharp nose twitching in a way that put Scanlon in mind of the rats.

"By the way. Daryl said it was OK to keep them in the teachers' room. Think I could borrow Danny Picard to help me carry them down?"

"Daryl told you you could keep those things in the teachers' room?" Kitchell's rat face expressed incredulity, Scanlon was delighted to see.

"That's right. Hey, Danny. How about giving me a hand?" Scanlon hailed Danny Picard who had appeared out from under a foreign car on a Jeepers Creepers.

"You sure he said it was OK?"

"Sure as shit, Dennis."

Danny got to his feet, a grin on his face. He wiped his oily hands on his coveralls.

"What do you need, Mr. S?"

"A hand with these cages." Scanlon pointed to the handsome rat cages stacked four high against the wall.

"Where they going?"

"Teachers' room," Scanlon said winking, "as if you didn't know."

"Let's go." Danny tried to pick up all four cages at once, but they were heavier than they looked. He grudgingly allowed Scanlon to carry one of them downstairs while he took the other three in one trip.

"Right here against the wall's the best place, I guess." Scanlon placed his cage against the wall just inside the door. He let the door swing all the way open to test for clearance. He told Danny to stack them on top of each other. Denise was built low enough to the floor so that the bottom ones wouldn't present a problem for her.

"Wait'll Cynthia finds out there's rats in here," Danny said, cackling.

"How much worse can they smell than her perfume?" Danny didn't react to the remark the way Scanlon expected. He didn't react at all, and Scanlon regretted saying it.

"What are you gonna do, dissect them?"

"No. I don't know for sure what we'll end up doing with them. Probably maze train them or something."

"What the fuck's that?"

"Teaching them to turn left at corners instead of right."

"What for?"

"To try and learn something about learning."

"Who gives a rat's ass about how rats learn?"

"Thanks for the help, Danny. You'd better get back underneath that Toyota before Mr. Kitchell throws a rod."

"Karman Ghia. Have fun with your rats."

"Thanks, Danny."

Scanlon waited in a state of acute agitation for ten minutes after the bell rang before marching down the hall to Winship's office.

"Samantha Burnham is missing from study hall again. What's the story with that girl?" he heard himself ask Winship, his voice shrill. Winship's eyebrows twitched, and he seemed to ask why the sudden concern for this sprite who comes to eighth period maybe two days out of the week, tops?

"I called her father to come get her. She had a note from Connie." Connie Gallagher was probably responsible for saving Scanlon's formaldehyde-scorched eye that he got from his botched attempt at cat dissection.

"Another medical excuse? She should be hospitalized if she's so frail she can't make it through eight periods twice a week."

"Jack, this has been pretty much the same story all year. I haven't heard you complain." Winship smiled. "You're beginning to sound like a schoolteacher. Like one of us."

"Sorry."

"No need to apologize. I sympathize. I'm afraid we've dropped the ball where Samantha's concerned. Too late now to change her ways."

"I'm surprised she gets so many excuses from Connie." Connie Gallagher was a no-nonsense woman, compassionate but not easily fooled, even by one with Samantha's apparent guile.

"Migraine headaches. Runs in the family on her mother's side. That's the word from Connie. I'm not so sure Samantha hasn't put one over on old Connie, though."

"I doubt it. Migraines. I worked with a guy who got them so bad he'd have to leave work. Laid him low for a week once. They were the real thing. Migraines are killers." Scanlon was full of sympathy for her now. He saw himself by her bedside applying a cold cloth to her forehead, taking care of her.

"I think they're all in the head," Winship said. Scanlon smiled, but Winship wasn't joking.

Doug Stambaugh made a rare appearance in the teachers' room as Scanlon was preparing his coffee. Scanlon's eyes shifted to the sofa where his open notebook lay. Stambaugh noticed.

"Don't worry, I won't look."

"What are you talking about?" Scanlon stirred his coffee with a tongue depressor provided for the coffee paraphernalia compliments of Connie Gallagher.

"You seem concerned that I might see what you're writing, and I'm merely assuring you that I won't look at what you're writing. Not without your permission. I confess to a mild curiosity, however." Stambaugh sat down and laid a stack of thick hardcover volumes on the scarred table.

"Look if you want. It's nothing that would interest you." Scanlon sat down beside his notebook and casually flipped it shut. "Haven't seen a lot of you lately. What's new?"

"Nothing. You've been scarce yourself."

"You know how it is without wheels. Or do you?"

"How are you getting along?"

"Fine and dandy, thanks in no small way to my good friend Lyle Higgins." Scanlon tried to imbue his laugh with irony. It still came out sounding tinny.

"I'd noticed."

"He's dying to know about you, Doug. About your subversive activities. It's sort of fun to listen to him. It's so transparent, the way he pumps me, it's funny." He had Stambaugh's attention, something he thought he'd lost for good.

"Well? Let's hear it."

"Oh, he'll start off on some innocuous direction, the weather, sports, whatever, trying like hell to sound casual and small-talky. Then out of the blue he'll say something like 'So how's our friend the draft dodger,' or 'Our friend booked his passage to Canada yet?' Stuff like that. Once he asked me how many kids you planned to take along with you to Canada. How do you like that for subtle?"

"How do you reply to questions like that?"

"I play ignorant, which is really not playing. I am ignorant. Higgins knows as much as I do about what's going on with you. He just doesn't know it. You got nothing to worry about."

"I don't relish being the object of speculation. You can appreciate that." Was Stambaugh suggesting that Scanlon knew firsthand what it was like to be the object of speculation? He supposed he knew it to be true. Still, hearing it spoken out loud caused him some uneasiness. It was like overhearing something unpleasant, but true, said about you.

"Yeah," Scanlon said.

"In any case, my appeal was denied so unless I can demonstrate in court that the board acted improperly in ruling on my petition, it's a certainty that I'll be called up."

Stambaugh's jaw muscle worked up and down. Scanlon could picture Stambaugh with his strong military jaw standing before a platoon of genetic inferiors, smart in his olive drab and his spit-shined shoes.

"I guess your choices are narrowing then." Scanlon flipped open his notebook and closed it.

"What exactly are you doing in there?" Stambaugh asked.

"Jotting down ideas. Ideas for experiments."

Stambaugh looked over his shoulder and made a face that expressed his distaste for the rats who were scuttling around in their new custom-built homes. The odor of animal life was already thick in the teachers' room; Scanlon had been cold-shouldered by Cynthia Sinclair, something that was definitely not in the woman's nature. Scanlon had been skipping lunch to come down to the lounge to write in his notebook, knowing that since the rats had taken up residence none of his colleagues was likely to interrupt. But here was Stambaugh.

"My friends offend you?"

"That would be putting it mildly. There is no other place in this entire building to house those creatures? They give miasma new meaning."

"Miasma," Scanlon said, pondering the sound of it. "I've always wanted to visit. Any ideas about how I might use our little friends?"

"You're the biologist."

"I teach biology, a subject I know very little about. That hardly qualifies me as a biologist."

"What would make you think I'd have any suggestions? My advice would be to put them to sleep."

"You mean kill them?"

"Yes."

"Why not say it? Kill them."

"I was trying for irony."

"Sounds more like you were trying for euphemism." Scanlon smiled before he said, "The rats stay."

"Your colleagues aren't pleased."

"Let them take it up with the principal. He's the one who approved the deal." Put them to sleep, Scanlon thought, and an idea began to take shape in his mind.

"I heard that. I find it a little difficult to believe, knowing Winship the way I do." Stambaugh scratched under his chin with the backs of his fingers like a rube. He'd picked up a few curious habits from the natives. He'd soon enough be learning the ways of Canadians.

"I didn't believe it myself. I'm pals with Lyle Higgins and Winship's falling over himself to accommodate me and my rats. How do you figure that?"

"I think it's poor judgment. Why should the rest of us be made to suffer for the sake of your rats?"

"I don't know, Douglas. Maybe it's a test of your loyalty."

"You're joking." Stambaugh looked at him as if he were witnessing instantaneous derangement. Scanlon offered him back a goofy smile. Stambaugh shook his head and gathered up his heavy books.

"Come back now, you hear," Scanlon said with his southern accent. "And be thinking of names."

"Names?" Stambaugh bit.

"For them." Scanlon pointed at the cages. "I've got three already. Shadrach, Meshach, Abednego. Like 'em?"

Stambaugh gave him one last pitying look before he left.

"No, Jack. Absolutely not. I cannot and will not allow that sort of thing."

"Why not? There won't be any pain. The animals will be treated humanely, I give you my word." Who did he think he was? He who couldn't operate a film-loop projector was suggesting that he could supervise operations on live animals.

"Parents would yell to high heaven. This is way beyond these kids. It's out of the question."

"Whatever you say."

Winship's eyes narrowed at Scanlon's acquiescence. He had cause to be skeptical because Scanlon had no intention of backing down.

"I promise you, Jack," Winship said in a low voice, "there'll be trouble if you defy me on this. Use the rats for whatever else you want, but there will be no operations of any kind in my school."

"I don't get it, Daryl. You'd have no qualms if I sacrificed them for dissection, but you don't want me to operate on them, and let them live. Operations, by the way, which have a very high rate of survival. I just don't get it."

"I don't have to justify anything to you. No operations on live animals. That's final." Winship closed his desktop checkbook with a clunk of finality. Scanlon was torn. Not that he was worried about what Winship would do to him if he went against his wishes, but because of the way Winship had been siding with him lately it seemed unfair somehow to defy him. Winship must have known that his decision to allow the rats in the teachers' room would be unpopular, to say the least. Here he was, going in circles again.

"Kids are saying that you're making your biology classes do unspeakable things to poor, little mice," Samantha Burnham said to Scanlon at the beginning of study hall. Disarmed, unprepared, his heart galloping, Scanlon could think of nothing to say. All he could do was stare at Samantha, this elusive object of his illicit, if pure, desire. "Well, is it true?"

"They're poor, little rats." Those pale blue eyes, those full, moist lips, red against that porcelain white skin. The long, unruly but silken hair glistening with good genes and good nutrition. How could such a creature as this abuse herself with sex and mind-blowing drugs and still present this portrait of wholesomeness? Except there was nothing morally wholesome about this chick, was there? Behind those eyes was knowledge that spoke of carnality, exasperation, cynicism—cruelty? Could this be true? Wasn't she standing up to him, a figure of authority, defending the rights of rodents?

"I can't believe you'd allow such a thing." She had her chin in her hands, her elbows on the lecture desk, and looked straight into his eyes with such fierce defiance that he had to look away. When he did bring his eyes back to her, he had to work to keep them off her unfettered breasts, which were poised to spill out of the top of her peasant blouse. He was supposed to be obsessed with platonic love for this child, not sneaking peeks at her creamy breasts. She kept her voice low, evenly modulated, not really appropriately pitched for her castigating message.

"Nothing like that is going to happen. What you've heard is idle rumor. None of it is true."

"If it's not true, it's not because of anything you've done to stop it. Even Mr. Winship wouldn't allow you to hurt those creatures. I can't believe you'd even think of doing something like that."

"Can we talk about this another time? This isn't really the place for a debate." Such blatant hypocrisy fell from his lips only because he was cornered, like one of his white friends downstairs, and could think of nothing more intelligent to say to the girl. Samantha turned angrily and strode to her chair. She jerked a paperback book from her shoulder bag and started to read, slouched in her chair. Scanlon stared at but did not see the page of his chemistry text, conscious only of his latest misery. His intentions had been good. And the operations were really simple; if he didn't believe that he was the last person in the world to try them. And now, here was the love of his life taking sides with Winship against him. Where had he gone wrong? He got out his notebook.

Chapter Thirty-five

"Could you possibly give me a ride home?" Samantha asked Scanlon in the parking lot as he was about to climb into Higgins' car. Here she was, the way she sometimes turned up in his fantasies, asking innocently for a favor. That is how it would begin, continue, and never end, in a kind of sublime innocence. Of course, he was always eager to grant her wishes.

"I'm afraid I still don't have a car. I'd be happy to take you home if I did have a car, but ..."

"My father was supposed to be here by now." Samantha glanced wistfully toward the road, holding her shoulder bag close to her side as if it could comfort her. Was that a tear in her eye? She shrugged her delicate shoulders. "He must have forgotten. He's sort of absentminded." A brave little smile appeared on her face for an instant then vanished. She wandered away in the direction of the school buses behind the gym. No good-bye, no parting words for him. Poor, lovesick Jack Scanlon.

"Denise, I think you may have mixed up the boys and the girls." Denise looked at Scanlon and blinked as if she hadn't understood. "The rats, Denise. I think you put males and females together in the same cages. Would you mind checking? And if you have mixed them up, would you please unmix them before we have a rat takeover?" Scanlon had no doubts that the males and females were together, but he didn't want to sound accusatory and risk upsetting Denise. If she decided that she wasn't appreciated, she could refuse to continue taking care of them and then where would he be? But neither could he have a rat population explosion.

"They should be together," Denise said matter-of-factly.

"No, Denise, they should not be together. Together they make more rats, and what we don't want, what we can't have, are more rats than we've got already."

"It's not natural for them to live in separate cages."

"That may be, Denise, but we're in no position to let nature have its way. Please, Denise."

Denise sulked out of the room, presumably to do as she was told. He had the cold feeling, however, that it was too late. How long they had been cohabiting he hadn't dared to ask.

"Your rats are beginning to stink upstairs, Mr. Scanlon," Lyle Higgins said on the way home.

"Denise cleans their cages every day. What more can I do?"

"Get rid of them would be my advice. What on earth do you plan to do with them? I haven't heard any talk from the kids."

"We'll be doing experiments soon, experiments on behavior."

Lyle chuckled his disdain. He drove his car at the most maddeningly slow speeds, like an old woman, both hands firmly on the steering wheel. Their conversations had been agreeable for the most part, if not actually friendly. Today Lyle was no doubt speaking for all of his colleagues when he observed that the smell of rat was, like communism, becoming all-pervasive.

There was now only the occasional patch of snow along Route 2; the pastureland was becoming jade-like, a deep spring green that reminded Scanlon of a bad painting. The warm air made Scanlon want to breathe deeply, to take in all that oxygen, to clear out and refresh his overheated brain. He'd never get to do experiments on behavior or anything else; he might as well face up to that fact. What then was to be done with the rats? Donate them to the university? That was the only alternative short of sacrificing them. There was no pet store in Groveton. He'd have to admit failure to Winship, who would pass it along to the others, and he would be scorned even more for having made his colleagues endure his miasmic folly. Not to mention the imposition on Dennis Kitchell to build the cages.

"How would you suggest I dispose of them?" Scanlon asked Higgins.

"I say kill 'em. What're rats good for except to spread disease?"

"They aren't those kind of rats. Haven't you seen them?"

"I've smelled them. That's enough for me. Same for everyone else. Lucky you depend on me for transportation, else you'd have nobody to talk to." Higgins smiled, but it was no joke. Scanlon was crushed to hear it put so starkly, even if he knew in his heart that it was the absolute truth.

"I can't kill them. Denise wouldn't allow it. What else can I do?" Scanlon must have sounded desperate because Higgins gently suggested that they might be kept outside, behind the gym by the dumpsters.

"It stinks naturally out there. What's wrong with keeping them outside?"

Scanlon had no answer. It seemed all too reasonable a solution, one that he should have considered two weeks ago.

"It still gets cold at night. They can't tolerate the cold."

"Rabbits stay out all winter. Why not rats?"

"Rats are different. They have a different metabolism." Scanlon didn't know what he was talking about. He felt compelled to bluff because suddenly the solution to Fairfield High's rat crisis seemed embarrassingly simple. For all he knew, rats could withstand nighttime low temperatures this time of year. It was too late, of course, to make such an admission even if it were true.

"All the better. Then our troubles would be over and you could claim ignorance," Higgins said. For Scanlon, there was a certain appeal to this logic.

Scanlon needn't have spent a futile evening in the Groveton library researching temperature tolerance in white rats because when he arrived at school the next morning he discovered all four cages empty, the doors wide open. He thought immediately of Denise, then Lyle Higgins. It was absurd to think that Higgins would do such a thing, and Denise would be too logical a suspect. She wouldn't risk getting into trouble, even for the sake of restoring the natural order. Or would she?

Scanlon panicked. He looked under the sofa, in all the corners. There was no evidence of rats in the room, unless their fetid scent counted. He thought of the pregnant females, their imminent offspring, and he panicked some more.

"Oh, lord in heaven," he lamented to the ceiling. The homeroom bell rang bringing on another wave of panic. For the time being, he would have to pretend that he knew nothing about the rats.

Smiles, the horny janitor, was sweeping the corridor outside the teachers' room, a big ring of keys hanging from his belt. He was a big man, maybe six-foot-two, with thick shoulders and a narrow waist. Rugged, as Danny Picard would describe him. If he ever got rape in his head, a high school girl wouldn't stand a chance. He was taciturn, communicating with a system of modulated grunts, eyes always averted. Scanlon was reminded of Quasimodo, except Smiles was actually not bad looking for a pervert. Should he ask Smiles about the missing rats? That would be a mistake, Scanlon realized, nodding at Smiles who grunted without looking up from his sweeping, somehow knowing that Scanlon had nodded.

"When're we gonna dissect them rats?" Romeo Boudreau asked as he had asked first thing every day since the rats had arrived. Did he look more supercilious than usual this morning? Did the little shit have a secret? Scanlon wouldn't have put it past Romeo to spring the rats. Scanlon, as he had every time Romeo asked the question, ignored him and launched into a description of the frog's cardiovascular system, of which he knew precious little.

"We gonna dissect them rats, or what?" Romeo asked again, more insistent this time. Scanlon tried a look of menace on Romeo knowing that this wouldn't faze Romeo, but he tried it just the same.

"They're not going to be dissected," Denise said. Denise had a fascination that bordered on true love of animal life, but he had never known her to be sentimental. Hadn't she been willing to sacrifice her pet snake to dissection? Maybe her sentiments ran only to fur bearers. It was looking to Scanlon like Denise was the culprit after all.

"You should listen to Denise," Scanlon said, watching her carefully, "she knows more about those rats than anybody. Don't you, Denise."

"Probably lettin' them diddle her." Scanlon heard Romeo's loud whisper followed by his cackling, hick laugh. If he acknowledged the remark and took Romeo to task for it, it would only draw attention to poor Denise, humiliate the kid whom no one would probably ever want to diddle. He wanted more than he cared to admit to himself to punish Romeo, punish the little shitkicker in a way he would not soon forget. He pretended he hadn't heard Romeo and ignored the honks and titters that ensued whenever Romeo Boudreau exercised his wit in class. Denise, as usual, was the portrait of stolid passivity. If she had heard Romeo's words, she wasn't about to let what he had to say get to her. How could something like that not hurt deeply? Or did Scanlon bruise easier than most?

Scanlon asked Denise to remain after class.

"Denise," he started, carefully, "what do you know about the rats?"

An angry pimple was blooming on the side of her porous nose; her forehead was a garden of blackheads. But her expression was guileless, all innocence. Scanlon asked her if she'd looked in on the rats this morning.

"No. I usually go down after fourth period." Denise frowned, sensing that something was wrong. "What do you mean, what do I know about the rats?"

"They're gone, Denise," Scanlon said, not being at all careful this time, "flown the coop. Tell me this is some kind of joke."

"Gone?"

"Yes. The doors of all the cages are wide open and there isn't a white rat to be seen anywhere. No droppings, no nothing. Do you know what this means?" Tears started in Denise's too-close-together eyes.

"Who could have done something like this?" Denise said.

"I don't know. I have no idea. What do you think?"

"I better go look for them." Denise started to leave.

"Wait, Denise. Listen. Maybe you better not say anything to anyone about this until we get to the bottom of it. I mean, they could be in a box somewhere in the building. You know, somebody's idea of a joke." Or, Scanlon thought, they could be free, all of them, free in the building, in the partitions, in the duct work, in the cafeteria, screwing and giving birth and screwing some more. An exterminator, or whatever it was you called people who rid high schools of white rats, would have to be hired. Scanlon would be the laughingstock of the whole school, and the news wouldn't take long to travel to Groveton and then all over the state. He'd be blackballed from teaching the way he'd been blackballed from industry.

"I should try and find them. They'll be hungry." Denise waddled out in search of her lost charges.

Cynthia Sinclair (it would have to be her) made the first sighting during third period English with her seniors. Her scream was heard in every second floor classroom. It was one of the smaller ones, one of the juveniles, and it had been crawling along the molding of one of the big windows against which Cynthia liked to lean when she was holding forth on Dickens. The kids had been particularly attentive this morning, actually rapt, as Cynthia rhapsodized over Bleak House, while barely inches away, over her rounded shoulders, the whiskered albino, myopic and trusting to touch and smell, hunted for food (Denise had said they'd be hungry this time of day). When the dawn came for Cynthia, the thing (probably trained by Denise to hop on her shoulder) was about to go aboard Cynthia's. Thus the robust screams.

All of this by Danny Picard's account, told with such exuberance, such relish, that for a moment Scanlon was almost certain that it had to have been Danny who had set them loose.

"Please tell me it wasn't you who opened those cages, Picard," Scanlon said to Danny in study hall, looking over the boy's shoulder to see what his beloved was up to. There she was, back in her crummy paperback book, her indifference blatant.

"Winship pissed?" Danny asked.

"Does the Pope shit in the woods?"

Danny liked that one. He laughed himself into a fit of out-of-control honking. Kids looked up, wondering what was going on, what was so funny? By now, everyone had to have heard about the rat fiasco, so what was to wonder about? Winship had been uncharacteristically calm at the news. Cynthia had to be sedated, but Winship kept his cool. He simply wanted to know where the rat had come from and Scanlon had feigned ignorance, made a show of going down to the teachers' room to make a head check, to see if any of his guests was missing. He gave a good enough performance for Winship to convince the principal that Scanlon had just discovered the fact that all rats were at large. He expected Winship to explode, but he didn't. He raised his eyebrows; he actually smiled. Was it because he thought they could be easily rounded up? That it was a harmless student prank? Scanlon nearly overacted, showing too much concern to be believed. In truth, he was concerned. After all, he was responsible.

"You could make the recapture a biology project. Tell them they'll be graded on creativity." Winship sounded almost playful. Scanlon smiled cautiously. He was relieved by Winship's attitude toward the affair, and if he thought about it, how could he really be held responsible? There was no lock on the teachers' room door. What defense did he have against adolescent hijinks? Yes, he felt better, much better. Bless Winship. Nevertheless, he preferred to characterize Winship as an angry principal to Danny. Why disappoint the kid?

"What're you gonna do? All them rats runnin' around, probably fucking like rabbits."

"I prefer that to having a lot of rabbits loose screwing like rats," Scanlon said, sending Danny into near apoplexy. Kids started to drift to the front of the room, their faces in half smiles of curiosity. All except Samantha, who remained sublimely above it all.

"I need a bright idea. Anybody got any suggestions as to how we might get our little friends back into custody before they reproduce tenfold?" Scanlon asked the kids gathered around the lecture desk.

"Just set out a mess of food and wait," Danny offered.

Phil Daigle said he'd bring in his mother's five cats. "There any reward?"

"I'd kind of like them back alive and in one piece. Think you could convince your mother's cats? Anyway, if I wanted cats I could provide plenty of my own," Scanlon said, though Alice's cats were too well fed to be motivated to hunt down white rats. All her cats seemed capable of doing, besides eating canned food and going to the cellar, was lolling around the house and coughing up hair balls. "Suppose we put food out like Danny suggested," Scanlon continued, "then we have the problem of catching them. How do we lure them back in their cages?"

"Ever hear of the rat trap?"

"I told you, I want them alive."

"Take forever to catch that many rats. You're gonna have to go for poison." This was Vance Cotter's sober assessment. He was a taciturn farmboy with a cowlick in the back of a shock of dry and unruly, blond hair. Scanlon was about to repeat the conditions of the recapture, namely that they must come back alive and well, when Samantha's voice intruded from her place among the empty chairs.

"It's so like you to suggest such a thing," she said.

"Jesus," Vance said, sighing, "here we go. What do you suggest? Let 'em run around free?" He uttered the word free with contempt for freedom as it was obviously perceived by Samantha Burnham.

"They've got as much right to freedom as you have," Samantha countered.

"She been hangin' around them hippies too long, Vance," Danny said to Vance Cotter. To Samantha he said, "Why don't you go and catch 'em. You can string love beads round their necks then let 'em go again."

Amidst laughter at Danny's remark, Samantha suggested that if anything should be caged perhaps it should be them, meaning her classmates. Scanlon didn't choose to include himself.

Danny stuck out his tongue and wagged it obscenely at Samantha. She stared him down, unfazed, enough contempt in her eyes to reduce five grown men to quivering insecurity. Danny was impervious to Samantha Burnham's haughty looks. Scanlon was envious of him.

"Why don't you all take your seats before we start rioting. Go on, sit down." Scanlon herded everyone away from the lecture desk. "You, too, Danny. Enough is enough."

Chapter Thirty-six

K: Responsibility. It's a slippery concept, Jack. There are so many variables to consider. The social context, the political. You say you feel responsible for those rats but ...

S: Careful, Bob. You're verging on bullshit. I didn't mean to suggest that I feel morally responsible. It's just that it was my idea, and I kind of got my way with Winship and the shop teacher by being allowed to keep them in the teachers' room, and goddamn it, I feel responsible for what happened even if I'm not totally to blame. Technically. What's so tough about that?

K: Well, you got your own way for a change. How did that feel?

S: Whatever good feelings I got from it were short-lived. It's as if someone is deliberately out there to thwart me. And don't look at me like that. I don't mean it the way you think.

K: How do you mean it?

S: What am I supposed to think?

K: You admitted that the things were a nuisance, that the teachers stopped coming around. Isn't that enough? You can't believe that someone would pull a stunt like this to thwart you because you got your own way.

S: Not really. No adult would stoop to that. It has to have been a kid. I think I know which kid, too.

K: So what do you think, the kids are out to get you?

S: You sound kind of like a jerk since you stopped providing juice. You know that? Aren't I allowed the occasional irrational feeling without you jumping all over me yelling paranoia?

K: So who's this Samantha? You never mention kids by name. What's the deal with this Samantha?

S: There's no deal. She's a student. Not my student.

K: Why does this one have a name when all the others are this kid or that kid?

S: I'm beginning to learn names. All right? About time, don't you think? The fucking year's shot.

K: You got the hots for this student whose name you just now learned?

S: Come off it. You're twisted and fucked up. First you look for incest, now ... what? What do you take me for?

K: So, it's true. How far has it gone?

S: How far has what gone, you asshole? There's nothing. I can't believe you.

Scanlon squirmed in his chair, knowing that Kennedy would interpret all his squirming as a sign of guilt. And of course he'd be correct. He knew that Kennedy was trying to goad him into disclosing his feelings about Samantha. With shrinks there could be no secrets. It would be in his best interest, he knew, to cooperate with Kennedy, but he had always balked at disclosure. Lack of trust? He trusted Kennedy, or he thought he did.

K: What's new with the insurance company? Any closer to a settlement?

S: Don't play with me. All right? Yes, as a matter of fact, I did get a settlement. Finally. A handsome one at that. I suddenly have more dough than I've seen all at once since I mustered out of the Navy.

K: Congratulations.

S: My uncle's trying to talk me into getting something used, but I'm leery of used cars and used car salesmen. I'll probably just turn over the check to the VW people. Living without wheels in the boondocks is impossible or else you know what I'd spend the money on.

K: Afraid I do. Don't you owe on the one you totaled?

S: A mere technicality.

K: You going to be more careful behind the wheel?

S: I learned my lesson, thank you. What do you drive, Bob, if you don't mind my asking?

K: Saab. Had it for years. Never a problem.

S: That's what I hear. Always starts in cold weather, just like my VW, only thirty times more expensive. What are you, moonlighting?

K: There's some dough on my wife's side.

S: Oh.

There was no money in Scanlon's family, in any direction. Whatever he accumulated in the way of material gain in this life would have to come from his own efforts. It was a depressing thought because he didn't feel all that ambitious these days. The material world was a formidable opponent.

S: Must be nice to know that if you fall there's someone there to catch you.

K: Do I hear resentment?

S: I didn't intend to sound resentful.

K: All the more reason to ask.

S: It's no secret that I have a hate-on for the rich, and the rich can be anyone from stinking to just about anybody who has more than I do. That's no secret, Bob.

K: Is it the fault of the rich they have more than you?

S: I never said these feelings were rational. You taking sides with the rich against me?

This wasn't so all of a sudden, Kennedy beating up on him, as it were. There was the time he'd taken Scanlon down for his views on womanhood.

K: Just looking for some answers.

S: There are no answers. Only questions.

K: This Samantha rich?

S: Richer than I am I would guess, but I don't think rich in any real sense of the word.

K: She got a crush on you?

S: Hah!

K: So it's the other way around.

S: Drop it, Bob. You're fishing in a dead pond.

K: Whatever you say.

They sat for the rest of the hour without saying another word. When Scanlon's time was up, Kennedy swept up his papers and left the room, giving up on the amenities, it would seem, with charity cases. Scanlon, unaccustomed to such treatment from Kennedy, was left shaken, with a queasy stomach. He sat for a while looking absently out the window at his familiar gully, free of snow now, patches of green showing here and there, the maples in some kind of bud. Was he expecting Kennedy to return? To apologize? Ask him to apologize? Either way would have been all right with him. A sunny day in Vermont. A rare phenomenon; his spirits should be brighter, should match the sunshine, should be free of trivial concerns. However trivial his concerns, today they packed the necessary weight to crush his spirit.

"Fuck you, Kennedy," Scanlon said out loud and got up to leave. "Fuck you and the Saab you rode in on."

Scanlon had only to see how Winship's shoulders sagged as he sat at his desk stirring his coffee with a pencil to know that something was wrong. He thought immediately of the rats, and in his mind's eye he saw Cynthia (who had sulkily consented to come back to her duties) standing on her desk, a desk surrounded by a swarm of teeth-baring white rats.

"Danny's dead," Winship said, without looking at Scanlon, his voice flat.

"What?"

"Hollis Trimble shot him in the head last night. Died this morning about three without regaining consciousness." Winship stirred his coffee.

"Who the hell is Hollis Trimble? Are you talking about Danny Picard?"

"Danny and Norma were parked below the hill where Hollis lives with his parents. They weren't harming anybody. Just going over the expenses they could expect to face after they were married. Just minding their own business when Hollis shows up. I guess neither of them, Norma or Danny, was surprised to see him. Hollis roamed around the road below the house all the time, talking to himself, acting crazy the way Hollis does. Danny knew him well, used to kid him all the time but not in any mean or unfriendly way—you know Danny.

"Last night, Hollis had a .22 pistol and Danny asked him what the hell he thought he could kill with a .22 pistol and Hollis shot Danny through the temple." Winship's voice cracked. He brought his coffee-stirring hand to his brow, shading his eyes.

"How do you know all this?"

"Norma told the police everything after she got over being hysterical. After he shot Danny, Hollis took off running. Norma held Danny's bleeding head in her lap and screamed for help, not knowing what else to do and of course being hysterical, naturally. When it was clear to her that no help would be coming she got her wits about her and got behind the wheel and drove to the emergency room in Groveton. The police were called, and the doctors gave Norma a sedative. Poor kid was covered with blood and out of her mind by the time she got to the hospital. The police had to wait until she came around from the sedative before they could get out of her what happened."

"And what about this lunatic?" Scanlon's voice sounded far away to him, as if it issued from somewhere deeper than his throat. "This can't be true. What the hell's the story here?"

"I'm afraid it is true. Everyone's in shock."

"I don't think I want to be here today." Scanlon felt dizzy. "You have any objections to my taking the day off?"

Winship hedged. "I guess not." How much education did he expect would get accomplished today? He should call off school period. What would be lost?

"Where's Danny now?" Scanlon asked.

"Homestead's in Groveton. On Winter. Visiting hours from six to eight tonight. Funeral's tomorrow at two. We'll suspend classes after lunch."

Scanlon tried to write in his journal, to come to grips with the reality of Danny's murder, but it was no good. Danny's tragic death inspired nothing but platitudes, trite philosophizing about the frailty of life. He closed his notebook in disgust, disgust with himself and with the poor demented soul named Hollis Trimble who, he learned from Winship, was now in police custody waiting to be sent to Waterbury. Hollis was an alumnus of that institution and was considered crazier than a bedbug but essentially harmless. How many other harmless crazies were out there with .22 pistols?

Higgins was the only faculty member present when Scanlon arrived, but it was early and Higgins was the only Fairfield High teacher besides himself who lived in Groveton. Danny's casket was mounted on a platform in a sort of grove of flowers and boughs. The cloying stench of hothouse flowers hung in the room like death itself. Norma Woodruff sat in a metal folding chair beside the casket. Beside her was a young woman to whom Norma had given herself over physically. She leaned helplessly limp against the woman who stroked her dull hair and moved her lips in whispers of comfort. In front of the casket kneeled a big, red-knuckled boy wearing a too-tight jacket with too-short sleeves. In profile he resembled Danny. Scanlon knew nothing about Danny Picard's family, didn't know he had brothers or sisters or even if his parents were still alive. He knew only Norma. There were many rough-looking farm people seated in the metal folding chairs arranged in semi-circular rows. Scanlon recognized none of them. There was no sign of any of Danny's classmates.

Scanlon lingered at the edge of the room by the entrance, conscious of the nauseating fragrance, the oppressive heat. He could see part of Danny's head, enough of the corpse to see that Danny was wearing a necktie, something he couldn't picture the boy wearing alive until he remembered the night he'd seen Danny and Norma in Hackett's Diner. He'd worn a tie that night.

What could have been the occasion? Still, neckties and Danny didn't go together. He should have been presented in his T-shirt and fatigues.

There was no way he could force himself up to that casket for a look at Danny. He made eye contact with Lyle Higgins. Higgins nodded and shook his head—what a shame, what a waste, his face said. Then Higgins was beside him whispering.

"What a damn shame."

Scanlon nodded. Higgins invited him to the front porch for a breath of fresh air. Scanlon lit a cigarette and gazed across the street at the elementary school playground, at the jungle gym and swings, and at the skatehouse and that merry-go-round contraption. Like Fairfield's playground, like every school playground in America, the world. For no reason, Scanlon wondered what Russian playgrounds looked like, Chinese playgrounds. Surely, even communist kids played.

"Yes," Higgins said with a big intake of the soft, early evening air, "it's a goddamn shame at best. They should've never let poor Hollis out in the first place. I had a bad feeling something like this would happen. That damn moron and guns."

Scanlon looked at Higgins. "He's had trouble with guns before?"

"Hell, yes. Ran amuck downtown a few years back with a thirty-ought-six. Shooting the windows out of the Masonic Temple. That's what got him sent to Waterbury in the first place. Two years and he's out running loose again. Tells you how much them head doctors know."

Did his uncle know Hollis Trimble? His uncle in Waterbury. Harold was in his own world there, a world populated by friends of his imagination. Kennedy had compared Waterbury to Bedlam. Probably overcrowded and understaffed. Looking for excuses to let patients out, to make room. They let Hollis Trimble out so he could snuff out Danny Picard's young life. Winship had told him that Danny used to kid Hollis. Kidded him once too often, it would appear. Where was Winship? Where was anybody?

"What time you got?" he asked Higgins.

"It's still early. They'll be here."

People were arriving, more people he'd never seen before.

Higgins asked him if he'd spoken to Danny's folks. Higgins had seen him come in. He had to know that Scanlon hadn't spoken to the Picards. He didn't even know who they were.

"No," Scanlon replied.

"They're taking it well. Better'n poor Norma."

People started to come out on the porch, to light up cigarettes and talk about the weather and other mundane subjects. Scanlon heard no mention of death. Pretty soon the talk got lively, and there was laughing.

The Winships arrived with Cynthia Sinclair. Tommy Winship barely acknowledged Scanlon, and Cynthia, he was sure, deliberately ignored him. Here he was at this sad and tragic occasion, feeling sorry for himself for being snubbed. Fairfield High kids began arriving in groups with their parents. Soon the funeral parlor was packed to capacity, and Scanlon began to feel closed in.

After a few minutes, he slipped away. He hadn't offered condolences to Danny's parents or to Norma Woodruff. He hadn't taken his turn at the casket. He drove back home in his new VW only because he lacked the money to stop by the Groveton House.

Scanlon must have been staring at the empty seat Danny usually occupied in eighth period study hall. Samantha Burnham's hand was on his, and he withdrew it reflexively.

"You're taking it hard aren't you, Jack." He was dreaming, of course. In his most potent fantasies she never said anything like this. But wait! It was no dream. Her eyes were real and they were on him, exuding tender sympathy. There was simply no acceptable way for him to get his hand back with hers, not with six attentive kids for an audience.

"No harder than a lot of people," Scanlon whispered.

"You're too sensitive."

"Jesus, Samantha." Scanlon turned away. Samantha remained in front of the lecture desk. There was a stifled laugh behind her. Scanlon was embarrassed and angry. Angry at himself for allowing this girl such complete control over him, angry at whoever it was out there snickering when Danny Picard hadn't been in the ground forty-eight hours. He hurried out of the room. To his dismay, Samantha followed him. She caught up with him on the south landing.

"Oh, Jack." She took his arm in both of her warm hands.

"Don't call me that," he said in a repressed, hoarse whisper. She squeezed his arm. A white rat scurried over his shoe and hers. A chill moved along his spine. Samantha moved her body against him; his arms opened automatically to receive her, and now his brain was full of her softness. He was visited with lust and helplessness there on the top landing of the south stairs of musty old Fairfield High School.

"That was a white rat," Scanlon said, "and I think it's on its way to Miss Sinclair's room." It kept to the wall, indeed seeming purposefully headed in the direction of Cynthia's classroom, and he finally understood the meaning of "scurrying." Samantha made no effort to disengage herself from him, as if to cuddle up to her study hall teacher was a natural thing to do.

"Cynthia will have a stroke." Samantha giggled prettily.

"You were in her class last time?"

"It was so funny. You should have been there."

"I heard."

"You really had to be there."

What if Winship should decide to poke his head out of his office? Or Patterson? Or anyone? What would they make of this sweet tableau?

Scanlon pushed her out of his arms. "We've got to get back."

"Are you all right?" She looked up into his face, melting his will, bringing fever to his mind and body.

"Yes."

She actually held his hand as they walked back toward study hall.

"You'd better go in first," Scanlon said. "I'll be along in a little while."

"Why?"

"How would it look if we walked in together?"

"I don't know. How would it look?" Was it possible that she honestly believed that this was innocent? If it were so, what was he to make of the fact that only moments ago they were practically embracing? And hadn't she held his hand? What was he to make of that?

"I've got to see Mr. Winship." Scanlon pointed toward the principal's office as if she didn't know where his office was. The corridor was empty. Samantha shrugged and opened the door. Scanlon could hear lively conversation coming from the room. He couldn't go inside, not with her. Someone howled like a wolf as Samantha closed the door behind her.

Scanlon wandered down the hall and stopped to put an ear to Cynthia's classroom door. He listened for her screams. There was no sign of the rat in the hall. He'd been too enveloped in Samantha's aura to track the rat's progress after it passed over their feet. How could it get into anyone's classroom unless someone opened the door and invited it in? Winship's door was open. If the thing had gone in there, surely he would have heard Trudy Lester's screams. It must have gone down the north stairs.

He hurried past Winship's office without looking inside. He descended the north stairs on tiptoe in case the beast was lurking on one of the steps.

"Jack?"

Scanlon turned around, startled, to discover Winship leaning over the railing, peering down at him. "Can I have a minute of your time? You busy?"

Scanlon took the stairs two at a time and followed Winship into his office.

"Your study hall is raising all kinds of hell. I tried calling you over the speaker. Sounded like a cocktail party in there."

"I spotted one of the rats in the hall. I was tracking it down the stairs when you saw me."

Winship looked skeptical, scratching at his cowlick, eyes averted so he wouldn't have to confront Scanlon with his skepticism. It was a lame excuse. What brought him out of his study hall in the first place was the question Winship would have been justified in asking.

"I'd almost forgotten about them." Winship wrinkled his nose as if he smelled something bad.

"They're still out there, I'm afraid," Scanlon said with a weak smile.

"Anyway, I wanted to talk to you about something else."

"Something else?"

"Yeah. I've talked to Sumner and he feels, as do I, that you've done a real good job for us this year and, well, it's that time of year when we talk about contracts, and I just wanted you to know where I sit."

"I don't know what to say. I ... I don't know what to say."

"Why don't you plan to sit down with Sumner in the next few days. We need teachers like you, Jack. Hope you'll consider staying aboard next year."

With rats running loose in the building, with his science teacher's lust for one of his female students out of control, he hopes Scanlon will consider staying on board? Scanlon was flabbergasted.

"You better get back to your study hall before they start a riot."

Chapter Thirty-seven

Samantha was standing next to his spiffy, new red VW when he came out of the building. The one he'd wrecked in January had been beige. It had taken not so much courage as he thought it would to return to his study hall, thanks in no small measure to Winship's remarks, which had Scanlon nearly euphoric. And now he was cashing in on that euphoria as he glimpsed his beloved leaning against the rear fender of his car. It must be sublime moments like these that inspired men to poetry, he thought. He would present her with a love poem and she would be his forever. Of course he was driven by sheer possessiveness, but wasn't that what love was all about?

She seemed enthralled. He'd never seen her so radiant, so full of color and energy. Her nose was raised, as if she were after a scent. And he noticed that in profile her nose turned up slightly, not enough to render it pug, but ever so slightly and beautifully. Her white peasant dress let in the light, and she was barefoot. Her long hair needed only a few garlands of wild flowers and she could have passed for a hippie princess, if such a personage could exist in the harsh egalitarianism of hippie culture.

Scanlon approached, or attempted to, with an air of studied indifference, pretending to be searching his pockets for keys.

"Could you possibly give me a ride home? Daddy was supposed to have been here by now, so he's obviously forgotten."

"Hop in."

Scanlon drove south to Burton, his body taut, as though he had high explosives on board—dynamite, TNT, the hydrogen bomb. Samantha concentrated, or pretended to concentrate, on the landscape. He was at an utter loss for anything to say. They drove for miles, it seemed, in this heavy silence. Then he thought he saw her, peripherally, turn to look at him. He tensed, stared straight ahead at the road.

"You missed the turn about a mile back," she said.

"I did?" Scanlon slowed down, and as it happened, found himself slowing down in front of the Pattersons' big, yellow house. Logic dictated that he turn around in their driveway, but he kept going. He felt Samantha's eyes on him.

"I hate to turn around in people's driveways," he said.

"I hate people's driveways."

Scanlon turned to her and smiled. "I can see where it would be easy to take a dislike to a driveway."

"Little houses with little driveways and little station wagons. I hate all symbols of possession and ownership. Nothing should be owned."

"This car will never be owned by me, I promise you."

"You're making fun of me."

"I certainly am not. I agree with you in principle, but we've got this unwieldy system to deal with. Besides, people like to own things. I'll bet you own a few things yourself."

"My father owns things." Did he hear resentment in her voice? It had a tone similar to the one she used in her argument against poisoning the escaped rats.

"What about that dress? You borrow that from your father?"

"Paid for with his money. Money." This time there was no mistaking the bitterness.

"Yes. I've heard that it was evil. Never had any personal experience with the stuff myself."

"You're different." He could feel her eyes on him. He didn't dare look at her.

"Help me with the turn."

"It's not for a while. Are you always so evasive?"

"Evasive?"

"Like now. Every time I try to give you a compliment, you take this evasive action."

"You're wise beyond your years, Samantha." Scanlon swept his arm in front of the windshield. "I can't get over how green everything is. Like emeralds. Seems like there was never any snow. Isn't nature a marvel?"

"They plow everything. It's disgusting."

The road to Samantha's house narrowed, becoming barely wide enough for Scanlon's little VW to pass. What if he should encounter an oncoming car? Low hanging branches created a bower over the road, shutting out sunlight, what little of it there was in Vermont.

"You weren't exaggerating narrow." And she hadn't exaggerated the condition of the road. Scanlon winced as his twenty-one-hundred-dollar VW Bug suffered clawing branches and root concussions.

Samantha's house was a small, shingled cottage, the kind you'd expect to find at the seashore, not in landlocked Vermont. It was situated on a knoll by a small pond. An idyllic setting, the perfect dwelling place for a wood nymph or a sorceress.

"Here we are. Come in and say hello to Daddy."

"This is nice." Scanlon hesitated, left the engine idling.

"Come on." Samantha got out of the car. Scanlon didn't move. "Come on. Have a cup of tea."

"I shouldn't." Scanlon surveyed the pines around the little house. It would be no easy task to turn his car around. He didn't want to meet the father, having been set up by Winship to think a certain way about him, and feeling the way he did about the man's teenaged daughter. And he was concerned about his ineptitude as a driver and how it would look to her to witness his inability to turn around in this labyrinth of pines. What if "Daddy" wasn't home? He saw no sign of a vehicle.

"Will you please come on!" Samantha turned and skipped toward the house like a nine-year-old. Scanlon opened his door, turned off the engine, hesitated, and finally climbed out of the safety of his new car. Samantha beckoned from her door. He must be dreaming. This had all the features of unreality.

Then he was inside. Samantha's father sat at a large, black typewriter in the middle of a surprisingly spacious room with a raised stone fireplace like the one in Lillian Bloemer's house. Mr. Burnham, dressed in shorts and T-shirt, didn't look up from his typing when Scanlon and his daughter entered.

"That's Daddy," Samantha said, dropping her bag on an overstuffed sofa. The room was dark because of all the pines, and bare except for the sofa, a single armchair that matched the sofa, and the author's niche accentuated by the black presence of that ancient typewriter. For all its bareness, the room looked messy: books and paper strewn around the bare, wide-pine floor. Wobbly stacks of books and papers flanked Daddy, hard at work at his craft, a single floor lamp for illumination. Daddy was younger than Scanlon expected, with long, wavy, blond hair and a muscular build. What was he, thirty-seven, thirty-eight?

Scanlon hung back by the door, awkward, self-conscious, not daring to speak for fear of breaking a spell, for Samantha's father was under the influence of something very much like a spell. Samantha disappeared into another room. He was peeved at her for inviting him in here against his will only to abandon him to her strange father. She was soon back, eating an apple.

"Say hello to Jack, Daddy," Samantha said before sinking her lovely teeth into the apple's dark, red skin.

"Hello to Jack," Mr. Burnham said, stabbing at the enormous keys with his two forefingers.

"Jack teaches at school. He's the coolest teacher there, aren't you, Jack?"

"The coolest by a mile. Nice to meet you, Mr. Burnham."

"His name is Seymour, not Mr. Burnham," Samantha said. "Everyone calls him Sy."

"Fetch me a new pack of cigarettes, will you, pigeon?" Sy said to his daughter, crumpling a spent pack with his hand and dropping it on the floor beside him.

Scanlon used to call Lucy that, pigeon. Hearing Burnham address his daughter that way did something funny to his insides. He sighed.

"I've got water on for tea. Want some?" Scanlon thought that she was asking him and he said no. Sy Burnham assumed the question was directed at him, and he replied yes in unison with Scanlon's no.

"Yes and no," Samantha said. "It's a nice herb tea we blend ourselves. Live dangerously, Jack."

"Why not?" He hated tea, except for the green tea he drank a lot in Japan when he was in the service. Seymour Burnham worked fast, not deterred in the slightest by the presence of a guest in the house. Scanlon wanted to inquire about his writing. Something told him this would be the wrong thing to do at the moment. It wasn't so warm in this drafty, dark room that he'd want to hang around in his skivvies. And he was embarrassed to be in the room with this man who was practically naked in front of his own daughter. It struck him as lurid, faintly perverse. Yet Samantha showed no sign of being bothered by her father's state of undress. Less than a year back in the sticks and Scanlon was already beginning to think and feel like a provincial.

Samantha returned bearing a bamboo tray with three steaming mugs of her homegrown herbal tea. To Scanlon, it tasted like something between garden soil and chicken soup. Her father's mug she placed on top of one the crooked stacks of books at his elbow. Then she plopped onto the sofa and tucked her feet under her thighs meditation style. She held her tea mug in both hands, pursed her lips and delicately blew away the steam. No one had invited Scanlon to sit down. There was room on the sofa beside Samantha, and an empty, matching chair. He stood where he was, holding his wretched mug of pungent tea, not knowing what to do with his free hand.

"Aren't you going to ask Sy what he's writing?" she asked Scanlon.

"Sy's writing the usual crap," Sy said, punching those fat keys for all he was worth. "Crap, crap, and more crap. God help us, he loves it."

"Particular crap, or general crap?" Scanlon dared to ask.

"Sy writes novels," Samantha said. "They are crap, just as he says, but he writes an awful lot of them, and they do get published, so how bad can they be? They even sell."

Scanlon wondered if he used a pseudonym, for even if he didn't read a novel a year he was aware, more or less, of who was out there writing them, or thought he was. Seymour Burnham was not a familiar name to him.

"It's compulsive with him," Sy said, referring to himself. "Like gambling, liquor, and cheap women. He can do nothing but churn out crap."

"He's right," Samantha said. "That's why his daughter has to depend on the kindness of strangers for things like rides home."

"But as Mr. Scanlon can hear, Sy hasn't neglected his daughter's literary education."

How does he know my name is Scanlon? Scanlon thought. He was introduced as Jack by Samantha. Say hello to Jack, she'd said. How did he know?

"Sy made his daughter read all of Tennessee Williams' plays after she turned fourteen," Samantha said.

Scanlon had an urge to put down his mug and run for it. Samantha patted the cushion beside her, and he came and sat down like the obedient, lovesick dog he was.

"You don't have to drink your tea if you don't like it. You don't like it, do you?"

"I was never big on tea."

"You're a coffee man, aren't you. Yes, hot and black and no sugar."

He was being taunted, and he couldn't understand why. In fact, he felt that Samantha and her father were ganging up on him and his urge to flee grew stronger.

"You've got me pegged."

"Make the man some hot, black coffee, no sugar, you lazy child," Sy said over the typewriter racket. Scanlon admired the speed Daddy got with just two fingers. He found himself jealous of Sy Burnham's compulsive-ness. He hadn't touched the cigarettes his daughter had brought him; he probably didn't drink. The first thing Scanlon would have done was go for the smokes. His cravings always took precedence. What he wouldn't give for a passion like Daddy's! He wished that he had his own notebook with him; he had crap of his own he'd like to get down on paper.

"You want Samantha to make you some nice, hot, black coffee, no sugar?" Her hand was on his arm; he felt her heat all the way through his jacket and shirtsleeve.

"Anyone ever call you Sam?" Scanlon asked her.

"No one who's ever lived to tell. I despise that name." Samantha unfolded herself and floated off the sofa like a sprite. He didn't want coffee any more than he wanted tea. He didn't feel in any position to refuse, sitting there like a hostage, being toyed with by his captors.

Alone again with Seymour Burnham whose talent for drawing the curtain down on the world around him was unequaled by anyone Scanlon had ever met. For his part, Scanlon was in no hurry to show any more interest, to grovel for this man, who in his opinion was just plain rude. Who did he think he was he could sit around practically bareassed in front of his daughter and a stranger, one of his daughter's teachers, even if he wasn't her teacher, technically? Who was he, he could indulge in such eccentricity? Samantha was back.

"I put water on. You don't have to have coffee if you don't want it. Let's go down by the water. Leave Sy to his crap."

"I ought to be going."

"I'll walk you out," Samantha said, making no protest.

Scanlon said good-bye to Seymour Burnham, told him he was glad to have met him. Sy waved, not saying anything, not once looking up from his typing.

"Don't be surprised if you have to drive me home again some time," Samantha said outside, raising his hackles. He was now her private chauffeur? He said no such thing. "Sy's not only not reliable transportation, he's kind of scary to ride with. He's always taking his eyes off the road, his hands off the steering wheel. When he's not typing, he talks a lot with his hands."

Scanlon stood holding his car door open, not getting in, really wanting to go down by the water with this girl, to sit with her on the grassy bank.

"He must not talk a lot, then." Scanlon was hard put to imagine Sy Burnham long away from his typewriter. Something dark passed over Samantha's face.

"You said something about having to leave." She turned and started to walk away.

"Samantha," he called and she stopped but didn't turn around. Her shoulders were thrust back as if she really were angry. "I didn't mean anything by that," he said. This time she turned. She had a sassy, playful smile for him, as if she hadn't been angry at all.

"Mean what? That Daddy doesn't talk a lot? Meaning that he doesn't communicate? That he's a bad Daddy who leaves his daughter to depend upon the kindness of strangers? I know you didn't mean that." She danced toward him. He thought for a second that she might throw herself in his arms; he almost spread them to receive her, wondering at the same time what Sy would think if he took it in his head to tear himself away from his work for a look outside and saw his young daughter in the arms of a man almost thirty. A schoolteacher yet, entrusted to protect and preserve the sanctity of youth. She skipped past him, whirling round and round, her arms waving like the graceful limbs of the weeping willow, her hair spilling all around her neck and shoulders. She was on the passenger side, playing peek-a-boo with him over the roof. He felt weak in the legs.

"Why don't you show me down by the water," he said, his voice lecherously husky. Samantha giggled, raised her arms over her head and whirled round and round again like a wood nymph and temptress. With all his might he resisted the urge to catch her, to pick her up and carry her to the pond's edge and have her on that plush grass.

"Next time you drive me home I'll show you down by the water." She laughed and danced toward the pond. Was this his cue to follow? Or was he to take her at her word? Why had he never learned to interpret the language of females? After some hard maneuvering, he got the car turned around. He kept an eye in the rearview mirror for the reappearance of his water nymph. She did not appear. Let her think he was playing hard to get, he told himself as he drove through the dark woods away from that strange household.

Chapter Thirty-eight

S: I might as well tell you now. It's too late, but I might as well tell you anyway. I'm hopelessly in love with this girl at school. The one you suspected.

K: How far has it gone?

S: It's gone nowhere, except in my head. But it won't stay that way much longer, I promise you.

K: Sounds like you've made a promise to yourself.

S: I suppose you're right. As I said, I'm hooked. There's no going back now.

K: You're crazy if you think this can amount to anything.

S: Haven't we both known this right along? That I'm crazy?

K: I'm disappointed.

S: Me, too.

K: I'm disappointed in you.

S: I'm disappointed in me, too. What did you think?

K: I thought you meant something else.

S: That I was disappointed in you? Don't make me laugh. I don't expect anything from you at five bucks a throw.

Kennedy let that one hang. He leaned back in his old chair, facing Scanlon, his meaty hands folded under his double chin, giant perspiration stains at his armpits. It was late spring and very hot in the room. The window was open allowing in the fragrance of spring if not the breeze. Scanlon had his jacket off, too. He also perspired heavily under the arms, but nothing to compare with Kennedy. Anyway, he'd decided to stop eating lunches, to lose weight for Samantha. If he was bent on seduction he should go into training.

K: What do you think about this?

S: Don't you mean to say what do I feel about this?
K: I meant what do you think about this.
S: What do you think I think?
K: Am I supposed to say *touché*?
S: I don't know what you're supposed to say.

Scanlon got up and stood in front of the window. Trees were nearly in full leaf; low-growing shrubs were filling out. Everything was green in the gully. Even clothesline wash looked more hopeful on those back porches. Scanlon closed his eyes and tried to picture all the snow from the long winter. There was only green and laundry white on the backs of his eyelids, and the peeling tenement blocks that looked fragile enough to disintegrate with the next breeze. He'd lived in one of those.

K: What're you thinking, Scanlon?
S: I'm thinking nothing.

Scanlon sat back down. He felt restless.

K: What're your plans for next year?
S: Next year? Why don't you ask me what I've got planned for this evening? I'm skipping supper tonight. Maybe I'll skip next year.
K: Losing weight for the chickee?
S: Fuck, no.
K: Fuck, yes. You think you're the first guy who's fallen for a young girl? Are you so self-centered that you think you're the first?
S: What the rest of the world does or doesn't do is no concern of mine.
K: I've noticed.
S: I can't help it. It's out of my control.
K: That's bullshit, even for you, Scanlon.
S: Thanks.
K: Don't force me to psychologize. I thought we could talk like men. You know as well as I do that you can't go through with a thing like this.
S: I don't know anything of the kind. Why can't I go through with a thing like this, as you put it? Didn't you hear me? I'm in love.
K: You're no more in love with this kid than you were with your wife. You're lying to yourself in a big way if you think you are.
S: You're sure of that?
K: I'm sure.
S: Why don't you tell me what's going on. Go ahead and psychologize if you have to. Shrink away.
K: Your mother was how old when she had you?
S: Jesus. He's being literal again. Eighteen.

K: And your recurring incestuous dreams?

S: You said those dreams were normal. You changed your mind?

K: And you haven't had a relationship with a mature woman since your marriage split up?

S: Since before my marriage split up. My marriage was anything but mature.

K: Where do you think a thing like this with the kid can lead?

S: Absolutely nowhere. Maybe to prison. But I got nowhere to go.

K: You'd better find someplace to go, chum. You've got to have some idea about next year. What about coming back to Fairfield? What are the odds?

S: Zero.

K: You were given an offer. Didn't you say you were flattered to get it?

S: I was, but I can't picture myself going through another year with those people. And if this thing with Samantha materializes, as I know it will, despite everything you say, I'll be tarred, feathered, and run out of town on a rail. I need to say more?

K: What about your aunt and uncle?

S: They've been saints, but they've got their threshold like everyone else. I don't think they'll go into deep depression after I'm gone.

K: You considered graduate school?

S: Are you my shrink or my academic counselor? I hate school, always have. Besides, how would I pay for graduate school?

K: Being broke is no reason nowadays not to go to school, what with all the financial aid and other boondoggles. You eligible for the GI Bill?

S: I'm not sure. I ought to be after giving Uncle Sam the four best years of my life, putting it on the line in Southeast Asian bars night after night. I wouldn't mind having those years back.

K: To do what?

S: To do exactly what I did then, except enjoy them more knowing that there are worse ways to pass your days on this planet.

K: And the kid's death? How are you dealing with that?

S: What's to deal with? He's dead, and there's nothing I can do to change that fact. I miss him. He was my favorite kid.

K: Except for what's her name.

S: That's different.

K: Why was he your favorite kid?

S: If you don't mind, I'm not in the mood to talk about it. How many more sessions do we have? Two? Three?

K: I'm clearing out on the fourteenth.

S: You don't have to get all sentimental. The fourteenth. That's my birthday.

K: You'll be how old? Thirty?

S: Yeah. Thirty years old. Sounds like a geological epoch. Thirty and over the hill. I'll tell Samantha I'm twenty-five. Can I pass for twenty-five, Bob?

K: Maybe without the mustache.

S: I've been dreaming lately I shaved it off. What does it mean when you start dreaming about facial hair? Lip hair? I wake up expecting to look clean-shaved and do a double take when I spot myself in the mirror. What do you make of that, Bob? Psychologically.

K: Easy. You don't know who the fuck you are.

S: Does anybody? Do you? Who the fuck are you, Bob? Tell me.

K: I know what I want and don't want. I know that I want you to know that much at least about yourself.

S: I'm pretty sure I know these things. Don't make me out a complete meatball. Ask me some stuff. Go ahead. Ask me what I want and don't want.

K: OK. How about a drink? Do you want a drink right now, right this instant?

S: Of course.

K: Good. Do you ever wish that you didn't want that drink as bad as you want it?

S: Sure. Wait. Maybe not. Not when I'm in the immediate need phase. It's later, when the recriminations start up that I have these feelings. Anyway, I'm giving up smoking first. Smoking's ten times worse than drinking if you want to consider health alone. I'm getting bored with smoking, bored enough to quit for good this time, I think. Too many logistics involved with smoking. You always got to worry about taking your smokes with you when you go out to the car; you worry about running out at night when the stores are closed. All that worry is beginning to bore me. I think I can actually do it this time. And if I quit smoking, how hard can it be to give up the booze?

K: I find it the hardest thing to do in the world.

S: Thanks. I needed to hear that.

K: Do you want to find out who your father is?

S: Yes and no. What if he's got some heritable condition like Huntington's or something lethal like that? I don't want to know. Ignorance is bliss.

K: Your mother wouldn't know?

S: What if she did? Do you think she'd tell me?

K: Why don't you take off your mustache instead of just dreaming about it?

S: I'd feel naked. Besides, I don't want to have to deal with all the attention I'd get at school. I hate attention.

K: Oh?

S: You look surprised. You don't believe me?

K: Not entirely. I think there's a part of you that enjoys attention.

S: I like it on my terms. I don't go around looking for ways to focus attention on myself, and I resent you for implying that I do.

K: I wasn't suggesting that you went around looking for it. There's an important difference.

S: You think I don't know that? I'm not as stupid as I look, and as you think I am.

K: I never thought you were stupid.

S: Why use the past tense?

K: How would you describe your relationship with the boy who was killed?

S: Oh, didn't I tell you? I don't feel like talking about that now any more than I did five minutes ago.

K: Can you tell me why you don't feel like talking about it at this particular time?

S: You're being kind of obtuse about this. It's still painful for me. It hasn't been that long. What's your rush?

K: What do you plan to do after you leave?

S: You mean after I leave this office? This afternoon?

K: You know that's not what I mean.

S: I haven't a clue.

K: I don't believe you.

S: Stambaugh's going to Canada to avoid getting killed. Maybe I'll go some place like that for the same reason.

K: I know you don't want to hear this, but I'm going to say it anyway. You're probably as suited to teaching as you are to anything. You could do worse things with your life.

S: Don't make me laugh.

K: This is no shit.

S: Are you advising me to sign up for another hitch?

K: Not necessarily. There's graduate school, other teaching jobs. The profession's wide open. You could do anything you want in the field.

S: If I wanted, which I don't. And I have no interest in graduate school for the same reason I gave you a few minutes ago. School is unnatural, like having sex with domestic animals.

K: You've shared your views on formal education with your colleagues?

S: Not exactly.

K: Are you really blackballed from industry? I find it hard to believe in this day and age.

S: The word is out on me. I'd never get a second look, not for a long time. I hate industry and commerce, too, by the way. It's as despicable as formal education.

K: I guess that leaves the monastery.

S: Don't laugh. I haven't ruled it out. Think they'd let me have a teenage tootsie?

K: These days you never know.

S: Whatever happens, it'll be on your head.

K: How's that?

S: You got me in this fucked-up introspective frame of mind. I was content to muddle through life until you came along.

K: You were the one to come along, as I recall.

S: What's the difference? It will be on your head.

K: Stay in the teaching racket. I wouldn't mind having that on my head.

S: You want me poor and dependent on cut-rate shrinks all my life?

K: You know how the saying goes about the poor.

S: Who'd want to inherit this scuzzy earth?

K: I'll bet you five bucks against a bottle of cheap bourbon you can't go through with this business with the girl. What do you say?

S: I say you're on.

Chapter Thirty-nine

"Want a ride in a really fast car?" Scanlon asked Samantha Burnham in the parking lot after school on Monday. He was supposed to be helping Josh Patterson coach the girls' softball team. Samantha was there for the asking, however, and Josh and his softball girls could get lost.

"You know someone who owns a fast car?"

"Hop in, I'll take you home. That is, unless Sy's picking you up."

Samantha opened the door and slid in with more grace than most people he'd seen get in or out of a Volkswagen. She had on an embroidered, low-necked peasant blouse and long white skirt. She was barefoot. On her legs grew a soft, blonde down. Blood surged to Scanlon's brain instantly.

"How about this weather?" Scanlon said. "Makes life seem almost worth living."

"How romantic, Jack."

"You want to go home or ride around a little?"

"Ride around. Let's just ride around and be free. You do know how to be free?"

"Just like you know how to be sarcastic." Scanlon had to work to concentrate on the road. He'd turned west out of the parking lot and was getting queer looks from kids walking along Route 2. He kept his eyes straight ahead trying to look innocent and adult. With Samantha there, only inches away from him, looking innocent was a feat.

"Let's go to Montpelier," Samantha said.

"What's there? I thought Montpelier was dull."

"I have friends there. We can turn on, have some fun. You turn on, don't you?"

"Do I."

"Great. Let's go."

Scanlon stopped at the store with the Flying A pump outside, the one with Dale and his voluptuous, young, high-school-drop-out wife, the store that today smelled of bleach. Neither Dale nor bride of Dale was on duty today. An older woman sat behind the linoleum-covered counter. She wasn't reading, or knitting, or working a crossword puzzle. She sat and stared at the opposite wall. Scanlon got two six-packs of beer out of the dirty cooler and laid two singles on the counter in front of the woman.

"That cover it?"

The lady (Dale's mother?) dragged the bills toward her with a shaky, veiny hand. Scanlon didn't dare look at her face. She had not spoken a word and Scanlon felt a chill as he hurried out of the store.

Samantha looked at him as if he'd asked her to do something nasty when he offered her a beer.

"You don't like beer?"

"No, and I don't like what it represents."

"I see. Do I dare ask what it is you think beer represents?"

"You wouldn't want to hear."

"I suppose pot is morally superior to beer. I imagine that's what you think. Am I close?"

"Very close."

"Pot never did anything for me. I think it must all be in the head if you'll pardon me."

"You obviously don't know how to use it."

"I was using it before you were born. Talk to me."

It was true that on the two occasions he'd tried marijuana he hadn't gotten the advertised results. He'd been told he was too uptight. But wasn't that the reason to smoke pot in the first place? To get loosened up?

Scanlon reached across Samantha's lap and got his church key out of the glove compartment.

"You'll suffer me a beer or two, I hope."

"Do your own thing. Wait till we get to Montpelier. I'll teach you the art of getting high."

"Sure." Scanlon flipped the cap, tucked the cold beer bottle between his thighs with only a fleeting spasm of doubt as he thought about the last time he embarked in his car with beer between his legs. "Montpelier or bust," he said, starting up the car.

Soon they were passing by the freak college where Mole Cheek and Goatee learned the art of social revolution. He was disappointed, and even jealous, when Samantha looked for a long time at the shabby sign at the school's entrance, as if that was where she really wanted to be instead of riding to Montpelier with this randy, aging high school teacher. He accelerated.

"Be careful. The pigs around here look for any excuse to bust kids for speeding and hassle them for dope."

"I'm not a kid, and I've got no dope."

Samantha laughed, and it was her laugh, finally, that made him wonder what in the world he thought he was doing.

"Why are you going here?" Samantha asked as he turned abruptly left onto a dirt road. She didn't sound concerned so much as curious.

"I don't feel like Montpelier. I remember this road. It's a nice road with a couple nice villages along the way. We can commune with nature. You'd like that, wouldn't you?"

"I know this road, too. I've been on it enough."

"Then you don't mind?"

"It's your car."

"I don't think we should stray too far. Your father is apt to worry. And to be frank, I don't know why I'm doing this with you in the first place."

"You don't have age hang-ups on top of everything else?"

"What do you mean, on top of everything else?"

"I mean, you're so uptight."

"So how come you agreed to ride around with me, being free? Why don't you go for rides with Mr. Stambaugh, or somebody free of hang-ups?"

"You sound like one of the kids you teach."

"Thanks."

"You're welcome." Samantha giggled and laid her head on his shoulder. She snuggled up to him, and he veered off the road momentarily. He wondered if she could hear his thudding heart and know for sure, if she didn't know already, that he was helplessly in her thrall. Or if she would be turned off by his unbridled physiology, think it uncool. Or think that he had a heart condition and be reminded that he was crowding thirty and was practically over the hill.

Her hand was on his thigh, next to the cold beer, as if to put her hand there was as natural as his putting a beer between his legs. He should put his arm around her soft shoulders. Wouldn't that be the natural thing for a boy in love to do with his girl, especially if she had snuggled up to him with her hand nearly in his crotch? Scanlon held onto the steering wheel with both hands for dear life.

They came to a steep downhill grade. Scanlon had to shift down to second gear. Samantha withdrew her hand and her body, turning her attention to the window at her side. Scanlon's thigh went cool where her hand had been; the beer was warm between his legs. He drank some, and it was warm in his mouth, too. At the bottom of the hill on Samantha's side of the road was a small pond.

"Oh, stop!" she shouted.

Scanlon braked. The car skidded a few feet in the loose gravel.

"What's the matter?"

Samantha flung open the door and slipped gracefully out of the car. Scanlon got out, too, looked both ways along the road, then followed her to the edge of the water. Was this like the pond near her house? There was swamp on the far side with long cattails and grasses, dense woods growing right up to the edge. The edge near the road was muddy, scummy with algae and emerging vegetation.

Samantha had two handfuls of her skirt held above her thighs and was up to her knees in the stagnant water.

"It's beautiful. Come on in. Karl and I went skinny dipping here last October. It's so beautiful."

It looked more cold and slimy than beautiful to Scanlon. And he was not about to take off his shoes and socks, roll up his pants. He drained his warm beer and tossed the empty out into the middle of the water.

Samantha turned to him with a dark look, but said nothing. She didn't have to. Neither did she repeat her invitation for him to join her in the water.

"Who's Karl?" Scanlon knew perfectly well who Karl was. His mouth was sour from warm beer and the mention of Karl.

"A friend."

"Your boyfriend?

Another look from her, over her shoulder. How hopelessly jejune, her look said this time. Sick at heart, and queasy in the stomach, and so tired he could have laid his head down on the fecund ground and gone instantly to sleep. He wouldn't want to wake up. Samantha waded out farther, up to her waist. She dropped the hem of her dress; it floated momentarily then sank out of sight. She abandoned herself to the cold water. She'd never get dry. Then she was swimming out in the middle, delicate arms dipping in and out of the black water, and he felt alone and helpless, and so tired. He could hear her breathing. It seemed like the only sound in the world, her swimming breath.

"Why don't you come out," Scanlon yelled, though there was no need to raise his voice to be heard in that utter quiet. "You'll catch cold."

Samantha laughed and went underwater. She surfaced near the far shore. What if she got in trouble? What if she drowned? How would he explain that to everyone who would need to know?

"I think we should be going." There was worry in his voice, worry even he could hear.

"Don't be so uptight. Drink another beer." Samantha went under again, and when she came up she had in her hand the bottle he had tossed. She held it over her head.

"That's a no-deposit, no-return. You didn't have to bother."

He was not prepared for how stunning she really was as she came out of the water, her thin skirt and peasant blouse clinging wet to her body, all lovely contours accentuated in the late afternoon light. She wore no underwear. Suddenly he was no longer tired.

"You'll catch your death," Scanlon said, taking off his jacket, like a courtier, and slipping it over her shoulders.

"I don't need that," she shivered. "It's delicious."

Scanlon feasted his eyes on her body, like a hick at a hootchie-koochie show. She must have known how she looked; she must have wanted him to see her like this. Otherwise, why refuse the jacket? Even flower children couldn't take that much pleasure in being cold and wet. He would have liked to take her in his arms, warm her with his body. She ran her fingers through her hair to straighten snarls. She cocked her head and stood up on one foot to shake water out of one ear, then the other. Scanlon sighed with desire.

"I suppose you're worried that your car will get wet," she said.

"That, believe me, is the least of my worries."

Samantha wrung water out of her hair with both hands. Scanlon was about to embrace her, while her hands were occupied with her hair, when a pickup truck came bumping down the road, raising a cloud of dust behind it that blocked out the horizon. Scanlon felt the needles of fear in his neck, knowing what some of these country boys were capable of doing out here, away from civilization, and remembering what happened to poor Danny Picard. The truck rolled by without breaking speed, enveloping them in a cloud of road grit.

"Shit," Samantha said, spitting, and brushing at her arms and wet clothes.

"Let's get out of here." Scanlon got in the car and opened a beer, glad that he wasn't made to find out today whether or not he was a coward.

Samantha's arms were all gooseflesh and bluish. "You sure you don't want my coat?" Scanlon started to shrug out of his jacket.

"OK." She allowed him to put it around her shoulders. She smelled of the stagnant pond.

They continued south on the dirt road, neither of them saying anything for a long time. Scanlon thought he heard Samantha's teeth chatter, and he turned on the heater. She leaned against him again and wound her arms around his biceps. He wanted to kiss her but didn't know how to bring that off with her face buried in his sleeve. He didn't want to stop the car with the chance of encountering people in pickup trucks. And suppose she didn't want him to kiss her? Kennedy would have shook his head in disbelief at Scanlon's ineptitude, would have demanded instant payment of their wager. Was this what Kennedy knew when he told Scanlon that he'd never be able to go through with the seduction of this girl? What if he took her hand and placed it on his thigh where she'd had it before?

"Where are we?" Samantha murmured into his sleeve, as if she'd been asleep all this time. He felt her hot breath through the cloth of his shirt.

"Somewhere in the wilderness. No sign of human existence since that pickup."

Samantha lifted her head and squinted out the windshield. "We should be coming to Granville pretty soon." Granville delivered two busloads of Fairfield High students every morning before seven-thirty. What time must they leave Granville? Scanlon felt as though he'd been driving for hours on this endless dirt road, hyperconscious of Samantha Burnham of the class of 1969 clinging to him like a limpet, he unable to do anything but think and drive and go crazy with lust and self-doubt. So he was relieved when they arrived in Granville, though there wasn't much to Granville to justify relief. A blip on the radar screen, a widening in the road—a square, two-decker building housing the general store, post-office, gas station, and local hangout. Across the road, a white Methodist church next to which was a freshly painted white town meeting house where pure democracy was allegedly practiced. If the good citizens of Granville knew what he, schoolmaster to their children, was doing with one of them, they'd show him a little down-home justice in the back roads. He'd heard how they'd taken care of business with one of their own farmers who'd neglected his livestock. His decomposed body was discovered one morning washed up on the bank of the Connecticut River. He didn't imagine Vermonters would take any more kindly to sexual deviance either. Just ask that poor black minister in Irasburgh. Was that what he was engaged in? Sexual deviance?

"You need to stop?" Scanlon asked.

"I have to pee."

Why didn't you go back in the pond he wanted to ask. "Doesn't look very promising."

"Drive around the back of the town hall."

"It's daylight, for crying out loud." He didn't want to take the chance of being seen with her by a Granvillian.

"It's daylight? What did you expect in the middle of the afternoon?"

"You could be seen." Which was to say she could be seen with him.

"Let them look. I have to pee."

"Hang on till we clear the village, and I'll find you some nice bushes."

"Well, hurry." She sounded little-girl pouty, and once again he was filled with lust and despair.

There was another dirt road that led east out of Granville. Samantha didn't take the trouble to walk to the thicket to do her business. She squatted on the edge of the road, car door wide open, and answered nature's call. Scanlon kept his eye on the rearview mirror, some of his ardor slipping away with the sound of her pee, like heavy rain, hitting the hard dirt road. But she was adorable in his jacket, the shoulders and sleeves way too big for her. Her hair was frizzy where it had begun to dry, and there was a blush on her cheeks like rouge. He decided to tell her he loved her when she was finished peeing. Instead, he shifted gears and got them on their way again without a word.

"I wish we had grass," she said. Scanlon tried offering her beer again. She refused. "I could really use some grass." She was starting to sound cranky. She had just voided her bladder, what did she have to be cranky about?

"Wish I could help you." He thought idly of Stambaugh, wondering what he would think if Scanlon, of all people, asked him for pot. Samantha leaned against the door, self-absorbed. The absence of her warmth was palpable.

"Go to Groveton," she said, sitting up straight. Scanlon could see the light bulb flash over her head. "I know where to get some in Groveton."

"I don't know about that, Samantha. Won't your father be wondering where you are? Won't he be worried?"

"Are you serious?"

"I guess not." Scanlon saw, in his mind's eye, Sy Burnham hunched over his big, black typewriter. On the sofa he saw himself and Samantha naked, going at it under Sy's nose, Sy interested only in making words appear on paper. "I don't know about Groveton. I'm pretty known there."

"You worry too much. Where we're going nobody knows you."

"That's easy for you to say."

"Take me home then if you're so worried."

"Maybe that would be best."

"Whatever you think is best." Now she was petulant, the way he got when he was deprived of his booze.

"All right. We'll go to Groveton if that's what you want."

"Don't let me force you to do anything."

Scanlon could only laugh at the irony and felt good that he was able to laugh after all this wallowing around in his randy muck and guilt. Part of him, a large part of him, wanted to drive her straight home, to be rid of her.

It was twilight by the time they reached Groveton. The sky was violet and the air was soft. Even the oppressive humpbacked hills that encircled the town gave off a benign light.

"Where to?" Scanlon asked, driving past the trade school and thinking, unaccountably, about Mary Alice McGinnis.

"You know where River Street is?"

"Yes." Could she have known that he lived on River Street? How could she? "Where on River?"

"Just before East Groveton. I'll tell you where when we get there."

Maybe Lyle Higgins dealt a little pot on the side. Smiling at the absurdity of this idea, Scanlon turned left on Main to avoid driving through town and risk being seen by Fairfield High kids who sometimes came to Groveton to shop. He swung down Winter Street past the gingerbread schoolhouse where Johnny Labalm had attended fourth grade. Across the street was the playground where he'd fought bare-knuckled with Leroy Bean, the playground bully, and bloodied his own knuckles but Bean's lip, as well. That may have been the act that got Laraine Comstock's attention. He was more the fighter than the lover, however, and Laraine Comstock made that painfully obvious to him. At eight years old she already knew enough to stick her tongue in your mouth when she kissed you. She wore pretty cashmere sweaters to school. She was cute, with freckles, an almost pug nose, and short brown hair that radiated light.

Scanlon spotted Lucky trotting purposefully along the sidewalk ahead of them. Lucky was known to roam occasionally, but never this far from home. Scanlon pulled over and rolled down his window.

"What're you doing way up here, you bad dog? Where's your father?" Lucky stopped and looked sidelong at the car. "Your father's not going to like hearing about you being way up here. Come on, get in." Lucky sniffed at the door, at Scanlon's pant leg. Scanlon patted his lap and Lucky jumped aboard.

"Who have we here?" Samantha reached over and stroked Lucky's snout. His tail slapped against the open door. He smelled like he'd been in stagnant water, like Samantha.

"This is Lucky, my uncle's neurotic hound."

"He's cute. What kind of hound?"

"A hound is a hound is a hound. Come on, pal. I'll take you home." Scanlon hoisted Lucky into the back seat. Samantha turned around to play with him, to pull his silky ears. Lucky groaned with pleasure, the way Scanlon would have groaned if she were to pull his ears in this fashion.

Then Scanlon spotted Ira's Ford parked in front of the Goodwin's house. Wasn't it early for Ira to be out of work? If Alice and Ira were visiting the Goodwins, Lucky wasn't so far afield after all. Lucky didn't get along with Duke, Willie's big lab, which was why he'd hit the road. On the other hand, Ira could be paying Althea a visit on his own, without Alice. If he brought Lucky home, Ira would worry about the mutt when he came looking for him. He stopped two houses past the Goodwins and opened the door.

"Bail out, Lucky. Go find Ira. Good dog."

"Oh, let him stay," Samantha said.

"My uncle would wonder what happened to him, worry that he'd been hit by a car."

"I thought he was a long way from home."

"He is. My uncle's visiting in the neighborhood. I saw his car." Scanlon didn't feel compelled to tell her which car belonged to his uncle, or which house in the neighborhood he was visiting. And he wouldn't have been able to actually deliver Lucky to his uncle's rundown house with Samantha in the car. Pride hangover from his days of living behind the storefronts on Main Street.

Lucky wasn't eager to leave the car, not with the attention he was getting from Samantha.

"Lucky, out." Scanlon got out of the car and pushed his backrest forward. "Come on." Lucky gave him a hangdog look, and buried his snout between his front paws with a half-whine, half-sigh. "Lucky." Scanlon pointed at the ground, and Lucky held his ground.

"That's a good dog, Lucky," Samantha said. "Don't listen to him. You stay right here with Samantha."

"You're a lot of help. Come on, don't play games. Get out of the car. He'll come if we're both out. He can't stand to be left alone."

"I don't want him to leave. I like him and he likes me, don't you, Lucky?" Scanlon reached in and grabbed Lucky's collar and pulled him out of the back seat. Samantha told him he was cruel to animals and that she intended to report him to the SPCA.

"What about cruelty to humans? My uncle would be literally sick if he couldn't find this thing." Scanlon pointed down the street and ordered Lucky to go find his father, knowing that what he should have done was take the dog to Althea's door. If Ira was too caught up in illicit love in the afternoon to look after his dog, why should he worry? Nevertheless, Scanlon drove away feeling uneasy with Lucky back on the loose.

He slowed down next to "Labalm's cat house" as Alice was fond of calling the place.

"How can people live like that?" Scanlon said, shaking his head. He glanced at Samantha for her reaction. She was intent on the road ahead and the East Groveton turnoff. She acted as though she hadn't heard him.

"The turn's coming up soon. We have to go left over an iron bridge and then go up a really steep hill. I've only been there at night so go really slowly, all right?"

Scanlon drove past the VW garage, past Fletcher's Fried Clam Shack where Ira cleaned two nights a week for a few extra bucks. They crossed the line into East Groveton. Scanlon was getting antsy here in Lyle Higgins country. How would he explain Samantha's presence in his car to someone like Higgins who'd already alluded to a relationship between himself and this girl that went beyond "professional." Higgins could have been kidding, or he could have been fishing, who knew?

"Here it is!" Samantha pointed, all excited, at the rusty iron bridge. "Turn here." The proximity of marijuana had her hyperactive. For his part, Scanlon was a little benumbed from all the beer he'd drunk since being in this girl's company. He should have been the one looking for a place to pee. His bladder, so far, had held fast.

The road on the other side of the bridge was indeed steep, and full of potholes. The old bridge with its corrugated metal surface didn't seem secure enough to hold his VW, let alone trucks with heavy loads, yet there was no warning sign for load limits. Below them, the swollen Manoosic was full to the brim, threatening to overflow; it moved with ferocious speed and turbulence.

Around the next bend Samantha shouted again, with even greater gusto.

"Here!" She bounced in the seat like a kid at an ice cream stop. "Turn here! It's only a little farther. I remember everything!" The road was rutted from water runoff and there was enough loose gravel to make the VW's tires spin. Scanlon shifted down to second and spun all the more. Samantha exhorted him to keep moving, they were almost there. He lurched the car forward, searching for solid ground.

Then he was in a clearing in front of a big house. Several vehicles were in the rutted clearing, parked with utter randomness, as if they had been abandoned: VW buses painted psychedelic colors, VW bugs like his own, only rusted out, fenderless, with bumper stickers that said things like "Jesus Saves Green Stamps," "Get Your Shit Together," "Jesus is Coming, And Is He Gonna Be Pissed."

"Who lives here?" Scanlon asked, "Norman Bates?"

Samantha was too excited to hear him. He had hardly come to a stop before she had the door open and was prancing for the doorless front entrance. Scanlon stayed in the car. She didn't look back; she just disappeared through that doorless maw leaving him feeling abandoned, like the hippies' cars—and desolate. He shifted into reverse with the intention of backing out of there, out of Samantha Burnham's life while he still had the chance. She could prevail upon her creepy friends to take her home, if she was inclined to return home.

He started the car, let it idle, eyes on the sinister house with its absurd Victorian architecture out here in the woods, wondering if Samantha hadn't already got herself mired in an orgy of sex and pot. The appeal of marijuana he'd never understand. And the hippies, or what passed for hippies around here, he understood even less. He thought of Mole Cheek and Goatee and how just as smug as the so-called "establishment" they claimed to despise, they had been that day in Doug Stambaugh's classroom. He let out the clutch and moved backward into a rut. Samantha appeared in the doorway, shouting and waving, beckoning him to come. He had no choice but to shut off the engine and go to her. He brought along a full bottle of beer for moral support.

"Where were you going, you silly man? You weren't ditching me?"

"I thought I'd pick up some more beer." Samantha took his arm. She'd left his jacket in the car. Scanlon wished he'd taken it with him; he felt exposed in only shirt and tie.

"You won't want beer in this house. Leave it outside." She reached for his bottle. He held it away from her at arm's length.

"Excuse me. I go nowhere without Father Knickerbocker. I'm not about to go in there unarmed."

"You'll be sorry." She pulled him inside a dark, narrow hall reeking of marijuana, old and new. She tugged him along the hallway into a room full of bodies in repose. It was dark in here as well, but light enough for Scanlon to see that there was no furniture, only pillows on which to recline on the floor. What little light there was came from a few guttering candles in saucers on the wooden cable wheel that was a kind of centerpiece in this austere room. Scanlon found it difficult to breathe in the heavy atmosphere of reefer smoke, and he experienced momentary claustrophobia. Samantha had a firm grip on his hand as they tiptoed through the strewn bodies. The faint sound of sitar music came from somewhere in the house. Scanlon noticed that paper hung in shreds from the walls, as if it had been clawed off, and he felt guilty for not helping Ira paper the living room.

Samantha let go of his hand and hurried through a door across the room. Scanlon hastened to follow and stepped on someone's hand.

A voice floated up from the floor. "Hey, man. Like watch your step."

"Sorry." Scanlon made it to the door and found more hippies on the other side, except these hippies were standing. Samantha spoke into the ear of a dark-haired, young woman with enormous breasts that seemed to originate somewhere around her waist. She had on a denim shirt and leather vest with colored glass studs, and she wore a headband.

"Hello, beery," a thin, young man with watery eyes said to Scanlon.

"What?"

"Want a hit?" The young man offered Scanlon his dirty reefer, pinched between the thumb and forefinger of his dirty hand with its ragged fingernails. Scanlon swigged beer. The hippie smiled and shook his head as if he heard an inside joke in there. Where was the music coming from? The tempo changed, quickened in intensity. Scanlon looked around at the joyless hippies. The music's intensity was lost to them, whose senses were blunted by dope. Scanlon swallowed some more beer. No one seemed to be talking to anyone else, except for Samantha to big-tits. At least at Winship's party there had been the illusion of social interaction. These people flew in their own orbits with no apparent forces of attraction at work.

Then Samantha was beside him, toking on a joint. He wondered if she would ask him for money to pay for the dope. She dragged earnestly on the reefer, inspecting it after each toke with utmost seriousness.

"Want some?" She offered but he could see that her heart wasn't into sharing.

"No, thanks. One of your charming friends already offered."

"These freaks aren't my friends. They always have grass and anything else you can name. We crash here, too, sometimes. Nobody bothers you."

"Who would have the energy? I'm getting that hemmed-in feeling. I'll wait for you outside." Scanlon found the door, and once he was outside, inhaled deeply. He could hear the heady beat of the sitar music outside, wasted on these zombies. He drained his beer and dropped the empty on the ground.

"Want to go now?" Samantha was beside him. She slipped her hand in his.

They drove around Groveton, holding hands, not speaking. Under the influence of marijuana, Samantha had become quiet instead of garrulous like his half brothers. Scanlon had always thought it made everyone hyper and giggly. He wanted another beer, but he didn't dare let go of Samantha's hand to get one. For the first time today he felt almost calm, somewhat at peace except for the nagging itch for another brew. As long as he held her hand there was harmony between them, something the hippies would probably describe as positive energy flow or some such nonsense. Whatever it was called, he wanted to keep it for as long as he could. The tension of lust had abated, and this strange girl who was not really a girl at all, but a woman by anyone's definition, was part of him in this quiet interlude. Words would have ruined the mood, and for once he didn't feel compelled to fill the void with his tinny voice.

His new VW had a radio, but he hadn't been able to pick up anything except the dreadful local station with its semi-classical renderings of Beatles' tunes, and the Arthur Godfrey show in the morning. So he didn't turn on the radio, and Samantha, unlike most girls her age, didn't ask him to. In his ears he kept hearing the beat behind the sitar music.

He drove the winding dirt roads around the outskirts of Groveton, not once thinking of parking and trying something with Samantha. Then he turned abruptly into the Lions Club swimming pool across from the house where Johnny Labalm had been born, and where Johnny had seen the act of love, as it was called, performed for the first time. Two-hundred yards from the pool was the trade school where as an eight-year-old Johnny had had the chance to perform the act himself on poor Mary Alice McGinnis, duped by magic and her own six-year-old innocence. Johnny had been unable to bring it off, had chickened out in fear and disgust. Thinking about it now, twenty years later, Scanlon wondered what it would have been like inside her dry little cunt. Would it have changed his life? He laughed out loud and Samantha withdrew her hand. She got out of the car. Scanlon followed. She grabbed the chain-link fence with both hands and looked in at the empty pool.

"It'll be opening for the season soon," Scanlon said, his voice throaty from beer and not speaking for so long.

"I wish there was water. I feel like swimming some more. We could go skinny-dipping." Samantha turned to him. "Wouldn't you like to go skinny-dipping?"

"I'm too modest for that. I shower fully clothed. Remember, I'm almost thirty."

"No you're not."

"I'm not?"

"Let's make believe there's water." Samantha started to climb the fence.

"What are you doing? Be careful."

"Come on." Samantha swung a leg over the top of the fence, her lovely thigh flashing in the moonlight. She dropped soundlessly to the ground on the pool side. They faced each other through the fence. "Are you coming over?" Her face was against the metal. "Kiss me."

Scanlon felt silly pressing his lips through the cold fence. Samantha giggled and backed away, leaving him with pursed lips through the metal opening. How silly he must have looked to her, too. She pulled off her blouse, unhitched her skirt. She stood naked in the moonlight, hands on her buttocks. She turned and jumped into the shallow end of the empty pool, leaving Scanlon holding on to the fence.

"Come on over. We'll make believe we're skinny-dipping. Come on, take your clothes off, you silly man."

"I can't, Samantha. I wish you'd come out of there. You can come through the bathhouse."

"I'll let you in through the bathhouse, if you're scared of climbing the fence," Samantha said, leaping out of the pool.

Scanlon jogged around the building to meet her, his breathing rapid and shallow. He was startled to find her framed in the doorway in all her stunning nakedness. This must be a dream. Nothing like this happened to him in real life. It was rare enough in his dreams. He moved toward her. She melted into the darkness of the bathhouse like an apparition. He hesitated before he entered himself.

"Samantha?" It was too dark inside to see, and there was a lingering smell of chlorine, pungent in his nostrils. He remembered the cage in the middle of the room where you paid admission, rented towels or umbrellas. Dressing rooms flanked the cage, men and boys on the left, women and girls on the right. He remembered a tunnel with a running shower before you came out on the pool deck.

"Samantha?" he called again, waiting for his eyes to adjust to the darkness.

"Take off your clothes, Mr. Scanlon. You won't be allowed in until you've removed all your clothes, and that includes shoes and socks."

"Samantha, the cops check this place out. We can't be found here."

She jumped out in front of him from the men and boys' dressing room. Her voice had seemed farther away, and he was startled.

"You're still uptight, aren't you. You should have had a smoke."

"Go get your clothes."

"Don't you like my body?" She pressed against him, wound her arms around his neck and kissed him. He felt his knees, along with his will, yield, begin to tremble. "Somebody's waking up," she said, pressing her lower body hard against him.

"Samantha. Dear God, Samantha."

"Let's get out of those old clothes." Samantha tugged at his belt buckle. Scanlon, out of control, took her breasts, one in each hand, expecting hard, aroused nipples, feeling instead smooth, flaccid skin. He saw in his mind's eye the high school kids Johnny Labalm had witnessed, when he was eight, humping outside the bathhouse door, the girl consumed by passion. Samantha Burnham was not consumed by anything that he recognized as passion, none at least to match his own. He was in its grip, and now the feel of her smooth, cool nipples broke that passion like an ice and alcohol bath.

"Please, Samantha," he said, letting go of her, "get your clothes and let's get the hell out of here before somebody comes along."

Samantha put her hand on his crotch. "Back to sleep? He doesn't like Samantha?"

"Get your things."

Samantha laughed crazily and skipped out of the bathhouse toward the pool. When she came outside, where Scanlon waited for her beside his car smoking a cigarette, she had on her clothes.

Scanlon drove her home. They didn't talk. They didn't hold hands. When they got to her house, Samantha got out of the car without a word. Scanlon didn't say anything either. He watched her all the way to her door with her long strides. She tossed her hair back before going inside, and he wondered if this gesture was for him, to show him a little contempt. But he was glad to be rid of her, if a little sad as well, and even hurt that she couldn't have felt for him something of what he had felt for her, if he really did feel anything at all for her beyond physical want. Well, that was that, and he realized, as he drove back down that dark, bowered road, that he felt almost carefree. What a strange and unusual feeling for him.

"I'm free," he said out loud, reaching for his last beer. "Halleluia, I'm not in love."

K: You sound almost glad that you struck out with Lolita. You owe me five by the way.

S: I don't look at it as striking out.

K: How do you see it?

S: As a sign.

K: A sign?

S: Yes.

K: A good sign?

S: A very good sign.

K: Tell me about it.

S: It wasn't just because her tits were soft. They only served to remind me that she was taboo.

K: You need soft tits to remind you about taboos?

S: Don't interrupt. I'm on the edge of an insight. Maybe they weren't soft at all. Maybe I only imagined they were, and this was how my conscience informed me of the wrongness of what I was doing, I don't know. I do have a conscience, you know, in case you were wondering. So the way I look at it, you can call it what you want—psychological repression, whatever—it was the old conscience doing its job. Samantha would call it uptight. I may be uptight, but I know that it's fundamentally wrong for a guy my age and in my circumstances to go around banging seventeen-year-old girls in bathhouses on warm, spring nights.

K: You didn't know that before you started out on this deliberate seduction?

S: Not in any way that affected my actions.

K: Before, when you were planning this whole thing, you said that she was no kid.

S: In many ways she's not. But she's a student at the school where I'm employed, where kids are entrusted to me, where I'm expected to behave like a responsible adult, not like some randy teenager. And this position assumes that seducing female students is wrong, no matter how physically and emotionally mature they appear on the outside.

K: Sounds like you prepared a speech on the subject.

S: I've given it quite a lot of thought, Bob.

K: What about your spontaneity?

S: What about it?

K: You've expressed concern in the past over your lack of it.

S: I've got an obligation, a kind of stewardship to consider. What's spontaneity next to that?

K: You sure you weren't simply scared shitless?

S: Sure, I was afraid. I admit it. But I'm pretty sure I wasn't acting out of fear alone. We used to say in the Navy that a stiff prick has no conscience. And no fear.

K: You're fired up over this, aren't you?

S: So don't throw water on my fire. Stop trying to queer it for me with penetrating insight.

K: Congratulations.

S: Thanks, you sarcastic fuck.

K: I mean it.

S: I hope so. I wouldn't want to think you resented me for making progress on my own. I'll give you forty-percent credit if it'll make you feel better.

K: Thanks. Forty-percent seems generous. You seen the girl since that night?

S: Sure. She hasn't gone away. Acts like nothing happened, you know how it is with women, with girls, even. I play along. What else is there for me to do? Any feelings I had for her I can see now were fraudulent, neurotic fantasies.

K: So you think she felt nothing for you?

S: Absolutely nothing. You'd understand if you could meet her father. She'll be lucky if she ever feels anything for anybody, except herself.

K: You feel sorry for her?

S: Of course.

K: She really busted your balls, didn't she, by not responding the way you thought she should?

S: You won't let go, will you. You can't stand to have me feel good.

K: I can't stand to have you kid yourself. What if she had reacted properly?

S: If I recall, it was you who always preached the instincts, the feelings. All you assholes from the touchy-feely school, right? Well, goddamn it, I do feel good for once in my life, or I did until I came here.

K: You're better off when you're ambivalent. It's as if you're looking for instant salvation. Join a religious cult if you want that.

S: You lied to me. You said I could always trust these so-called feelings. What are you saying now? That it was all bullshit?

K: I was talking about honest feelings. I repeat my earlier question.

S: I never lied to you about myself. I always said I was a liar, that I wouldn't know the truth if it sat on me. You're telling me now that I shouldn't trust my good feelings, that I'm only true to myself when I'm feeling lousy and ambivalent. Is that about it, Bob?

K: Close.

S: Why did I bother coming here today? Why did I ever come here?

K: How you doing with the drinking?

S: Go and fuck yourself.

K: Have you written to your mother?

S: Leave me alone.

K: What will you do with yourself next year?

S: Drown in shit.

K: Are you going to show for our last session? I'm betting that you think you won't.

S: I wouldn't bet against you, Bob. Save your money. What would be the point of my coming next week? To say good-bye? To reminisce about the productive months we've had together?

K: I want you to come. I think it's important that you show.

S: What do you want from me? I've spilled my insides out in front of you, told you things I've never told anybody in my life, things I wouldn't admit in a confessional. What do you do? Trivialize everything. I dream of incest, you tell me it happens all the time; I tell you about my lust for a seventeen-year-old girl, you tell me I couldn't bring off her seduction, as if anybody could see that but me. I tell you about my feelings, feelings that bother me, keep me awake nights, drive me to drink, and you shrug them off and tell me they're natural. And the final insult, you stop serving refreshments which, if you want the truth, is the real reason I kept coming back here. The free hooch. Believe me.

K: I don't believe you.

S: What else is new?

K: If I promised to have something next week would you promise to come?

S: I can't believe you, Bob.

K: Throw around insults, expect to get a few back.

S: I'm paying you to insult me?

K: You're not paying me, pal.

S: Thanks for the reminder.

K: You want to know why I think it's important you come next week?

S: I can guess.

K: All right. Let's hear it from you.

S: It's all ritual, like rites of passage, formal closure, a final exam. And I think you want off the guilt hook a little. You feel guilty for abandoning me? Don't tell me I'm the only one around here bearing guilt.

K: Why do you feel guilty?

S: I haven't really been that good a patient. I haven't been as forthcoming as I say I have. Have I? You're a clever fellow. I don't have to tell you. I suppose it's normal for us patients to get dependent on you shrinks, but I never thought it would happen to me. I can't even remember what it was that brought me here in the first place. I'm the last guy in the world who'd ever seek out a head man. Why did I come?

K: You were scared by your dreams.

S: I've been scared by dreams before.

K: Somebody planted the idea in your head that you needed to talk to some one. I remember you saying that.

S: How can I be sure? Don't you keep notes?

K: I'm sure, Jack.

S: Anyway, I don't dream anymore. At least I don't have dream memories. I must be suppressing them. I've eased up on the drinking, too. What do you think of that?

K: Good for you.

S: There are times, lately, when I don't even feel like a drink. I drink out of habit. How do you like that irony?

K: Habits have their degrees.

S: This business with the girl had me preoccupied, took my mind off important things like getting shitfaced every chance I got. One obsession at a time is apparently all I'm capable of handling.

K: So the need isn't as acute?

S: I don't think so. I'm also on the verge of giving up cigarettes. You got a light, Bob?

K: Next, you'll be entering that monastery we talked about.

S: I can think of worse fates. I could grow peas, make scientific breakthroughs.

K: I don't see you in a monastery.

S: Any of the nuns ever come around here, for old time's sake, for nostalgia?

K: I've seen no nuns.

S: How long have you people occupied this place?

K: You make us sound like conquerors. Three years.

S: So what happened to the school? The nuns?

K: Reassigned, I guess. I never saw nun one.

S: You're looking at your watch. My time up, or are you bored, or both?

K: None of the above. Force of habit.

S: Nice, Bob.

K: Thanks.

S: Want to know the real reason I won't come next week?

K: I think I know. All the more reason you should make an effort, force yourself.

S: I don't know, Bob.

K: Force yourself.

S: I'll force myself.

K: See that you do. I'll be very disappointed if you don't show.

S: Yes, Dad.

K: In fact, our time is about up. Next week. Don't forget.

S: How could I forget?

Chapter Forty

"I'll want copies of your final exams for my files."

Winship is testing me. He's worried that I haven't made them up yet.

"Jack? You hear me?"

"Yeah. I'll drop them on your desk this morning."

He wants desperately to ask me what I'm writing, and he's annoyed at me for ignoring him.

"What in God's name are you writing in there?"

"Last will and testament."

Winship chuckled and sipped hot coffee from his Styrofoam cup.

"What will you leave Fairfield High?"

"My legacy is running around breeding in the partitions."

"No sightings for quite a while. Maybe they've struck out for greener pasture."

"They're waiting for a critical mass. Then they'll take over the building. You know, Cynthia hasn't spoken word one to me since that day?"

"Poor Cynthia."

He says poor Cynthia as if she were a child. I never heard him condescend to her before.

"Stop writing in that confounded notebook. Makes me feel like you're taking notes."

"What's a notebook for if not to take notes?"

"Well, just stop it when I'm in your company." Winship laughed. Scanlon heard strain behind it. For Winship's sake, Scanlon closed his notebook. He gazed up at the broken asbestos sleeving on the overhead pipes. In the June heat the room had become clammy, the way it had been in early September when he first set foot in here. The walls perspired. New organic odors arose from the sofa.

"I'll miss this dungeon. This room is one of a kind."

"When the new wing goes on, there'll be a proper teachers' lounge."

"I like this one."

"Easy for you to say, now that you're leaving."

"I'll miss this school, too. I mean it."

"You can change your mind. I mean about staying. Sumner hasn't hired anybody on yet."

"I couldn't do that. Did you mean it when you said you thought I did a good job this year?"

"Yes, I did."

Scanlon opened his notebook. *He's lying. He must be lying.*

Winship said, "There you go again with the damn notebook."

"I got a new way of improving my life. Every time I think about something that pertains to the future I write it down. From now on, think of me as a memo man. And I'm working on organization, too, thanks to you. I'm told that organization is the key to true happiness and fulfillment. Memos are signs of the organized mind, aren't they?"

"Organization is important, but I don't know about the key to happiness." Winship scratched at his cowlick and wrinkled his forehead. "But who's to say it isn't?"

"Not this cowboy."

If I hadn't done the good job he said I had, why would they want me back? Don't tell me, I know the answer. Warm bodies are hard to find these days. Everywhere, teacher shortages. They'll hire anybody who's willing and isn't brain damaged or a convicted felon.

"It could very well be that your memos are the path to good organizational habits, Jack, but I personally find them annoying. Can't you write them in private?"

"Sorry."

Winship wound his wristwatch. "I've got to get behind the desk. Don't forget those final exams."

"I'll have them for you before noon."

This time I'll make you proud of me, Daryl. I have them finished. All I have to do is run them off. There's always the possibility that the mimeo machine will chew up my masters, of course, but you'll have to know that I had the best intentions. Ah, here comes Cynthia. I'll pretend I don't notice her. But she's so fragrant this morning, like rotting gardenias, how could anyone not notice her? She's pretending not to notice me, too. She's making her coffee with her back to me. I'm invisible as far as she's concerned.

Now she's giving me her chinless profile. Is she giving me a second chance? I can play her game. Brave of her to come down here alone, what with all those whiskered carnivores lurking in the building. She could be angry with me for some completely different reason. Who knows how many people I've offended, or how often, without knowing it?

"I think it's rather rude to be taking notes in the presence of a colleague, Mr. Scanlon. Haven't I scolded you before about that?"

"What? Are you addressing me, Miss Sinclair? I must be hearing things."

"I was addressing you, indeed, young man."

"Sorry. I'm not accustomed lately to being addressed by you, Miss Sinclair, so forgive me if I'm rusty in the practice of reply."

"Your sarcasm hasn't gathered any rust, I assure you. And what nonsense are you writing in your silly notebook this time?"

Oh, Cynthia, I want to embrace you. What would you think if you could read this?

"Mr. Scanlon?"

"I know, but it's this new habit of mine. I can't help myself."

"Well, it's a blessed bad habit."

"I'm grateful for anything habitual. Almost anything."

"Oh, you silly man."

Silly man? Surely Samantha couldn't have picked up that expression from Cynthia. Just as surely, Cynthia couldn't be stealing phrases from the imperious Miss Burnham.

"You're doing it again, Mr. Scanlon! You can be so rude. And I'm not sure I've forgiven you for your dreadful rodents."

"That wasn't entirely my fault. There was sabotage."

"They were your responsibility. And the very idea of keeping them in here."

The idea, in this sanctified room, indeed.

"And would you please refrain from scribbling while we are engaged in conversation? As if I haven't reminded you too many times already."

"I'm sorry, Cynthia. For everything. The writing, the rats, last winter, everything."

"Last winter?"

"Daryl's Christmas party. Don't be polite and say you don't remember."

"That?" Cynthia laughed too heartily. "Mr. Scanlon was a little in his cups that evening, wasn't he? Weren't we all?"

"My cup was bigger."

"All that was forgotten a long time ago. Mr. Scanlon, please."

"Sorry." Scanlon put away his pen, and closed his notebook. The closed notebook made him antsy. He fingered the pen in his shirt pocket.

"My, aren't we fidgety this morning."

"Daryl doesn't believe I've written my exams."

"Have you?"

"Of course."

"What makes you think he doesn't believe you?"

"I can tell."

"Land sakes."

He wanted to fling open his notebook and write down "land sakes" for history. Lyle Higgins and Rob Sorenson, of all people, came in. Since the rats' escape, teachers were showing up in the lounge more regularly. Sorenson he hadn't spoken to in ages. There were greetings and a burst of effusiveness from Cynthia. The coach and Lyle Higgins prepared coffee for themselves. Scanlon's hand fell on his notebook.

"He's been warned," Cynthia said to the others, "not to write in his precious notebook in the presence of his colleagues. Haven't you, Jack?"

"Yes ma'am." Sorenson flashed one of his low-watt smiles, the kind one uses for jokes one doesn't get. Scanlon would have written that down if he could. Lyle had on one of his tight-fitting, short-sleeved shirts and a plaid bow tie. His forearm muscles rippled as he stirred his coffee. Sorenson had on a white shirt and knit tie. He combed his straight, black hair over one side of his skull like Adolph Hitler. As a stereotypical jock it was too easy to compare him to someone like Hitler, but Scanlon would still like to see what he looked like with a small mustache.

Cynthia used her hands actively when she talked. It was to her credit that she was able to keep from splashing coffee over everybody within range. She was back to Styrofoam, Scanlon noticed. What happened to Snoopy? Styrofoam with red lipstick stains on the rim would be etched in Scanlon's memory for a long time. This morning it had the power of invoking nostalgia in him.

"Got your exams made up yet?" Higgins asked Scanlon with that playful needling he'd grown accustomed to getting from the math teacher.

"Plenty of time for that."

Higgins chuckled. Not a bad shit, after his fashion, Scanlon would have written had he been permitted access to his notebook.

"Glad I don't have to make up exams," Sorenson announced, tempting Scanlon to make a crack about Sorenson's ability to write exams even if he were required to. But Scanlon was at thirty's threshold and he must learn the art of restraint.

"We all know that coaches don't know how to write," Cynthia said, with absolutely no malice.

Sorenson smiled like the village idiot. Could it be true, Scanlon thought, that jocks were a breed of moron? Or was he simply harboring an old grudge for the Sorenson who had gone behind his back about his use of the gym? All he had was Stambaugh's word for that.

"Year's gone before you know it was there," Higgins said. He looked almost wistful, staring into his coffee cup. No, wistful and Higgins were as alien as Sorenson and verbal communication. Oh, to have his notebook!

"Yes," Cynthia murmured, "we'll all soon be old and out to pasture."

"Speak for yourselves," Sorenson said with a laugh.

Even as he crowded the big three-O, Scanlon didn't feel particularly old. To Samantha and her dirty companions he was practically an old geezer.

Cynthia and Lyle talked about their summer plans. Sorenson sat at the table looking into his own coffee cup with a goofy half smile that was probably inspired by an ill-formed sense of nostalgia. Was he still angry with Scanlon and his extra-help kids for scuffing up his precious floor? Did he actually see evidence of damage? Scanlon had never gone back to the gym floor to check. Why hadn't he?

Scanlon surreptitiously flipped open his notebook while Cynthia and Higgins were engaged in conversation and Sorenson was preoccupied with his inner life. He reached for his ballpoint.

I just had this most wicked thought, along with an image of Cynthia and Lyle going at it in the dry goods storeroom. Didn't I have a dream along those lines once? Why didn't I check the stupid gym floor myself? What was going on in my head at the time? What do they talk about, Rob, and Jackie, and the baby? I'm an uncharitable son-of-a-bitch. Here come Josh and Winship. Haven't seen Stambaugh in maybe a week, and it's been so long since I've laid eyes on Lillian I couldn't say for sure that she still exists. Patterson's giving me the once over, wondering, like everyone else, if I'm writing nasty things about him in here. Time for homeroom. I'll get back to you.

"Why don't you plan to come over to the house after graduation? Doug will be there. We'll perform a postmortem on the year," Patterson said to Scanlon on the stairs. Scanlon was taken off guard and was stuck for a quick reply. "What do you say? Bring some chips and a six-pack. We've got the new Hair album."

"Is that like a hair shirt? Thanks, but I'll have to get back to you. There's another thing I may have to do."

Patterson looked down the barrel of his long nose at Scanlon, skeptical of Scanlon's other "thing."

"Rache wants to give you guys a little send-off. I hope you can make it. She'd be disappointed if you didn't come."

"I'll have to see."

Homeroom was bristling with end-of-the-year energy. Kids milled around the lab benches, had chairs turned for head-to-head conversations, hung out the windows and shouted at the shop kids on the ramp below. Scanlon stood behind the lecture desk and watched them, waiting for his mere presence to be felt and order to be instantaneously restored. He opened his notebook.

Some authority figure. These kids think of me more as one of them than a teacher. Or do they? I'm neither an authority figure nor one of them. What does that make me? If Winship walked in now they'd be in their seats in a flash, mouths shut, hands folded on their desktops.

Scanlon dropped his chemistry textbook on the floor to get their attention. The book's impact he could barely hear over the noise.

"Shut up and sit down," he yelled. A few heads turned in his direction, then turned away as if he were invisible. Nobody sat down, nobody shut up. Scanlon moved out into the room and accosted individuals. By the time he got everybody seated, if not quiet, the bell rang for first period.

"I hope you all suffer unbearable pain in your lives," he shouted after them, his shout feeble against their exuberance.

Why don't these little shits take me seriously? And now I have to face the darling sophomores. Oh, Lillian, how right you were. I'll miss you, Romeo Boudreau. I hope you smother in cow shit. Denise, will I ever know the truth about the rats? I know in my heart of hearts that it was you. But you'll take the knowledge to your grave you demented child. Tommy Winship, I hope you outgrow your natural sneer because it's not at all becoming. Was I as surly at that age? As callous, as callow?

"Why don't we have class outside today?" Rachel Perkins asked fourth period.

Scanlon closed his notebook. "Thanks for that observation, Romeo." Romeo grinned as if to say fuck you, Scanlon, with your sarcasm.

"We could go for a nature walk," Junior Darling offered.

"Nature's not all it's cracked up to be," Scanlon said. "I'd think you'd be concerned about the final exam. There's a lot of material to review in three days. What do you say we get going?"

"What the hell's the use of final exams?" Romeo asked out loud of no one in particular, and Scanlon thought, with a stab of sadness, of Danny Picard.

"I still don't understand the law of the heart," someone said, and Scanlon, his own heart weighty in his chest, tried to explain Starling's principle.

I'm making it my business to drop in on Stambaugh this afternoon. Too bad if he doesn't want to see me. Nothing I can do about what he wants, is there, Bob? What am I going to do with myself next year? I've forgotten. Did I tell someone I was going to graduate school? Don't you have to apply first? Romeo and I have this one thing in common. We both loathe and detest school.

Loved the look on Winship's face when I dumped my final exams on his desk. He even offered Trudy's services in running them off. I wouldn't mind Trudy on loan; I wouldn't waste her talents on the mimeograph machine. Listen to me! I'll never learn, will I, Bob? Will SB show for study hall today? Is she deliberately avoiding me now? If she is, perhaps I should feel triumphant, but what I feel is a dullness, a nothing. A part of me wants to go to Patterson's party after graduation. It's my birthday, the end of my youth. Why not a party? I could have one more go at Rachel.

I'll miss this old sofa, the smell of mildew, the springs up my ass. I'll miss the flies in the fall, the flaking asbestos in winter, the great coffee. I half expect to see Danny push through the door, a case of evaporated milk on his shoulder. I can see his shit-eating grin, his tiny dark eyes full of inside dope on our secret lives. Did he really know anything about SB and me? He would have never opened his mouth if he did. To needle me in study hall with his smirks and innuendo would have been enough for him. They should hang that Hollis Trimble fucker. What gives him the right, just because he's looney-tunes, to go around plugging eighteen-year-old kids planning to get married? Hang him in public in case there are other crazies out there thinking about doing the same thing. How do you like that for law and order, Dick? Make me attorney general, I'll clean up your streets. I'll make last summer in Chicago look like a show of solidarity between the cops and the yippies. Look who's here? This has got to be more than coincidence.

"Hello, Jack. Still scribbling in the notebook?"

"Doug Stambaugh. Long time no see. Would you believe me if I told you I was going to pay you a visit this afternoon?"

"Oh?"

"No shit."

Stambaugh looked a little dazed.

"You flying?" Scanlon asked and Stambaugh looked even more puzzled. "You heading for the border?"

"Right after graduation. Saturday to be exact. I hope you're planning to come to Josh's party."

"You're really going through with it? Congratulations, friend. You've got gonads."

"Thanks for saying so. I'm frightened, I don't mind telling you."

"Who wouldn't be?"

"Somehow I imagined you wouldn't be."

"You're shitting me."

"I'll miss this place, in spite of everything. I'll really miss it." Stambaugh searched the ceiling for what it was about the place he'd miss. For once, Scanlon understood.

"What'll you miss most?"

"The cafeteria lunches."

"Ah, yes. Those soggy peanut butter and jelly sandwiches should provide nostalgia for many years."

"Oddly, I'll miss the kids. I know I've said some unflattering things about them, but this spring I've come to see them in a different light."

"No more Hitler Youth in this new light?"

"On the contrary. They're decent, thoughtful people. I've really grown to respect them."

"Good for you, Doug."

"I envy you their respect."

"I suppose you've got everything packed and organized. Seems like you've been living out of boxes since last winter."

"I've packed and unpacked twice since the last time you were up. I'm shipping everything I can't get in the car to my parents."

"They approve of what you're doing?"

"Dad doesn't, of course. Given who he is, I'm not surprised. Mother is behind me. In a way, she's relieved."

"Is there going to be some way to correspond with you?" What a joke, Scanlon corresponding with anyone.

"As soon as I'm settled, I'll be in touch with people. What are your plans?"

"Nothing definite. Maybe a little yachting, some polo, the usual stuff. When I'm bored with all that, I'll choose another career. I haven't made up my mind between law, medicine, or nuclear physics."

"I'm still curious about the notebook."

"Dear diary? It wouldn't interest you."

"My interest is piqued nevertheless."

"Sorry. You know how it is with diaries, you've got a sister, right?"

"She never kept a diary, to my knowledge."

"You know, Doug, you're the only person I've ever met who drinks straight hot water. What do you get out of plain hot water?"

"Warmth."

"Coffee and tea are warm."

"Water soothes me. Coffee and tea have the opposite effect. The way marijuana has no effect on you."

"Interesting."

"Isn't it strange how all of sudden the year is over, vanished?"

"Very strange, indeed. I remember very little of it to tell you the truth."

"Perhaps that's why you've become a diarist. So you won't forget entire years again."

"I doubt it. This won't last. Too much effort. What are memories for if not to be selective? Most of the crap that happens isn't worth remembering."

"I should be going. I have letters to write."

"Farewell letters?"

"Sort of. See you, Jack."

Chapter Forty-one

Ira was reading the paper at the kitchen table when Scanlon got home; Alice was on the sofa in front of the *Merv Griffin Show*. Scanlon's first thought was that his uncle was home early because of illness.

"You all right, Ira?" Scanlon asked his uncle.

"Oh, yeah. Slow at the shop this time of year. Got sick of hanging around with nothing to do. Punched out early."

Scanlon laughed, the idea of his uncle punching out early striking him as absurd.

"Mr. Rockefeller can punch out an hour early if he feels like it," Alice shouted from the living room. "What's an hour's wages to a rich man?"

Ira winked. "Mother's pissed."

"Goddamn right mother's pissed." Alice stood in the doorway now, beer bottle in hand, hair in curlers, and dressed in her bathrobe and slippers. It was her Merv Griffin outfit. And she looked pissed, too, her eyes narrowed, jaw quivering. In fact, Scanlon hadn't seen her looking this angry since that night at the American Legion when Ira wanted to go home early and all Alice wanted to do was drink shots and beers, and dance. That night she'd been drunk. She wasn't drunk now. Scanlon had never actually been present when Alice and Ira squabbled over money, and this scene was a painful reminder of how irresponsible he'd been all year, living off these people like a parasite. He didn't believe for a minute that Ira had punched out early because there was no work for him to do. His uncle looked pale; even his wink lacked vitality. And Alice, no doubt, saw the same thing. Out of fear, she'd gone on the attack. Having had her say, Alice turned and went back to Merv, her correspondent.

"Don't pay no attention to her," Ira said, folding the paper against his chest. "We're having supper at Althea's. Why don't you come along."

"Thanks, but I've got a ton of work to do tonight."

"Althea's not that bad a cook."

"I know that. I also know what happens at the Goodwins after the eating is over. I've got final exams to make up." Scanlon lied about the exams, and for once he didn't have a lot of papers stacked up waiting for grades. He didn't feel equal to an evening with Willie and Althea, however.

"May be the last time you get to see them, if you're bound and determined to leave after school's over."

"All right, but remind me when I'm matching Willie with shots and beers that I've got work to do."

"Sure thing."

Upstairs, Scanlon found a letter from his mother on the bureau.

Willie and Althea were roaring drunk and in the middle of a loud, hoarse argument when Scanlon arrived, just after his aunt and uncle. Donny and little Dave were stretched out on the living room floor watching TV, deaf apparently to the vile threats and scurrilous insults being passed back and forth between their sodden parents. Scanlon's impulse was to bolt. He'd anticipated such a scene, which was why he'd driven here in his own car—in case he had to make a separate escape.

"Jesus Christ," Alice said, drawing out the words, "you two at it again?"

"I'm not takin' no more of her shit," Willie said, flashing his vicious grin.

"Then why don't you take your ass down to the VFW to your girlfriends, you cocksucker." Althea gave Willie her falsetto voice for "girlfriends."

The odor of good cooking filled the room. Scanlon marveled at Althea's ability to function in the midst of such quarreling with her husband. Katie had been a lot like that. Some of her most creative housekeeping got done in the middle of a pitched battle with Scanlon.

"Come on, Mother," Ira said, "let's go home."

"You better not leave, you son-of-a-bitch," Althea cried, her eyes bloodshot and watery. She was getting a tummy. Pregnant? Ira? She had on the same tight-fitting, mohair sweater she wore that Thanksgiving morning and here it was June, and hot enough tonight to be July. She must have believed it turned Ira on.

Willie had on his green work pants, mud-caked boots and a khaki T-shirt. His big-knuckled hand surrounded a beer bottle. On the coffee table was a bottle of Canadian Club, no glasses. The top was off the bottle. No one had yet offered Scanlon or Alice a drink. The last few days had been so filled with the business of making up exams that Scanlon hadn't had time to think much about drinking. Nor had he made time to think about it. He wasn't too busy now. He couldn't take his eyes off the whiskey, and he despised Canadian Club. Willie intercepted his stare, grabbed the bottle by the neck and thrust it at him.

"Glass in the kitchen, you want," Willie the mind reader said. Willie gave his wife a hateful look, and Althea gave him back in kind. Scanlon hurried into the kitchen with the whiskey not so much to fetch a glass as to get out of the crossfire. He poured himself half a water glass full of CC and leaned against the sink, glad to be away from the maelstrom in the living room. He sipped whiskey and swallowed cautiously. The CC left fire in its wake. He went to the refrigerator for a cold beer chaser. The back door was inviting, but to run out under these circumstances would not win him any points with Alice. Ira would understand, but Alice and Althea would be hurt. Who knew how Willie would take it? What was left for Scanlon to do except get drunk? If he'd thought to bring his notebook, he could have been chronicling all this instead of merely getting loaded.

Alice and Althea came into the kitchen. It looked like another men-in-one-room-women-in-the-other night.

"I won't sit at the supper table with that bastard," Althea said, her voice thick, her words slurred. Alice had an arm around her sister's waist.

"Get me a beer, will you, Johnny? Better put a shot with it. Not that CC."

"Velvet's under the sink," Althea said. Scanlon got Alice a beer out of the fridge, the Black Velvet private stock from under the sink.

"Pour Althea one," Alice said. Scanlon did as he was told.

"I'd better go see what's going on in the other room," Scanlon said, delivering the drinks to the women, who sat across from each other at the kitchen table like negotiators.

"Thanks, Johnny," Althea said with a wan smile.

Willie lay out full length on his side on the sofa. Ira sat in his favorite straight-back chair way across the room. They looked at TV and from the silence Scanlon could tell that Ira was not pleased with Willie. Perhaps it was Willie who was not pleased with Ira. Had he caught his wife in an afternoon tryst with his brother-in-law and former drinking buddy? Scanlon was very glad he was on his way out of their lives, as much as he loved Alice and his uncle and these pathetic Goodwins. Somewhere there had to be less chaotic lives for him to share.

"Johnny," Willie mumbled in greeting.

"Willie."

"How's the prince of poon tang?"

"I'm all right, Willie. Yourself?"

"Happier'n a pig in shit."

"Dad," Donny whispered, "we're tryin' to watch the show."

"Don't Dad me, you little shit. You ain't careful I'll lay a strap acrost your ass." Donny was silenced. Scanlon wondered if Willie ever actually had to take a hand to his kids. His menacing voice seemed adequate to strike terror in the heart of any child, sufficient to maintain order and discipline. Althea he couldn't imagine hitting anyone except Willie.

Bill Scanlon had struck his stepson only once. Young Scanlon had it coming to him, too. Bill Scanlon had been an unconscionable thief in his time, but when his stepson had tested the waters of petty theft and was caught, Bill Scanlon reacted like the village chieftain. He struck Jack a vicious backhand across the face. Jack had been fifteen. He held his tears back in defiance, and Bill Scanlon seemed to cave in. He hit him only that once and later told him that it had not been easy for him to do. Pounding on Billy and Keith had come easily enough to him, but Jack, because he wasn't his flesh and blood, didn't hit so easy. Jack Scanlon learned something about passive resistance that day then promptly forgot it.

Poor Willie. Poor Althea. The poor Goodwin family should be on emotional welfare, the way he'd been all year with Bob Kennedy.

"Think we'll get fed tonight, Ira?" Willie asked with his phlegmy laugh.

"Don't look good." Ira's reply was clenched, his voice brittle. Scanlon hadn't seen Ira angry all year. He couldn't remember ever seeing him mad at anyone.

"Hand us over the jug." Willie reached out his hand and Scanlon passed him the bottle.

Willie raised the bottle to his lips and took several long gurgling swallows, as if he were drinking soda pop. He wiped his mouth with the back of his hand like the tough guys in the movies. Was this Willie showing his upset? By acting like a swine? Reflexively, Scanlon drained his glass; again the CC went down like a flamethrower. He belched and almost threw up. He had to kick out a wad of saliva and swallow like a fiend to keep from tossing on Willie's living room floor which would have been a most unmanly thing to do. Eyes watering, insides erupting, Scanlon felt very much like a pig himself. It was dark enough in the room with the shades drawn that his distress passed unnoticed. Scanlon settled his stomach with a swallow of beer. He leaned back and relaxed, blessedly drunk.

Was this the way it would always be with the Goodwins? At each other until they died of exhaustion? What was to become of Ira and Alice? Ira was ill, Scanlon just knew it. If Ira were to go, Alice would not survive long, even with her considerable extended family. They were the kind of married couple who followed each other closely to the grave.

"What're you brooding about over there, Johnny? Here, have a snort." Willie dangled the near empty bottle from his first two fingers. Scanlon splashed a little whiskey in his glass and swirled it carefully, as if it were explosive. He sipped. No more chug-a-lug for him with rotgut. "You look like your goddamn dog died," Willie said. "Cheer up."

Alice stuck her head in the room to announce that they could come in and eat anytime they wanted. It was serve yourself tonight. The boys leaped up off the floor and sprinted to the kitchen. Ira lifted himself off his chair. Did Scanlon see a grimace of pain on his face? It was too dark to tell for sure, but it looked to him like getting out of the chair caused his uncle some pain. Willie held fast to the sofa. Scanlon wasn't hungry. Neither was he comfortable alone in the room with Willie. He wouldn't have been comfortable alone in the room with anybody. He knew he shouldn't have come tonight.

"You going to eat, Willie?" Scanlon asked, getting up.

"Not in the same room with that bitch."

"Come on, Willie. Come on in and eat."

"You go ahead. I'm stayin' right where I am."

Donny and Dave were hunched over their plates at the kitchen table, literally shoveling lasagna into their maws. Althea sat on a stool by the cupboard, smoking a cigarette and drinking a beer. Her face was swollen and mascara streaked down her cheeks. Ira and Alice must have been in the dining room where Althea had set up a buffet table.

"Get yourself something to eat, Johnny."

"I'm not really hungry, Althea. Maybe I'll wait."

Althea shrugged her shoulders. His appetite, or lack of it, was of no concern to her tonight. Donny and Dave snorted over their food like two little hogs. Maybe the Goodwin household was a pigpen after all. Scanlon got another beer out of the refrigerator.

"Wanna go bowlin' after we eat, Johnny?" Donny asked, mouth rimmed with tomato sauce. Scanlon hadn't seen much of the Goodwin boys since Thanksgiving. Donny had changed; he looked older, like a little boy transported prematurely into old age. His jaw line had lengthened since November, and he was beginning to take on his father's sharp features—mouth, nose, and jaw. And his hair was still crew cut which accentuated the geometry of his aging face. How old was he? Ten? Ten going on thirty-five. Not mentally. Donny grinned at Scanlon with his lasagna face, and Scanlon swore he looked crazy.

"How's school?"

Donny's old face sagged. "Boring. All you do all day is sit around."

"You could try once in a while to understand what's going on," Althea said from her stool. "He's so goddamn hyper. Can't sit still five minutes at a time. Grow up stupid like his father."

"Don't feel like sittin' around all day," Donny mumbled into his plate, eyes downcast, as if he didn't like hearing about himself and school any more than he liked sitting around all day.

Dave stifled a laugh, his mouth crammed with food.

"And you ain't no Abe Lincoln, neither, mister," Althea said to Dave.

Scanlon wondered what Alice and Ira were doing in the other room. He hadn't seen Alice take food in so long. Could she be feeding secretly? She was down to eighty-five pounds he'd overheard her say to Althea. She simply had no appetite. Beer was all that kept her going—beer and butts. Scanlon was tempted to look in on his uncle to see if at least he still had some appetite. The day Ira didn't pack it away was the day Scanlon knew for sure that he was a sick man. But then Ira was in the room rubbing his belly, an empty and soiled plate in his hand.

"That good," he said to Althea with his impish grin. Alice followed, plateless, beer in one hand, cigarette in the other. She looked preoccupied, distracted by something. What was up? Ira? The Goodwin's ongoing domestic fracas was like a script from one of Alice's afternoon TV melodramas. He hoped it was the Goodwins who had her out of sorts and not Ira's failing health. Where was Eddie, the youngest, Billy the oldest? What kind of family was this, with people going this way and that?

"Well, folks," Scanlon announced, "I've got to be shoving off. *Mucho* work to do."

No one protested. No one suggested that he stay just a little longer. No one seemed to even hear him. He stood by the kitchen table for a while, peeling his beer label, feeling stupid, ill at ease, out of place. He finished his beer and bid everyone good-bye again.

"You didn't eat nothing," Althea observed in her flat, full-of-grief voice.

"Nothing to do with your cooking, Althea. Just one of those not hungry nights."

"Come back if you want. There's plenty. Shithead in there won't eat nothin' just to spite me."

"Thanks, Althea."

Only when he was behind the wheel did Scanlon think that maybe this could be the last time he'd ever see the Goodwins. He felt mildly anxious because he'd left so unceremoniously, and for a moment considered going back inside to say good-bye properly. But he just drove away. And though he tried not to give the matter any further thought, it became self-evident to Scanlon that what he had witnessed at the Goodwins tonight, and every other day or night he had been in their company in the months that he had lived here, was what they were. Furthermore, whatever it was that ate at Ira and Alice was likely to have no lasting effect on their lives either. It was the kind of stasis that he dreaded, the subtle imprisonment that had no doubt driven him away from his own marriage, as ill-fated as it was anyway.

So he drove into a lovely sunset that had everything bathed in a purplish light; the kind of twilight that could offer new hope, if only for a moment. He should have driven around the back roads, savored this rare light. Instead, he drove straight home, home to his notebook and his inner world where the light had been dim for so long.

Chapter Forty-two

We'll be down here in Lyle Higgins' classroom all morning recording exams and final grades, deciding on who should receive academic honors at graduation tomorrow night. I'm the first one here if you can believe that. My kids didn't do so badly on their finals. I must have made the exams too easy. It's all over now. It's hot down here, the temperature outside already in the mid-seventies and it's not even nine o'clock. Everything ending like this is very strange. I would have thought there'd be more to it than this. Maybe the graduation ceremony will do it. I haven't ruled out going to the Pattersons tomorrow night. Here comes Sophie Metcalf, of all people. Have I spoken three words to her all year?

"Mornin'."

"Good morning, Sophie." *Sophie looks so sad this morning. Even librarians get it. Why shouldn't they? I hear kids give her tons of shit in the library, and in her study hall. She makes the mistake of rising to their bait. She gets pissed at them and yells and throws them in detention for whispering or chewing gum. Kids leave notes on her desk quoting prices on mouthwash and make mean cracks about her dragon breath. They love to hate Sophie the way they get off dumping on old Lillian Bloemer, only Lillian's tough and cynical and Sophie's really a marshmallow underneath her stone-faced exterior. She takes everything the kids hand her personally. She's dying to ask me what I'm writing. Poor woman wouldn't know how to ask such a question. She's wondering, who is this person with the mustache in Vermont? I've seen him around here and there this year, but I have no idea who he is. I'm the guy who pinch-hit for you on detention duty that time you went home with a migraine. One lousy kid. I was half way home and had to turn around and come back for one lousy kid. Remember? Did I get a thank you? Poor Sophie with her migraines. Here come my colleagues. Bye-bye for now.*

Well, it has finally arrived, the day you've been dreading all year. Happy Birthday! You're thirty and over the hill. Still, it's a glorious day, if a little on the muggy side. Do you feel any different today at thirty than you did yesterday at twenty-nine years, three hundred and sixty-four days?

Yes, I do feel a little different, wise guy, if you have to know. It's not so easy to explain but somewhere, probably in my groin, something feels different.

You've been set up by expectation. A few hours can't make any physiological difference unless it's the time that a nice family of cancer cells goes into bloom. They have to have their beginning, like everything else. But don't let me depress you.

I refuse to let this depress me. I take it back. I don't feel any different at all.

Remember when you reached puberty? When you sprouted hair on your balls, the way Eddie Leclerc always promised you would?

Can't say that I do.

Well, I remember. You were so full of yourself you spent maybe an hour in the bathroom playing with your whang, running your fingers through your new pubic hair thinking, I'm a man, I'm a man. Look where your whang got you.

How can you remember something like that?

I remember.

How reliable do you think your memory is?

It gets me by.

When did you first get the sense that there was no hope?

I can't give you dates and times, only ballpark.

I'll settle for ballpark.

When we went to live with our mother.

Would it have made any difference, do you think, if we had known then what we know about our father?

Who knows? Do you believe her story? How does it make you feel to know that you're the product of a gang rape?

I'm more devastated by the fact that she thinks the guy that shot the magic bullet was named Henry Bascomb! Henry fucking Bascomb! I can't accept that my father would have such a pedestrian name.

Looks don't lie. Wonder where the old boy is now? She mentioned that he'd shipped out to Pearl. Maybe he got wiped out in the sneak attack. What if he was on the Arizona or something?

This is not the way I imagined it, not the way at all.

It only goes to show that you're woefully deficient in imagination along with everything else.

We should tell Bob about this news. He would want to know. In a way he deserves to know.

No.

Why not?

I can't say. I agree, he does deserve to know, what with everything we've put him through all these months. It's just that something tells me we should keep this to ourselves. Bob's given us the confidence to get on with the rest of it on our own.

Spare me.

You asked.

Should we at least say good-bye to Bob? Keep our appointment?

No.

Why not?

We hate good-byes. Remember?

Bob will be disappointed. He'll blame himself.

I know.

We just go? No how do you do, nice to have met you, see you later?

That's right. We just go.

What about tonight? What about the Pattersons?

We stay away from there, too. We say our good-byes at the handshaking then we split. We don't look back.

You're one cold son-of-a-bitch.

Don't you mean one cold bastard?

What about Alice and Ira? We leave them cold?

Let's not think about them. We just go, all right? How many times do I have to say it?

Why don't we get out of here? We're going nowhere with this conversation. What do you say we go over and do a final lab cleanup? We wouldn't want to leave our pal, Winship, with a bad taste.

Yeah, let's do that.

It's way too hot in here. The men are taking off their jackets first thing, those that are wearing jackets. Most of them look like they just finished their chores and didn't bother to change clothes. Ventilation system's on the fritz again. Smiles, the stupid shit, is running around acting like he knows what he's doing which he does not. On stage there's a lectern with a reading lamp and mike attached. Cynthia all gussied up for the occasion (in her usual bad taste), pacing back and forth in front of the stage like a cat, actually wringing her hands. Winship leaning against the edge of the stage talking to featured speaker, a big guy dressed in dark, pin-striped, three-piece suit. He looks cool in it while everyone around him sweats likes horses. Big, wide, florid face. Montpelier lawyer Patterson says, ex-jarhead, Korea, law-and-order buff. Winship's cowlick acting up; he's sweating through the underarms of his favorite green jacket. Sweating myself, hands all clammy, I can barely hold my pen. Don't dare take off jacket. Shirt plastered to my body. Higgins sitting next to me. Has all he can do not to lean over for a peek at what I'm writing. Made to sit on these ass-numbing metal chairs. All they do is draw the sweat out of your butt. Could be a very long evening ahead. No sign of the seniors. Band in place down on the floor in front of stage. Cynthia reading over her list of names she'll call for diplomas, as she's done for maybe last twenty years. Has to be close to seven o'clock. More bodies here than I would have guessed. Getting more restless by the minute, fanning themselves with programs. A hick in the back row just yelled, get this show on the road.

Pattersons are in the row in front of me. Doug's with them. Exchanged polite nods, a little grin from Rachel, my fairest Rachel. Higgins wants to say something to me.

"Damn," Higgins said as the lights went out. "Just what we need in this heat. Guess you won't be taking any more notes now, will you, Mr. Scanlon."

"Guess not. This is kind of funny. I'd laugh if I didn't think it would consume too much oxygen."

"Goddamn Smiles. Don't know his ass from a hole in the ground. He's been fooling with the electrical circuits. That nincompoop's to blame for this."

Emergency spotlights came on over the exits. Catcalls and hoots and cynical comments from the irate audience filled the gym. Winship jumped on stage and attempted to speak into the mike. He was greeted with boos and more catcalls. He tapped the dead mike with his forefinger. With only emergency lights for illumination, he looked ghostly.

"I'd better go see what the hell's going on," Higgins said, standing up. Scanlon would have offered to go with him, but he wouldn't have been much help with a broken down electrical system. As if Higgins, rising out of his chair, had cued the band, they started playing, the musicians squinting at their sheet music in the poor light, turning out a lot of errant notes and choppy rhythm. Scanlon didn't recognize the piece, but it was meant to be a rousing march with flourishes. Loud enough to compete with the disgruntled parents, friends, and relatives milling around the gym floor, and that was all Winship desired for the moment. Then the band abruptly segued to "Pomp and Circumstance" as the seniors filed on stage from the wings, capped and gowned, bearing, each of them, a single white taper, casting their faces in eerie, sepulchral light. Scanlon worried about wax runoff.

Higgins had remained standing in front of his chair, never getting off on his mission to save the evening from electrical disaster.

"I'll be damned," he said. "That's nice."

"Looks like Cynthia's touch," Scanlon said. Then the lights came back on. The fickle audience groaned its displeasure.

"That's too bad," Higgins said. Then the overhead fans began to whir and this brought a cheer from the crowd. On stage, the seniors blew out their candles and placed them carefully beside their chairs, arranged in a semi-circle, an arc that spanned the full width of the stage, giving the illusion that there were more of them than there actually were. Thirty-seven seniors were listed in the Fairfield High class of 1969, a list that included Danny Picard. When they were seated, Scanlon noticed that there were two empty chairs. It didn't take him long to realize that the other missing senior was Samantha Burnham. A mass of emotion formed in Scanlon's throat. The lights were on, so he opened his notebook.

What is this feeling? Where is Samantha? Metal chair conspicuously empty, the way the little square in the yearbook where her photograph should be is empty. The way Danny's chair is empty. Where is she? Takes sang-froid to skip your high school graduation. Off with the hippies, that's where she is. Can she lose her diploma for not showing? Would she care? What is this thing lodged in my chest? Thirty years old today. I'm having a heart attack. The hippies have been right all along.

Robbie Trishman, valedictorian, stepping to the lectern, unfolding a piece of paper. He speaks in a low, measured voice. I don't remember such depth, such resonance. He's worried about social injustice. He cites lyrics from a song by some rock group called Spanky and Our Gang. All about view of some black city ghetto from train. Now, he's on the country's case over illegal, immoral war in Vietnam. Here come the catcalls. Stambaugh's jaw working overtime; the sneak has been coaching Robbie. Hicks squirming in their sweaty pants. Not the message they want from their valedictorian.

Winship's head bowed. He's wondering, why didn't I look at Robbie's speech? It's all over. He's finished. Short, sweet to some ears, and to the point. Applause too thin to be even called polite, except for Robbie's classmates, clapping and stomping their feet. A few even raise fists. Stambaugh and Patterson banging the flesh, wild-eyed.

Here comes the war hero, decorated in Korea. Smug-looking, red-faced bastard in his pin-stripes. Tosses a condescending look over his shoulder at Robbie and the other seniors, shakes his head as if he's witnessing something distasteful. Whips out a huge, white hanky and mops his big face, like Satchmo. Pulls this folded paper out of his vest pocket like a dramatic jackass, then puts it back. Where have I seen this act before? Looks back at Robbie then plants his elbows on the lectern, mike practically in his big mouth.

Listen to the prick attack Robbie, calling him a fuzzy-headed liberal. Such an original thing to say, like the fact that he wants everybody to think he's shooting from the hip with his speech now that the prepared text is back in his pocket. Stambaugh's jaw back in motion. Patterson's head going back and forth like a metronome . Rachel leans over every two seconds to whisper in his ear. The jarhead is on a roll: attacks the hippies, the doves in Congress, people with eccentric hair growth. Is he looking at me? He's defending Mayor Daley and his storm troopers, law and order. Audience getting restless again. Guy in the back yells for him to sit down and dry up. They're not impatient with the blowhard's message; they just want out of this oven. They need fresh air. The big guy's into a rant now, sweat pouring out of his glands, down his face. Here comes the hanky. Guy needs a trumpet. Winship ought to gaff this jerk off stage. More shouting from the audience for him to quit. He finally does. Cheers for the end of the speech. Diplomas are awarded. People stampede the exit. Parents climbing on stage to congratulate their kids.

Seniors have to line up on front walk for handshaking with faculty. Can I say good-bye, shake their clammy hands? I'm feeling a little panic. Who are these kids?

"Too bad the man had to run off at the mouth at an occasion like this," Higgins said. "He had no business singling Robbie out like that. Just because he's right doesn't excuse it."

"Higgins, you sentimental slob."

"Your hand's going to drop off you keep writing in that thing. Why don't you put it down, be sociable for a change."

"Sorry, Lyle. There are a lot of things I have to get down while there's still time."

"Time? What's the hurry? You got a terminal condition?"

"No more than anybody else. I meant time before we have to go outside for handshaking."

"What in the name of Christ are you writing in there?"

"Personal stuff."

"Well, if you want my opinion, you're wasting your time. And it makes people think you're snubbing them, that you're uppity and making fun of them. Like talking behind their back."

"Is that what people think? It's not like that. I don't mean to be rude."

"Well, it is rude, so put it away and let's go out and say our farewells."

"I'm not sure I'm up to it."

"Not up to what? A Vietnam veteran not up to saying good-bye to a few kids? I don't buy it. Come on, let's go." Higgins put his vise grip on Scanlon's arm and pulled him out of his chair. "How would it look to the kids if their favorite teacher wasn't there to shake their hand on the most important night of their lives?"

Scanlon tucked his notebook under his arm.

"Leave that," Higgins commanded.

"Leave what?"

"The notebook. Leave the goddamn thing on the chair. You don't want to be lugging it around while you're shaking people's hands. It don't look right. Just leave it there on the chair until after this is finished."

"I can't. What if someone takes it?"

"Who the hell would want it? Do like I say. Leave it on the chair. It'll be there when you come back."

Scanlon looked back at his notebook on the gray metal chair, as he filed out of the gym behind Higgins. He looked back and worried.

Outside in the warm June evening, clean and refreshing after the fetid closeness of the gymnasium, people stood around talking, smoking, laughing, swatting mosquitoes. Lighted paper lanterns rigged on long poles were strung along the handshaking route which began at the front entrance, flanked right over the lawn, and ended in the parking lot. The seniors, still in academic regalia, were starting to form a receiving line to shake hands with their teachers and friends. All that was needed was a signal from someone in authority for it to begin. Where was Winship? Cynthia? Thirty-five seniors waited, some hugging and crying, others laughing it up, yelling out war whoops with a toss of their mortarboards in the air. There should have been thirty-seven. Danny was gone, Samantha a no-show.

Winship came into view, looking harried and confused as if he'd never gone through such an experience before. He steered people here and there by the elbow. What was so difficult about getting people started down this simple handshaking gauntlet?

"I'd better go see what I can do to get things started," Higgins said, and left Scanlon standing by himself with a strong urge to make a run for it. He couldn't go through with this. He was thirty. Thirty years old.

High thin clouds passed across the moon nearly full tonight. Something on the hill beside the school caught his eye, the hill on which stood the elementary school and Sumner Purnells' office. Scanlon made out three figures silhouetted in the moonlight. Yes, three people. Samantha and two others. No doubt that it was Samantha with her diaphanous white peasant dress and her wild blonde hair. And the other two? Who else but her hippie friends? Samantha had her elbow up on the shoulder of one of them, from that distance he couldn't tell which one. They passed a joint between them; he could see the intermittent glow as they toked. Samatha witnessing her high school graduation from the hill. Scanlon hesitated, then stepped to the head of the receiving line to say his good-byes, to pass through to the end of that line if it was the last thing he did.

The End

Michael Burns was born in St. Johnsbury, Vermont. His family moved to New Hampshire in 1950 where he attended high school, graduating in 1957. He deferred entrance to college, and served in the U.S. Navy for four years, seeing duty in the Far East in the early days of the Vietnam War. After mustering out of the Navy, Burns returned to New Hampshire where he met and married his wife, and matriculated into the University of New Hampshire.

Encouraged by his freshman English teacher, Burns first became interested in writing fiction in 1963. He continued writing after being inspired by the late Thomas Williams, National Book Award-winning author and mentor to many young writers, among them John Irving.

In 1971, Burns joined the faculty of St. Paul's School, a college preparatory boarding school in Concord, New Hampshire, where he continues to teach chemistry and life science. He lives there with his wife Nancy, and is at work on another novel, *Where You Are*. *Gemini* is Burns' first novel.

Portrait by Wendy Cahill

Michael Burns, Author